AN IMAGINED LIFE

AN IMAGINED LIFE

a novel

ROHAN SRINIVASAN

ISBN: 979-8-9914713-0-5
eISBN: 979-8-9914713-1-2

Cover design by Xavier Comas
Interior design by Euan Monaghan
Author headshot by Shubha Jagannatha

First edition 2024

10 9 8 7 6 5 4 3 2 1

For my parents

MARATHI FAMILY RELATIONSHIPS
AND PRONUNCIATION GUIDE

Grandfather—Ajoba <*ah-zoh-bah*>

Grandmother—Aaji <*ah-JEE*>

Mother—Aai (traditional) <*ah-yee*> //
Mama (informal) <*muh-mah*>

Father—Baba <*bah-bah*>

Maternal uncle—Mama <*mah-mah*>

Maternal uncle's wife—Mami <*mah-mee*>

Maternal aunt—Mavshi <*mauw-shee*>

Maternal aunt's husband—Kaka <*kah-kah*>

Older sister/cousin—Tai <*thah-yee*>

Older brother/cousin—Dada <*dhah-dhah*>

TAMIL FAMILY RELATIONSHIPS
AND PRONUNCIATION GUIDE

Father—Appa <*uh-PAH*>

PART ONE

CHAPTER 1

THE WEDDING

THE EARLIEST MEMORY I feel confident enough to narrate extensively is my uncle's wedding reception. I remember fragments of prior events—certain images that have remained unwaveringly intact over the years—but many other characteristics of those early memories are distant and muddled. Colors bleed into one another like a watercolor painting. Objects are in incongruous dimensions, and faces are constructed purely by the way I see them in photos now. When I try to expand on each memory and weave the fragments together, I end up with a perplexing mix of fact and fiction. As an adult now, I know that memory is fleeting and often untrustworthy. If I attempt to recapture forgotten details, imagination begins to take over.

Nonetheless, very little escapes me from Suhail Mama and Kiara Mami's reception. My senses were unusually astute that evening. They sought out the surrounding environment and lapped up whatever they could find. I can still see the fiery glow emanating from the standing lights, beaming on some guests and deepening a shadow across others. The lingering scents of rose perfume and warm vada pav make my mouth salivate now as much as they did then. Mostly, I remember the unbearable stickiness of the East Coast summer heat and how it forced women to pat their foreheads and men to air out their sweaty underarms.

There were numerous aspects of the reception, including the regal decorations and large number of guests, that make it a particularly memorable day for me. But my recollection of this event has endured for one primary reason: the wedding was the first time I ever experienced a significant change in my life. Before that night, I moved seamlessly through each day, surrounded by the same people, following a routine handed to me. However, the wedding marked the departure of Suhail Mama, my beloved uncle, from our family home. At the end of the night, he would retire to the apartment he'd recently bought with Kiara Mami, and there would be an empty room in our house he would never fill again.

I arrived at this realization an hour before the reception was supposed to begin. I was sitting at the edge of a large, unpaved oval area that had been sectioned off for the event. Although I'd come to help set up, Kiara Mami's mother, Kalpana Aaji, had banished me to the side so that I was far enough away not to interfere with her preparation. Hired workers hustled in front of me, unpacking folded chairs and meticulously arranging table decor. Sweat dripped onto their white uniforms as they scrambled under Kalpana Aaji's vigilant gaze. Unfortunately for one of the workers, Kalpana Aaji caught sight of her misarranged cutlery before she could realize her mistake.

"I told you two spoons on the right side of the plate, the napkin on the left. Just—" In frustration, Kalpana Aaji grabbed the tray out of the worker's hands and started rearranging the utensils. The frightened girl stood with her head bowed, unsure whether to leave or stay.

Noticing the worker's lack of movement, Kalpana Aaji barked, "Is the ground paying you?"

The girl scurried away. Kalpana Aaji muttered a few exple-
tives, loud enough that the other workers around her could
hear.

With nothing to do but wait for further instruction, I
ruminated over Suhail Mama's departure. My family had been
tiptoeing around this subject in order to avoid the impending
sorrow, but the imminence of this change was difficult to
ignore any longer, especially when the anticipated event was
coming to fruition before my very eyes. An intense pang of
dread disarmed me. The thought of an incomplete house was
incomprehensible, sickening even. Loss was a disorienting
emotion for my eleven-year-old mind, and I desperately
wished to rid myself of it.

Luckily, a deep hum from my right side interrupted my
thoughts. I turned and saw a man sitting cross-legged on the
ground. A bulky, spoon-shaped instrument lay flat on his lap.
Taken aback, I lurched away and raised my hands in defense.
I'd been perched at the edge of the oval for half an hour and
hadn't noticed someone was sitting a foot away from me.

The man did not acknowledge or even flinch at my sudden
movement. He took a deep breath in and let out an "Om" this
time, steadily holding the bass note until his lungs gave out.
He sucked in another breath and continued the note while
his hands softly plucked the strings of his droning instrument.
I observed this mysterious figure, studying how his protruding belly rose and contracted in his white cotton kurta. His
concentration was impeccable. He did not move even when a
fly landed on his balding head and crawled from his wrinkled
forehead to his bushy eyebrows. The fly took its time exploring
his visage, resting momentarily on his hooked, pore-infested
nose before finally settling on his peppered mustache.

Intending to shoo the fly without disrupting the singer's meditative state, I blew puffs of air in his direction. The

stubborn fly remained adamantly rooted in the thick forest of hair. My efforts to push air out became noisier and more vigorous. The singer's chant stopped. He opened his left eye and peered at me. Sensing the singer's movement, the fly swiftly left to search for another resting spot.

"Can you please do whatever it is you are doing elsewhere?" the singer asked with irritation. His raspy voice sounded like two pieces of sandpaper rubbing against one another.

"I was trying to get rid of the bug on your face."

"What bug?" His hand instinctively reached up to his cheek.

"It flew away," I replied, ashamed my evidence was no longer present.

The singer sighed. He readjusted in his seat and closed his eyes. "Then, please do not disturb me anymore."

I pulled my knees in closer and tried to focus again on the event preparation, but the singer had piqued my interest.

"Are you performing at the reception tonight?" I asked as he sucked in another massive breath. The air came out in a bellowing groan.

"Is there nowhere else you can be?" he pleaded. "Nothing else you could be doing?"

"I was ordered to sit here and wait. I'm not allowed to leave this spot."

He thought for a moment before lifting the wooden instrument from his lap. "Fine. Why don't you help me then? Better than distracting me."

He handed the instrument to me. I grabbed its long neck and positioned it on my lap like he had. Though the instrument's large size made me assume it was going to be heavy, I couldn't feel even the slightest weight on my thighs. The density wasn't light or minute—it was nonexistent. If I had closed my eyes, I could have easily convinced myself that there was nothing but air hovering over my legs.

"What is this?" I asked.

"A tanpura. It helps me know what key I am singing in. Pluck from the furthest string to the closest one. Use your middle finger for the first string and your index for the other three."

I followed his instruction, firmly plucking each string. The sound that came out was harsh and unpleasant.

"Gently, gently," he said, motioning for me to slow down.

I began again, this time allowing my fingers to roll between the strings. After a few cycles, the sound was smooth, just like when the singer had played.

"Good. Very good," he said, impressed. "What is your name?"

"Akash," I replied, lifting my chest confidently. "What about you?"

His brow furrowed, and he muttered to himself, "My name ... my name ... Baba only says my pet name ... but I will not let a stranger call me that."

I was deeply confused why a simple question was taking him this long to answer. "What do people normally call you? What am I supposed to call you?"

He waved his hand in the air. "What is the need to call me anything? I am the only one you are speaking to right now. If you were to say something, it would only be directed at me."

"I guess that's true."

"Enough talking. Help me warm up," he said, pointing at the tanpura. I heeded his instructions and began plucking the way he'd taught me. His meditative chant resumed. I closed my eyes and concentrated on his hypnotizing voice.

A shattering noise ended the brief trance. I stopped plucking the strings and focused on the scene before me. A group of workers stood around shards of broken glass. Kalpana Aaji marched over to them, and her eyes widened with fury when she saw the mess. She let out a stream of curses, prompting the panicked workers to pick up plates and napkins from nearby tables and sweep the glass off the ground.

"Why did you stop playing?"

My attention returned to the Singer. "Didn't you hear that?" I asked, thinking the answer to his question was rather obvious.

"Hear what?"

"The glass breaking. It was so loud!"

"When I sing, I allow myself to be lost in the notes, lost in the emotion, and all other noise is blocked out."

I tried to decipher this strange man's response. "If that's true, how could you hear me blowing the fly away while you were singing?"

The master of answers became silent. "Hm."

"Teach me," I said, intrigued by this special ability he was boasting.

He smirked. "Teach you? This type of meditation requires deep concentration. A child like you cannot learn it."

"I am not a child," I huffed. "I'll be twelve soon enough."

He examined me, testing my confidence with his eyes. I unwaveringly met them.

"Fine. Let's see what you can do. But do not expect any results."

I started plucking the tanpura again, taking the initiative before he could ask.

"I will sing a song—a thumri, to be exact," the Singer continued. "I want you to focus on a memory, one that you wish you could relive. Concentrate on the music and the emotion you feel thinking about the memory. Let your mind connect the two."

"Okay," I said, closing my eyes, preparing for his test. I was usually docile against authority. My voice would catch in my throat, and I would timidly bow my head. But I was ready to challenge the Singer's arrogance and prove to him that I was capable of more.

He began to sing a tune, commencing in the deepest part of his voice before ascending into his upper range. He moved fluidly between the notes, curving and dipping like he was swimming along a windy river. I was conscious of the pace at which I was breathing and the afternoon light warming the right side of my face. Remembering his instructions, I searched for a memory to concentrate on, trying to find a joyful one with my family. The task proved difficult, as the Singer's voice was filled with a doleful urgency, as if he were longing for something or someone. I wondered what memory he was focusing on to convey such raw emotion through his voice. His singing reminded me of the moments before he'd appeared, when I'd been preoccupied with the unfamiliar feelings of dread and sorrow regarding Suhail Mama's departure.

An unexpected image materialized in my mind. Suhail Mama was lying on his bed in a tank top, tossing a football in the air. Rap music was blasting from the boombox next to him, and he was bopping his head to the beat. I grappled with the fact that I would never see him like that in our house again. My crippling dejection returned, even stronger than before.

The raucous sounds of chairs being pushed around and glass being swept up faded away. An invisible shell swelled around me and the Singer, rising from the ground, bricks upon bricks, until we were cocooned in our own world, sheltered from the chaos of the environment around us.

Suddenly, even with my eyes closed, I could see clearly. I was floating in complete darkness except for a tiny source of baby blue light above me. The light grew larger, and I realized that whatever was issuing this glow was rapidly shooting toward me. As it approached, the light took form in what seemed to be a large droplet of luminous paint. I recoiled, preparing for impact, but the meteor-sized droplet morphed before me into a small rectangle with a cross in the middle, resembling the shape of a window frame. Another droplet was racing down, this time a shade of dark brown. It fell beneath me and spread into a hardwood floor that I could stand on. Soon, many droplets of paint, all various hues, were raining around me, each adding to a composition that slowly began to resemble an exact replica of Suhail Mama's bedroom.

An echo of a shrill voice diverted my attention. The falling droplets paused where they were, leaving the composition incomplete. The echo grew louder, and I realized that Kalpana Aaji was calling my name. As if my surroundings could sense my distraction, the composition came undone, and the morphed colors transformed back into their original droplet forms before shooting up into the darkness above me. The shell around me crumbled. I could once again feel the gravel beneath me and hear the commotion of the wedding preparation. Returning to my body at the edge of the oval area, I opened my eyes and saw a blurry image of Kalpana Aaji. She was waving at me.

"Akash! Are you sleeping? How many times I've been calling your name!"

"Sorry, Kalpana Aaji!" I said, quickly standing up.

"Go check on the rest of your family. Tell them to get ready fast. Guests will be arriving soon."

I nodded and turned back to the Singer. He wasn't singing, but he looked deeply involved in his meditation. The weightless tanpura was back on his lap.

"I have to go now," I whispered.

"Were you able to block out the noise?" he asked with his eyes closed.

"Yep. I focused on a memory of my uncle, just like you told me to. After a while, I couldn't hear anything but your voice."

He smiled. "I stand corrected. You are a fast learner."

"Something else happened."

"Oh?"

"I felt like I was back in that memory. I wasn't just thinking about it anymore. I was standing in the same room I saw in my mind."

The Singer's smile faded. He opened his eyes. "What do you mean?"

"It's hard to describe. It was completely dark at first. But then these drops of paint fell from above and built the room around me."

The Singer did not respond. He examined me intensely.

Realizing how silly I sounded, I tried to recover from embarrassment. "I was just imagining things."

He murmured to himself, "It can't be. A child? Unless …"

"I need to go," I interrupted, worried that Kalpana Aaji would yell at me if I did not move. I was surprised she had not made an irritated remark to the Singer yet. Everyone else in the oval had already been threatened. I assumed she was allowing him to warm up in peace if he was supposed to perform later that night.

"Stay. Please. I need to know more about what you saw," insisted the Singer.

"I'm just going home. I'll come back soon."

"Do you promise?"

Confused by his emphatic tone, I replied, "Yes. I promise."

The Singer hesitated. "Then, goodbye for now, Akash."

He closed his eyes and continued to meditate. I walked away from this bizarre character, his chant fading until it was nothing more than a sound of the past.

My walk broke into a jog as I left the oval space and proceeded to Main Street. A line of caterers and decorators carried boxes of cutlery and table decorations in the opposite direction I was headed. I continued to the source of their procession by turning right onto the first cul-de-sac and jogging to my home at the very end. It was an unassuming abode—two stories with a coat of graying beige withering on the outside. The houses on our street had ample space in between one another. They each had a small lawn and cement walkway leading to the front door. Behind them was an open grassy space we treated like a shared backyard.

I entered a busy home. The living room was being used as a base to hold the various supplies needed for the reception. The workers were unpacking and organizing their equipment before heading to the oval area. I sidestepped flower garlands and other puja items that had been used for the intimate, family-only wedding ceremony earlier that day and leapt up the stairs to the second floor.

The master bedroom was at the end of the hall. I slept there with my mother and grandmother, my Aaji. When I opened the door, I found my Aaji fast asleep on the king bed. Several outfits were strewn across the bed and floor. Her black, torso-length hair flowed around her, the strands on her face blowing slightly from her loud snores. She was in a loose kurta and salwar, not at all ready for the evening festivities.

I tiptoed past her, making my way to the bathroom door. I slowly pushed it open. My mother faced away from me. Her loosely curled hair tumbled down to the middle of her back. She wore an elegant navy-blue sari with silver designs on the border of the pallu. Her silver earrings and blue bangles glistened from the coral light that delicately spilled through the bathroom blinds.

The door creaked as I pushed it open further. My mother's head turned toward me. A smile opened on her face, starting from her full lips and extending to the dimples on her plump cheeks. She retained childlike features, with her button nose and naturally curled eyelashes. Her teeth were milky white and her eyebrows thick and subtly arched. She wore her signature kohl, which made her round eyes appear especially striking. I pore over this abiding image of my mother to this day, even though many years have passed in the interim. I can only remember her from that night in one way: carefree and happy.

She waved me over. I ran to her, wrapping my arms tightly around her waist. She wobbled from the impact but quickly stabilized herself. Her fingers gently ran through my hair.

"Hi, baby," she whispered. Her distinctive voice had a husky yet melodic tone. "Did you get bored downstairs? I thought you would enjoy helping out."

"Kalpana Aaji didn't let me," I said, my face still tightly pressed against her, my arms refusing to let go.

"God, that woman. We'll go down together in a bit. Let me wake your Aaji up."

"Mama?"

"Yes?"

"Do you feel sad that Suhail Mama is leaving?"

She pulled me away from her so she could look into my eyes. "Of course, Aku. He's my little brother!"

I lowered my head. "Do you think the house will be different once he's gone?"

My mother lifted my chin back up to meet her gaze. "It will, but this is the best decision for him. And he'll only be a short ride away! We'll see him so much that you won't even realize he's gone."

I still wasn't convinced.

She continued, "You'll have your own room now. You won't have to be smushed in between me and your Aaji when you sleep."

"I don't mind being smushed."

"You don't mind?"

She tugged me toward her and ferociously smothered me in kisses.

"Mama, stop!" I said, giggling and trying my best to break free.

"You don't mind, huh? Cool boy?" she said, amid her kisses.

We were interrupted by a creak in the adjacent room. My Aaji rose from her slumber and looked at us with sleepy, half-open eyes. "What's all this racket about?" she mumbled.

My mother and I looked at each other with momentary guilt. Then, we burst out laughing, the type that erupts without an end in sight. My eyes began to water when I saw the confused expression on my Aaji's face. My mother leaned over and kissed my cheek once more.

—

By the time my Aaji had changed into her sari, the sun had tucked itself behind the trees. We exited the house to the tender violet of dusk and the resounding hum of cicadas and crickets hiding in the nearby forest. I offered an arm for my Aaji to hold on to as we walked. We rounded the corner toward the oval area and were pleasantly surprised to see that the setup was complete and that many guests had arrived already.

The circular tables were organized into three semicircular rings. Tall lamps were placed in the outer circumference, separating the reception space from the surrounding trees. On the left side, select Indian dishes, from papdi chaat to jalebi, were laid out on a long table. A slightly elevated stage with two majestic chairs on top was on the far end opposite us. Hung on poles behind it was a banner that read in a curvy pink font:

Suhail Patil weds Kiara Kulkarni
♥ *06.12.11* ♥

Suhail Mama and Kiara Mami were standing in front of the chairs, greeting guests and receiving gifts like they were royalty. Suhail Mama sported a tight, cream-colored sherwani that showed off his defined shoulders and chiseled jaw. His hair was short and styled up in a fauxhawk. Kiara Mami's attire was as vivacious as her personality. She wore a bright red lehenga with gold patterns running down it, complemented by a labyrinth of mehndi designs on her arms. Her tight curls were tied up in a bun, but a few strands were left hanging by her temples. They bounced vigorously as she chattered away with the guests in front of her.

The other three inhabitants of our house were standing on the steps to the stage. Vaishnavi (or Vaishu) Mavshi, the eldest sister to my mom and Suhail Mama, was perched on the highest step, her arms crossed, her lips in a slight frown. She watched the crowd like a hawk, her eyes narrowed and focused. Her husband, Harsh Kaka, was standing beside her, a kind smile resting on his face as he gazed lovingly at the wedded couple. He stood with a slight hunch, his bald spot sparkling from the glow of the lamps. Animatedly dancing in front of the two of them was their son and my best friend, Sagar.

I pulled on my mother's arm, trying to lead her toward the stage, but she'd already struck up a conversation with Aneesa Aziz, a good friend of the family and a teacher at my elementary school.

"Mama, let's go!"

Aneesa Aunty smiled at me. "Ready to start sixth grade soon, Akash?"

"I still have a couple months of summer left."

She laughed. "That you do."

"I'll catch up with you later, girl. Come over for coffee sometime," my mother said, embracing Aneesa Aunty.

"Of course, Mahi." Breaking away from the embrace, she waved at me and my Aaji. "Bye, Akash! Bye, Gayatri Aunty!"

We continued to the stage but were repeatedly interrupted by other familiar faces from our small community. Bhaskar Uncle peered down at me through his boxy spectacles and gave me a high five. A group of ladies from the salon my mother worked at ambushed us with rapid-fire gossip. My Aaji derailed us once more by complaining to Adi Deo, a cardiologist, about how high her blood pressure was. Fed up with these distractions, I left my mother and Aaji, pushing my way toward Sagar. I called out his name. A group of thirty-year-old men with bloodshot eyes and vapid stares blocked my line of sight to him. I tried to maneuver between them, but they were oblivious to my attempts to get past.

A hand tightly grabbed my arm. It tried to yank me past the group, but one of the men pushed against us. The connection between our arms was about to break, but another arm shot out and solidified the grip, finally hauling me out of the mayhem.

I bent over, catching my breath. Sagar, my savior, grinned at me, his misaligned teeth poking out over his bottom lip. Though we were related, we had few physical characteristics in common. His complexion was darker than mine, and his coarse black hair fell onto his forehead in a classic bowl cut. His eyelashes were long and luscious, shading his wide eyes. He was shorter and skinnier than me, slightly undersized for his age, with fragile-looking arms and legs.

"Thanks for pulling me out," I said, dusting myself off.

"My dad said they're on drugs. Maree-something," Sagar whispered. "I was thinking we could prank them later. I'll tell you my plan—"

"What mischief are you boys talking?" Harsh Kaka called out.

"Nothing," we replied in unison.

Vaishu Mavshi raised her index finger. "Sagar, if I see you messing with anyone tonight, I'm warning you …"

Sagar and I stiffly looked at each other.

"Oh, great! The whole family's here," my mother said as she and my Aaji caught up to us. "Why didn't you come back to the house? We could have come together."

"We were waiting with Suhail and Kiara for Mariam to finish their alterations. Took her forever to stitch them up," said Vaishu Mavshi. "Anyway, let's take the family photo now. God knows where everyone is going to be throughout the night."

"How can you be stressed already? The party has barely begun."

"I'm not stressed," snapped Vaishu Mavshi as the creases on her forehead became more prominent.

My mother smirked. "All right, fine. You're not stressed."

"There she is." Vaishu Mavshi waved to a lady snapping photos on the other side of the stage. "Photographer! Photographer!"

"You can't call her like that," my mother whispered. "It's rude."

"Do you know her name, Mahi? Why don't you call her?"

My mother did not respond. Vaishu Mavshi continued to wave, muttering, "I thought so."

The photographer noticed the excessive beckoning and walked over to us. Vaishu Mavshi instructed her where to stand while we all joined Suhail Mama and Kiara Mami on the stage. My mother and I approached the couple to say our congratulations again, but Vaishu Mavshi interfered and ordered us into a straight line for the photo.

"Okay, one, two, three, smile!" said the photographer, clicking away.

I heard a light sniffle coming from my left side. My Aaji had tears rolling down her face.

My mother noticed as well. "Aai, why are you crying?"

We all broke away and huddled around my Aaji.

"What's wrong, Aai?" Vaishu Mavshi chimed in, rubbing her supportively on the back.

"Nothing, nothing. It's silly. Let's continue with the photos," she said, trying to wipe the tears away.

"Tell us, Aaji," Sagar said, grabbing on to her arms.

"It's just … one by one, you will all leave me and go on with your lives. I want that for you. But I fear that someday soon, I will be all alone."

"We're not going anywhere," said my mother, hugging her tightly.

"Even if we do move, you'll always be with at least one of us," reassured Vaishu Mavshi.

My mother glanced at my aunt. "But we're not moving, right?"

"Right."

My Aaji hugged them back. "My two beautiful daughters."

Kiara Mami nudged Suhail Mama. Taking the hint, he jumped in. "Come on, Aai, it's supposed to be a happy day, not a sad one."

Vaishu Mavshi rolled her eyes. "Thanks for your contribution."

"I'm trying, okay?"

"Just hug her, idiot."

We all laughed as he joined the family embrace. Feeling left out, Sagar and I added ourselves to the hug and were welcomed by our mothers' warm arms. Harsh Kaka and Kiara Mami were swiftly pulled in as well. The photographer snapped away, capturing this heartfelt moment.

My Aaji sighed. "I wish your Baba was here to see this day."

"I know, Aai, I know …" my mother murmured.

"Test, one, two."

I broke away and saw a DJ speaking into his microphone on the opposite side of the stage. He was standing in front of a small table with his laptop and mixing equipment.

"Looks like it's almost time to dance!" squealed Kiara Mami.

Seeing the DJ reminded me of the promise I'd made to the Singer earlier that night. I stood on the tips of my feet, trying to locate where we'd been sitting. I was unable to get a good view from the stage, but I caught a glimpse of what looked like a man sitting upright on the ground.

"Who are you looking for, Aku?" my mother asked.

"The singer I was sitting with earlier. Will he be performing soon?"

"Singer? What singer?" my mother asked. "Suhail, did you guys hire a singer?"

"Not to my knowledge. Unless your family …" he said, looking at Kiara Mami. "Sorry, our family."

"Thanks, sweetie. No, I don't know of any singer. Just the DJ."

"I was sitting right next to him while everyone was getting ready," I persisted. "He was warming up his voice."

"Who was he? Do we know him?" my mother asked.

"I don't know. He was old and kind of grumpy at first."

"You didn't know who he was?" asked Vaishu Mavshi with concern. "And you were still talking to him?"

"Yes," I replied cautiously, worried that I had said something wrong.

"Aku, you can't do that!" scolded Vaishu Mavshi. "You can't just strike up a conversation with any random stranger. Mahi, say something!"

"Yes, Akash, very bad," added my mother.

"He was nice!" I insisted. "He showed me how to use his instrument ... what did he call it ... a ... a tanpura!"

"Your grandfather used to love his tanpura," my Aaji said wistfully, tears springing to her eyes once more.

"Aai, please! No more crying," chided Vaishu Mavshi.

My mother regarded me with confusion. "Are you sure that's what you saw? I don't think someone would bring a tanpura to this event."

My cheeks reddened. "Yes, I'm sure! Come, I'll show you."

I pulled on my mother's arm. She relented and shrugged at Vaishu Mavshi. We exited the stage and made our way through the crowd. "He showed me this cool meditation thing. Everything went quiet, and then paint started falling from the sky and—I'll just ask him to show you."

"Okay, okay, slow down," she said as I tugged her forcefully.

"Here." I pointed to where I thought I'd seen the Singer a moment ago. My hand fell. He wasn't there.

"I'm sure he was very nice."

"I don't understand. He was sitting right there."

I searched for his face through the throng of standing guests, but I couldn't find him.

A screech erupted from the speakers. The familiar beat of "Dhoom Machale" reverberated around us.

My mother gasped. "Aku, we have to dance to this."

"But ... the singer ..."

It was her turn to pull me. She guided me to the middle of the oval, where uncles, aunties, and children were letting out their moves. As more guests joined in, the dance floor became crowded and claustrophobic. When we found the rest of the family, all thoughts about the Singer's mysterious disappearance left my mind. The music pulsed through me, and my shoes smacked the floor with each beat. I was sucked into the turbulence of bodies against bodies as brightly colored saris and kurtas whipped around me. Vaishu Mavshi and my mom were holding on to my Aaji, occasionally twirling her. Sagar was doing his own interpretation of the moonwalk, punching his hands up and down in the air while Harsh Kaka cheered him on. Suhail Mama and Kiara Mami were slow-dancing through each song, lost in their own romantic euphoria.

Besides being my first notable encounter with change, the reception was one of the last times as a child I felt complete. Love connected my family as we twisted, turned, and held each other into the depths of the night, unaware of the misfortune that would soon tear us apart.

CHAPTER 2

THE TOWN

A MAN STUFFED as much of his life as he could within his tweed suitcase. He packed the possessions he could not do without—spare clothes, brass idols of Hindu deities, a photo of him and his wife on their wedding day—and figured the rest he could purchase at his destination. He mentally went through his neighbors, friends, and ex-coworkers, confirming to himself that he had said all his necessary goodbyes. Then, he kissed his pregnant wife, the only one he desired to see again, on both her forehead and belly. She fed him a spoonful of sugar and yogurt, praying for his good fortune. Once he stepped out of his Bombay flat, the man waved at the children frolicking near the end of his complex and gifted the kind watchman a box of laddus he had purchased earlier that morning.

He inhaled deeply, letting the salty, dusty, humid smell of the city fill his nose, unsure when he would get a whiff again. His elder brother pulled around on his scooter with a bright smile. Though they hadn't spoken in a while, his brother had insisted he be the last one to see the man go. On the ride to the airport, his brother eagerly recited what he knew about New York. He told the man that he was a lucky son of a bitch to have an opportunity like this and that he would be a fool if he ever moved back.

So, the man kissed his brother goodbye and boarded his flight, starting the voyage to the imagined oasis, his chest puffed with pride. He knew that he was the crown jewel of the family—the one who received the opportunity to study where none of them could, the one who had married the woman of his dreams. The man looked out at the clouds floating alongside him, exhilarated by the prospect of his future.

Like most anticipated dreams, the reality of living in America was far from what he had envisioned. Though the man soared through his engineering courses at the esteemed New York University, he found himself to be lonesome. His American peers enviously watched him answer complex questions within a few minutes while they clumsily sorted through equations. Friendships formed among the low-ranking students, and they withdrew themselves from the foreign one occupying the top spot. While his classmates went to chase lust at bars on a Thursday night, the man stayed in his cramped, acrid apartment in the Bronx, poring through textbooks. Despite his initial enthusiasm to move away, the man began to miss Bombay. Distracting himself with his studies was the only way he could cope with the biting separation from his homeland. He tried his best to love his new surroundings. He spent a few hours every weekend exploring the turbulent metropolis that was Manhattan, but it provided him little satisfaction when he had no one to share it with.

His wife would send lengthy letters of the happenings in her life, chronicling the squabbles of their neighbors and the highs and lows of raising an infant daughter. He would reread the letters countless times, helplessly clinging on to every word that provided him a window into his old life. As every penny was going toward his education, a trip home was out of the question. He spent many nights crying over his solitude. The man secretly harbored a desire to relinquish his dream of staying in America, but the voice of his brother played over and over in his mind, once again reminding him how lucky he was to be here. His pride was replaced with a crippling sense of duty to chase after a life his relatives were unable to pursue themselves.

He and his wife had discussed her moving to America after a year, but she was content with her life in Bombay. She piled on excuses to postpone leaving. Her mother and aunt lived less than a mile away from her, and it was better to raise a baby around familiar faces. She promised to come once he graduated from his program, but even when he obtained his degree with honors and secured a civil engineering job in Manhattan, she told him that she could only move once he had a community she could rely on. Their daughter was attached to Bombay folks; a transition would be difficult for her. His wife encouraged him to come back, and though he considered it, the paycheck he received every couple of weeks elicited the torture of his brother's words. His salary was greater than it would ever be in India; the life he needed to build for his wife and daughter had to be in this country. Regrettably, the burden of saving up for a house replaced his educational costs, and a trip to Bombay was still unjustifiable.

Years passed, and his loneliness grew worse. The man had lost sight of himself in the relentless activity of the boroughs, surrounded by thousands of nameless faces that rushed past him without any acknowledgment. One Saturday, he woke up without any plans for the day and decided he wanted to get away. No, he *needed* to get away. Something deep within him, a sort of divine responsibility, propelled him to leap out of the bed he usually moped in, put on a fresh set of clothes, and walk outside. He bought a railway ticket without checking where the train was headed and got off at a random station.

He boarded a bus, traveled for a while, hopped onto a different one, and disembarked when he felt like it.

He walked and walked through suburbia, losing track of time. He saw homes with big yards and tiny shops with families in them. He breathed in the subtle sounds of the open space, the rustle of leaves on the oak trees, the singing sparrows flittering above him. He walked and walked until there were no more sidewalks or homes or shops around him, until he was delicately tailing the edge of an isolated road.

A dirt pathway appeared before him, veering off into a broad, uncultivated thicket of trees. Golden afternoon light rained through the yellow leaves. A collection of butterflies and bees swam around him. He trusted his instinct to explore whatever was at the end of this alluring, solitary path.

What he found was an unexpected space, an unnamed town with worn-down buildings and empty roads. The almost-abandoned neighborhood had one central street with two biker bars and a slew of closed businesses. A few cul-de-sacs branched out from the main road, with dilapidated houses that looked as deserted as the businesses. It was a sleepy community, one most would not take a second look at.

But the man was intrigued. He felt a pull to this settlement so far removed from established civilization. Disillusioned with the chaos of metropolitan life, he envisioned what his future could be like if he moved to a malleable place. In this town, there was no precedent on how life should be, only opportunity as to what it could be. He believed that God had willed him to find this quiet area. He had a vision, and if he could figure out how to bring others, if he could build a community of his own making, he could convince his wife to come. He would finally have found the perfect location to raise his daughter.

After tracing his way back to the Bronx, the man contacted the only other Indian immigrant he knew. This friend was also motivated to move out of the boroughs, having had his own experiences with crude discrimination. Still, he hesitated when he saw the empty strip the man was so excited to show him. Although he admired the vision, the friend was uncertain that others would follow, especially given how difficult it would be to connect to Manhattan for work. The man confidently persuaded his friend, once again recounting how spiritual his discovery of this land had been. The friend caved and joined his project.

They were the pioneers, the first immigrants to move to this relatively unknown place. The man continued his job, waking up very early to leave for Manhattan and returning to his new home late in the evening. His friend refurbished a home appliance shop along the central street and convinced his cousin in the New York area to relocate as well. Like wildfire, word of mouth carried the news through a tiny network of Indian, Pakistani, and Sri Lankan immigrants. One by one, new faces found themselves drifting to this remote area, hoping to find some semblance of their dearly missed homeland among other outcasts. Anyone who was wary to move needed to talk to the man for only five minutes to be convinced that it was worth it. Hoping to expedite the formation of this budding neighborhood, he lent money to folks who needed financial support to buy and renovate their homes. He sacrificed the funds that would have been used to visit India with the sole objective of relocating his family as soon as possible and ensuring that his wife wouldn't feel as lonely as he had after moving. Soon, novel businesses were built along the central street, otherwise known as Main Street, and large families occupied almost every house within the cul-de-sacs.

Ten years had passed since the man had left his home. Ten years since he had last seen his wife. He cried when he saw her and his daughter emerge from the arrivals area at the airport. He fell at his wife's feet and kissed his daughter's face for the first time. He packed their luggage in the back of his vehicle and drove them to the refuge he had built for them. Over time, this pocket of houses and businesses became a hub of South Asian immigrants—a home for lost souls seeking familiarity within a foreign land.

This story of the man, my grandfather, my Ajoba, was often told at gatherings within the Town. Even though he had passed on a few years before I was born, I was fully aware of his brilliance and sacrifice. Our neighbors still regarded him with utmost respect. He was the glorious founding father of the Town.

My Aaji, the masterful storyteller, would narrate this tale to the children of the Town, brushing her long black hair with one hand and using the other to exaggerate every detail with copious gestures. The subject of my Ajoba's journey was very emotional for her. Every time she reached the part of the story where my Ajoba picked her and nine-year-old Vaishu Mavshi up from the airport, she would devolve into an inconsolable fit of tears. We would try our best to comfort her, but she was unable to recover for many hours.

Vaishu Mavshi tried to limit the discussion of my Ajoba around the house in order to prevent my Aaji from reaching this state. When I was very little, she hid the few photos we had of him, eliminating all visual reminders. If anyone in the house mentioned him, she would shoot them a vicious glare until they were silent. Unlike my Aaji, Vaishu Mavshi despised dwelling on the past. She felt that it removed focus from the myriad of ongoing issues our family was dealing with. Especially with regard to my Ajoba's death, Vaishu Mavshi believed it was better for everyone to sweep irrevocable trage-dies of the past under the rug and swiftly move on. Still, Sagar and I were curious about this relative that had left such a large impact on our family and community. We used to implore our Aaji to tell us more about him, but Vaishu Mavshi would find us within seconds and order her to begin another story. They would argue, as my Aaji believed that we should know about our grandfather. But in the end, Vaishu Mavshi would always win by bribing my sugar-crazed Aaji with sweets if she chose a different topic.

Even though Sagar and I were disappointed when the story changed, our Aaji would quickly recapture our interest with another riveting tale she pulled out of her enormous collection. She would introduce us to bizarre characters she'd known back in India, such as her clairvoyant childhood friend or the ghost of a maid that had haunted her apartment building's stairwell. When she needed a break from her personal accounts, she would tell us classic tales that had been passed down orally for generations, stories that she'd heard from her Aaji, who'd heard them from her Aaji, and so on. We learned about the famous court of Akbar, the Dashavatara of Vishnu, and the glorious love between Ram-Sita. She emphasized the importance of knowing these stories, no matter how old they were. According to her, learning about those who lived before us was the only way we could understand the foundation of our being.

However, the week after Suhail Mama's wedding, my Aaji temporarily lost her storytelling abilities. She no longer had the will to narrate with her dear son gone. The sentiment was shared among the remaining family. After the caterers and decorators packed up the last remnants of the wedding, we trudged around the house, staring blankly at the door, hoping Suhail Mama would surprise us with a visit.

Walking into his bare room was like stepping into a pit of nostalgia. He was the little brother my mother and Vaishu Mavshi fiercely protected and the cheerful uncle who taught me and Sagar about basketball and hip-hop. His animated, polite, generous personality was deeply missed.

The only consolation to Suhail Mama's departure was that Sagar and I were shifting into his old room. Previously, I'd slept with my Aaji and mother, and Sagar had slept with his parents. But in our new room, Sagar and I would each get a twin bed and could decorate our half how we saw fit. I was happy that I was not moving into a room by myself. The thought of sleeping without anyone beside me was terrifying. Having only ever lived with my extended family, I was unfamiliar with the concept of privacy and personal space.

Our home was one of many in the Town inhabited by a multigenerational family. Sharing a home was the most financially viable option, and we could easily rely on each other to complete the numerous tasks that overwhelm a domestic space. But we primarily stayed this way because it was what we were used to. Before Suhail Mama got engaged, none of the adults had even entertained the possibility of leaving. Our Ajoba had bought this house with the intent of cultivating a large, lively family. Separation from one another seemed lonely and unnecessary.

The weekend after the wedding, my family heaved the last pieces of furniture into Sagar's and my new room. We subsequently collapsed in the tight confines of our living room. I was sprawled out on the couch, my head on my mother's lap and my legs on my grandmother's. My Aaji had put on one of her daily Marathi TV serials, and she and my mother were watching earnestly. I was unable to follow Marathi well, so I had only a vague idea of what the characters were saying. From what I could see, each episode had little dialogue advancing the plot, filling the time instead with dramatic shots of the actors' faces. I was drifting in and out of a lull induced by the gentle caress of my mother, but whenever I was on the verge of falling asleep, a loud sound effect from the show would swiftly pull me back to the room.

My gaze drowsily shifted to the connected kitchen. Sagar was sitting on the counter, eating the leftover sweets from the wedding. Vaishu Mavshi reached over and wiped the crumbs that stuck to Sagar's chin.

"You've had enough," she reproached.

"How come you're only telling me to stop?" said Sagar. "Daddy had five this morning."

Harsh Kaka paused chopping coriander leaves on the adjacent counter. "Sagar!"

Vaishu Mavshi rolled her eyes. "You both want to treat your health like a joke? Fine."

Harsh Kaka swung his arm around Sagar and faced Vaishu Mavshi. "You have to learn how to let loose, Vaishu."

"Yeah, Mama. You have to let loose."

Vaishu Mavshi shook her head. "Why did God give me two boys?"

Harsh Kaka grabbed Vaishu Mavshi's hands and started awkwardly dancing with her. She protested at first, but after a few seconds, she gave in and smiled, her lines of worry fading.

Watching them, I couldn't help but envy Sagar for having two doting parents under the same roof. I never dwelled on my jealousy for long. There was no need, given that Harsh Kaka and Vaishu Mavshi treated me like a second son. But seeing Harsh Kaka transition from his stiff, shy self to a jovial father and husband made me wonder what life would have been like if my father was living in this house as well.

I reached my hand up to my mother's cheek, but she brushed it off.

"Almost done, baby," she said.

The show finished on one last dramatic bang and moved to an ad for an astrology reading.

My Aaji stopped massaging my legs. "What an episode."

"I really didn't think the uncle was in on it," added my mother.

Vaishu Mavshi came out of the kitchen and stood by the television. "Lunch is ready."

I swung my legs off my Aaji. She put one arm on her thigh and tried to hoist herself up.

Vaishu Mavshi rushed to her side and helped her sit back down. "Stay, Aai. I'll bring it."

A thunderous roar emerged from the television speakers as the next show began. Vaishu Mavshi yelped and snapped around. She stormed to the TV set and pressed the power button, silencing the deafening noise.

"What the hell!" my mother exclaimed. "We were still watching."

"Aai, why do you watch this crap?" said Vaishu Mavshi. "I expect this from Mahi, but you're better than this."

My mother stood up. "What are you trying to say?"

"That your threshold for quality cinema is lower than anyone in this house."

Before my mother could respond, my Aaji gloomily said, "What else is there to do at my age, Vaishu? How else can I bide my time waiting for it all to end?"

Vaishu Mavshi raised her hand. "Not this morbid shit again. Please."

"Don't change the subject," said my mother. "Why are you trying to kill our happiness?"

"I'm not trying to kill anything. I just want to eat lunch with my family without this horrible background noise. Don't you want to spend quality time with us? … Hello? … Mahi?"

Instead of paying attention to Vaishu Mavshi, my mother stared at the TV remote on the coffee table. Vaishu Mavshi must have caught her gaze too because they both lunged for the remote at the same time. Vaishu Mavshi tugged the remote toward her, causing my mom to dive over the coffee table. Sagar and I were excitedly cheering for our respective mothers.

"Let go! What are you doing?" screamed Vaishu Mavshi as my mother pinned her to the floor and tickled her.

"Mahi ... stop ... crazy ..." Vaishu Mavshi squealed, attempting to block my mother's attacks.

My mother finally pulled the remote out of Vaishu Mavshi's hand and held it triumphantly in the air. "Ha!"

Harsh Kaka emerged from the kitchen holding a steaming platter of khichdi. "What is going on out here?"

Even Vaishu Mavshi couldn't stop herself from giggling at his dumbfounded face.

———

After lunch, Sagar and I decided to go play in the forest, our routine on most summer afternoons. Sagar loved to reenact the stories that our Aaji would tell us. We would transform into warriors, kings, or deities that were mortal enemies with one another. Sagar would dictate what the imaginary world looked like and which characters we would play, and I would dutifully follow his instructions.

Sagar and I were about to run out the front door, but we were stalled by Vaishu Mavshi.

"Where are you going?" she asked.

"To the forest," Sagar responded.

Vaishu Mavshi crossed her arms. "Why don't you play here? We have so much space in front of the house."

Sagar rolled his eyes. "Mama, we can take care of ourselves."

Vaishu Mavshi's face scrunched up with concern. She relented and hugged him. "Be back before dark."

Sagar pushed himself out of her embrace. "You worry too much."

Vaishu Mavshi smiled. "Of course I do. You're my son."

"We're leaving," I called out to my mother. She was lying on the couch, reading a magazine.

Her eyes did not leave the page. "Have fun, baby."

Sagar was already outside, calling my name. I followed him as he hastily ran away. The soles of my shoes whacked against the tough gravel. My hair, which had grown long over summer, whipped past my face, catching between my lashes and stinging my eyes. We turned the corner of our cul-de-sac onto Main Street. It was hard to imagine that the street had been nearly vacant when my Ajoba first discovered it. I only knew the version of Main Street that was crowded with shops. Residents in the area would hang around the sidewalks to gossip and laugh, typically over tea and biscuits. Immigrants from nearby areas would frequent the Town to take advantage of the various South Asian stores. Even with the light traffic that came for the businesses, there was never an overwhelming number of unknown faces. The Town remained its own comfortable, private bubble.

The unpaved clearing where Suhail Mama's wedding reception had taken place was at the south end of Main Street. We saved that space for festivities throughout the year, including Diwali, Navaratri, and Eid Mela. The Town's planning committee would hang up lights on every shop and bring out large speakers to blast folk music. Families in the Town would dance down Main Street and in circles around the clearing, clapping and twirling to the beat of the dhol.

Continuing our trek to the forest, Sagar and I ran toward the north end of Main Street, waving to Bhaskar Uncle as he smoked a cigarette near the curb. His store, Ghosh Goods, sold home appliances as well as a substantial assortment of puja items. It was also occasionally used as a makeshift temple and venue for community meetings. Wanting to continue the legacy that he and my Ajoba had started almost forty years back, Bhaskar Uncle remained the Town leader, taking charge of events and mediating any personal or business disputes like an old-time village chief would.

Uma Aunty yelled at us to slow down when Sagar crashed into a table outside her vegetarian restaurant, Sangeetha. We crossed the road, and I caught the ill-tempered eye of Simran Kaur, the owner of the beauty salon my mother worked at.

"Tell your mother to show up on time for her shift tomorrow," she called out. "I'm done dealing with her tardiness."

I nodded in acknowledgment, knowing that if I told my mother this, she would flippantly say that Simran needed to "get laid," which made no sense to me at the time since Simran Aunty looked very well rested.

We passed by Das Electronics, Harsh Kaka's pharmacy, and the Mahmoods' tailor shop, before leaving Main Street for an adjacent cul-de-sac. We ran to the end of the road and entered the forest.

"What are we playing today?" I hollered as we zigzagged between towering trees.

"Arjuna and Karna?" Sagar shouted back. We revisited these two characters from the *Mahabharata* often, in awe of the epic battle our Aaji told us took place between them. Embodying the powerful archer Arjuna and warrior Karna provided Sagar and me with an imaginary strength we normally did not possess. Within moments, we left the forest and entered a vast battlefield with thousands of soldiers and chariots. It was customary for Sagar to play Arjuna, the victor in the story, and the game was not finished until he successfully tackled and killed me.

"Draw your weapon, Karna," said Sagar, pretending to raise a bow and arrow. "Ready ... set ... go!"

He shot arrow after arrow into the air. I deflected each one and quickly altered my path to create distance between me and him.

"You can't run from me!" he shouted.

My legs tore through the low-growing plants covering the forest floor. The land dipped slightly into a small stream, and I jumped over the water, only to realize that Sagar wasn't behind me.

"Sagar?"

He shot out from behind a tree and rushed toward me. "Got you!"

"Not yet, you haven't!" I yelled, nimbly running away. I continued dodging his attacks and swerving around trees until the shade from the forest canopy vanished.

I stood before a towering glass building with a border of yellow caution signs. Two elevated train tracks, held up by standing steel supports, jutted out from either side of the building. The sun's rays reflected off the glass, and I had to shield my eyes from the blinding glare. Construction workers in white safety helmets and orange vests moved around the formidable edifice, using machinery to transport metal and glass.

"Now I got …" Sagar's voice trailed off, as he saw why I'd stopped. He tugged my arm. "Let's go back."

As blinding as it was, the nearly finished train station commanded me to fixate on it and recognize its imposing architecture. I'd seen the structure many times before, but my mouth still hung open in awe.

"I'm leaving. Stay if you want," muttered Sagar, turning back to the forest.

I pulled my eyes away and followed him. The noise of the machinery became a distant hum, and the unrefined sounds of the forest overpowered once again.

"Do you still want to play?" I asked.

"Let's go to our spot."

Whenever we were tired of running around, Sagar and I would head to a place deep within the forest where three of the tallest trees were organized in a triangular formation. We would lie parallel to each other on a small bed of grass in the center of these trees, our heads facing opposite directions.

After comfortably settling into our spot, I stared at the pocket of sky that was visible between the leaves. I closed my eyes and smiled, unburdened by responsibility.

"I want to live like this forever," said Sagar.

"Me too."

"What are you thinking about?"

"Nothing," I replied. "Nothing at all."

CHAPTER 3

VARUN

ON THE LAST Saturday morning before summer vacation ended, my mother came to my room to wake me but was surprised to find me sitting on my freshly made bed, already changed into slacks and a checkered shirt. I had been up for hours, unable to fall back asleep. For as long as I could remember, every other month, my mother and I would undergo the long journey into Manhattan to spend a day with my father. My father refused to visit the Town, claiming that it brought back painful memories for him. I didn't mind. I enjoyed these excursions, considering my mother and I rarely left the Town otherwise. The towering skyscrapers and boisterous crowds provided a stimulating escape.

Even so, our visits were mellow. The three of us would typically walk around Central Park, grab a slice of pizza, and retire to my father's apartment in Brooklyn. Despite partaking in unremarkable activities, I cherished this brief time with both of my parents, especially when they were amiable. Though they mostly joked with each other like the old friends that they were, they occasionally devolved into arguments about topics neither of them knew enough about (chiefly politics). As headstrong people, they hated admitting when they were wrong. These arguments would explode out of proportion, resulting in the two of them not speaking to each other for the rest of the day. I walked on eggshells around them, adopting the role of a pacifying mediator between their volatile personalities. I'd learned what subjects to stay away from to reduce the risk of these precious days turning sour.

Regardless of his disagreements with my mother, my father never showed anger or annoyance toward me. He would enthusiastically ask me questions about my life to make up for the missed time in between our visits. I loved when he doted on me, which is why this Saturday visit was notably important. My father had gone above and beyond by reserving tickets for the new Broadway show, *The Book of Mormon*. I hadn't heard of this musical before, but I appreciated his transparent initiative.

"Let's leave in a bit?" my mother asked.

I put my finger to my lips, shushing her. Sagar was fast asleep on the other twin bed, his pillow stuffed between his legs, his comforter thrown on the floor.

"Sorry," mouthed my mother. She tiptoed out.

I lifted Sagar's comforter and repositioned it on him. "Bye," I whispered.

I left the room and shut the door gently behind me. My mother was not at the front door, so I searched for her downstairs. I was shocked to find her in the kitchen, buttering toast and brewing coffee.

"What are you doing?" I exclaimed. "The show starts at two."

My mother calmly finished one last stroke on her toast and set down the butter knife. "We have plenty of time."

"What if the bus is delayed? Or there's a line outside the theater?"

Startled by my burst of emotion, my mother set her toast aside. "Relax. I'll take my coffee to go."

I did not breathe easy until my mother finished pouring

her coffee into a disposable cup and we were out the front door. As we sped down Main Street, I was more confident that we were going to make it on time. With a significant weight off my shoulders, my thoughts deviated to the distressing events of the previous day, and I wondered how my mother was acting so nonchalant, despite the high tensions in the family.

Around midafternoon, my mother had stormed into the house, tossed her apron on the floor, and plopped herself on the living room couch with a huff. Vaishu Mavshi and Harsh Kaka were at work, and my Aaji was fast asleep, so Sagar and I were the only ones available to confront my mother. She was aggressively scrolling through television channels.

"Mama? Are you okay?" I asked.

She threw the remote on the floor. "Goddamn Simran Kaur. I hope that bitch ends up in hell. Who gave her the right to order me around?"

After a tense moment, Sagar meekly asked, "Isn't she your boss though, Mavshi?"

"I still deserve *respect*!" she yelled.

Sagar and I knew this was a conversation better left to the elders. We crept away as my mother picked up the remote from the floor and flipped through the channels again. We hid in our room upstairs, listening to my mother hurl insults at the TV. We did not leave until Vaishu Mavshi returned home from her nursing shift. She plodded up the stairs in pink scrubs, her eyes drooping. We told her everything that had transpired with my mother, watching her expression transition from confusion to seething rage.

She stormed into the living room. Sagar and I followed cautiously and sat behind the pillars of the staircase, wanting to see the action but afraid of being in the vicinity of our mothers' fury. Vaishu Mavshi slammed the TV's power button. My mother stood up, startled by my aunt's hostility.

"Hey, I was—"

"You left the salon in the middle of the day?"

My mother sat back down. "Yes, and I would do it again."

"There better be a good reason behind this, Mahi. I mean it."

"You don't have to be condescending."

Vaishu Mavshi sighed. "I'm not trying to be—listen, I've had a very long shift. Can you just tell me what happened?"

My mother flipped her hair. "I was working on Aneesa's eyebrows, and Simran had the nerve to tell me not to thin them out so much. Obviously, I was pissed! I've been working there for how many years, and she's telling me how to thread? In front of a customer?"

Vaishu Mavshi's jaw clenched. "Then what?"

"I mean, I had to tell Kavita about this. I pulled her into the back room so I could warn her what a bitch Simran was being. But Simran, that nosy cunt, was standing outside, listening to everything! She burst in and yelled at me for leaving Aneesa alone for like two seconds and talking to Kavita about her." My mother paused. "So, I told her to fuck off."

Vaishu Mavshi's eyes bulged out. "You did what?"

"Yeah." My mother held her chin up. "No one talks to me like that."

"Let me get this straight. Simran gave you some criticism—"

"It wasn't just criticism—"

"She gave you criticism," Vaishu Mavshi said, raising her voice. "And then you left a customer—"

"Aneesa is a regular! She was fine."

"I don't care if she lives in the salon! You left her—to bad-mouth your boss? At your job?"

My mother threw her hands up in the air. "Why do you have to twist everything I say?"

"Please!" Vaishu Mavshi clasped her hands together like she was praying. "Please tell me what part I'm twisting."

The steps creaked above us. My Aaji hobbled down the stairs, wiping her eyes.

"What's all this noise?" she asked.

I put my finger to my lips and beckoned her to join me and Sagar in hiding. She caught on and perched herself behind us.

My mother put her hand on her chest. "You don't care about my well-being at all, do you? How can you be okay with her treating me like this?"

"I get criticized all the time at the hospital. Do you see me leaving?"

"That's because you're ... you," my mother said, exasperated.

"What the hell does that mean?"

"You're just better at this stuff."

"Better at what stuff? Being an adult? If so, then yes. Because I seem to be the only one here who understands that we need money to keep us in this house and properly fed. When was the last time you picked up a bill? You can't even comprehend the amount of stress I've been under since Suhail left."

Vaishu Mavshi's voice quivered. She turned away and covered her face. My mother was taken aback. It was rare to see Vaishu Mavshi cry or express any form of vulnerable emotion.

My mother placed a hand on Vaishu Mavshi's shoulder. "You know how dramatic Simran is. She's obviously going to take me back."

"When are you going to start acting like an adult, Mahi?"

Vaishu Mavshi pushed my mother's hand away and darted toward the staircase. She did not acknowledge any of us hiding on the steps. She pushed past us and charged straight to her bedroom, slamming the door shut behind her. We did not see her for the rest of the evening. Even Harsh Kaka had to beg her to be let in to sleep. She cracked the door open, and Harsh Kaka slipped in before she could change her mind.

As my mother and I walked down Main Street, I debated whether to ask her about these events and spoil her pleasant mood. My curiosity got the better of me.

"Is everything okay with you and Vaishu Mavshi?" I said.

She looked startled by the question, as if she had forgotten all about the fight. "What? Oh, I haven't talked to her yet."

"She sounded pretty mad."

My mother smiled. "We're sisters. We have to forgive each other, no matter what. She'll get over it by the end of the day. Trust me."

We turned right at the end of Main Street and trailed alongside a lone road. A van honked as it passed us. We distanced ourselves from the road and stood closer to the elevated train tracks under construction. We followed the path they lined out for us until we reached the towering glass building.

My mother stopped to examine it. "Looks like the station is going to be running any day now."

One of the construction workers lugging a crate into the building paused to stare at us. Rather than scolding us for stepping past the caution signs, he cheerfully waved.

"Mama, let's go," I said, tugging at her sleeve.

She didn't budge, and instead smiled back at him. "It's coming along."

"We're working hard," he responded. "Lot of sore muscles."

"I can tell."

He grinned and adjusted the crate so that his biceps were flexing. "Oh, yeah?"

She giggled and waved goodbye, finally succumbing to my tugs. As my mother and I walked away from the construction site, the worker dropped the crate and frantically called after us, "Hey! Wait! Do you live near here?"

"Maybe!" my mother responded, without looking back at him. This was not the first time I'd noticed the way men outside of the Town would interact with my mother. Many would stare at her with woozy grins, and some were bold enough to introduce themselves. Most of the time, she would entertain them for a minute and then politely excuse herself. With a select few, she would laugh at their senseless jokes, throwing her head back with vigor. She would graze their arms and lean in, making deep eye contact. Right when it seemed like they were about to fall over from infatuation, she would walk away with a mischievous smile, as if she had won a contest.

My mother and I entered a dense arrangement of suburban homes, part of what we Townsfolk referred to as the City. It was an ironic name for an area devoid of skyscrapers and other metropolitan structures, but in comparison to our tiny bubble, the title was fitting. It contained a hospital, where Vaishu Mavshi and a few other Townspeople worked, as well as stores of larger corporations like Target and Home Depot.

Technically, the Town was part of the City. According to published maps, our neighborhood was well within the City's limits. "The Town" was merely a made-up name we Townsfolk used to differentiate our secluded, immigrant-dominated area from the other parts of the City. With the short strip of forest that divided us and the even more prominent cultural contrast, the Town and City felt like two opposing worlds with little uniting them. Most people living outside of the Town, especially those not of South Asian descent, assumed we were just an extension of a standard, run-of-the-mill suburb and didn't bother visiting our side of the forest. I'm sure there were people in the City who hadn't even heard of Main Street. Because of these generalizations, the Town was able to remain relatively anonymous. Information about our South Asian businesses traveled mostly through word of mouth. Those who moved to the Town did so because they were connected to someone in the community. The anonymity was an asset for most Townsfolk. We weren't overrun by tourists, drew little attention from the news, and were rarely harassed by local politicians. For many years, the Town stayed true to the detached vision my Ajoba had devised for it.

My mother and I approached a bus stop, reaching the next step of our complicated journey into Manhattan. Our usual route to Penn Station necessitated taking a bus to a station outside of the City, riding a connecting train, and transferring lines once again midway. It was a long and arduous task.

When we stepped on the bus, my mother checked her purse to look for quarters. "Shit. I must have left my wallet back at the house."

"Seriously?" I asked, panic rising within me.

"We'll have to go back and get it," she groaned. "It's such a long walk."

"But the show!"

"We'll still make it," she said, leading me back to the sidewalk.

"How do you know that?" I turned away from her and crossed my arms. "Vaishu Mavshi was right. You are irresponsible."

"Hey!" She jerked me back to face her. Her hand gripped my right shoulder, and I winced in pain. "I'm still your mother. You do not get to talk to me like that."

"You're hurting me," I said, and her grip loosened.

"Dammit," she said as the bus took off. "Maybe I can ask Vaishu to bring the wallet."

"It doesn't matter. The bus is already gone. I wish we had a car."

Suhail Mama was the only person in our family who owned a car, a secondhand Honda Civic he'd bought when he was in college. The car had gone with him to his new residence, leaving the rest of the family reliant on the complicated public transport system.

My mother's face lit up. "I have an idea."

She procured her cellphone and walked away from me as she dialed. I sat on the bench by the bus stop, my shoulders drooping. I dreaded what would happen if we didn't make the show. Would my father ever book something like this again? Would he be mad? Or even worse, disappointed?

My mother jumped up and down, repeating "Thank you" loudly into the phone. She skipped back to me with a wide smile on her face.

"I found us a ride! A friend of mine is going to drop us off."

"Who?"

"You'll see. I've been wanting you two to meet properly anyways."

She plopped herself beside me and clasped my hands. I was curious who this secret friend was, especially since my mother rarely left the Town without me. Any friend she had would likely be someone I knew.

We waited for about five minutes before a blue Toyota Corolla pulled up to the curb. Just like Suhail Mama's Civic, the exterior of the car was worn out from great use. Sitting in the driver's seat was someone I would have never guessed could be my mother's friend.

Nikhil was the shy and reclusive son of Pronoy Das, the owner of Das Electronics. I'd occasionally seen him when passing the store on Main, but we hadn't spoken before. He was in his early twenties, and his features made him look even younger. He had a light complexion with round cheeks and pink lips. His wavy hair poked out from under his black beanie and fell over his brown glasses. He usually wore a graphic tee with an obscure science fiction character on it. Sometimes he would add variety by throwing an unbuttoned flannel shirt on top of the tee, like he did when picking us up at the bus stop.

A few years earlier, Nikhil's family had been involved in a much-discussed scandal. Pronoy had woken up Bhaskar Uncle in the middle of the night, claiming that his wife was missing and that they needed to search for her. The following day, the search suddenly stopped. Pronoy withdrew himself for a few months, and Nikhil took over the store. Through our Aaji, my family learned that Nikhil's mother had run away. She'd admitted to her friend that she was having an affair with someone from the City. This boyfriend of hers had promised to leave his family and take her far away from the mundanity of the Town. The day after Nikhil's mother left, the friend confessed what she knew to Pronoy in shame. Since then, Pronoy, Nikhil, and Nikhil's older sister were rarely seen at Town events. If they were, none of them would participate greatly. Nikhil would meekly smile and avoid eye contact when spoken to. Having seen him only in this context, it baffled me how such a reserved person could ever get along with my vivacious mother.

I opened the back door with caution and entered the vehicle. The inside of Nikhil's car was cleaner than the exterior.

My mother sat in the front passenger seat and kissed Nikhil lightly on his cheek. "Thank you so much for doing this."

"No worries. Happy to help," he said with a slight lisp. His voice was soft and high pitched.

We made eye contact in the rearview mirror. He smiled at me.

My mother grabbed the neck of her seat so that she was facing both of us. "Aku, you know Nikhil, right?"

"Kind of," I replied.

Nikhil asked my mother, "Does he like video games?"

"I don't think he's played any. Have you, Aku?"

I shook my head no.

"Anytime he wants to try some games out," said Nikhil, "he can come to the store."

"How does that sound?" my mother, the middleman, asked me.

I shrugged.

My mother rubbed my cheek. "Let's go, shall we?"

"Let's do it," Nikhil said, shifting his hand on the steering wheel and pulling the car away from the bus stop.

———

Even though we were stuck in bumper-to-bumper traffic, the drive to Manhattan was peaceful. Nikhil played a radio station with classic rock songs. My mother rolled down her window, and the warm breeze wafted through our hair. She and Nikhil talked to each other in low voices, broad grins plastered on their faces. My mother did not force an unnatural laugh with Nikhil the way she usually did with other men. She sounded more like how she was around family: bubbly and uncontrolled. Her arm grazed his on the armrest. They maintained this sort of subtle physical contact with each other the entire ride.

Oddly enough, I felt jealous on my father's behalf. Even though he and my mother had lived apart for as long as I could remember, I'd always hoped that they would find their way back to each other at some point. Seeing her laugh so naturally with another man curtailed this dream of mine.

"Let's stop here. I need to pee," my mother said, pointing to a nearby exit.

"Right now?" I asked, hassled by my mother's continued efforts to delay our arrival.

"Don't worry. We have a ride now, so we'll be super early."

I fiddled with the car handle as Nikhil took us off the freeway and into the empty parking lot of a run-down diner.

"I'm gonna go in," my mother said, opening the car door. She paused, and then asked Nikhil, "Do you want to come with me? You can get a milkshake or something while waiting."

"Um … all right." He looked back at me. "What about …"

"You'll be fine, won't you, Aku?"

"Yeah," I replied.

"Do you want us to get you a milkshake?"

"Only if it doesn't take too long."

My mother and Nikhil left the car and walked toward the diner. Nikhil towered over her, but my mother's presence was much larger than his. She clutched his arm and fixed his hair, bouncing next to him with a slight spring in her step.

I unbuckled my seatbelt and decided to snoop until they returned. I reached into the back pouch of the front passenger seat. There were video game cases as well as sci-fi DVDs. As I dug further into the pouch, I felt a thin piece of fabric. I pulled out a bright yellow shirt and recognized it as one of my mother's throw-away tops, something she wore on hot days while lazing on the couch.

The car suddenly felt revolting. What were my mother's clothes doing in Nikhil's car? Even though the window was cracked open, the stifling heat was making me lightheaded. I sat in discomfort for another fifteen minutes. Finally, the two of them emerged from the diner's front doors. My mother walked toward the car with a confident strut. Her hair was tousled, and she shook it out with her hands. Nikhil followed behind her. His beanie was removed, and tufts of his hair poked up into the air. His T-shirt was a little uneven, his face a little flushed. As they neared, he glanced at me guiltily, as if he knew what I'd found in his car.

"Sorry that took a while, Aku. There was a long line," my mother said while reentering the car. Nikhil smiled weakly when I caught him looking at me in the rearview mirror.

They hadn't brought milkshakes with them, but I wasn't going to remind them about it or ask how the line could have been long when we were one of the only cars parked in the lot. I was determined to reach my father without any more distractions. This goal kept my mind off the nausea.

Soon enough, abundant trees and single-family homes were replaced with high-rise buildings and flashy billboards. Whenever I returned to Manhattan, I felt like I was seeing the metropolis for the first time, mesmerized by the vibrancy of it all. Outside my window was a cacophony of honks and curses, of flashing lights and stained sidewalks, of young people trying to look older and old people trying to look younger.

Unfortunately for Nikhil, driving in Manhattan was a cursed endeavor. His hands anxiously rubbed the steering wheel as he combatted the impudent drivers swerving around him. The quick brakes and sudden merging made me feel like I was on a terribly maintained roller coaster. To make matters worse, my directionally challenged mother was guiding him on how to get to the theater. Two blocks after he was supposed to make a right, she would realize her mistake and slap her forehead. Through an act of God, we made it to the correct building, and a relieved Nikhil braked at the curb.

"There's Dad!"

My father, usually dressed in knitted sweaters with holes and paint stains, was unrecognizable. He wore an oversized suit with a bright-red tie. The jacket and pants were two disparate shades of gray and looked mismatched in size. His poofy, curly hair was slicked back, which made his receding hairline apparent. Though he typically had slight scruff tracing his cheeks, he was completely clean shaven. My father looked like a walking contradiction. He had all the right components to appear groomed, but he did not know what to do with them, leaving him looking uncomfortable and a little foolish.

"What the hell …" my mother said, her perplexed expression reflecting that she was as thrown off by his appearance as I was. She rolled down the window and yelled, "Varun!"

His face snapped in the direction of our car. He grinned and jogged across the street, brashly sidestepping cars until he reached my mother's window. "Hi."

"Hey," she said.

"A car?"

"Missed the bus."

"Glad you could make it."

"What's with the …" My mother pointed to his outfit.

"It's the theatre. You gotta be fancy," my father said, looking down at his suit. "Don't I look sexy?"

Nikhil cut in with a small cough.

"Right!" My mother leaned away from the window. "You remember Nikhil."

"Mm, I don't think so," my father said, his grin fading.

"That's okay. I was a kid when you left the Town," said Nikhil, outstretching his hand for a fist bump. "I'm Pronoy Das's son."

My father ignored the attempted greeting. "Oh, yeah, I remember now."

Nikhil awkwardly brought his hand back to his lap. My mother jumped in. "Nikhil was very kind and drove us in."

"That's nice," my father said. "How are you returning the favor?"

My mother rolled her eyes. "Varun …"

My father pushed his head further into the car and looked at me. "Hey, buddy. You ready for the show?"

I nodded vigorously.

He reached behind my mother's seat and ruffled my hair. "Let's go. Show will start soon."

I climbed out of the car, but my mother did not budge. She looked between my father and Nikhil. "If you don't need me, I think I'm going to stay with Nikhil for the day."

"What!" I exclaimed.

"But I have your ticket," my father said, equally confused.

"You should go," whispered Nikhil.

My mother grabbed Nikhil's arm. My father clenched his jaw.

"You went to so much trouble driving us," she whispered back.

A car attempting to pass Nikhil's car honked. My father responded by holding up his middle finger.

"What am I going to do with your ticket?" he asked, irritated.

"There are like a thousand people waiting outside to buy one. You'll sell it off no problem."

My father raised his hands incredulously. "Okay. Do what you want."

I was annoyed with my mother. This day was supposed to be about the three of us, and she was spoiling it.

"Don't worry about me," Nikhil murmured. "I have to help my father with inventory tonight anyways."

My mother bit her lip, contemplating. She faced my father. "Why don't I stay with Nikhil while you both are at the show, then I'll join you for an early dinner? Akash and I can take the train back after that."

"You sure? You don't have to," Nikhil said.

She smiled and rubbed his arm. "I want to."

"Great. See you then," my father replied tersely. He grabbed my hand and yanked me toward the theater.

"Bye, Aku!" my mother yelled out the window. "Have fun!"

—

My mother's prediction was right. We sold the ticket within a minute of advertising it in front of the box office, infuriating my father even more. As we waited for the doors to open, he did not ask me any of his usual questions. Instead, he incessantly kicked a loose trash bag on the ground, muttering to himself. He took off his jacket and loosened his tie so that it sloppily hung off his neck. The hair gel's strength was wearing off, and his hair began to poof up. He looked more like the unkempt father that I knew well.

During the show, I tried my best to follow the story, but I was too stunned by the abrasive content. I wondered if my father had known what *The Book of Mormon* was about before he'd bought tickets, as the cursing and innuendos steadily increased after the song "Hasa Diga Eebowai," translating to "F--- You, God." My mouth was agape. If Vaishu Mavshi had been there, she would have yanked me out of the theater immediately. I sneaked a glance at my father. He was staring at the stage blankly, as if he wasn't even processing the words being sung before him. I enjoyed my few moments of vulgarity, trying to mask my awe so that he would not catch on to how little I was exposed to this type of content at home.

Toward the end of the first act, he leaned over and whispered in my ear, "Who was that man?"

"Nikhil," I whispered back.

"I know that. But like, who is he?"

"I don't understand."

"How long have they been seeing each other?"

"Um …"

"No, you know what, I don't even want to know."

He slumped back in his chair. I stayed silent, unsure how

to appease his irritation. The old couple sitting next to us stole uncomfortable glances at my father.

"How irresponsible can she get?" he seethed. "Dating a literal child and bringing him around you? Now that's irresponsible."

On stage, one of the characters started yelling about mutilating women. The old man next to us tried to shush my father.

"Oh, fuck you," my father snapped at him. The old man blinked in shock.

Continuing his interrogation, my father asked, "How many times has she brought him to the house?"

"Zero," I replied.

"Does the rest of the family know?"

"I don't know."

"Does Vaishnavi know?"

"I don't know."

An usher came by our seats and whispered that we could either quiet down or leave the theater.

My father stood up. "Let's go."

"What?" I asked, my eyes glued to the stage.

"Let's get out of here."

"Right now?" I asked, desperately wanting to savor this rare window into maturity.

He crouched down. "Do you want to stay?"

I could see in his eyes that he was looking for only one answer. Relinquishing my desire to see the musical until its end, I said, "Not really."

"Then let's go."

My father and I followed the usher up the aisle. The devoted theatergoers glared at us. My anger toward my mother ripened. What could have been a wonderful day for the three of us had been ruined because of her decision to stay with Nikhil.

I regularly interrogated my mother as to why she and my father were not married. Although they did fight, my parents enjoyed sincere moments with each other, especially when reminiscing on their childhood together. My mother would share the mischievous antics my father used to devise to annoy his parents. My father would recount how my mother bullied the boys who played with them. I once asked my mother if she loved my father. She responded that she always would, but it was better to love him from a distance. As much as I prodded, this was the only answer she would give me.

Fed up with her riddles, I tried to pry out their history from other family members. Vaishu Mavshi and Harsh Kaka were faithful to my mother and said that she would tell me when she was ready. My Aaji was easier to crack; I had to subtly weave my questions into conversation while she was distracted. Based on the fragments I picked up from her, I learned that my mother and father had grown up as best friends and neighbors. My father was the only child of strict, dictatorial parents. Their constant academic pressure had pushed him to rebel, and he'd started to ditch class to work on his art. After my Ajoba's death, my heartbroken mother turned to my father for comfort. She couldn't handle seeing the rest of the family and being reminded of her pain. My father was the perfect escape for her because he wasn't associated with my Ajoba in any way. As they spent more time together, she began to adopt his defiant attitude and would regularly skip school as well.

While describing this turbulent period, my Aaji would shake her fist and declare that my father had led my mother astray. He'd encouraged her to make horrible choices while she'd been dealing with her grief. He'd compelled her to pick fights with the family and threaten to run away. He'd lured her into disappearing for days, tempting her to engage in sinful activities that my Aaji would not elaborate on. And, according to my Aaji, he would have continued to instigate my mother's unruly behavior if she hadn't found out she was pregnant with me in her last year of high school.

Usually by this point in the story, my Aaji would figure out my plan to extract information from her and give me a tender smack on the back of my head. Like Vaishu Mavshi and Harsh Kaka, she assured me that the rest would be shared by my mother one day. She added that it was good my father never visited the Town; he was not welcome back by our family. Hoping to push my luck a little further, I meekly asked her once where my other set of grandparents were. I knew my father was estranged from them, but nothing more. All my Aaji disclosed was that they had moved far away from the Town.

The lack of transparency was frustrating. I was led down a rabbit hole of theories as to what had transpired between my mother's pregnancy and our routine visits to Manhattan. Why had my father moved out of the Town? Why did his parents no longer speak to us? I speculated that my mother was the main one opposed to permanently bringing him back into our lives. My father used to suggest we meet more often, an idea I fully supported, but my mother stayed firm in our routine. She always seemed reluctant to meet him and would triple-check with me days before we went whether I still wanted to go. She was not giving him a chance when it was so obvious that he was trying. She was holding us back from having a perfect life together.

I brooded over my bitterness as my father and I rode the subway to his apartment in Brooklyn. He lived in a tiny two-bedroom with an aspiring actor. The place had a rustic design with brick walls and dark, moody lighting. With the right decorations, the apartment could have been charming, but my disorganized father left the general living space in disarray. Unwashed plates lay on the kitchen counter alongside his stained sweaters and torn magazines.

After we entered the apartment, he asked, "Want a snack?"

"Sure," I said.

He opened the fridge and perused its sparse contents before removing a loaf of bread. He checked if it was stale. "Jam sandwich it is."

I entered his room while he struggled with the jam lid. My father's bedroom was a perfect physical representation of what I imagined his mind to be like: cluttered, turbulent, and packed with potential. On top of being a place to sleep, it was an art studio and storage space. His bed was unmade, and piles of clothes were strewn across the floor. He had a dusty guitar in one corner from when he'd thought that music producing was his calling. Likewise, a tennis racket, used film cameras, and a collection of philosophy books were piled in other corners from the additional ventures my father had picked up and lost interest in.

The most fascinating part of the room was what I liked to refer to as "the wall of incompleteness," a collection of sketches and paintings on the wall across from his bed. My father's love for visual art stayed consistent throughout his other undertakings, but he lacked the patience to see most of his pieces to the end. On the wall, he had half-completed watercolor paintings of people or landmarks around New York, as well as printed graphics for the occasional freelance design work he did to pay his rent. Meticulous detail was applied to one portion of the artwork before his interest tapered off to pursue another idea. Scattered among these formal compositions were indiscernible sketches. My father prided himself on his creativity. These sketches would sometimes be as simple as a circle with a dot in the center or a spiral collection of abstract squiggly lines. I loved guessing what my father had intended when he'd drawn them. I would spend hours examining the wall, wondering what he was seeing that others couldn't, or rather, what the larger vision was in these disconnected drawings.

When my father first noticed how engrossed I was with his designs, he introduced me to the basics of sketching and painting. Some visits would pass by with my mother curled up on the bed, reading a book, while my father and I lost ourselves in the limitless manipulation of colors, shapes, and textures. My father would repeatedly instruct me not to let anyone ever deter my creativity, expressing that it was my one claim to individuality in this world.

I accidentally stumbled over an easel while approaching the wall. My reflexes kicked in, and I steadied it before it tipped over. The easel was covered with a black cloth, but I could tell from the bulky shape that there was a canvas underneath. I made sure my father was still busy making the sandwich before lifting the cloth to observe what he was working on. I was astonished to find an acrylic portrait of me, him, and my mother. He wasn't using a reference photo—this painting was purely derived from his memory. As a result, there were parts of the image, like the shape of my mother's face and my smile, that were not entirely accurate. Still, the similarity was there, and my heart soared seeing a dream of mine put down on paper.

"Akash!"

I dropped the cloth and faced my father. He was standing by the bedroom door, holding a plate with the jam sandwich on it. I was searching for anger in his expression, but he looked more startled than anything.

"I'm sorry, I—"

"That was supposed to be a surprise," he said.

"What … what is it?"

"I was going to gift it to you and your mother."

He wanted it too. The three of us. Together. It all made sense now—why he'd booked the show, why he'd worn a suit, why he'd been irritated when my mother had left us.

Expressing excitement, I continued, "It's so good, Dad."

He walked over to the easel, lifted the cloth, and examined his painting again. "Do you think your mother will like it?"

"I think she'll love it."

"Good, because today … well, today I have something important to ask you both. Something I think will make you very happy."

This was it. This was the moment I'd been waiting for. The chance for my entire family to be reunited.

"What is it? Please tell me."

"Patience. I'll tell you when we see your mother," he said, ruffling my hair. "Why are you grinning, Aku? You don't even know what I'm going to say."

I tried to hide my smile, but it proved impossible. My father hugged me and handed over the plate. I sat on his bed and happily ate the worst sandwich I'd ever had in my life, waiting in excruciating agony for the dinner with my mother.

At six sharp, I hurried my father to the Chinese restaurant where we were meeting my mother. He'd changed from his suit to his usual paint-stained sweater and baggy jeans. For forty-five minutes, we sipped our canned Cokes and stared at the entrance. Whenever the door swung open, we jumped up, only to sit back down in disappointment when another customer came through.

Finally, my mother entered. Her hair was damp with sweat. We waved to her, and she walked over to our table.

"Hi, baby," she said, setting down her purse.

"Where were you?" I asked pointedly. "We've been waiting."

"I'm sorry. I'm here now. Did you have a good time with your dad?"

"Yes. A great time, actually!"

"That's awesome!" she said with amusement. She kissed my father on the cheek before sitting down. She reached for the menu. "I'm starving. What should we eat?"

My father grabbed his own menu. "We can start with some potstickers?"

I impatiently tapped my hand on the table. How was he thinking about food? Our order was the last thing on my mind.

"Potstickers sound good. Maybe some chow fun too," my mother replied.

My restlessness took over, and I blurted out, "Dad, you said you had something to tell us."

My father blushed. "I have to work up to it, Aku."

"Anything we should be concerned about?" my mother asked, placing her menu back on the table.

"No, no. Actually, I—"

"Can I get something started for you guys?" A young waitress stood at the head of our table. She poured water into our cups from a steel pitcher.

My mother collected the menus. "Yes, we'll have two orders of veggie potstickers to start. Also, some chow fun and fried rice to share."

"I'll get that going." The waitress took the menus and walked away.

"Continue," I said.

My father cleared his throat. "Right, well ... Mahi, many years ago, I made a promise to myself. A promise that one day I would make something of myself and, when that day came, the three of us would become one."

At last, he was saying the words that would open a lifetime of happiness for us. I was optimistic that once my father expressed his wishes, the family would welcome him back to the Town with open arms. I glanced at my mother, expecting to see elation in her eyes. But I found only apprehension. Her fingers were red from how tightly she was squeezing her hands.

"Varun—" she said.

"Let me finish everything I have to say first," interrupted my father. "Something exciting has happened in my life. Last year, I started working with one of my buddies on this new technology he'd been researching. We decided that I would lead the creative design while he focused on the business and technical side of it. We didn't know if it would lead to anything, but we got an angel investor to put in enough for initial development."

"What does this have to do with us?" my mother asked with caution.

He exhaled slowly. "I'm moving to San Francisco to work full time on this. And I want you both to come with me."

My hands went limp. The excitement I'd felt instantly vanished. He wanted us to move to the other side of the country? That would mean we would be separated from the Town. From our home. From the family. From Sagar.

My mother shook her head. "Varun, stop—"

"I know it's a lot to ask. But someone believes in me, Mahi. I could finally achieve something great, and I want my family to be beside me when I do."

"Now that you've found a new fad for a bit, we're supposed to drop everything and join you?"

"This isn't a fad. This is a chance for us to have a good life together. A successful one. Akash wants this, don't you, buddy?"

My voice was stuck in my throat. I was torn between the choice my father was presenting us with and the life I knew.

"Don't bring him into this," my mother said, leaning toward

my father. "If you wanted a life with us, we could have started one a long time ago. You know that better than anyone."

He glanced at me. "Mahi, think about our future."

"Even if we wanted to go, we have too much tying us to the Town to leave."

"You have to leave your family's house eventually."

"It's not just about them."

"What else is holding you back? Don't tell me it's that kid who brought you here today."

My mother's eyes narrowed. She stood up and outstretched her hand to me. "Aku, let's go."

"Mahi, wait." My father reached out to grab my mother's arm. "Mahi, I love you so much. Both of you. I always have. Give us another chance."

For a moment, she searched his eyes. Then, she shook his hand off and grabbed the purse on the back of her chair.

"We should leave," she said. "Nikhil lent me some money for the train back."

I cautiously stood up, unsure whether to leave or stay.

My mother outstretched her hand again but dropped it when she saw that I wasn't budging. "Say bye to your father. I'll meet you outside."

She marched out of the restaurant. My father looked utterly deflated.

"Well, I guess this is it, then," he said.

I walked around the table and hugged him. "We'll see you soon. Very soon."

My mother and I rode the train in silence. When we reached the house, we found Vaishu Mavshi reading a book in the living room. Still vexed from the fight with my mother, Vaishu Mavshi uttered a curt hello without looking at us.

"Vaishu," my mother croaked.

Vaishu Mavshi did not acknowledge her.

"Vaishu, can I talk to you alone please?"

"What do you want?" Vaishu Mavshi snapped.

Sobs erupted out of my mother. She covered her face and doubled over. Vaishu Mavshi rushed to my mother's side and led her to the couch.

"I ... I don't ... know what to do ..."

Vaishu Mavshi instructed me to go to my room. I retreated, bewildered by the sudden change in my mother's mood. Sagar was in our room when I entered.

"How was the—"

I shushed him, motioning to join me at the door. We pressed our ears against the wood, listening to the conversation between my mother and Vaishu Mavshi downstairs.

"Did he forget that he was the one who disappeared to Illinois when you were pregnant? One day, he promised to take care of you and the baby. The next, he vanished with his parents. For three years, we heard nothing from him."

"We were so young, Vaishu. And he came back eventually."

"He came back to get away from his crazy parents! Not because of you! He chose to live in Brooklyn rather than be here. He worked only to sustain himself. He didn't take any initiative to care or provide for either of you."

"But he didn't have to tell us that he moved back. He didn't have to ask to be involved in our lives again. We could have gone our separate ways."

"The bar cannot be so low, Mahi. He got the best of both worlds. He could see Akash whenever he wanted while also pursuing his passion. He got the title of being a father without any effort."

"Then why now? Why does he want to live with us if this other setup worked so well for him?"

"I don't know why. I wish I did. What I do know is that he finally has a good opportunity after messing around for years, and he's acting like this dream life with you is all he's ever wanted. It's complete bullshit."

"He told me he loves us."

"I don't doubt that he does. But he loves himself more."

Sagar fell asleep after an hour or so, but I stayed up, listening, trying to understand. I'd assumed my father had moved from the Town to Brooklyn directly. I hadn't known he'd disappeared to Illinois with his parents. If this revelation was true, my father was the reason he and my mother were not together. I'd antagonized her for so long, but her wariness to meet my father had come from fear that he would leave again. She'd kept our distance to protect me.

I was in disbelief that my father could have deserted her in a time of need. There had to be a proper explanation for why he'd left. He loved us. He loved me. I adored him too much to believe that he was as selfish as Vaishu Mavshi made him out to be. Whenever the family had expressed their dislike for him before, I'd assured myself that they weren't giving him a fair chance. But overhearing my mother cry was not easy to push past, and it brought forth a smidge of doubt about my father that I couldn't shake off. I wasn't sure where to place my blame anymore, but I resolved that, for the time being, my anger toward my mother was unjustified.

Eventually, the conversation ended. I cracked the door open, and it made a loud, deep groan.

Vaishu Mavshi's voice rang out. "Who's there? Akash?"

I left my room and walked down the stairs. My mother lay across the sofa, her head in Vaishu Mavshi's lap. Vaishu Mavshi ran her fingers through my mother's hair. Their fight from the previous day had clearly been forgiven and forgotten.

My mother raised her head. "Aku?"

"Yeah?"

She outstretched her arms. I ran to her and climbed onto the sofa. There was hardly any room for one more person, but we managed to squish.

Vaishu Mavshi gently hoisted herself up. "I'm going to bed."

My mother's arms were wrapped around me, and I buried my head in her chest. I felt immense regret for having thought such nasty things about her earlier that day.

"I'm sorry. I'm sorry," I repeated, my words muffled by her shirt.

"Shh. My baby."

We fell asleep in less than a minute, comforted by each other's embrace.

CHAPTER 4

GROWING PAINS

CHANGE BEFELL OUR house like a quiet storm. Heavy clouds began to gradually sag over our roof, and the sun slept much earlier than before. We bid farewell to the sweltering heat and bundled up within the comfort of our living room. While summer provided a pleasant routine that was stable but never tedious, fall brought with it an array of personal developments that surreptitiously pronounced a new era for our family.

My Aaji was the first one affected. Before leaving for the hospital one morning, Vaishu Mavshi asked her to buy chicken breast for dinner. When Vaishu Mavshi returned from work, there wasn't any sign of the chicken, and my Aaji couldn't recollect the conversation. Vaishu Mavshi had to detail exactly where they'd been and how the exchange had progressed before my Aaji could remember it. To dismiss Vaishu Mavshi's concerns, my Aaji joked that she tunes out most of the orders given to her.

Her nonchalance could not hide her failing memory much longer, as these forgetful episodes recurred frequently. She would ask for the time even though she'd asked for it five minutes earlier. She needed my mother to recount the previous day's episode of her Marathi serials to be able to understand where they'd left off. Unable to swallow my Aaji's excuses, Vaishu Mavshi scheduled her for a consultation with a physician. The two of them returned somberly from the hospital with a diagnosis of early-stage dementia.

Vaishu Mavshi acted as expected. She made sure my Aaji was accompanied whenever she left the house and took her for numerous checkups, even though the practitioner said it wasn't necessary. Every morning, Vaishu Mavshi would quiz my Aaji extensively on the events of the previous day. If there was anything that my Aaji forgot, even if it was the most minute event, Vaishu Mavshi would start to panic. Harsh Kaka would soothe her, saying that it wasn't good for my Aaji to constantly be reminded of her illness.

My Aaji took the news better than the family thought she would. We used to refer to her as the ultimate drama queen because of how often she would mention her impending death. But after the diagnosis, her dismal remarks ended. She no longer fought Vaishu Mavshi's demands, even if some were ridiculous. When Vaishu Mavshi overreacted to forgotten details, my Aaji would shrink, her eyes sinking back like those of a helpless puppy. She looked dazed, as if through all the endless comments she'd made about her demise, she hadn't considered it a reality until the doctor confirmed the shortcomings of her mortality. She was at the bidding of an intangible force controlling the rest of her decline. All she could do was wait, and that powerlessness crippled her.

The mood in the house would lighten after Vaishu Mavshi left for work. I couldn't tell if my mother didn't understand the gravity of my Aaji's situation or if she chose to ignore it, but regardless, she treated my grandmother no differently after the diagnosis. The two of them would watch countless shows on the couch and play cards around the living room table. My Aaji remained at my mother's beck and call with stories, massages, and hot meals, an arrangement that served my mother well after she was fired from the salon.

The Monday after the fight with Simran, Vaishu Mavshi implored my mother to go to the salon and apologize. My prideful mother said that she would only go if Simran called her first. She waited for a week, but no call came. Trying to throw hints at Simran, my mother strode up and down Main Street, passing the salon without peeking inside. Another week passed with no contact.

Fed up with Simran's lack of initiative, my mother stormed to the salon. I accompanied her to see firsthand what would unfold. When my mother entered, Simran held up her hand.

"Uh-uh, you are not stepping one more foot in here."

"Come on, Simran! I've worked here for a decade."

"I don't care. I've had enough of your drama."

I clutched the door handle, afraid that my mother's response would be explosive. However, she turned away from Simran with her head held high.

"You'll be sorry. Come, Aku."

"Crazy woman," muttered Simran.

My mother halted, pursing her lips. In an instant, she whipped around, grabbed a box of hair dye by the entrance, and threw it across the room. The box split. Red liquid exploded on the walls, floors, and salon workers. Simran shrieked as thick globs dripped off her.

"*Get out!*" Simran screeched.

My mother hurried me out of the salon. She smiled triumphantly the rest of the way home, reveling in her victory. I was in terrified awe of her.

Vaishu Mavshi begged my mother to seek new employment, but my mother would shrug these concerns off, vowing to look eventually. Though she wouldn't admit it, she seemed to be in shock that Simran hadn't reinstated her. Simran had threatened her before, but consequences had never been doled out. My mother had only worked in this one place, having started at the salon shortly after giving birth to me. Without the routine of her job, she was unsure what to do with herself. She spent hours in front of the television and only rose from the sofa if she needed a bathroom break. She rarely changed out of her pajamas and passed off most chores she was assigned to other family members.

Through the thin walls, I could hear Vaishu Mavshi privately expressing to Harsh Kaka that the income being brought in was not enough to support everyone, especially with my Aaji's increasing medical costs. Harsh Kaka gently comforted her, as he always did, promising that they would figure it out.

I paid little mind to these mounting anxieties, as the return to elementary school brought forth its own set of challenges. I began sixth grade, and Sagar, a year younger than me, started fifth. We attended Accelerated Academy, a small school that most children from the Town went to as well. The school covered kindergarten through sixth, after which students would have to transition over to junior high within the City. From the first day back, my classmates tried to act more grown up than they had in fifth grade. Many of them discarded their immature tendencies for more middle school–appropriate behavior. During lunch, Bilal Hadi and Sameer Rahman hung out on the outdoor bleachers, giggling over stolen lingerie magazines. Sania Reddy appointed herself the leader of a group of girls who traded lip gloss and intensely discussed the latest vampire-romance novel. Brainiac Kunal Deo sat with his Math Olympiad friends, battling them to solve the highest number of problems. Unlike the previous year when we would all play with each other, the sixth-grade class separated into exclusive, tightly knit groups. Unfortunately for me and Sagar, our friends had dispersed into other circles, leaving us on the outskirts.

At first, I couldn't grasp why the rest of the class would choose these dull activities over the excitement of our imaginative worlds. There weren't any limits or rules to our fantasies, just endless fun. But the sixth graders' judgmental stares when Sagar and I threw invisible swords at each other made me feel increasingly self-conscious. When I saw the way we behaved through their critical eyes, I began to see how our antics could appear ridiculous to those not directly involved. Without an understanding or acceptance of the invented world, Sagar and I did just look like two kids goofing off. I used to take my make-believe roles very seriously, believing wholeheartedly that I was a warrior immersed in an intense battle. But my conviction in the illusion declined the more distanced I felt from my peers. I continued to play with Sagar, but I couldn't shake the feeling that it was time to evolve along with the other sixth graders and find a more age-appropriate source of entertainment.

An opportunity to do so was ignited after Mayuran Selvaratnam tapped me on the shoulder during a math test. He leaned in and whispered, "Let me see your answers."

I stiffened, having never cheated before. My peers and I were used to completing our work like we were asked, especially since many of the teachers at Accelerated Academy were integrated within our community. My sixth-grade teacher, Aneesa Aziz, was a dear friend of the family and someone I deeply respected. I glanced up to see if she was watching me and Mayuran, but she was copying the homework assignment onto the whiteboard, oblivious to the misconduct happening behind her. Mayuran was waiting for my answer. I set aside my guilt and pushed my Scantron into his line of sight.

When everyone in the class had finished their tests and conversation was allowed again, Mayuran tapped me once more. He had a dark complexion and a buzz cut so short that I could see his scalp. An elongated, cracked scar stretched across his temple to the right side of his cheek. He wore an oversized T-shirt with a faded, washed-out logo. His eyes were narrow, and his nose was wide, like a flattened mountain above his mouth.

"Thanks," he said. "No one else lets me copy off them."

"No problem," I replied.

The lunch bell rang, and I stood up to leave the classroom.

"Wait," he called out.

"Yeah?"

"What are you doing after school?"

I was thrown off by his question. "Going home."

"Not today. Let's hang out."

"O-okay," I stuttered. "What do you want to do?"

He shrugged. "What do you like to do?"

I scrambled for an answer. His prominent, disconcerting scar matured his face, making him appear tough and intimidating. I was embarrassed to tell him about the games that Sagar and I played in the forest, expecting him to ridicule them. While trying to think of an activity that would make me seem cool, I recalled Nikhil's offer and blurted out, "Video games."

"*You* play video games?" he asked with a doubtful smirk.

"Yes. All the time," I said, shoving myself deeper into the lie.

"What do you play?"

I answered with a title I'd seen in Nikhil's car.

I hoped that Mayuran would not know the game and instead suggest another activity I didn't need to lie about.

He nodded, impressed. "Never would have taken you to play shooter games. Got any at your house?"

I squirmed. "No."

"Then where do you play?"

"Well, um, you know Nikhil Das? He has a ton of games at his store. But we really don't have to—"

"Great! I'll meet you outside the cafeteria when school ends, and we can walk over there."

He strode away. I was left dizzy from the conversation, unsure how I was going to sell my unanticipated lie.

———

"Mayuran?"

"Yes."

"Mayuran Selvaratnam?"

"Saying his full name doesn't change who it is."

"But-but why?" asked Sagar. We were standing by the entrance of the playground, where we typically met at the end of the school day to walk home together.

I shrugged. "He wanted to. Do you want to come?"

"No way! I don't even understand why you're going. He's scary."

"You've never spoken to him before."

"Duh. Because he's scary!"

Mayuran and his father were known for their reclusiveness. Unlike most houses in the Town that were part of the cul-de-sacs, Mayuran's house was built on a detached path in the forest. His father, Selvaratnam (Ratnam for short), was a gruff and unpleasant man. He owned a small construction business that operated mostly in the City. Our community knew little about his past except that he'd lived in Sri Lanka before moving to America. It was rumored that his wife had been killed in the violent civil war, leaving a resentful and devastated Ratnam with a broken home and an infant son. How he'd come to the United States and found refuge in the Town was unclear, but the inhabitants of the Town knew better than to ask. Ratnam tried to lead as private a life as possible, only appearing to cause conflict. He would pick verbal fights with shop owners on Main Street over pre-written prices, and he had a longstanding feud with Bhaskar Uncle. Although Bhaskar Uncle approached every person in the Town with respect, Ratnam resisted his authority and wished to challenge him at every opportunity. The only events Ratnam showed up to were the monthly town hall meetings in Bhaskar Uncle's shop, where he deliberately acted as a contrarian.

Because of Ratnam's disagreeable behavior, parents urged their children to stay away from Mayuran. Most lunches, Mayuran would eat by himself in a corner, not making eye contact with anyone. In class, he sat in the last row and would rarely contribute to group activities. Unsettling rumors spread about him. Sania said that she saw him torturing snails for fun. Sameer claimed that Mayuran sold drugs for Ratnam. Although the verity of these statements was questionable, I'd previously refrained from speaking to him out of caution. But ever since he'd asked me to hang out, I'd been wondering whether he really was as bad as others made him out to be. I might have still been able to back out, but I was intrigued by the individual behind this enigmatic persona.

"I should find him," I said.

"We'll play together after, right?" asked Sagar.

"Of course. Whatever game you want."

He was pleased with my answer.

Before walking away, I added, "Can you keep this between us? Our moms will worry if they find out."

Sagar rolled his eyes.

"Promise?" I asked.

"Promise."

Sagar and I parted ways. I walked to the cafeteria and

found Mayuran standing outside, tossing a few loose rocks against the wall.

I cleared my throat. "H-hey!"

He whipped around. "I didn't think you'd come."

"You still wanna hang out?"

He nodded, and the two of us shuffled together toward Main Street. I asked him again if there was another activity he wanted to do, but he was set on video games. I wasn't sure if Nikhil was working that afternoon, but I prayed that he was. I didn't want to lose face in front of Mayuran, even if it meant fraternizing with my father's enemy.

Nikhil and I hadn't seen each other since he'd dropped me and my mother off in Manhattan. My mother had pleaded for subsequent meetings, contending that the first one had been too abrupt for a proper introduction. I'd resisted her attempts out of loyalty to my father, but my efforts hadn't been able to prevent her and Nikhil's burgeoning relationship. My mother spent copious time with him after she was let go, and I was the only one she'd swoon to about their dates. She still hadn't told anyone else in the family. I could tell she enjoyed the secrecy—the sneaking out during Aaji's naps and the coy smiles she would hide from Vaishu Mavshi. Nikhil made her happy in this generally melancholic period of her life. As much as I wanted their liaison to end, I couldn't bring myself to spoil her excitement.

When Mayuran and I reached Das Electronics, I was relieved to see Nikhil behind the counter. He took his earbuds out when he saw me approaching.

"Akash? What are you—is your mother all right?"

"She's fine," I responded. I checked to see if Mayuran had picked up on the question, but he was surveying the store, unaware of our conversation. "We wanted to play a video game."

Nikhil relaxed, pleasantly surprised with my request. "Sure. Any particular game?"

I looked to Mayuran for an answer, but he replied, "Whatever you want to play."

I gulped and said one of the titles I'd seen when searching through Nikhil's car.

Nikhil scratched his beanie. "Aren't you a little too young for that game?"

"No. It's my favorite."

"Really? It has a lot of violence. Tons of blood and gore."

Mayuran grinned. "Cool."

I was too committed to the lie to back down. I prayed that Nikhil would catch on. "I play it all the time here, remember?"

Although he was visibly perplexed, Nikhil did not ask any more questions. His eyes flitted between me and Mayuran, assessing our relationship. "Okay. Come over to the back."

"This is so cool. I can't believe he lets you play here anytime you want," whispered Mayuran as we walked around the counter to the back room. Das Electronics was a narrow, cluttered shop that sold used electronics, such as DVD and VCD players, as well as cheap copies of Indian films. The back room had a blue cloth couch and mounted TV amid a collection of other wires and gadgets. Mayuran and I situated ourselves on the couch while Nikhil set up the game.

"It's on Xbox," said Nikhil. "You know how to use it?"

"Yeah," I replied, hoping I could pick up the game from Mayuran.

"Yep, me too," Mayuran chimed in.

Action music blasted from the TV speakers as images of a simulated war-torn country popped up. Nikhil handed me and Mayuran weirdly shaped game controllers with an assortment of buttons.

"Let me know if you have any questions. Have fun."

After Nikhil bowed out, I peeked at Mayuran to see if he knew how to play. I assumed he would know more about video games since he'd expressed interest in playing them with me. However, he seemed equally confused by the controller. He glanced over at me for guidance.

Trying to save both of us from embarrassment, I said, "It's been a while since I've done this. I'll ask Nikhil for some help."

"Good idea," said Mayuran. "It's been a while for me too."

I went back to the main store. Nikhil was organizing DVD players on the shelf.

"What's up?" he said.

"We don't know how to play," I admitted.

"I thought so. I remember in the car your mom said you hadn't played video games before. Why'd you say you had?"

I hung my head. "I was being dumb."

Nikhil smiled. With a kind voice, he responded, "No, you weren't. I remember trying to fit in when I was your age. I'll come help."

"Thanks."

"Before we go back, I want to ask you something. Has your mom said anything about me? Maybe about how she feels?"

I could have lied. I could have planted doubt in support of my father, but Nikhil's act of allegiance made me reconsider. "She likes you a lot."

He perked up, grinning widely. "Really? She's something else, man. I've never felt this way about anyone before."

"Please don't tell my mom that I came with Mayuran."

Recognition dawned on Nikhil's face. "Ratnam's son, huh? I won't say a word. I'll tell her you came to play on your own."

He patted my shoulder and led me back to the Xbox. He gave me and Mayuran thorough instructions on how to play before leaving us alone. We scoped out the game for our first few rounds, testing out the guns and grenades, shooting at bots and watching blood spurt out of them. Once we got the hang of it, we were ruthlessly competitive. During intense moments of the game, Mayuran would yell at the television, squeezing the commands on his controller. We leaned against each other, trying to hinder the other person's ability to move or see the screen.

One round, I was so invested in trying to beat him that I jumped on him, punching my buttons with one hand, while reaching for his controller with the other. As I tried to locate it, I grasped at Mayuran's hip, triggering a fit of laughter with my inadvertent tickling. His face contracted, as if he was about to let out a sneeze. An uncontrollable, throaty, horse-like sound erupted from his mouth. His cheeks turned dark red, and tears formed around the corners of his eyes. I couldn't look away.

Nikhil interrupted us when the shop was about to close. Mayuran and I left the back room and went back onto Main Street at the peak of dusk. Soft pink clouds shone above us, a rare sight in this somber fall. So much time had passed since we'd started playing, even though it had only felt like a few minutes.

"I had a lot of fun," I said.

"Me too," said Mayuran. "Let's do this again."

He walked away, adjusting his backpack straps. He turned around once more to wave at me. I drifted home, charmed by my new and unexpected friend.

Sagar was waiting for me in our room. "I thought you were dead."

"We hung out for a long time," I said. "It was fun."

"Weird. Ready to go play?"

"It's getting dark, and I'm tired."

Sagar's face drooped in disappointment.

"We can play tomorrow?"

"Promise?"

"Sure, yeah."

I fell onto my bed and covered myself with my comforter. Though it was much earlier than my usual bedtime, I succumbed to my drowsiness. My sleep was accompanied by a strange set of dreams. I was sitting in the oval where Suhail Mama and Kiara Mami's wedding reception had taken place. There was nothing around me—no tables, no people—except for the Singer.

He sat in front of me, tanpura in his lap, singing the same tune he'd sung before the reception. His voice was strained, the song even more harrowing than before. He suddenly stopped singing and locked eyes with mine.

"You have a gift, Akash."

The trees began to sway, and one by one, the leaves vaporized into strands of paint, joining the blue that dripped off the sky. The colors swirled around us … and, suddenly, I was back in Das Electronics.

Mayuran was sprawled out next to me, and he was laughing heartily. He grabbed my hand. Our faces were only a few inches apart, and I could feel his warm breath tickling the tip of my nose.

I woke up in a frenzy, my skin drenched in sweat. It was nighttime, and Sagar was fast asleep next to me. As I regained awareness of my body, I sensed something unusual under my covers. I reached my hand down to my underwear and felt a thick, sticky substance the same consistency as glue. I threw my covers off and tiptoed out of the room. The common bathroom was in the tiny hallway between the living room and kitchen. I tiptoed downstairs and heard a crunching noise coming from the kitchen. Harsh Kaka was standing by the coffee machine, eating a slice of toast.

"Harsh Kaka?"

He jumped. "Akash! You startled me!"

"What time is it?"

"It's very early. I'm going to head to the pharmacy soon. You must be starving. We wanted to wake you up for dinner, but you were fast asleep."

My stomach growled. I looked down and saw the dark circle on my pajamas. Harsh Kaka's eyes followed mine.

"Oh," he said, clearing his throat. "Nothing to worry about. I'll, uh, I'll start you a bath."

———

Harsh Kaka made me eggs and toast while I cleaned up. After I devoured my breakfast, he explained the bodily changes that I would experience as I transitioned from boy to man. He emphasized that it was nothing to be ashamed of. I could tell that he was uncomfortable with the conversation—his eyes flitted around, and his voice shook every time he said the word "sperm." But he powered through and explained puberty to me with as much clarity as I needed.

"It's tough undergoing this much change," he said. "I remember how angry I was with myself at your age."

I was stunned. "You? Angry?"

"The bodily changes will be tough, but the changes of the mind will be the most difficult to grapple with."

"What does that mean?"

"During this transition, you are going to feel like you're splitting in two. There will be an adult version and child version of yourself. As the adult version takes over, you will slowly lose the child inside of you. It happens every time someone tells you a story about your younger self and you can't remember why you acted that way. And, although you're losing this child version, you won't have fully grown into the adult version either. It's too new. Too unknown." Harsh Kaka's expression became distant, and his voice quieter. "That's when the anger sets in. You'll develop emotions that are hard to control and learn many uncomfortable truths about life. You'll get mad at the world for taking away your innocence, and you'll feel frustrated with yourself for not being able to recognize the person you are inside. But as time passes, you'll figure out a way to adjust. We all have to accept at one point or another that change is inevitable."

Off my puzzled expression, Harsh Kaka asked, "Does any of that make sense?"

"Not really."

He chuckled. "It might one day."

"Do you still feel angry with yourself?"

His eyes clouded. "Sometimes. But not as often anymore." He checked his watch and stood up. "I should go to the pharmacy. Are you feeling okay?"

"Yes. Thanks, Harsh Kaka."

He caressed my cheek. "You're going to make a great man, Aku."

After he left for work, I finished breakfast in the cold light of dawn and went up to my bedroom. Sagar was still fast asleep, snoring as loudly as ever. I couldn't imagine Sagar experiencing any of the changes Harsh Kaka had described. His personality was defined by his immaturity. He cherished his innocence and shunned all that interfered with his child-like reverie. I was slightly envious of his stagnant ignorance, of the trust and wonder he had when he looked at the world.

If only I'd understood then what I know now as an adult, I would have counted my blessings that my metamorphosis began when it did. Although Harsh Kaka's advice was hauntingly prophetic, he left out one key detail. Change within us is not only inevitable, it is necessary. This volatile world is unforgiving to those who are not able to transform alongside it.

CHAPTER 5

THE STATION

I HAVE SPENT many years of my life trying to comprehend the unfortunate event that unfolded within the Town. I've come to understand that what seemed like an isolated incident had been in the making for some time, building silently like steam in a pressure cooker.

As mentioned, the Town and City had little in common; the dividing strip of forest between us concealed our immigrant community. These two localities stayed as quiet, respectful neighbors until a project propelled by the City threatened to disrupt the Town's solitude. The looming opening of a fully constructed train station, the formidable glass building tucked away between the Town and City, inspired in our community celebration among a few and concern among most others.

Construction for the station began long before I was born. The aim had always been to ease transportation from the City into larger metropolises. The onerous trek to Manhattan that required multiple train and bus transfers would be condensed to one direct line, reducing the travel time in half for commuters.

This project, however, had a history of ill luck. It was subject to numerous erratic halts, so construction would occur only in brief intervals. Leadership would change, or the workers would strike, or an economic crash would divert City resources, causing the station to be put on hold. This on-off pattern made the project seem unattainable, and most residents in the Town believed that the station would never be completed. From what I was told, the tracks lay for years as a dormant, rusted metal backbone. When I was six years old, a new mayor was elected to power, and the fate of the station was decided. Mayor Rivera had a bold vision for the City's future, with accessibility being the central focus of his platform. He declared that the station would be a revolutionary step for the visibility of the City. If better transportation was implemented, more people would be attracted to live in the City and, consequently, more property would be developed.

With the goal of expanding business and population, the City acknowledged the Town as an underutilized space within their bounds that had great potential for development. The Town hadn't received such attention from the City before, and the newfound focus on enhancement instilled confusion among Townsfolk as to what changes should be expected after the train lines were opened.

Bhaskar Uncle would hold meetings in his shop to encourage open conversation about the station. The majority of Townsfolk were in favor of ensuring that the station didn't see the light of day. Though some just didn't want construction noise going on for years, the primary concern was that further development would uproot the secluded foundation of the Town. Most families had moved to this neighborhood because of its isolation. Being separate, rather than integrated into the City, allowed residents, especially those of the older generation, to find comfort among neighbors with similar experiences and imagine the Town as a close reproduction to their places of origin. They feared that if the Town grew, the community and shops would expand and shift to echo those of any other American suburb. The illusion of our unique neighborhood would be broken, and the strong cultural connection maintained through this slight distance from American life would decline.

Bhaskar Uncle brought the Town's concerns to the City council, but he was quickly shot down. Only one member of the City's governing body was from the Town, so the pleas for privacy were trivial when compared to the economic promises of the project. He attempted a few more times, but it became clear that the mayor and council were already set in their plan.

Trucks, cranes, and gear-clad men appeared in full force to expedite the station's completion. Property developers meandered around Main Street, observing the stores from outside and scribbling on their notepads. Once, a neatly dressed woman stood on our cul-de-sac, her hands clasped behind her back. She peered at our house for about ten minutes before Vaishu Mavshi waved from our window. The woman pursed her lips into a thin smile and cruised away.

The Town endured the obstreperous construction and unsettling interactions for years. Though frustration was rampant among residents, all anyone could do was hope that construction would be halted again. For a while, discussion about the station subsided. But disquietude permeated the Town again after the station's opening ceremony was set for December of 2011, around six months after Suhail Mama's wedding. Conversations along Main Street shifted from light gossip and stories to more serious dialogues about what people predicted would result from the opening, and whether they would stay if the Town expanded to a point of unrecognizability.

I discovered much of the station's history later in life. As an eleven-year-old, I had limited knowledge and no opinion whatsoever on this matter. I was aware it was a heavily discussed topic, but beyond that, I was much too focused on my budding friendship with Mayuran to closely follow the issue.

It became routine after school that I would find Mayuran by the cafeteria and walk with him to Nikhil's shop. Sagar would inquire profusely about our hangouts. I could sense his jealousy, but I didn't invite him again. I enjoyed the private time I had with Mayuran, away from Sagar. Mayuran was someone I respected, someone I wanted to be. The more time I spent with him, the less I wanted to engage in Sagar's games. They seemed silly in comparison to the brutally violent video games Mayuran and I played. I would have liked to spend lunches with Mayuran as well, but out of guilt, I felt I owed those thirty minutes to Sagar. This split of time between the two of them was working well enough, until one day in October, Sagar decided to disrupt it.

"Akash Dada!"

Mayuran and I were heading over to Das Electronics when I saw Sagar sprinting toward us, his massive backpack flopping up and down his tiny frame. Sagar stopped in front of us, catching his breath.

"Sagar? What's going on?" I asked.

"I thought I could join you guys today," he replied.

"Join us?"

"Yeah. We could all play together."

"I don't think you'd enjoy what we do."

Sagar faced Mayuran. "Hi. I'm Sagar."

"I know," replied Mayuran.

"What do you say? Can I join you?"

Mayuran shrugged. "Why not?"

His indifference disappointed me. I'd hoped that Mayuran would want to spend time only with me. Any excuse I came up with to deny Sagar's request would seem malicious if Mayuran was okay with it.

I sighed. "Fine."

The three of us walked to Nikhil's back room. Mayuran set Sagar up with a controller. Mayuran and I had become pros at multiplayer shooter games, and we took turns explaining the rules to Sagar. The first match was Mayuran against Sagar. Within seconds, Mayuran shot at Sagar and killed him. Sagar gaped at the screen as his avatar's lifeless body leaked blood.

"You have to shoot," I advised. "You can't stay in one place."

Sagar recomposed and pressed the button for a new game. He immediately ran away from his starting position, but Mayuran found his avatar shortly after and demolished it with rapid gunfire. Sagar winced while the thunderous theme score roared on screen. Mayuran chuckled.

Sensing Sagar's frustration, I grabbed the controller from Mayuran. "Let me play."

I gave Sagar the upper hand in the next round and ran as far away from him as possible. He cowered at every gunshot and recoiled when gore splattered across the screen. The violence was paralyzing for him. Although most of our fantasy games in the forest were on a battlefield, imagination softened the violence. With video games, Sagar was forced to see the grisly images displayed on screen. Sensing movement near my avatar, I swiveled around and threw a grenade. Sagar's avatar blew up. The game was over.

Sagar jolted up, throwing the controller on the couch. "How can you like this? It's so- it's so- horrible!"

"You wanted to come," I pointed out.

"Why don't you play with me in the forest anymore? Those games are way more fun than pressing dumb buttons."

"What do you do in the forest?" Mayuran inquired.

"Nothing," I quickly said.

"We could show you," pressed Sagar.

"Mayuran's not interested—"

"Sure. Let's go," Mayuran interrupted.

I looked helplessly between the two of them. I feared that if Mayuran saw what Sagar and I played, he would judge me for engaging in something so juvenile. I wanted him to regard me as his equal, not as inferior or immature.

Before I could protest, Sagar stood up, triumph shining in his eyes. "Follow me."

———

Among the three trees, Sagar instructed Mayuran. He paced from side to side, retelling the story of Arjuna and Karna, building the imaginary world with theatrical dramatization. His arms swung with overzealous passion. I used to love how invested Sagar was in his storytelling, but this time, his enthusiasm made him look incredibly foolish. Mayuran main-tained a subtle smirk the entire time. Out of embarrassment, I frequently interrupted to assure Mayuran that he didn't have to play if he didn't want to. Sagar would shush me, and Mayuran mockingly imitated him.

"As usual, I will be Arjuna, the archer," said Sagar. "Akash will be his nemesis, Karna. And you can be one of the soldiers."

"What exactly do we do?" asked Mayuran.

"We act out the story, of course."

"But we're in a forest."

"Haven't you been listening? You have to imagine the battlefield. Pretend that you're covered in armor and other soldiers are fighting around us. We can be somewhere else without ever having to leave the Town."

"What if I see the battlefield differently than you do?"

Sagar blinked. "What do you mean?"

"Let's say I see a soldier standing over there." Mayuran pointed in an arbitrary direction. "I imagine that soldier to be running at you, but you don't know that since you can't see him. Then, in my mind, that soldier cuts off your head and you die."

Sagar was stunned. The mechanics of his game hadn't been questioned before. My eyes darted between the two of them, apprehensive of the rising tension.

"None of the other soldiers can kill us," replied Sagar.

"Fine. But let's say you run into a soldier. Shouldn't you at least fall—"

"None of the other soldiers can touch us! Can we please just play the game!"

"I have one more question."

"What is it?" Sagar snapped.

"Didn't you say this story already has an ending? Doesn't Arjuna defeat Karna?"

"Yeah, so?"

"That seems unfair. We fight, but you win at the end no matter what. Don't you think so, Akash?"

"I don't know. It's not that big of a deal," I said, nervously glancing at Sagar.

"Akash, do you ever get to win?"

My palms were sweaty. "Not really."

"Don't you ever want to win?"

"Sometimes, I guess."

"You never told me that," said Sagar.

"Well, why don't we switch it up?" announced Mayuran, his eyes glinting. "We can keep the same characters, but this time, we won't decide beforehand who's going to win."

"That's not how it's supposed to go!" exclaimed Sagar. "Arjuna has to defeat Karna."

"It's just a story. We can change the ending for one game. What do you say, Akash?"

"O-okay," I stammered.

Though I anticipated further objections from Sagar, he quietly responded, "Fine. But it's unfair if you both are on the same team."

Mayuran smiled. "I'll join yours."

I closed my eyes, commencing my count for Mayuran and Sagar to get a head start. "One, two, three …"

After reaching thirty, I jogged around the surrounding area to find them. The magic of the game was lost for me, knowing Mayuran was a part of it. I couldn't pretend that the forest was anything but a forest or that I was anyone but myself. I moved sluggishly, with discomfort and disinterest. The routine I had grown up loving was becoming slightly tiresome and boring.

A rustle caught my attention. My head whipped around, and I saw movement behind a tree.

"Got you," I murmured. When I reached the tree, I was surprised to find that no one was behind it. Where could Sagar and Mayuran have darted to within those few seconds?

The tune began so softly, I assumed it was the call of a bird. But soon enough, the haunting, melodic voice crystallized, echoing around me. I looked around with unease. I had convinced myself after Suhail Mama's wedding reception that I'd probably dozed off and dreamed up the whole interaction with the Singer. There wasn't any other plausible explanation for why a strange, unnamed musician would randomly be at a wedding without an invitation from the couple. But the voice I heard then—undoubtedly the Singer's voice—was too loud and concrete to be imaginary. I was engulfed by doubt. Why would the Singer be practicing here? What could he possibly be doing in the middle of a forest? I ran to where I thought his voice was coming from, but with each step, the tune grew fainter. I pivoted, dodging bushes and leaping over fallen branches.

"Hello?" I yelled.

I caught a glimpse of a white kurta peeking out behind a tree. The Singer's face wasn't visible, but seeing a sliver of his clothing was enough for me to sprint in that direction.

Bam! I slammed into another body, and we toppled to the ground. My vision took a few seconds to readjust and register that I'd collided into Mayuran. I lay on top of him. Our faces were an inch away from each other. We were breathless, our bodies motionless.

"Aren't you gonna get off me?" teased Mayuran.

"Oh, right, sorry." I climbed off and scanned the surrounding area. The singing had stopped, and the kurta was nowhere to be seen. "Where's Sagar?"

"I lost him a while ago. Why were you running so fast?"

I stood up. "I thought I saw … never mind. Let's go find Sagar."

"Wait. Do you wanna keep playing this game?"

"Not really …"

"Then let's go back to Nikhil's."

"Okay. I'll find Sagar, and we can head back."

Mayuran brushed the dirt off his trousers. "Does he always boss you around like that?"

"What are you talking about?"

"Why do you play with him if you don't enjoy his games?"

"I used to."

"Come on. You don't have to lie. They're stupid."

"Sagar enjoys playing them."

"But you should do what you want."

"I know that."

"Then let's leave."

"Without Sagar?"

"He'll throw a fit if we take him back there. You know he won't want to play."

I hesitated. "Maybe, but I should at least tell him."

"He'll figure it out. We could be back at the store in less time than it'll take to find him."

Mayuran was right. Sagar knew the forest inside out and would be difficult to catch. I was conflicted, but Mayuran had already begun walking away. After a moment of indecision, I followed him, reassuring myself that Sagar was sharp enough to eventually figure out that we'd left.

When Mayuran and I resumed our video game in Nikhil's shop, I forgot all about Sagar. For two hours, we engaged in our usual antics, playfully pushing and taunting each other. Only when I walked home did I contemplate Mayuran's advice. Why did I play with Sagar if I didn't want to anymore? I enjoyed spending time with Mayuran much more. I didn't dislike Sagar; I still considered him close family. But I didn't want to force myself to do what he wanted solely because of our relation to each other. My mind was made up.

Or it was until I reached the front of my house and registered that I would have to face Sagar shortly. I played out scenarios of how he might have reacted to us leaving. I imagined him wandering through the forest, desperately searching for us, and then finally trudging home, defeated and hurt after piecing together what I had done. I wanted to believe that I wasn't in the wrong, but a twinge of guilt gnawed at me for purposely excluding him.

The entire family, including Sagar, was gathered in the living room. My Aaji was in the middle of recounting an old memory involving my mother. Vaishu Mavshi, Harsh Kaka, and Sagar sat on the floor around the living room table, while my mother and my Aaji lounged on the couch.

"… I'm telling you she was such a terror. When I asked her who broke the vase, she looked at me with wide eyes as if she had no idea what I was talking about."

"Aai, I didn't know better! You never disciplined me," said my mother, hugging my Aaji's arm tightly.

"How could I yell at that sweet face?"

Vaishu Mavshi caught me watching from the side.

"Aku, come sit here," she said, patting the floor between her and Sagar. I approached cautiously. Sagar did not make eye contact with me.

"Sagar told us what happened."

I stiffened. Of course he had.

"You had some sort of group project after school?"

I didn't reply.

"Akash?"

"Yeah, um, he's right. For ... for science."

I took my seat, nodding at Sagar in gratitude.

"We're just sharing stories from our childhood," said Vaishu Mavshi, hugging me with one arm.

"From *our* childhood? They're all embarrassing stories about me," said my mother. "This isn't fair. I don't have bad stories about Vaishu."

"Obviously. I'm more than a decade older than you. And I was much better behaved."

"Oh, if your Baba was here, he could tell you about Vaishnavi," said my Aaji pensively.

"I highly doubt that," said Vaishu Mavshi. "We were apart for most of my childhood."

"You were still young when we moved here."

"Didn't make a difference," muttered Vaishu Mavshi.

"Hm? I can't hear when you talk softly-softly."

"Aai, why do you pretend like he knew anything about us? He was aloof for most of his life."

"That isn't true. He showered you with affection."

"Only on his good days."

My Aaji knitted her eyebrows. "Enough, Vaishnavi."

"I'm tired of having this same argument with you. Believe what you want." Vaishu Mavshi picked up the empty cups on the table and walked over to the kitchen.

"How dare you?" my Aaji whispered. "How dare you speak about him like that?"

Vaishu Mavshi turned around, shocked. "I'm not denying—"

"Stop," my Aaji said, putting her hand up. "There is no respect in this house. No respect for the sacrifices that have been made."

"Aai, calm down. She's joking," my mother whispered. She glared at Vaishu Mavshi. "Cool it."

"I'm just being honest. I had to step up and take care of this family because he was off doing God-knows-what with God-knows-who—"

"Is this the way you are going to talk about me after I've passed?" my Aaji asked, her voice quivering. "Is this the respect I'm going to be shown?"

"Aai ..."

My Aaji covered her face. She hobbled out of the room and up the stairs. We flinched when we heard her bedroom door slam shut.

"What's going on with her?" Vaishu Mavshi asked my mother. "Did she have memory issues today?"

"It's not related to that," my mother replied in a hushed voice. "Uma was telling Aai this morning that she might shut her restaurant. Apparently, the mayor and some other City officials were talking to business owners along Main about potentially tearing down and redeveloping the street to make it more of a downtown area."

"Why? Because of the new train station?"

"Must be. Aai was in a bad mood the rest of the day. Kept muttering that it's a disgrace to Baba's memory. That's why I tried to distract her with these stories."

Vaishu Mavshi bit her lip. "I'm sure they were just talking hypothetically. Things won't change that much after it opens. Right?"

She looked around for reassurance, but none of us knew enough to provide it to her. She sighed and started toward the staircase. "I should go apologize."

———

"Why didn't you tell them what happened today?"

Sagar and I were lying underneath our covers. This question had been eating at me since I'd returned home, and in the privacy of our room, I finally found the courage to ask.

"Why did you leave?" he responded.

"We couldn't find you," I lied. "You're too good at hiding."

"Akash Dada, I don't like him at all. He gives me a bad feeling."

"You don't know anything about him."

"I know he's a bad influence."

"Just because he's different than you doesn't mean he's a bad influence. I like hanging out with him."

"Our parents would agree with me. They wouldn't want you hanging out with him either."

I sat up. "Have you said anything to them?"

"Not yet."

"Sagar. You promised."

"What would you do if I told them?"

"I would be really, really mad."

"Because you know they don't want you hanging out with him!"

"What is your problem?" I asked, annoyed. Sagar and I hadn't fought before, but his possessiveness was aggravating. "Sagar, just because you're jealous—"

"I'm not jealous!"

"You don't have to lie."

"I said I'm not! You can hang out with him if you want. One day, when he does something bad, don't say I didn't warn you."

I haughtily drew my covers over my head, shutting off the conversation.

Sagar and I didn't speak to each other the next morning. When lunchtime came, I looked between him prancing on the field and Mayuran sitting on his own. Taking a deep breath, I strode over to Mayuran and joined him on his bench. He was startled, as were many others on the playground. I noticed Bilal and Sameer whispering to each other and Sania pointing at us. But most importantly, I saw Sagar, his wide eyes brimming with betrayal.

CHAPTER 6

DREAMS AND CIGARETTES

SLEEP BECAME A painful source of anxiety for me. My dreams of the Singer intensified as winter neared. The situation was always the same; we were sitting at the same place we'd sat at before the reception, only this time the oval was empty. He would sing while the ground, trees, and sky deteriorated into a muddled array of hues. Midway through the song, I would shoot out of my slumber, panting and covered in sweat.

Afflicted by the discomfort, I longed for these dreams to end. I tried to suppress any thoughts about my encounter with the Singer at the reception, but the more I tried to forget him, the more I fixated on every word we'd exchanged. I wondered if these dreams were leading me to something, but what that destination could be was a complete mystery.

Although I still wasn't certain if he was real or a character I'd conjured up during an unfortunate nap, I attempted to hunt the Singer down. I quizzed my mother and Vaishu Mavshi about his presence at the wedding. My mother repeated that she wasn't aware of a singer being there. Vaishu Mavshi became concerned with my persistent mention of him, so I refrained from pushing her. I didn't divulge my troubling dreams or the glimpse I'd caught of him in the forest, afraid that it would cause them additional stress. I prodded my mother to call Suhail Mama and confirm that he hadn't booked a singer. He swore to her that he'd only hired a DJ.

Deciding to expand my questioning outside of the family, I approached Aneesa Aunty. In addition to teaching at the elementary school, she hosted classes at her house for semi-classical Hindustani music. I described the Singer to her and even tried to hum the thumri. She assured me that she was well connected with other Indian and Pakistani singers in the area but hadn't heard of someone who fit my description.

Without any leads, my last option was to wait for him. On the weekends, I would sit for hours at the oval, hoping he would show up. But the Singer was nowhere to be found, and the torturous dreams continued.

———

Once I began hanging out with Mayuran during lunch, our relationship evolved from solely playing video games to having conversations about our lives and interests. Mayuran shared his love for heavy metal music with me. He would sneak his father's iPod into school and play his favorite bands, one earbud in his right ear, the other in my left. Although I didn't enjoy the genre, I loved watching Mayuran mimic the drum flourishes and tap his feet to the beat. I listened to it because he adored it.

Mayuran dreamed of the day he could leave the Town. He would express his plans to be a world traveler, listing all the countries that he wanted to visit in the future.

"The Town is like a jail. You stay here, and you miss out on a lifetime of experiences. Will you come, Akash? Will you see the world with me?"

I eagerly told him I would.

The only subject Mayuran avoided was his family. He rarely mentioned his father. It seemed accidental when he did, and he would swiftly pivot to another topic right after. I waited for him to mention his late mother. I was certain she constituted the most vulnerable part of him, and I wished for Mayuran to share that critical piece of his past with me.

Because of my association with Mayuran, my classmates regarded me with a hint of respect in their eyes and fear in their voices. Bilal and Sameer interrogated me about Mayuran's personality. They wanted to know if any of the rumors about him were true. I would respond with nothing more than a coy smile and shrug. They pleaded with me, offering to do my homework anytime I wished, but I always declined. I preferred that the contents of my relationship with Mayuran remained a secret, preserved between the two of us.

Mayuran and I continued to play shooter games after school. I became numb to the violence of the simulated world, unabashedly sending out a flurry of bullets, smiling with glee as blood spurted out of made-up soldiers. I dreaded the moment Mayuran would say he had to head home, but I was elated when he left each hangout asking if we could continue the next day.

Returning home to Sagar sucked away any jubilation I retained from the hangout. After my decision to spend lunches with Mayuran, Sagar played mostly by himself in the schoolyard. He tried to replace me with some of his fifth-grade friends, but they reacted poorly to being bossed around. Without a companion, Sagar's battle cries and imaginary swordfights appeared even more outlandish. I wished Sagar would control his untamed imagination, let go of these ridiculous worlds, and join the rest of us in this new, grounded stage of adolescence.

Hoping to optically build distance between us at school, I avoided Sagar every lunch and recess. Whether it was guilt for leaving him or shame for having once looked as silly as he did, I became cold toward Sagar. At home, unless we were surrounded by family, we rarely spoke to each other. I would close myself up in our room, replaying each moment spent with Mayuran, while Sagar sat in our Aaji's room and listened to her stories. Although there wasn't any verbal acknowledgment of the rift, we both knew that our relationship was strained. Neither of us fully understood why or how, but I made little effort to reconcile.

One afternoon in late November, Mayuran and I were surprised to find Nikhil's father, Pronoy, working the front register at Das Electronics. Due to a sustained injury Pronoy had in his right leg, he mostly handled the back end of the business and rarely came to the shop, leaving the bulk of customer service to Nikhil. Mayuran and I were unsure whether Pronoy knew about the video game arrangement. We decided it was better not to expose ourselves and have our privileges taken away. Mayuran suggested that we go to Juhi's Groceries instead and pick up snacks. I agreed, eager to continue spending time with him.

Juhi's Groceries was a one-stop grocery market for many familiar brands from India and Pakistan, including Shan masala, Amul butter, and Laxmi dals. Juhi Aunty was one of the old-timers, just like Bhaskar Uncle, and her shop had been around since the early days of the Town. As a result, she had formed close relationships with almost every family in our community, and her store was frequented by Desis living in surrounding areas. She and my Aaji were close friends; a simple grocery visit would take hours as they chitchatted their way through a whole bunch of this and that. She wore hefty circular spectacles and perpetually smelled of garam masala and coconut oil. Although trusting and kind-hearted, Juhi Aunty had a reputation for being a bit kooky. She strongly believed in astrology, often engaging in lengthy discussions with her customers about their future. Although she was selective about what she said, her predictions unfailingly came true.

When Mayuran and I entered the store, Juhi Aunty was perched behind the counter, bundled from head to toe in warm clothing. She set her newspaper down and looked at me. "Hello, dear. It's chilly out today, huh?"

"Yes, Aunty," I replied.

"I see you've brought a friend, Akash."

"This is Mayuran."

"I know who he is," she said, staring him up and down, her expression turning grim.

"We just came in to get some snacks."

Her gentle smile reappeared, and she returned to her newspaper. "Of course. Let me know if you need any help."

Mayuran and I meandered through the aisles. We each picked up a packet of Kurkure Masala Munch chips near the back of the store. I checked my backpack for loose change and found only a stray quarter.

"Do you have any money?" I asked.

Mayuran shook his head no. I started to put the packet back on the shelf, but Mayuran grabbed my arm.

"What are you doing?" he whispered.

"We don't have money."

"Watch this." He slid his bag of chips under his thick wool jacket. His layers were bulky enough to hide it.

"Mayuran, you can't do that!" I glanced at Juhi Aunty. She was still reading her newspaper, unaware of Mayuran's actions.

"It's fine. I've done it before. She's too gullible to notice."

I gulped. Although I knew it was wrong to steal, Mayuran's audaciousness was inspiring. I stuffed my bag of chips under my jacket too. My fingers tingled from the adrenaline of this immoral stunt. I crossed my arms over my chest so that the chips wouldn't slip out.

"See?" he whispered. "Tell me that wasn't fun."

"It was."

"I think we can shoot even higher. I need you to create a distraction for me. Break something, make a mess, I don't care. Got it?"

I nodded, curious what he was planning. I handed my chips to him and walked to an adjacent aisle filled with sacks of dal. I grabbed as many as I could fit in my arms before tossing them on the ground. The smacking sound startled me, even though I was the one that had thrown the packets. Juhi Aunty hobbled around the corner of the aisle.

"Everything okay?"

"I was trying to reach for one packet, and they all came tumbling down. I'm sorry, Juhi Aunty."

"No worries, dear. Come, help me pick them up."

She walked over, and we began rearranging the packets on the shelf.

"Let me," I said, as she struggled to lift herself back up from bending over. I felt remorse for having caused a ruckus in her store. Whatever Mayuran was planning wasn't worth this.

"All good, dear, all good." She winced as she straightened out her back. "Weren't you here for a snack? Why were you picking out dal?"

"Vaishu Mavshi!" I blurted, my guilt increasing with each lie. "She wanted to make some tonight."

Juhi Aunty picked the last bag off the ground and held it out to me. "Here. You can take this bag of moong dal for her free of charge. Wish her my best, okay?"

"Thank you, Aunty." I hesitantly took the bag and went back to where the Kurkure chips were. Mayuran wasn't there. I searched for him around the store.

"Have you seen Mayuran?" I asked Juhi Aunty at the counter.

"He must have gone outside."

"Right. Thanks again for the dal, Aunty." I turned to the exit.

"Akash."

"Yes?"

"Beware of that boy," she stated, her eyes steadfastly peering into mine. "Those who pretend to be someone they aren't end up being the most dangerous."

"I don't understand." Did she know about the chips we were stealing?

Instead of responding, Juhi Aunty fluffed out her newspaper and began humming to herself. I took that as my cue to leave.

Mayuran was leaning on the wall outside. He grinned at me. "Mission accomplished."

"What did you do?"

"Shh," he said, yanking me behind the building so we weren't visible to anyone on Main Street. "You can't make too much noise."

"Why? What's going on?"

He reached under his jacket and pulled out a pack of cigarettes and a lighter.

"What? How did you …" I visualized where Juhi Aunty kept the cigarettes. They were hung up on the wall behind her counter, away from the reach of children. I hadn't paid much attention to them before, since no one in my family smoked.

"Your distraction helped me sneak behind the counter and grab them."

"I don't know if I want to do this, Mayuran."

"One ciggy won't hurt you." He plucked one out of the pack and held it up to me. "What do you say?"

I was conflicted, thinking back to Vaishu Mavshi's lectures about the dangers of cigarettes. She had shown me and Sagar horrifying, graphic images of people dying from lung cancer. Still, it was only one cigarette, and I didn't want to appear weak in front of Mayuran.

I yanked it from him. He clapped me on the back.

"What do I do?" I asked.

He guided the cigarette to my lips.

"Suck in," he said, bringing the lighter to the end of the cigarette.

I sucked in as hard as I could, and a rush of thick, putrid smoke swept into my mouth and burned my throat. I coughed, and the smoke spewed out of my mouth, dissolving in the chilly winter air. Each cough intensified the pain in my throat. "That was horrible."

Mayuran laughed. He held the cigarette to his lips and sucked in. He did not cough like I had, but instead, puckered his lips and let the smoke smoothly exit in his exhale. "It takes some time to get the hang of it. Try another drag."

"No way."

"You won't know if you like it unless you give it a few more tries."

I reluctantly took the cigarette from him and clenched my throat to prevent too much from going in. I coughed only a couple times after exhaling. "How are you so good at it?"

"My dad smokes a lot around the house. I steal some from his stash while he's asleep and practice."

I took advantage of this opening into his home life. "Does your dad care that you smoke?"

Mayuran snickered. "He doesn't know. If he found out, he would … it wouldn't be pretty."

"What is he like?" I asked, seeing how far I could take this.

"My dad? He's okay. He can be scary sometimes, but I know it's just because he's sad."

"From losing your mom?"

Mayuran regarded me suspiciously. "What do you know about my mom?"

"Nothing," I said, worried that I had overstepped. "I just know you don't have one anymore."

Mayuran softened. "My dad misses her a lot. He misses the rest of his family too. All of them died in Lanka. You probably knew that already."

"I didn't."

"Sometimes I think he hates living here. But he doesn't know where else to go."

"What if he went back?"

"To Lanka? No way. There's nothing left for him there. Nothing for me either. The stories he tells me about what he saw there …"

Mayuran shuddered and tossed the cigarette to the ground. The biting cold stifled the remaining spark.

"Do you miss your mom?"

"Why are you asking me this?"

"I'm sorry. We don't need to talk about her."

We remained quiet for a few minutes. Then, he lit another cigarette and replied, "How could I miss someone I've never met?"

I feared that I had gone too far, but I couldn't help myself. I needed to know more about him, what he thought about, what he felt every day, why he sheltered his life so much.

"It's possible," I said.

His expression grew distant. He passed the cigarette to me, and we continued to smoke in silence. My throat felt as if it were on fire from the toxins I was breathing in, and yet, I persisted.

"My father says I look a lot like her. My eyes, my nose, pretty much my entire face. He tells me this after he's done being angry with me. He'll just stare at me for a bit and cry.

It's strange, isn't it? That so much of me can be like someone I've never known?"

I sensed movement and thought that he was passing the cigarette to me. As I turned to take it from him, I realized his face, not his hands, was moving toward me. Suddenly, his lips were on mine. I had no time to react before they fled. The action was so abrupt that the intention behind it was unclear.

"Take this. Practice for next time."

He handed the pack of cigarettes to me and disappeared around the corner of the building. I was paralyzed, my body warm despite the frigid winter. The traces of smoke from his chapped lips lingered on mine, and I frantically clung on to the sliver of him I could taste.

—

The pack of cigarettes was securely tucked under my jacket when I returned to my room. Sagar lay on his bed, staring blankly at the ceiling. Neither of us greeted each other. I hopped onto my bed and stealthily stuffed the cigarettes under my pillow before removing my jacket. I glanced at Sagar to make sure he had not seen me hide them. We made brief eye contact, and his eyes darted away. I nonchalantly picked up a random book next to my bed and began to read. After a few minutes, Sagar sat up and sniffed the air.

"What's that smell?"

I lifted the top of my shirt to my nose. The stench of cigarette smoke drenched my clothes.

I shrugged. "Must be a skunk or something."

"A skunk? No. It smells more like … like smoke."

"You're imagining things. It's definitely a skunk."

"I should tell Mama."

"No, no," I said hastily. "I'm sure the smell will leave soon."

"I can't stand it. I'll wait downstairs until it goes away."

After Sagar left the room, I took off my clothes and stuffed them under my bed. I changed into a T-shirt and shorts, but the stench remained. I needed to shower and wash the smoke off me, but the only bathroom I could use was downstairs, where the adults and Sagar were sitting. I suspected that my mother and Aaji might not pick up on the smell, but Vaishu Mavshi, home from work early that day, had the nose of a hound. I tiptoed out of the room and down the stairs, trying my best not to draw attention to myself. Vaishu Mavshi, my mother, and Sagar were sitting around the kitchen table, past the bathroom. I couldn't avoid them.

"Aku? Where were you?" Vaishu Mavshi asked. "You didn't come home with Sagar?"

"They don't walk home together anymore," said my mother.

"Really? Why not?"

I shrugged, trying to inch to the bathroom, afraid that the cigarette smell would somehow waft toward them. Sagar was twiddling his thumbs, his eyes downcast.

"I hang out with another friend," I replied.

"Which friend?"

"Bilal. We play basketball together."

Sagar momentarily stopped moving his thumbs.

"Why can't Sagar come with you? You shouldn't leave him out like that," Vaishu Mavshi scolded as she ran her fingers through Sagar's hair.

"Okay. I won't anymore."

Before she could reply, I shut the door to the bathroom. I exhaled in relief, happy to have safely made it to my destination. For the next twenty minutes, I scrubbed myself clean, only leaving the bathroom once every part of me smelled like lavender soap.

No one was around the kitchen table anymore. I headed upstairs and opened the door to my room.

Vaishu Mavshi was standing over my bed, holding my clothes in one hand and the cigarette pack in the other. My mother and Sagar were sitting on the bed, their expressions uneasy.

"Sagar. Leave the room," Vaishu Mavshi ordered.

Sagar bowed his head and slowly walked toward the door. He glanced at me as he passed, discernible guilt in his eyes.

"Sit."

I obeyed Vaishu Mavshi's command. It took her less than a minute to extract the truth. I couldn't even attempt to lie with her terrifying stare locked in on me. Her eyes bulged as I narrated the events of the day. She yelled at me for hanging out with Mayuran and lying about it, for tricking Juhi Aunty, and for bringing such dangerous items around Sagar. I was supposed to be the older role model, and I'd failed at that. My mother was silent throughout Vaishu Mavshi's tirade.

"Do you have anything to add, Mahi?" snapped Vaishu Mavshi.

"No," said my mother. "You covered it all."

Vaishu Mavshi groaned in frustration. "The worst part about this is that he stole. I don't want him smoking, but stealing? Mahi, what type of behavior are you teaching him?"

My mother shriveled in her seat, mumbling an incoherent reply.

Vaishu Mavshi decided that we would first speak to Mayuran's father and then apologize to Juhi Aunty. My mother, Vaishu Mavshi, and I sped across Main Street in a single file, shivering. We turned left after Accelerated Academy and proceeded along a dirt road that led us further into the forested area. Mayuran's shack-like home sagged in solitary confinement, trapped by the trees around it. Black muck tarnished the washed-out wood, and vines snaked up the sides, gnawing into the boards.

"Let's get this over with," muttered Vaishu Mavshi.

She knocked. No one answered, so she hit the door forcefully with her palm three times.

"Bloody hell, I'm coming," a gruff voice responded.

Ratnam opened the door. He was short and broad, his hair thinning and gray. He had sunken eyes, deep creases surrounding them like a family of tree roots. He wore a tank top stained with yellow grease that barely fit over his stomach. The inside of the house was dark and messy. Take-out boxes and tools were littered across the dilapidated furniture.

"Whatdya want?"

"Hello, Ratnam. My name is Vaishnavi, and this is—"

"I know who you are. I asked what you wanted."

"We're here to talk to you about your son. You see, your son and my nephew—"

"*Mayuran!*" he yelled. Mayuran immediately crept out of the shadows and approached us.

"You know these people?"

Mayuran nodded, his frightened eyes fixed on the floor.

"What is this about?"

Mayuran shrugged.

Vaishu Mavshi attempted to insert herself back in the conversation. "As I was saying, my nephew came home today with a pack of cigarettes—"

"What does that have to do with my son?"

"Your son convinced him to steal it," Vaishu Mavshi said with irritation. She hated being interrupted.

"Did you do this?" Ratnam asked Mayuran. Mayuran timidly shook his head no.

Ratnam smacked Mayuran on the back of his head, causing the latter to stumble forward. My mother gasped.

"Speak up!" Ratnam bellowed.

"I didn't do it," Mayuran whispered.

Ratnam glared at Vaishu Mavshi. "If he says he didn't do it, he didn't do it. Don't come here blaming us again."

Ratnam slammed the door shut.

"Let's get out of here," my mother said, shuddering. Vaishu Mavshi and I agreed, and we all sped back to our house. Thankfully, Vaishu Mavshi was so shaken up by the interaction with Ratnam that she forgot about going to Juhi Aunty's store. The entire walk home, she kept repeating, "Such a rude man. Who treats people like that?"

When we locked ourselves in the safety of our living room, Vaishu Mavshi declared that I needed to face some sort of consequence. She hadn't disciplined me or Sagar to a high degree before, so settling on a fitting punishment took her a while. My mother said that I'd learned my lesson, to which I vehemently agreed. After a bit of contemplation, Vaishu Mavshi concluded that I wouldn't be able to leave my room over the weekend and that was punishment enough.

I expected the two days to fly by, but confinement proved to be lonely and dull. I paced from wall to wall, and when I got tired of that, I would lie on my bed, counting all the areas on the ceiling where the paint was peeling off. I explored every nook and cranny of the room and found a stash of Suhail Mama's old *Playboy* magazines in the closet.

Mayuran occupied my mind the entire weekend. I hadn't seen him as powerless, as devoid of confidence, as he had been in front of his father. I lingered on the moment when Ratnam had hit him, ruminating over the panic and humiliation that had sullied Mayuran's face. I hoped he could understand that my family wasn't supposed to find out about the cigarettes. I needed him to forgive me.

On Monday morning, I awoke to my mother banging on my bedroom door.

"Akash, you need to go to school now. I've let you sleep in for long enough." Her stern voice indicated that she'd taken Vaishu Mavshi's blame to heart.

When I went down for breakfast, my mother informed me that Sagar had already left. I walked to school alone. Arriving ten minutes late, I slipped into class while Aneesa Aunty was lecturing. The seat behind me, normally occupied by Mayuran, was empty. I scanned the room and found him on the opposite end, slouched over, his hood pulled over his head. His chin was the only visible part of his face.

Each time the bell rang for recess, Mayuran would run out of the room before I could catch him. I searched for him in the hallways and field, but he would disappear until the next period began. At the end of the school day, I saw him across the lot, about to walk home, his hands forced down his pants pockets, his hood still covering his head. I rushed to him.

"Mayuran!"

He sped up his pace away from me. I broke into a jog to keep up.

"Can we talk?"

"Leave me alone."

"I'm really sorry about yesterday. Sagar ratted me out."

"Get the fuck away from me."

I reached for his jacket, attempting to slow him down. In doing so, I accidentally pulled his hood down. He whipped around and lashed out at me. I stumbled back and fell on the pavement.

Mayuran's uncovered face revealed a bruised, bloated eye, opposite his scar. His expression turned to shock as he raised a hand to his exposed wound. He sprinted away, tugging his hood back over his head. I picked myself up and found a stream of blood running down my wrist to the tip of my finger. I was shocked; I hadn't even felt any pain.

———

Vaishu Mavshi and Sagar were sitting in the living room when I returned home. I went straight to my room without acknowledging either of them. I used a couple of tissues from my desk drawer to wipe away the blood on my arm.

A knock at the door startled me. I jerked my sleeve down and hid the bloody tissues underneath the desk. Vaishu Mavshi and Sagar entered. He tried to hide behind her, but she pulled him in front.

"I don't know what's been going on with the two of you," said Vaishu Mavshi. "But you need to sit down and fix it."

She left the room. I plopped myself on top of my covers, ignoring Sagar. I was enraged. He'd ruined my relationship with Mayuran.

"This is what you wanted, right?" I said. "For me and Mayuran to stop hanging out?"

"I'm sorry, Akash Dada. I just wanted to make sure it wasn't a skunk. I didn't want to get you in trouble."

My fists were tight. The more he said, the angrier I felt.

"How did she know the pack was under my pillow?" I said through gritted teeth. Silence, then—

"Please don't be mad at me."

His quiet voice quivered with fear. Fear of me. My irritation wavered. I relaxed my fists and rolled over, about to reach out, but the door had already gently closed behind him.

That night, my dreams were the most intense they'd ever been. The visceral storm of colors suffocated me. The Singer's voice tormented me. I wanted to escape this horrible nightmare, but I didn't know how. I could only brave through it.

CHAPTER 7

SUHAIL MAMA'S APARTMENT

DECEMBER WAS A grim month in my home. Sagar and I were off for winter holidays, and though endless snowfall trapped us in the house, we spent our time dawdling in separate rooms. After our falling out, Sagar moved back to his parents' room. Vaishu Mavshi didn't make any further effort to have us rekindle. Her trust in me dwindled, and I caught her on multiple occasions searching my room for other contraband. Harsh Kaka assured me that her suspicions would blow over, but the gloomy weather and despondent attitude within our house made me doubtful. Without the sun, my family was fatigued. We were forced to stay under the same roof, but we lived separately.

I escaped the house one afternoon and trudged down Main Street, but I found even less comfort in the empty Town center. There weren't any Townsfolk chatting on the sidewalks, and the doors to the businesses were shut to prevent snow from entering. Flyers announcing the opening of the station were hung on every telephone pole and open wall. To attract exposure and interest, Mayor Rivera had decided that the opening ceremony would be combined with a holiday event. The inside of the station would be decorated with red streamers, and the bottom floor would have booths of free snacks and hot chocolate. The opening was strategically set to take place the day after Christmas, when people wished for the festivities to continue, even though they had finished their own personal celebrations. The event was publicized considerably across county and state channels, radios, and newspapers. Based on the enormous lengths of advertising the mayor was going to, I expected the opening to garner a substantial crowd.

The event was being promoted as a joyous occasion, but unrest pervaded the Town. On Christmas Day, Bhaskar Uncle held a last-minute town hall at his shop to discuss the approaching changes. My mother and I joined in the early evening and squeezed through the overflowing crowd, perching ourselves in a less dense corner. Aneesa Aunty passed us chai in Dixie cups and rolled her eyes, indicating that no substantive conclusions had been reached. Bhaskar Uncle stood at the front, unsuccessfully attempting to calm the meeting participants. Ratnam obstructed Bhaskar Uncle's peacemaking by shouting from the other side of the room. Mayuran sat next to Ratnam, watching his imposing father with reverence.

"How can you all be okay with this?" roared Ratnam.

"What are we supposed to do? The station is built," said Mariam Mahmood, the tailor. "We already tried approaching the mayor with our concerns."

"And since when do you care about the Town?" retorted Simran Aunty.

Ratnam's jaw clenched. "I don't, but this is about power. Like many of you, I want to be left alone, not overrun with new houses and buildings. I moved here to get the hell away from government control, but it looks like I haven't escaped yet. We have to take matters into our own hands!"

A few of Ratnam's construction buddies grunted in agreement.

"How?" Mariam Aunty responded.

"We need to delay the station from opening. Think about how many times this project has been abandoned before."

A chorus of disapproving exclamations erupted. Bhaskar Uncle waved his hands to shush the crowd.

Farah Rahman, mother of Sameer, jumped in. "Who do you think we are, Ratnam? Don't make this station a bigger deal than it is."

"Not to mention the fact that it's opening tomorrow," added Mariam Aunty. "Even if we wanted to do anything, it's too late."

Ratnam raised his finger. "I'm warning all of you! Don't be foolish."

Adi Deo, the cardiologist, stood up. "Why are we approaching this station with such a disapproving outlook? It can help us too. We can look for more jobs in Manhattan with this shortened commute."

"The difference, Mr. Deo, is that your job can be found anywhere," said Bhaskar Uncle. "Those of us who own shops along Main will not be as lucky. More profitable businesses will crush us."

Ratnam glanced at Bhaskar Uncle, surprised that they were arguing for the same side. Bhaskar Uncle noticed Ratnam's look and readjusted his position. "And while it does worry me, I don't believe we can do anything at this point."

"I agree. Please let's end this pointless discussion," chorused Mariam Aunty.

Simran Aunty stood up. "I own a shop along Main, and I still support this station."

"Of course this bitch does," my mother whispered to me.

"So what if things change a little? We'll adapt. A few developers came by to discuss building larger stores. Can you imagine if we had a supermarket here instead of having to walk to the City every time?"

"But is that worth losing what we have?" asked Bhaskar Uncle. "The community that we've built together?"

"More housing means that more Desis will move here. Every year, thousands of Indians are immigrating to this country."

"You're absolutely right. More might move. But based on the mayor's vision for this place, so will many other people. The question is not how large or small our community is. It's how easily we can remain connected. If the Town becomes like any regular part of the City, we won't enjoy the benefits that come with being concentrated in this area."

His words received a few scattered claps and murmurs of approval. Simran Aunty shook her head. "You're overthinking this, Uncle."

"Who the hell cares who comes!" shouted Ratnam. "The point is that most of us don't want this bloody thing to open. Let's get back to how we can stall it!"

Ratnam's buddies grunted in support. Others across the store jumped in with reactionary retorts, sighs, and jabs. A disgruntled Bhaskar Uncle sat down and freely let the clamor continue.

"Let's go," my mother said. "It's getting late."

Suhail Mama and Kiara Mami were hosting Christmas dinner at their apartment later that evening. I was ecstatic. I had barely seen Suhail Mama since his wedding. He'd visited our house a few times, but his trips were primarily motivated to retrieve items he'd forgotten. His busy work schedule prevented him from having much time to meet up or call. In fact, Kiara Mami was the one who'd informed us about Christmas dinner. Though my family and I hadn't celebrated Christmas before, we were thrilled to have an excuse to see our beloved relative.

My mother and I shuffled out of Bhaskar Uncle's store. I

bundled myself in my coat and briskly began walking back home.

My mother reached out to stop me. "Slow down."

"I'm c-cold," I said, shivering.

"I have to tell you something. It'll only take a moment." She sat on the curb and patted the ground next to her.

I reluctantly joined her. She put an arm around me and rubbed my shoulder.

"Aku, you know how much I love you, right?"

"What's going on?" I replied warily.

"I know you miss your dad, but I think him leaving was for the best. We can think about what's next for you and me."

I was surprised she was discussing my father. His move to San Francisco was a sore subject for her. My father called me once a week, and though he asked each time to speak with my mother, she refused to be handed the phone. Instead, she would listen in on my conversations with him. Her eyebrows would narrow as he gushed about the beauty of the Bay Area and the abundant creative energy he'd found in the tech world. He stated once that this was the happiest he'd ever been, which instantly prompted my mother to storm off to her room. He ended each call by saying how much he missed me. He hoped that my mother would change her mind about moving. I wanted to know why he had waited this long to ask about living together, but I couldn't bring myself to broach the topic. After learning that he'd run away during my mother's pregnancy, I was wary of learning more about my father and having my perception of him tarnished.

"Why are you telling me this?" I asked.

"Nikhil proposed to me." She reached into her coat pocket and procured an engagement ring with a diamond band. "It must have cost him a fortune. I don't know why he bought something so expensive."

I was stunned. "Wow."

"I haven't said yes yet."

"Why not?"

"Because this is a decision for the both of us."

"Do you want to marry him?"

She hesitated. "I don't know."

Her eyes searched mine expectantly, begging them to provide her the correct answer.

"He's pretty cool."

She smiled. "He is, isn't he?"

"Are you going to tell the rest of the family?"

"Of course. When the time is right. I wanted you to be the first to know."

The idea of Nikhil marrying my mother would have repulsed me once, but I'd considerably warmed up to him in recent weeks. He had replaced Suhail Mama as an elder brother figure in my life. Even after Mayuran stopped speaking to me, I continued to play video games on my own at Das Electronics. If the store was empty, Nikhil would join in and teach me his gaming techniques. I also appreciated how stable Nikhil was for my mother. He was calm and adaptive—qualities my father lacked severely.

"I think you should do what makes you happy."

She grinned and kissed my cheek. "Let's go get ready."

———

Harsh Kaka, Vaishu Mavshi, and Sagar were dressed up and waiting in the living room when my mother and I returned home.

"What was it like?" asked Vaishu Mavshi.

"Chaos," replied my mother.

"I don't even know why you bothered to go. Such useless fighting."

"Is Aai not coming?"

"She said she needed a few more minutes. I'll go check again."

Vaishu Mavshi headed up the stairs. We heard her knock on my Aaji's door. "Aai, we're leaving."

"Go without me," my Aaji croaked back.

"Come, na, you've been wanting to visit Suhail's place."

"Go without me."

"Are you sure?"

Silence.

"Okay, well … we'll bring you back something to eat."

Vaishu Mavshi came back to the living room and shrugged. My Aaji's mood swings had been frequent since the diagnosis. The emotional toll of dementia was even more damaging to her than the actual impairment. Doubt crept into every joke, story, and recollection, often halting her speech midway through. She spent more time locked in her room than she did with us. The vibrant matriarch of the house had become reclusive.

The remaining family headed to Suhail Mama's apartment in a taxi van. Sagar was unusually quiet, somberly gazing out the van window. He hadn't spoken a word to anyone the entire evening, even though he'd been the most upset over Suhail Mama moving out. I thought the prospect of seeing our uncle again would have excited him, but his face reflected no joy.

We reached Suhail Mama's building an hour and a half later. Vaishu Mavshi paid the large taxi fee with vexation and commented that it was a good thing the station was opening soon.

Suhail Mama and Kiara Mami were waiting in the lobby. Kiara Mami tightly hugged each of us. Her curls bounced as much as they had at the wedding, spilling over her maroon dress. "*Soooooo* glad you all could make it! Mom and Dad are already upstairs."

Vaishu Mavshi awkwardly attempted to reciprocate Kiara Mami's animated hug. "Sorry we're late."

"Not at all, not at all! We're just preparing drinks."

Kiara Mami turned to me and Sagar, bending down even though I was nearing her height. She pinched our cheeks. "Hi, cuties. How are you?"

Sagar blushed. "Good."

Suhail Mama reached out to Harsh Kaka for a handshake. My mother swatted Suhail Mama's hand away and ruffled his hair. "Too good to give us hugs now, huh?"

A visibly annoyed Suhail Mama ran his hands through his hair. "Seriously? I'm not fifteen anymore."

My mother chuckled, though I could tell she was stunned Suhail Mama did not play off her teasing like he used to. "Who got your panties in a twist?"

Suhail Mama softened. "Sorry, sorry. Work's been crazy. My head's all over the place."

He outstretched his arms, and after a moment's hesitation, my mother relaxed into his embrace. He kissed the top of her head. "Aai didn't come?"

"She's not feeling well."

"That's too bad. Haven't seen her in a while." He turned to me and Sagar. "You guys been shooting hoops since I left?"

"We don't have anyone to teach us," I replied. "Mama doesn't know how to throw a ball."

My mother endearingly smacked my head. "Aku!"

Suhail Mama chuckled. "Next time you come, we'll play at the courts here."

Sagar and I eagerly nodded. Suhail Mama broke away and led the group to the elevator, shoving his hands deep into his pockets. He was dressed in a freshly ironed sweater vest and tan pants. He was slimmer too, having lost a bit of the muscle weight he used to pride himself on. His cheekbones stood out prominently, aging his face with a dignified seriousness. When he'd lived at our house, his outfits had been casual: mostly tank-tops and shorts, maybe his Rutgers sweatshirt if the house was cold. In all fairness, we were meeting up for a Christmas dinner, and the other adults were wearing nicer clothes than usual. But the way he carried himself in his semi-professional attire made him look unapproachable, intimidating even.

My uncle's appearance wasn't the only development of his that caught me off guard. The Suhail Mama that I'd known in the Town had been easygoing, with a lopsided grin perpetually hanging off his face. He hadn't been a slacker, but he definitely hadn't been a hard worker either. He'd had a laid-back approach to life, focusing more on sports, rap music, and the hundred girls he was flirting with than his grades or career goals. Work stress wasn't something I would have ever expected my uncle to express, but the current creases in his forehead and the weariness in his eyes proved to me that he hadn't been exaggerating about how busy he was. Whether or not it was a direct result of the stress, he seemed to be colder and less engaged with the family. On the elevator ride up, Kiara Mami led the bulk of the conversation. Suhail Mama was silent, staring at his shoes. I tried to gauge if he was angry at us, but he acted more standoffish than vengeful. I chalked it up to an off day for him, just like it was for my Aaji. The winter was seemingly harming everyone's moods.

Suhail Mama and Kiara Mami's apartment was on the fifth floor and had a decent view of downtown Stamford. The living room was accessorized with generic modern art, framed digital prints that did not speak to the personality of the couple. Although the detached decor fit the sleek black-granite style, the apartment felt impersonal, almost like a hotel room.

Kiara Mami's parents, Kalpana Aaji and Manav Ajoba, were seated on a stiff couch against the wall. Kalpana Aaji wore a dark blue sari without frills or designs. Her hair was pulled so tightly into a bun that the wrinkles on her face were stretched back as well. She examined us with cold stares through her thin spectacles. Manav Ajoba, on the other hand, was red faced and jovial when he greeted us. He was dressed in a checkered sweater vest, similar to Suhail Mama. In his right hand, he held a glass of liquor that sloshed around as he shook hands with us.

"This chap doesn't speak much, huh?" he said, thumping Sagar on the back.

"He's usually quite talkative," replied Vaishu Mavshi.

Manav Ajoba plopped himself back on the couch. A bit of his drink spilled onto his sweater.

"Sit up, Manav," said Kalpana Aaji, reaching over to dab the stain. He swatted her hand away with a grunt. Kalpana Aaji rolled her eyes and stood up. "Do you need help with the appetizers, Kiara?"

"I got it," Kiara Mami said, bringing out two trays of cheese and crackers to the table.

My family and I crowded the opposing couch. I had to constantly adjust to find a comfortable position on the tough surface. Suhail Mama sat on a chair in between us and his in-laws.

"It's a lovely place, Suhail," said Harsh Kaka. "Very spacious."

Manav Ajoba chuckled. "Thanks to me for funding it."

"Daddy," Kiara Mami reproached, setting the trays down on the central glass coffee table. She inserted herself between her parents.

"Teasing," said Manav Ajoba, clapping Suhail Mama on the back. "One day, my son-in-law will be earning much more than me."

Suhail Mama smiled. "I don't know about that."

I observed Manav Ajoba and Suhail Mama with curiosity. I'd initially thought the similarity between their outfits was coincidental, but I was slowly noticing how Suhail Mama emulated Manav Ajoba in his actions and mannerisms as well. For instance, Suhail Mama was drinking liquor, which was odd since he used to despise alcoholic drinks. He also sat with the same confident slouch as Manav Ajoba, legs spread apart, shoulders slumped forward. His eyes constantly flitted over to his father-in-law as he observed and replicated. When he'd lived with us, the female influence in our household had encouraged flamboyancy in his behavior. But under the guidance of Manav Ajoba, Suhail Mama's demeanor was stiff, cocky, and unrecognizable.

I was confused why Suhail Mama would want to imitate Kiara Mami's father. The few times I'd met Manav Ajoba prior to then, he'd forcibly drawn attention to himself with loud, crude commentary. Regardless of the conversation topic, he'd always found out a way to inject boasts about his self-made fortune into his speech. My Aaji loathed him with such intensity that she tried to persuade Suhail Mama early on to reconsider marrying into the family. Suhail Mama had assured her then that Manav Ajoba wouldn't have influence over him or the relationship. But the way my uncle was acting in his new apartment made me doubt how devoted he was to this promise.

"We miss you, Suhail," my mother said. "You should visit us more."

"I tell him the same thing," added Kiara Mami.

Suhail Mama sighed. "I'm helping oversee the development for two new rows of townhomes. I barely have time to breathe."

"He comes home really late. I think he should take a step back or something."

Suhail Mama lowered his voice. "We've talked about this. I already said I can't right now."

Manav Ajoba interrupted. "It's good he's putting in hard work, Kiara. That's what living in this country is about. I don't want my baby married to a slacker." To Suhail Mama, he added, "You're doing the right thing, son."

Suhail Mama nodded sheepishly at Manav Ajoba before switching subjects. "What's new in the Town?"

"The station's opening tomorrow," said my mother.

"Oh yeah, I forgot that was happening this year! Exciting stuff."

"I don't know if everyone shares your enthusiasm."

Suhail Mama rolled his eyes. "Are people in the Town still against it?"

"It's normal to be scared of change."

"Don't they understand that this is going to generate more profit for stores?"

"If people in the Town only cared about money, I think they would have chosen a different place to live."

"What's going on? What station?" Manav Ajoba inquired, leaning forward to remain included in the conversation.

"They're opening a train station next to the Town," responded Suhail Mama. "It'll make travel easier to Manhattan for commuters."

"So, what's the issue?"

"There is none. People are worried that it will attract more development to the community, as if that's not a reality of the age we live in."

Manav Ajoba wagged his finger at us. "I never understood the mentality of your Town. You're in America, one of the most diverse countries, and choose to live within this small Indian bubble? It's ridiculous to me."

"A strong community can be wonderful for those that want familiarity," said my mother defiantly.

"Why move in the first place, then? You'll find all that in India."

"Everyone immigrates for different reasons. It's not our place to question why our Baba came here. But we're settled now. This is the life that we know."

"You need to learn how to adjust. We did and built a great life," Manav Ajoba said, his chest puffed out. "Tell them, Suhail, how your life has improved since you moved out of that place."

Suhail Mama looked nervously between my mother and Manav Ajoba. "I agree with Dad."

I was taken aback by Suhail Mama's response. It was unsettling hearing him refer to someone besides my Ajoba as his father.

Frustration was laced in my mother's voice. "What about everything our Baba built?"

"Nothing is being destroyed. Development will just add on to what he began. And if you're not happy with it, then you can always move out like I did."

"He's right, Mahi," said Vaishu Mavshi. "Maybe it is time to consider a change."

We all turned to her, shocked by this unexpected comment from Vaishu Mavshi.

My mother stammered, "I-I can't believe you just said that."

"I've been thinking about it for some time. With Aai's dementia and Sagar transitioning to middle school soon, it could be nice to live in an area that offers more." She turned to Harsh Kaka. "What do you think?"

"You know I've always been open to it," he said warmly. "I'm ready whenever you are."

"But … but you've always been the one that said we need to stay together," my mother said, perplexed.

Vaishu Mavshi frowned. "We'll talk about this later."

"What changed? Did I do something?"

"Mahi, I don't want to get into this now."

"We're already talking about it."

"Fine. I don't have the energy to take care of everyone in the house anymore. Especially when the only one helping me is Harsh."

My mother crossed her arms. "That's not fair. You know I've been looking for a job."

"Really? Where exactly?" Vaishu Mavshi retorted. Before my mother could respond, another voice beckoned attention.

"We're moving?" Sagar whispered. This was the first time he'd spoken all night.

"Not this second, but maybe one day," said Vaishu Mavshi.

"I don't want to move," Sagar replied, his voice rising in volume.

"We're not leaving anytime soon, honey," said Harsh Kaka. He reached out to Sagar's face.

Sagar deflected his hand and stood up, his eyes glistening. "Everyone in this family is so selfish."

"Sit down. Stop making a scene," ordered Vaishu Mavshi.

"No."

"I'm not going to say it again."

"Let's change the subject," said Suhail Mama. Kiara Mami nodded.

An awkward silence hung over the room. Suddenly, Sagar ran into one of the bedrooms. He slammed the door and locked it.

Kalpana Aaji tsked in disapproval. Harsh Kaka stood up, about to follow Sagar.

Vaishu Mavshi grabbed his wrist. "Don't. We are not going to condone this behavior."

Harsh Kaka hesitantly sat back down. Kiara Mami encouraged everyone to take cheese and crackers, but the conversation was ruined after the outburst. Harsh Kaka was disengaged, focused on the room Sagar had run into, while Vaishu Mavshi sank into the couch with her arms crossed.

A few minutes later, Harsh Kaka stood up and went to the door. He knocked and whispered, "Sagar, come out."

When no response came, Harsh Kaka looked at Vaishu Mavshi with desperation. "Please."

"If he wants to come out and apologize, he can do so. What's with the two of you acting up so much recently?" she said, frowning at me.

"Aku, can you please try?"

The panic in Harsh Kaka's eyes compelled me to stand up. He moved aside when I reached the door.

"Sagar?" I whispered.

"Go away," said Sagar from behind the door.

Harsh Kaka motioned for me to keep talking.

"We're worried about you."

"Stop lying."

"I swear I'm not." I jostled the door handle, but it was locked tightly.

"You don't care about me. You forgot about me."

I sighed. "Please let me in, Sagar."

Vaishu Mavshi appeared at my side and motioned for me to step back. She banged on the door with her palm. "Sagar, we are in someone else's house. If you don't open up right this second, I swear to God ..."

Suhail Mama came up behind Vaishu Mavshi and tried to gently pull her away from the door. "Tai, it's okay—"

"No, Suhail, this is ridiculous."

Kiara Mami and her parents anxiously watched the scene unfold.

"One ... two ... Sagar, if I reach three ..."

Vaishu Mavshi halted her count and slowly tilted her head down. I followed her gaze to the crack at the bottom of the door. A stream of yellow liquid seeped out, forming a puddle around the base of her feet.

Kiara Mami gasped. "Is that …?"

No one needed to confirm what she'd been about to say. Kalpana Aaji squealed with disgust, and Manav Ajoba released a bellowing laugh. The rest of us watched in horror as Sagar's urine trickled between the polished tiles.

CHAPTER 8

THE INCIDENT

MY MOTHER'S HUSKY voice woke me. I stirred and found her kneeling by my bed. Her hair was curled, and she wore bright red lipstick. I could smell her favorite perfume, a floral scent she reserved for special occasions.

"Wake up, honey."

"Why?" I asked groggily.

"Nikhil wants us to join him for the station opening. Maybe we can even take the train to Manhattan after."

"Okay." I pulled my covers off.

"There's one more thing," she said, tucking her hair behind her ear. Nikhil's ring was displayed on her finger. "I thought about what you said, and I'm going to tell him yes today. I want you to be there when I do."

"That's great, Mama."

She tightly hugged me. "I'm so happy, Aku. You promise you're okay with this, right?"

"Yeah, he's pretty fun to hang out with."

We broke away from each other. Her face glowed as she said, "Let's find you something nice to wear."

She went to my dresser and tugged the stubborn top drawer. The old hinges made a loud, unpleasant squeak. My mother and I froze as the lump of blankets on the other bed shifted. I was expecting Sagar's head to pop out, but only a groan emerged from underneath the mound, followed soon by heavy snores.

Sagar hadn't spoken to anyone since the previous night's outburst. After Vaishu Mavshi overcame her initial shock of seeing Sagar's urine oozing beneath her feet, she aggressively banged on the locked door until Sagar opened it. He stood within the shadows of the room, fear plastered on his face. Vaishu Mavshi raised her hand to deliver a strong slap, but Harsh Kaka jumped in and pulled her back. Vaishu Mavshi's fury was shocking. Whenever Sagar had misbehaved in the past, Vaishu Mavshi would discipline him with firm threats. I'd never seen her that close to administering a physical punishment. Vaishu Mavshi ordered Sagar to clean up his urine while the rest of us watched. Kiara Mami tried to help, but Vaishu Mavshi insisted he deal with his own mess. After Sagar finished cleaning, we all ate dinner in silence. Manav Ajoba threw in the occasional joke, but his audience was unresponsive.

When we returned home, Sagar immediately ran into our room. I entered later that night and heard him sniffling under his covers. I wanted to talk to him, understand him, but I did not know where to begin. Even though he was only a few feet away, the previous months had stretched us far enough apart that approaching him felt like an insurmountable challenge. It baffled me how less than a year before, we'd been able to strike up a conversation at any moment with ease. With my voice caught in my throat, I turned away and lulled myself to sleep.

My mother, however, was much less afraid of approaching Sagar than I had been the previous night. She stepped away from the dresser and walked to his bed.

"What are you doing?" I whispered.

"He should come with us and get some fresh air. He's going to be stuck in here for a while."

"Vaishu Mavshi will be mad."

"She's going to be mad regardless."

"I-I don't want him to come. Yesterday was disgusting."

"Show some empathy for your brother, Aku. He's clearly acting out because he feels lonely."

"He's not my brother," I muttered.

My mother pretended not to hear as she sat on the edge of Sagar's bed. She nudged him. "Sagar, baby."

Sagar lifted the covers from the top of his head. "What's wrong?"

"Nothing's wrong. Aku and I are going to the opening ceremony. Do you want to come?"

"I'm supposed to stay in my room."

She playfully poked him. "Life's no fun if you don't break the rules a little. Your parents are in their room. We can sneak out now."

He glanced at me. I averted my eyes.

"Okay, I'll come."

———

The station was a spectacle. Displayed at the entrance was an enormous pine tree decorated with ornaments. Snowflake stickers were pasted in intricate patterns on the exterior glass surface. Enlarged photos of Mayor Rivera smiling and posing with construction workers were erected on stands by the entrance. The excessive promotion for this event seemed to have worked extremely well, as flocks of people, most of whom I did not recognize, swarmed outside of the station. The guards were struggling to organize the horde into straight lines. Camera operators from local news stations panned around, capturing the excitement and disorder. My mother, Sagar, and I walked past the news anchors to join the line for the ticketing booth. We purchased four tickets to Manhattan in case Nikhil hadn't bought one for himself.

After crossing the sliding doors, Sagar and I held my mother's hands to prevent losing each other in the crowded first floor. On our left-hand side was a coffee shop selling holiday-themed lattes. To our right were rolling carts offering free hot chocolate, popcorn, and other sugar-coated treats. There was a photo station with a costumed Santa, as well as booths for children's carnival games. Twirled red and green streamers were shoved on every wall, and classic Christmas songs blasted through speakers over the hubbub of laughter and conversations. If I hadn't known prior to coming, I would never have guessed this event was being held to promote a train line. The mayor's objective of attracting people through the holiday activities was evidently succeeding.

My mother, Sagar, and I shoved our way up the stairs toward the platform. Glass walls bordered the long, horizontal sides of the rectangular floor, and a translucent roof covered the top. Two tracks extended out of both open, unobstructed ends of the platform. Mayor Rivera stood on an elevated stage right by the tracks, beaming as he looked out at the tremendous number of attendees. Security was directing us into smaller clumps to better manage the traffic and movement onto the strip, but the platform itself was congested, almost overflowing beyond capacity. People were crammed against each other, and breathing room was impossible to fight for.

"Do you see Nikhil? He was supposed to meet us here," my mother yelled over the noise.

She craned her neck to search for him while dialing his number. None of her calls went through. She directed me and Sagar through the cramped crowd while continuously checking her phone. I was suffocated by the volume of taller bodies I had to shove past. I turned my face up in order to capture any air I could. We stopped by a bench packed with senior citizens far away from the stage. Sagar and I panted while my mother unsuccessfully tried calling Nikhil once again.

"Shit, I have no clue how I'm going to find him in this mess." My mother contemplated her options and then bent close to me and Sagar. "I'm going to look for him. Promise me you both will stay here. Okay? You cannot move."

I nodded.

"Sagar, baby, promise?"

"Yes, Mavshi."

"See you soon," she said, caressing my cheek before disappearing back into the crowd. Sagar and I squeezed ourselves onto the bench. I observed those standing on the platform and caught glimpses of Bhaskar Uncle near the stage and Mariam Aunty by the stairs. There were too many moving faces to find anyone else from the Town.

"Akash Dada?"

"Hm?"

"Do you hate me?"

I faced Sagar. His eyes were glistening, his lips trembling.

"No. I don't hate you."

"Then why won't you talk to me like you used to? Why won't you play with me?"

"I don't know. I'm older. I'm interested in other things now."

"But you used to like playing with me. How did things change so fast?"

I was beginning to get irritated. "No, Sagar, *you* liked to play. We always did what *you* wanted."

"Then tell me what you want to do. If you want to play those violent video games, I'll play with you. I can change. I promise."

"No one is asking you to. We're two different people. We don't have to do the same things."

His eyes searched mine with anguish. "Do you think we'll ever be as good friends as we used to be?"

I opened my mouth, about to reassure him that we were just stuck in a transitionary period. Soon enough, he would naturally experience a similar transformation in interests, and we would be able to understand each other again. If I hadn't remembered his tantrum the previous night, I would have said all of this. But the image of his urine, once conjured up, was impossible to forget. Disgust rose in my throat like sour bile, preventing the words from coming out. I could not see Sagar developing beyond what he was: an immature boy. I shuddered at the thought that I used to be like him. I no longer wanted to associate with the juvenile version of myself, but I feared that I would be stunted around Sagar, unable to reestablish myself because of his resistance to maturity.

I shrugged, intending this response to be more assuaging than telling him no. Still, Sagar's face fell. His shoulders slumped forward. Our arms were pressed against each other, but the emotional gap between us was vast. I was sure in my decision to distance myself, but acknowledging how detached I was from him brought forth an unexpected emotion within me. It was the same feeling I'd had at Suhail Mama's wedding reception, when I'd known a significant change in my life was approaching, but I hadn't been sure what to expect once it took effect. I'd happily mimicked Sagar's personality for most of my childhood, but I was finally growing into someone new. Someone I wasn't familiar with yet. Who was I supposed to be if completely independent and removed from him? I didn't have an answer, and that uncertainty troubled me.

Fortunately, Mayor Rivera drew my attention away by tapping on his microphone. The crowd quieted.

"What a turnout!" he said, grinning widely. "Building this station has been a passion project of mine since I was elected.

To see it completed ... well, it truly is a dream come true! In a few minutes, the first train will come by to take passengers to Manhattan—"

An indiscernible shout from the audience interrupted Mayor Rivera. He briefly paused and looked around for the source of the heckler, as did others in the crowd.

"Please keep your questions for the end!" he continued. "As I was saying, this station will be a gamechanger in terms of accessibility—"

A higher-pitched voice yelled out. The syllables were clearer this time, and I could distinguish that the source was speaking in Gujarati. Though I wasn't familiar with the language, I gathered that the shout was intended to distract more than convey a message. I stood up for a better view and saw that one of Ratnam's construction buddies was shaking his fist at the stage.

"I'm sorry. I didn't quite catch that," said Mayor Rivera, his smile wavering. More shouts emerged from the throng in fragments of Tamil, Hindi, and other Desi languages I was not familiar with. They came from Ratnam's troupe as well as the few that had sided with him at the town hall. Suddenly, Ratnam stepped on the stage. Mayor Rivera backed away from the microphone stand in alarm, and security guards pushed their way forward.

"Ratnam, get off!" yelled Bhaskar Uncle. Confusion proliferated through the audience, as most were unable to see the stage clearly. Ratnam resisted the guards' attempts to grab him.

"Open your eyes and see what's happening! This is only the beginning of their changes to this area!" he cried into the microphone. The guards forcefully tugged him away before he could speak further. Agitated murmurs spread through the crowd.

Mayor Rivera took control of the microphone once again.

"Sorry for that momentary interruption, everyone! It is being dealt with."

"Where is your mom?" Sagar asked, his voice trembling.

I was about to respond, but I was stalled by the sight of a familiar face. Through the thicket of restless bodies, I saw one that was stationary. His eyes were closed, his lips downturned in a solemn frown. Strands of his hair fluttered in what seemed like an illusory gust. Ripples stretched across his billowing white kurta. He was undisturbed by the surrounding commotion. There he was, no longer a dream or a hallucination. The Singer was standing on the platform, his face fully visible.

I began moving toward him, but a sharp pull on my wrist tugged me back.

"Where are you going?" asked Sagar.

"I'll be back in a minute," I said.

He stood up. "I'll come with you. We're supposed to stay together."

"No, just sit here. We might lose each other in the crowd."

His eyes swelled with panic. "Please don't leave me, Akash Dada. Please."

But the mysterious Singer continued to draw me away. I needed to find out who he was and why he was so prominent in my dreams. I needed to understand why he'd been present before the reception, and why I hadn't been able to find him after. Most importantly, I needed to speak to him and confirm to myself that he wasn't made up.

I pushed Sagar's hand off my wrist. "Wait here."

Before he could protest any more, I entered the crowd and began driving my way through, fighting through the suffocation. The Singer's face was my singular focal point when the movement of others confused my path. I was about to reach him, shoving my way through one final obstruction, when a stray elbow knocked me in the face. I doubled over, covering my cheek in pain. Bodies swirled around me, confusing my sense of direction.

Two sturdy hands grabbed my torso, lifting me back up to my former standing posture.

"Thank you," I said, facing my protector, only to realize that it was Mayuran. We were squished against one another.

"Don't mention it," he replied.

I craned my neck to find the Singer's face, but he had disappeared from view. I wanted to continue searching for him, but I was afraid of losing my way if I didn't have his face to latch on to. I decided to stay put until he popped up again.

Meanwhile, Ratnam was fighting the security guards to get back on stage. The attendees around him were backing away, not wishing to get involved in his conflict.

"Mayuran, what's going on?" I asked. "Your dad—"

"He's not going to hurt anyone. He's just sending a message."

"This doesn't feel right. Why is he doing this?"

"We asked them to leave this place alone, and they didn't listen."

"I know you. I know you don't care about this. What happened to leaving the Town one day? What happened to traveling the world?"

Mayuran's face hardened. "You don't know me. My dad is the only one that does. He's looked out for me my whole life. He's the only one I can trust."

A push on my back propelled me forward. I grabbed on to Mayuran's jacket for support and felt something protruding out of his pocket. He reached inside and produced a small firearm, hiding it in the tiny space between our stomachs.

I gasped. "Mayuran—"

"Don't worry," he whispered in my ear. "It only shoots blanks. I found it in my dad's dresser a while ago. I thought I could use it to scare the mayor. Kinda cool to see one outside of the video games, right?"

His finger toyed with the trigger. The barrel was pointed at the ground, directed in between my feet.

"See, nothing to be afraid—"

Someone tried to move past Mayuran and inadvertently shoved his body into mine. I stumbled back as a thunderous blast rocked the platform. The force of the push had caused Mayuran to press the trigger of his gun. For a moment, the world felt suspended. I couldn't hear anyone on the platform, nor could I feel the bodies pressed against mine. All I saw were Mayuran's eyes and the utter fear within them. His tough, armored exterior was stripped away, and standing behind it was a boy who was terrified, confused, and unaware of how dire his actions were. I used to admire Mayuran for how mature he presented himself to be, but in that moment, I realized that there wasn't any difference between him and Sagar. He was just as vulnerable and ignorant, just as much a child. Mayuran opened his mouth, about to say something, but it was already too late to prevent the turn of events initiated by the gunshot.

Ringing shrieks punctured the platform. I was separated from Mayuran and taken by a frenzied stampede of people trying to escape what they believed was an active shooter among us. The typhoon of bodies tossed me around as they pushed and squeezed toward the staircase without regard for those who stood in their way. I had absolutely no agency over where my body went. Between the flurry of clothes and flesh pressing against my eyes, I saw flashes of people who had fallen. One of Ratnam's buddies was curled on the floor, tangled in between a wave of legs. Blood trickled along his temple. I reached my arm out to help him up, but I was pulled away before we could make contact.

After seeing his injury, my only objective was to stay standing. It was a strenuous goal to achieve, considering that I was shorter than most adults at the station. My airflow was severely constricted because of this difference in height, and I gulped for oxygen every time the suffocation was briefly alleviated. I arrived at the stairs and concentrated on my balance, avoiding any stray legs that could trip me. A knee struck my stomach. I lost my footing and reached up, hoping someone would grab me.

"Akash!"

My mother appeared before me, lifting me up. She hugged me tightly. "Are you all right?"

I nodded. I hadn't even noticed through the shock that I was crying. We were being pushed apart by people clawing past us, but we held on to the staircase railing and fought to keep our bodies close together. Nikhil was perched on the lower step behind my mother, holding her waist for stability.

"Where is Sagar?" my mother yelled.

I shook my head.

"Akash, where is Sagar?" she yelled again, her voice shrill and panicked.

"I don't know."

"What do you mean you don't know!"

"I left him. I-I thought I saw someone I knew."

"I told you to stay together! I told you!" Distressed, my mother looked up at where the stairs and platform met. "I have to see if he's up there."

She stepped forward, but Nikhil held her back.

"Take Akash and get out of here," he said. "I'll look for him."

"Nikhil—"

"Go!" he shouted. He sidled past her and wrestled his way up the stairs.

My mother tried to watch Nikhil, but the crowd forced us down without a second to spare. We neared the end of the stairs and finally found space to breathe. We ran past the sliding glass doors and slowed down only when we tasted the reassurance of fresh air. Heavy clouds covered the sun. A strong gust whipped around us.

My mother was paralyzed with fear, her hand covering her mouth in shock. We were two of the only people outside who had stopped. Most were continuing to run as far away as they could from the station, while a few were also searching for family or friends who had been separated in the disarray. Distraught children were wailing. Panicked adults were yelling.

"Nikhil will find him," I said. I had to believe that he would.

I'm not sure how much time passed. It could have been five minutes, or it could have been twenty. Fewer people were emerging through the doors. Police sirens blared as two cop cars drove up to the front. Soon, Nikhil jogged out of the station. My mother immediately ran to him.

"Where is he?" she asked, grabbing the front of Nikhil's shirt.

"I tried to go up to the platform, but security wouldn't let me through. I looked everywhere I could downstairs."

My mother turned away from Nikhil and started yelling out, "Sagar! Sagar!"

She frantically ran between the sparse clumps of people outside, asking, "Have you seen a small boy? About this height?"

They said they hadn't, offering sympathetic glances instead. My mother tried calling Vaishu Mavshi and Harsh Kaka's cellphones, but her calls didn't go through. After the third attempt, she screamed, "Fuck!"

Nikhil hugged her. She tried to push him off, but it was of no use. He held on tightly.

"I have to go back in and look for him," my mother said.

"You won't be able to," replied Nikhil. "The guards are sectioning the entire area off. I'll get them to make an announcement. Go home and tell your sister."

"But ... no, I have to stay."

"He could have run home, Mahi, and we just didn't see him leave. Go and check." Nikhil held on to her face so that her eyes were forced to look into his. "It'll be okay. Make sure you and Akash are safely indoors. I'll be here waiting in case there's any news."

My mother nodded. He tried to kiss her, but she broke away. I took her hand and led her toward Main Street. I looked back at Nikhil. He was anxiously watching us leave.

As we ran home, my mother cried in erratic intervals. She would whimper for a few seconds, devolve into sobs, collect herself, and then repeat the process. I didn't have it in me to comfort her. I continuously replayed the moment when I'd pushed Sagar's hand off. I should have stayed with him. Why had I felt the need to leave him in pursuit of the Singer, who, for all I knew, had just been an illusion?

Main Street was peaceful compared to the station. My mother and I were the only ones on the sidewalk. I wanted to forget everything that had happened, just pinch myself and wake up from the horrible dream I was living in. I prayed to God that Sagar had come outside in the time since we'd left.

After what seemed like an eternity, my mother and I reached our house.

"One second," said my mother.

She took a long, deep breath before opening the front door. Vaishu Mavshi, Harsh Kaka, and my Aaji were sitting on the living room couch. Vaishu Mavshi jerked up, holding a scratch piece of paper.

"'Taking Sagar to New York. Be back soon?' That's all you write? And then you don't pick up any of my calls?"

"Vaishu," my mother croaked.

"No, Mahi. I don't want to hear it. I've been sitting here worried sick—"

"Vaishu," my mother repeated, more forcefully this time.

"Why are you crying?" She looked between the two of us and the door. "Where's Sagar?"

My mother began to cry.

"Mahi," said Vaishu Mavshi in a low voice, "where is Sagar?"

The truth was unraveled through broken, incohesive sentences. Harsh Kaka raised his hand to his mouth as he began to register the extremity of the situation. Vaishu Mavshi was expressionless.

"I tried to call you—wait, Vaishu—"

Vaishu Mavshi marched to the front door. "Grab the keys, Harsh," she ordered, her voice choked up.

"Let me come with you," pleaded my mother.

"You've done enough."

Vaishu Mavshi ran out. Harsh Kaka swiftly followed behind her.

"Stay with Aai," he said before slamming the door shut.

And with that, the house was quiet. The only sound that disrupted the silence came from the mantel clock. *Tick, tick, tick.* My Aaji stared blankly at the dark television screen. It was unclear how much of my mother's story she had processed. My mother sat on the couch and put her head on my Aaji's shoulder, but my Aaji did not offer her any solace. After a minute or so, my mother shuffled to the opposite end of the couch. She looked at me, her eyes searching for sympathy.

"I was just trying to help."

CHAPTER 9

A BITTER AFTERMATH

I REMEMBER THAT earlier that year—before the opening, before the wedding—I'd caused an unusually frantic afternoon by losing Sagar during one of our games in the forest. Although the specific game we were playing has now slipped my mind, I know it necessitated that we split up. I listened to Sagar's footsteps for as long as possible, but once the sound of him faded away, I couldn't pinpoint where exactly he was. I called his name and ran around the nearby area. I went back to the three trees, our home base, but did not see him lying among them.

As the sun began to set behind the forest canopy, I decided to enlist adults in helping me find Sagar. I sprinted back to the house and burst through the front door. Vaishu Mavshi was sipping coffee on the living room couch. She immediately set her mug down when she saw how frightened I was.

"What's wrong?" she asked.

"Did Sagar come back?"

She stood up, her forehead creasing with lines of worry. "No."

"W-we were playing and-and then we separated and—"

Before I could say another word, she sprinted out. We searched the forest, inspecting every possible hiding spot, but

Sagar was nowhere to be found. When it became too dark to see, we reluctantly started back to the house, contemplating our next course of action. I apologized to Vaishu Mavshi, but she wasn't acknowledging anything I was saying. Her head was tilted up to the sky, her eyes glazed over, and she repeatedly muttered, "You can't do this. It's not fair."

When we arrived home, Vaishu Mavshi and I were shocked to find Sagar munching on biscuits in front of the television. Vaishu Mavshi rushed toward him. She frantically ran her hands through his hair and felt every part of his face. Sagar looked at me with utmost confusion, and I instantly recognized how silly my initial reaction had been. How could I have doubted that he would find his way home? He knew the forest and Town better than I did. I had caused panic over nothing.

That same night, lying in between my snoring Aaji and mother, I mulled over Vaishu Mavshi's words. I woke up my mother to help me understand them.

"What is it?" she asked drowsily.

"When we couldn't find Sagar today, Vaishu Mavshi kept saying how unfair it was that he disappeared. What did she mean?"

"Unfair? She used that word exactly?"

"Yeah, I think so."

She sighed. "I don't know if I should tell you any of this."

"What? Tell me what?"

"You know that Vaishu Mavshi is many years older than me, right?"

I nodded.

"Well, Harsh and her were trying to have a child long before Sagar was born, but she couldn't get pregnant."

"Why?"

"She has a medical issue that makes it difficult to have a child. I can't explain more than that right now. But a year or so after the doctor told her this, I was pregnant with you by accident."

My mother paused and turned onto her back, staring up at the ceiling. "I felt responsible, like somehow God had taken away her ability to have a child and given it to me. After you were born, she told me that she would help in any way I needed, but her kindness made me feel even worse."

"If she couldn't have a child, how was Sagar born?"

"No one knows. I pleaded with God to give her a baby. I hated that guilty feeling clawing at me. A few months later, she was pregnant. As you know, Sagar was born on the same day your Ajoba first discovered the Town."

"As if Ajoba was watching down on us."

"Right? Pretty coincidental how connected those two events are. I was relieved after he was born, for your aunt's sake, of course, but for my own conscience too. Since then, I've wondered if Vaishu's overprotectiveness comes from a place of fear ... like she thinks she wasn't supposed to have Sagar in the first place, and that somehow, someday, he'll be taken back."

"Taken back where?" I asked, afraid.

My Aaji let out a guttural snore. My mother glanced at her.

"Anyways, it's all in the past," whispered my mother. "She has Sagar now. Forget about this. And don't tell Vaishu Mavshi anything I said, okay?"

My mother turned over, shutting me off from further questions.

———

Harsh Kaka and Vaishu Mavshi were sitting morosely in a corner of the waiting room. Vaishu Mavshi was hunched over. Loose hair from her ponytail sagged in front of her face.

Harsh Kaka's plaid shirt was untucked. His red eyes were blank and unfocused. The City hospital was busy. Doctors, nurses, patients, and family members dashed in and out of the emergency waiting room. But Harsh Kaka and Vaishu Mavshi sat still and detached, trapped in their own apprehension.

My mother cautiously approached them. She walked toward the empty seat by Vaishu Mavshi, but at the last moment, changed her mind and sat next to Harsh Kaka. My Aaji and I took the seats my mother had abandoned.

"Suhail and Kiara are on their way," said my Aaji, placing her hand on Vaishu Mavshi's shoulder. "Any news?"

"Not since I called you," replied Harsh Kaka, struggling to push each word out. "They said he's in critical condition."

My Aaji muttered incoherently and rubbed Vaishu Mavshi's back.

"Where did they find him?" my mother whispered.

"He was unconscious on the platform. A few others were trampled on as well and had to be brought to the hospital," answered Harsh Kaka.

My mother rubbed her temple. "I can't believe this happened."

Vaishu Mavshi scoffed. Her piercing eyes shone through the slivers of hair shielding her face. "What can't you believe? You left a child unattended on a crowded platform."

"Vaishu, now is not the time," whispered Harsh Kaka.

"I don't care."

"If I could go back and change everything, I would," said my mother, her voice shaking. "But to be fair, there's no way I could have predicted what was going to happen."

Vaishu Mavshi narrowed her eyes. "Are you kidding me, Mahi? Are you seriously trying to redeem yourself right now?"

"No, that's not what I'm saying—"

"Vaishu, please, let's discuss this later. None of us are

thinking clearly," Harsh Kaka urged. People in the waiting room were staring at us.

Vaishu Mavshi's voice was controlled and firm. "My thinking is perfectly clear. I have put up with her irresponsibility for too long. Time and time again I let it go because she's my sister. But I can't anymore. I'm done."

My mother sniffed, trying to hold back tears. "Tell me what to do, Vaishu, please. Tell me what I should do."

Vaishu Mavshi didn't respond.

My mother slipped out of her chair and knelt in front of Vaishu Mavshi. "Please forgive me. I won't be able to live with myself if you don't."

Vaishu Mavshi looked away from my mother, her expression unreadable.

My mother began to cry. She tried to hold Vaishu Mavshi's hands, but they were limp. "Vaish— Tai, please look at me. Tai, please, I beg of you."

Unable to procure a reaction from Vaishu Mavshi, my mother turned to my Aaji. "Aai, tell her to forgive me. Tell her that it was a mistake. Tell her Baba would have wanted her to forgive me."

My Aaji looked off into the distance, as if she couldn't hear my mother's pleas. My mother fell back on her calves. Her eyes helplessly flitted between the four of us towering over her, begging for pity.

"Mr. and Mrs. Khare?"

A nurse waved in our direction. Harsh Kaka and Vaishu Mavshi stumbled out of their chairs and rushed to him. I followed them, though my mother and Aaji stayed back.

"He's still in critical condition, but immediate family can see him," said the nurse.

"Please," croaked Harsh Kaka.

"Come with me." The nurse held the door open for the

three of us. He must have assumed I was Sagar's sibling. Too stunned to tell him the truth, I walked through the door into a long corridor with bright overhead lighting. The nurse led us to a gigantic room with two vertical rows of beds. Most beds were covered by curtains, but through small gaps in between the partitions, I was able to catch glimpses of patients. Their injuries were hidden by bandages and blankets, but the lifelessness in their expressions was sickening to see. I had to force myself to look straight ahead so that I wouldn't vomit before reaching Sagar's bed.

The nurse stopped and pulled one of the curtains back. There was a gentleness in the way Sagar was positioned on the hospital bed. Like an infant, he was swaddled in thick baby-blue blankets. He lay flat on his back, his head cocked to the side. At home, he would sloppily spread out on his bed, but here, he was oriented in a much calmer and more composed manner. I could have convinced myself that he was absorbed in a tranquil nap if his physical appearance hadn't been so jarring. He was unconscious, and his eyes were firmly shut. Under his oxygen mask, his breathing was shallow and erratic. Bandages covered most of his face, exposing only a bruised temple and leaving the rest up to a violent imagination.

Harsh Kaka fell on his knees beside the bed, crying and whispering Sagar's name. Vaishu Mavshi was frozen, her petrified eyes betraying her otherwise apathetic face. I backed away, unable to look any longer at the mutilated figure vaguely resembling the boy I knew. The boy, the sweetest boy. My cousin. My best friend.

Heat swelled up inside me, engulfing my ears, eyes, and nose. I could no longer hear any sounds of the hospital, no longer see anything but the cuts and bruises I imagined to be underneath those bandages. I ran back down the glaring hall and burst into the waiting room. I found my mother's expectant eyes. I knew that from my expression, she could see Sagar's injuries too. Her hand slowly rose to her mouth.

———

Overnight, the City, and consequently the Town, went from being relatively unknown to one of the most discussed places in the Northeast. Many print and television news outlets—far more than what had promoted the station beforehand—reported on the catastrophic event. Ironically, the abundance of conversation around the opening brought forth the attention Mayor Rivera had wanted for the station, though not the kind he'd hoped for. Despite the mayor's promises to increase security measures and training around public events, the new train lines were indefinitely put on hold.

Journalists combed through the Town for potential interviewees. Our door was knocked on multiple times, but we declined the requests. Though I didn't interact with any reporters, I closely followed what was being said about the station. My mother hated having the news on. She adamantly said that she didn't want to hear anything more about the opening. I switched it off when she was downstairs but quietly kept it running in the background when she locked herself in her room, which was most of the time. I found the news more comforting than silence. It was better to tune out my thoughts with the commentary of the reporters, even though the information they presented was always communicated to me first through the grapevine of our community.

Our house was kept alive by the support of friends and family. Suhail Mama and Kiara Mami called every day to ask for updates. Aneesa Aunty dropped off sweets, Juhi Aunty brought homemade pav bhaji, and Mariam Aunty offered to do our laundry for us. The donated food was left untouched by everyone in the house but me. From the various visitors, I was able to gather that three people other than Sagar were injured from trampling and asphyxiation. Recovery was in sight for them, as their wounds were much less serious than Sagar's.

No one—no news channel or bystander—knew what exactly had happened at the station. The sound of the gunshot had been the undeniable source of panic, but across all stories, there wasn't a consensus on who the suspect was or why a gun had been fired. Most blamed Ratnam, and one person even claimed that they'd seen him pull a gun out of his back pocket. Surprisingly, no one had seen Mayuran holding it. No one suspected that a child was to blame. I was relieved to be the sole person who knew the truth. Even at my young age, I was certain Mayuran would face severe consequences if anyone else found out, but I didn't believe he deserved to be punished for an accident. Remembering his terrified expression only brought forth sadness and sympathy within me, and so, I decided to keep his secret to myself.

Nikhil was the most consistent visitor to our house. He showed up every day, desperate to see my mother. I followed the same routine each time. I would tell him to wait by the door while I went up to my mother's room. I would stand in the hallway and tell her that Nikhil was downstairs. Without opening the door, she would respond that she was resting. I would then run back down and pass on this message to Nikhil. He would nod and say that he would try again the next day.

On December thirtieth, four days after the incident, Nikhil did not leave after I repeated my mother's message to him. He looked fraught, like he had not slept in days. He ran his hands through his hair, an action that reminded me of my disheveled father. He pleaded with me to ask her again. I ran up once more, but my mother insisted that she could not speak to anyone, let alone him. Nikhil was on the verge of tears when I delivered her response.

"Listen, man, I don't know what to do. I just need to talk to her, but she won't return any of my phone calls. One minute she's telling me she'll marry me, the next I don't hear from her. I love her, Akash. Tell her that for me, okay?"

I wanted to comfort him, but he shuffled away before I could figure out what to say. I went back up to my mother's room to convince her to talk to him. When I opened the door, I found only my Aaji inside. She lay on the bed, staring somberly up at the ceiling.

"Come sit with me for a minute, Aku."

I went to lie beside her.

"Your Ajoba founded this Town with the hope of always keeping our family together," said my Aaji. She sounded as if she was speaking to no one in particular, just releasing words into the air. "He would be so sad if he saw what has become of us."

"Don't say that, Aaji. Sagar will be fine. He'll come home, and everything will go back to normal."

"I don't know anymore. I don't know anything anymore."

I couldn't bear to see her morose. I wanted to cheer her up with fond memories. "Aaji, tell me about Ajoba."

"I don't have energy for a story, Akash."

"Please."

"What do you want to know?"

"Anything. Just talk to me about him."

"He was a kind man. Considerate. He always wanted the best for everyone in the family."

I waited for a twinkle to return to her eyes, but none came. Instead, she diverged from her usual description of my Ajoba.

"He was troubled, though. Every so often, he would spend hours—sometimes even days—away from the house. He wouldn't tell us where he went or when he was leaving. His moods were sometimes unpredictable, but they came without fail if there was conflict in the house—any fight between the kids or between us. He could not handle an unhappy household."

I was stunned. "Why haven't you told me this before?"

"Because when someone you love passes away, the bad moments don't matter anymore. I want to remember him as a good man, one that showered us with love when he was present."

She turned away from me with a heavy sigh. I left her and went out into the hallway. I heard a faint voice coming from Vaishu Mavshi and Harsh Kaka's bedroom. I went to the door and pressed my ear against it. My mother was rapidly whispering inside.

"I just feel so trapped here. It's like all the time, I feel suffocated. I don't know what to do. I need to … No, I need to fucking get out. I need to leave."

I listened for another voice, but I heard only hers. She sounded like she was talking to herself. I walked to my room and crumpled on top of my bed. Sagar's messy covers leered at me.

When the television was off and no visitors were at the house, I felt lonely. My Aaji and mother were locked up in the bedrooms. Vaishu Mavshi and Harsh Kaka spent each day at the hospital next to Sagar, whose condition had not improved from when we first visited him. In those long stretches devoid of distractions, I would mull over the events at the station and experience a knot in my body, one that twisted my stomach and made the hair on my arms stand up. It felt like a gigantic rock had been glued to my shoulders. Whenever I thought about Sagar alone on that platform, I would feel physically drained from trying to lift the rock up. This was my first time encountering the merciless effect of guilt, and no matter how much I tried to push the rock aside, it would not budge. I felt so foolish for having chased after the Singer. How could I have left Sagar for a mere glimpse of a person? Why had my curiosity coerced me to prioritize someone I barely knew over family?

On New Year's Eve, I slept well before midnight, knowing that no one in the house would be participating in festivities. Vaishu Mavshi and Harsh Kaka were still at the hospital, my Aaji had fallen asleep on the downstairs couch, and my mother was cooped up in her room. My sleep was disturbed a few hours later by vigorous shaking. It was pitch black in the room, but I could make out my mother bending over me.

"Aku."

"Wha …What time is it?"

"Shh. Don't make noise," she whispered.

"What's going on?"

"I'll explain later, but I need you to pack some clothes."

I was fully awake at this point. "What? Why?"

"We're leaving for a bit. To your father's place. I've figured out all the details with him."

"What! We can't just leave."

"It's only temporary. Think of it as a vacation."

"B-but what about Sagar? Is he okay? We need to wait until he gets better."

"Aku, stop." She massaged her forehead. "I know what's best for us. I'm your mother."

"I'm not going."

"Aku, don't you care about me?"

I was taken aback by her question. "Of course."

"Then you need to understand that I can't be here right now. I can't breathe. I can't sleep. I need to get out of here."

"Mama, once Sagar gets better, everything will go back to normal."

Her eyes shifted down to her hands. She hesitated before saying, "Fine, then when Sagar gets better, we'll come back."

"What about Vaishu Mavshi and Harsh Kaka? They need us right now."

She grabbed my arms. "Don't you understand? They're the ones that want us to leave. They don't want to see us."

"I don't believe you," I said, wincing in pain. I tried to break free from her grasp, but she held on tighter.

"I'm telling you the truth!"

"I don't believe you," I repeated defiantly.

"Don't you see that I'm trying to protect you?" she hissed. "Don't you see that I'm doing this for you? They know you left him alone when you were told to wait with him. This is your fault as much as it is mine, Akash."

Once again, the rock of guilt weighed down on me, stronger than ever. She was right. It was my fault. I could have prevented this from happening if I had stayed with Sagar.

My mother loosened her grip on my wrists. "Do you trust me?"

"Y-yes."

"Then believe me when I tell you this is the only way."

She was my mother. How could I doubt her when I hadn't before? "You promise we'll come back after Sagar gets better?"

She hesitated again. "I promise."

"When are we leaving?"

"I already ordered a cab. It's coming in half an hour."

"Aren't we going to say goodbye?"

She stroked my cheek. "It's better this way. It's what they want."

———

I finished packing in twenty minutes. I left most of my belongings, assuming we wouldn't be gone for longer than a week. My mother and I tiptoed past my sleeping Aaji in the living room. The cab driver was waiting outside in darkness. My mother and I handed him four bags—she'd packed much more than I had. We fit one bag in the front passenger seat and one in the middle back seat.

My mother and I sat on opposite sides of the bag. The driver pulled away from the curb and turned onto Main Street. As we passed by Das Electronics, I thought about Nikhil and wondered if he knew we were leaving. I looked over at my mother's hand and noticed that she wasn't wearing her engagement ring. She was intensely focused on a small pouch in her lap. She pulled out a wad of hundred-dollar bills from it and counted through them.

"What did you do with your ring?" I asked.

She tucked the money back in the pouch. "I returned it."

"Back to Nikhil?"

My mother reached for my hand. She looked out of the window. A tear rolled to the edge of her jaw before falling on her pouch. I realized then that this was the first time I would be leaving the Town for longer than a day.

The cab continued down the dark road, taking two lost individuals toward a blind hope for a better future.

PART TWO

CHAPTER 10

A TEMPORARY HOME

WE ARRIVED AT San Francisco Airport shortly after dawn. The crowd at the arrivals section was scant. The New Year's rush hadn't begun yet, as most people were either asleep or still celebrating. We trudged to baggage claim, passing by electronic signs that wished us a wonderful start to 2012. I caught a glimpse of our reflections in one of the screens. My mother and I looked exhausted. Although I'd managed to seize a few hours of sleep on the flight, I doubted my mother had gotten any. She'd been staring out of the plane window the entire time I'd been awake.

My mother informed me that my father would ride a taxi to the airport and accompany us back to his apartment. We began a prolonged wait for his arrival after collecting our bags. Each time a car rounded the bend, we rushed to the curb, expecting it to be him. Once we realized the faces inside the car were unfamiliar, my mother and I would plop ourselves back on our bags. We watched with envy as drivers rushed to whomever they were picking up and bestowed them with hugs and well wishes for the new year. They would drive off soon after, leaving me and my mother to repeat the same disappointing process with the next car.

"Are you sure he's picking us up?" I asked.

"Yes. I told him we could manage on our own, but he insisted he come," replied my mother.

"Can you call him and find out where he is?"

My mother looked away from me. "I don't have my cellphone. I got rid of it."

"What? Why would you do that?"

"Doesn't matter. I thought he would be here."

She reached into the front pouch of one of her bags and pulled out a slip of paper. "I wrote his number and address down in case of an emergency. I can ask to borrow someone's phone."

My mother approached a woman in sweats sitting on an adjacent bench. The woman seemed wary of my mother's request but eventually relented. My mother tried to call my father's number three times, but each attempt went to voicemail.

"What do we do now?" I asked.

"I guess we could figure out the transportation ourselves." She looked at the bend once more. "But he swore he'd be here."

"Maybe he hasn't woken up yet. Or he mixed up what time we were landing."

"There's no way. I called him last night."

"What else could it be?"

I knew both of us were thinking of the other possibility: what if he hadn't come because he'd changed his mind? What if he no longer wanted us to stay with him in San Francisco? What if this was his way of telling us to go back?

"We've waited for over an hour," I said. "Can we please just go to his apartment?"

"Fine," said my mother. "There has to be some sort of explanation."

A help desk attendant recommended that we ride a BART train if we wanted more affordable transit. He helped us map out our route to my father's apartment. As helpful as he was, he spoke so fast that by the time my mother and I were on the train, we couldn't agree on which station he'd told us to get off at. She swore she'd heard him say Powell, while I was certain he'd said Montgomery. Seeing how tense she was, I didn't argue with her. We exited at Powell, found none of the signs the attendant had told us to look for, and wearily resumed our journey to the correct Montgomery stop.

We hiked crowded streets, pausing every couple of minutes to catch our breath. The Chinatown district was buzzing. Hordes crowded the sidewalks and wove between the Chinese-owned stores, markets, and restaurants. As we walked past shopkeepers and patrons interacting in their native tongues, I was reminded of Main Street and the various languages that would seep through the sidewalk conversations. Although the Town could not be more dissimilar to Chinatown in terms of density and commotion, these communities shared a closeness among their immigrant residents and businesses. Strangers were brought together by simply possessing an understanding of similar cultural concepts. This parallel was both comforting and agonizing, as it brought back fond memories of the Town while forcing me to ruminate over how far I was from it. I shook my head, dispelling all gloomy reflections of my distant home. I was too tired to focus on anything but the task at hand: making it to my father's apartment without collapsing.

"I think this is it." My mother stopped in front of an old yellow building tarnished with smudges of city grime. A small bakery occupied the bottom floor. The door next to the bakery was opened by someone I assumed was a tenant of the apartments above. My mom darted toward the door and beckoned for me to enter. I dragged the bags inside over two trips. My head was spinning from the windchill, lack of sleep, and strenuous exercise of the morning.

"Seriously? They couldn't have put an elevator in here?" my mother groaned, peering up at the winding staircase. I slid down against the wall, jaded by the mere possibility of carrying the bags up the stairs.

"What floor is he on?" I asked.

My mother stared at the sheet of paper with my father's address. "Shit. I didn't write down his apartment number."

"Mama!"

"I know, Akash!"

She paced back and forth in front of the staircase. "I'm going to have to knock on every door until I find him. What other option do I have?"

She climbed a few steps and hesitated. "Come with me."

"What about the luggage?"

"Leave it. I'd rather you be by my side."

I obliged and followed her up the staircase. Every so often, I would poke my head over the railing to make sure our bags had not been taken. We made our way up the building, knocking on each door. Most tenants answered. Some were wary, others annoyed. One man interrupted my mother and threatened to call the cops if she disturbed him again. We reached the top floor with two apartments left to approach. A short middle-aged woman living in one of the units opened her front door before we could even knock.

After my mother described my father's physical appearance, the woman responded in a squeaky, high-pitched voice, "Oh yes! Always coming in and out so late at night! He rattles his keys—*chukchukchukchuk*." The woman demonstrated the action with imaginary keys. "Disturbs me every night!"

My mother perked up. "Do you know where he lives?"

"Right there." The woman pointed at the apartment across the hall. "Tell him to stop being so noisy."

Relieved to be near the end of our journey, my mother and

I sped to the other apartment. The short woman kept her door open a crack and watched us.

My mother knocked. She smiled at me as we waited for my father to appear.

"Varun!" my mother said, rapping on the door a little harder.

We waited again. After another failed attempt, she banged on the door using an open-faced palm. "Varun, come on, open up!"

"Mama, I don't think he's in there."

The female neighbor clucked disapprovingly. My mother whipped around and shouted, "Oh, just shut up already!"

The neighbor closed her door in fright. My mother stormed to the staircase railing and bent over. "I think I'm going to be sick."

I patted her on the back, unsure what words would be comforting.

She began muttering to herself. "This was a mistake. I should have known better."

"He'll come," I said, trying to emulate Harsh Kaka's soothing tone.

She breathed heavily for a minute. After slowing her exhales to a normal pace, she slumped down the stairs and collapsed next to our luggage. I knew from her sullen face that she didn't have another plan. Whether or not my father wanted us there, we had nowhere else to go. I sat next to my mother and rested my head on her shoulder.

For the next two hours, we stayed in that spot. Tenants entering and exiting the building shuffled around us, shooting puzzled looks in our direction. I was dozing off when my mother finally stood up.

"Let's go," she said.

"Where?"

"Away from here."

We wearily grabbed our bags and walked to the exit. As my mother reached for the handle, the door suddenly swung open, and she had to leap back to avoid it hitting her.

"Mahi?"

My father stood before us, his eyes widening with surprise. He rushed inside and embraced my mother.

"Oh my God, I was so worried! I waited for hours at the terminal thinking maybe your flight got delayed, but then … you're here! I'm so happy."

My mother stuttered incoherently.

My father let go of her and hugged me. "Aku! I'm so glad to see you!"

He tried to lift me up in the air but soon realized that I was too big for that. He awkwardly set me down. "What happened? I thought you were going to wait at the terminal."

"We did. We couldn't find you there," said my mother hesitantly.

"Impossible. I got there maybe fifteen minutes after your flight landed. I asked the United agent—"

"Wait what? United?"

"Isn't that the airline you took?"

"We flew American."

"No, I wrote it down," he said, pulling out his wallet. "I put it here after we hung up. Flight arrives at seven and the airline is … oh shit. Fuck me. Mahi, I'm so sorry."

"I called you."

"I'm a fucking ass and didn't charge my phone last night. I was rushing out when I realized, and it was too late by then."

"You swear you waited at the other terminal? It was a genuine mistake?"

"I thought you would be there. I'm so stupid. I should have at least looked at the paper one more time before leaving, but I was so sure you said Unite—"

"Varun," she interrupted, "it's okay. You're here now. Can you help us carry our luggage up?"

"Of course!" He grabbed the two largest bags and struggled to carry them up the first flight of stairs. He sheepishly handed one over to my mother.

"I'm so glad you guys are here," he chirped. "There's a lot I want to show you."

When we reached his apartment, my father unlocked the front door and ushered us inside. "I know it's a bit small."

Small was an understatement. A full-sized bed with a wiry metal frame was crammed in the back corner of the studio. To the right of the bed was an open kitchen with an old stovetop. The only other furniture my father possessed was a circular wooden table, two folding chairs, and a stained purple couch that was pressed against the wall closest to the door. Despite not having proper furnishings, my father made sure to transfer his mess from Brooklyn to this apartment. The drawings from his wall of incompleteness were taped up on the left-hand wall. His various instruments, books, and hoarded items were scattered across the room. They were in neater piles and not strewn across the floor like at his previous place. I gave him the benefit of the doubt, believing he'd cleaned for our arrival. The imperfect painting of the three of us hung by the door, welcoming us in.

My mother stood still. "Varun, you said we could all fit here."

"We can. You and I can take the bed, and Aku can sleep on the couch. How does that sound, buddy? And this is only temporary. I swear, once my project takes off, we'll have more space than we'll need."

My mother kicked off her shoes and fell on the bed. "I need to rest."

"What about you, Aku? Wanna go for a walk?"

Although I also wished to wind down from the hectic morning, I couldn't bring myself to disappoint my eager father. "Sure."

———

"Your mom told me what happened with Sagar. What a shitshow."

My father and I were strolling on a sidewalk bordering the bay. White sailboats roamed leisurely along the glittering water. Seagulls swam in gentle patterns above them. Compared to Manhattan, San Francisco seemed mellow, a place where people meandered more than they rushed. The air was crisper than the East Coast, and I had to constantly lick my lips to prevent them from drying out.

"It's a good thing you both came here," he continued. "Better to get away from all of that."

"We're going back, though," I said. "Right after Sagar wakes up."

My father stopped walking. "Huh?"

"Once Sagar gets better, Mama promised that we would go back to the Town. You know we're not staying here forever, right?"

He looked at me quizzically for a moment. Then, he shook his head and continued forward. "Of course, buddy. I'm just glad you're here now. Hey, I wanna show you something."

He led me to a perpendicular street away from the water. He stopped in front of one of the many high-rise buildings in the area and used a badge from his pocket to unlock the front glass door.

"Where are we?" I asked.

"This is where my dreams come true," he responded, winking mischievously at me.

We rode the elevator up to the eleventh floor, after which my father guided me to the end of the hall. He unlocked an office door and switched on the lights, powering up a luminous work studio. The spacious room resembled an expanded version of my father's wall of incompleteness. Posters of his designs were hung up on the walls. I recognized his unique style instantly, from the swooping curves to the vibrant neon colors and lack of uniformity. There were no rules in my father's drawings; the pattern that began in one corner of the frame did not necessarily end in the other. Diagrams of a human face wearing black glasses were drawn on a massive whiteboard. Computers and tablets rested on collaborative desks in the middle of the room.

"What is all of this?" I asked, awestruck.

"It's hard to explain without showing you first."

My father took me to a smaller office in the back, sectioned off by glass panels. He gestured for me to sit in a chair facing the wall while he hooked up a projector. He went behind a computer and, on the wall before me, launched a wide image of bleak homes.

"I want you to stare directly at the screen," my father ordered. "Don't look away."

The image became brighter once he switched off the lights. He pressed play on a remote, and the image turned into a handheld video. Barking dogs and screaming children could be heard in the background. The camera stayed focused on the homes, despite the occasional shaking from the camera operator's grip. I examined the houses. Nothing about them seemed out of the ordinary.

A red speck appeared on the wall of the leftmost home. As if a thin pen was commanding it, the speck grew into a curve and connected with itself to form a circle. Extending tangentially from the red circle, a green arch stretched toward the roof. Other neon colors branched off from these shapes and formed their own patterns. Within seconds, the designs, so clearly my father's, had expanded to fill the exterior of the other homes with color and vivacity. They lived, breathed, moved, and pulsed as if they were a part of the video, not an addition to it. When the camera shook, the designs remained imprinted on the houses. I was entranced, unable to take my eyes off.

Flashes of the undecorated homes disrupted the radiant visuals. The designs disappeared one moment and reappeared the next. My eyes had difficulty readjusting to the back-and-forth between the original video and the enhanced one.

"Dad, stop it," I said, covering my eyes to eliminate the sharp pain that surfaced in my head. I felt the flashes end and cautiously dropped my hands.

"Shit, I thought it was ready to view," muttered my father. He turned the projector off. "The engineer's gonna be pissed I touched her equipment."

"I still don't understand what this is. What's your job?"

"See, it all started with my friend Sean. He's a total geek about all this tech stuff. I usually tune him out, but this one night, he was explaining this thing called augmented reality. Ever heard of it?"

I shook my head.

"Neither had I. Simply put, it's technology that allows us to see the world we know but with a few imaginative additions that make it better. Like right now, for example, you were looking at normal, boring homes, right? But then they were improved once you could see my designs on them. Does that make sense?"

"Kinda."

"It's confusing. Even I don't fully understand. But when Sean first told me about AR, I joked how cool it would be if people could see the world through my art. He loved the idea, especially since he'd always been a fan of my work. We brainstormed for months and somehow got this twenty-something dude with a shit ton of money to invest in it. We're still in early stages, which is why I could only show you the animation concept through this video. But could you imagine one day looking through a pair of special glasses and seeing my art all over sidewalks, buildings, clothes, basically everywhere you look, as if it were just a natural part of the environment?"

Even though I was still nauseated from the glitching video, I responded, "It looks great, Dad."

He walked around the computer and kissed the top of my head. "You don't know how much that means to me, Aku. Sean told me that larger companies are developing projects in this same field. That's the beauty of the time we're living in. It's all about ideas, ideas, ideas. Ideas are your currency. But none of them have what we have. None of them have my vision. Don't you agree?"

I enthusiastically nodded, sensing that this was the reaction he was looking for.

My father beamed. "I've been looking for a greater purpose my entire life. I've wanted to create something that would live on long after I die. I admit, I've jumped around trying to find it, but it's because I've never been able to pinpoint the right thing. Until now."

He bent down and looked straight into my eyes. "You're lucky to have a father like me. I'll always encourage you to pursue whatever your heart tells you to. My parents tried to stifle me when I was younger. They wanted me to study subjects I hated, get a mind-numbing job at some fucktard corporation, and settle for mediocrity, like all the other kids from the Town. But I knew I was destined for more. And you are too."

I thought back to what Vaishu Mavshi had said about my father's disappearance. I decided it was better to confront him rather than hold any form of resentment.

"Why did you leave for Illinois before I was born?" I asked. "Did you ... did you not want me?"

My father's brow furrowed. "Who told you this? Was it Mahi?"

"Um ..."

"Whatever, doesn't matter. How can you even ask me this, Aku? You have to understand—it was all my parents' idea. They forced me to move because they thought that having a child before college would ruin my chances of a good life. I realized how wrong they were and ran away. I came back to you."

"Why didn't you live with us in the Town?"

"Because ... that place reminds me too much of feeling suffocated. Running away from my parents was the best decision I ever made. It gave me freedom. I didn't want to lose that again."

Sensing my hesitancy, he grabbed my face in his palms. "Look at me, Aku. The timing was never right before. I still needed to figure myself out and what I wanted to do in life. But now that I have this project, I'm ready to make this family work. I can't even express how much I love you and your mom. I've been waiting for this moment my entire life."

The sincerity in his eyes convinced me. His reassuring statement dismantled my already minimal doubt, and he was back to being the faultless man I adored. I hugged him around the neck and told him I loved him too.

——

My mother was asleep when we returned to the apartment. My father joined her and began snoring like a bear. I sat on the couch, watching my mother twist and turn in her sleep, wondering what she was dreaming about. Though I was physically drained, I couldn't fall asleep. There was too much nagging at me. The day had been a string of constant movement, helping keep my thoughts mostly away from the Town. But the stillness of the apartment brought out an insatiable restlessness within me.

I took my father's apartment keys and cellphone off the wooden table and went outside, softly shutting the apartment door behind me. I perched myself on the stairs in between the second and third floor. Staring at the phone screen, I contemplated calling home. I wanted to know how Vaishu Mavshi and Harsh Kaka were doing. I wanted to know if Sagar's condition had improved. Did they know where we were? Were they worrying about us?

I dialed our landline number, holding my breath as it rang once. Twice. Three times.

"Hello?" murmured Harsh Kaka.

I choked up. The anguish in his voice debilitated my ability to respond. I was reminded of what my mother had said before we'd left. They blamed us for what had happened to Sagar. They didn't want to hear from us.

"Hello?" he repeated.

I hung up the call, feeling guilty for even dialing the number. I vowed not to contact them again until my mother told me that Sagar was better. For the first time since the incident at the station, I cried.

CHAPTER 11

THE IMAGINED

LONELINESS WAS A new obstacle for me and my mother. My father spent most of his time at the office, often leaving before we woke up and returning once we had finished dinner. We would eagerly await his arrival, since the rest of our day was spent listlessly passing time. He would come back to the apartment enthused by his work and ready to entertain us with stories of his office drama.

The day after we landed, my mother and I recognized that we had absolutely nothing to do: no work, no school, no people we could meet. I tried to convince her to explore San Francisco with me, but she didn't want to leave the apartment except to buy groceries from the corner street market, and that was only out of necessity. My mother mentioned once that we should check out elementary schools nearby, which I considered a silly comment since the move to SF was only temporary. There wasn't a need to enroll me if we were eventually going to return to the Town. I didn't bring up the topic again, and she seemed too preoccupied with her own thoughts to remember. She was two separate people when my father was there and when he wasn't. When he returned in the evening, she was her usual vivacious self, giggling at his stories as if she had lived with him for years. But when he wasn't present, she would gloomily lie in bed for hours and stare out of the window, as if her personality had vacated her body.

Meanwhile, I spent most of my time sketching on my father's scratch paper. I captured observable parts of the apartment such as the tiny kitchen, the ugly couch, or my mother sprawled on the bed, observing the shadows and lines and contours and re-creating them on the page the way my father had taught me to. None of the drawings I completed ever satisfied me. The claustrophobic apartment was too drab and monotonous. I would rip up my sketches once I finished them, hoping a fresh page would open my eyes to something more interesting in my environment. It never did, and the dissatisfying process repeated itself each successive day.

At the end of the first week, my mother abruptly jumped up from the bed and announced that she was going to find a job. She instructed me not to leave the apartment while she was gone. Hours later, she returned grinning. She said that she had walked around searching for a Desi-owned beauty salon. The first one she'd come across was run by an older lady with a blunt, no-nonsense personality. This lady, who my mother referred to as Nabeela Aunty, calmly listened as my mother detailed her previous experience and begged for an opportunity. After my mother finished her long-winded speech, Nabeela Aunty pointed to her own eyebrows and said that my mother would have to successfully thread them if she wanted to be hired.

"I was so scared, Aku! What if I messed up? That would have been horrible! But I did it! I did it, and I got the job!"

The next day, she left for work as early as my father did, abandoning me in the apartment. I attempted to read one of my father's philosophy books but quit out of boredom three pages in. I fiddled with his guitar next, strumming hopelessly out of tune. Midway through my daily drawing, I decided that

I needed to escape the apartment. Although my mother had instructed me not to go outside, I reasoned that if I returned before she came back, she wouldn't find out that I'd left in the first place. I packed a tote bag with savory pastries from the bakery downstairs and spare change from my father's stash. I used a toothbrush as a door stopper so that I had a way of reentering.

When I exited the building, fear of my unfamiliar surroundings momentarily prevented me from proceeding. The lack of a set path, as well as the possibility of getting lost, terrified me. Faced with a choice to either explore the area or return to the apartment, I forced myself to walk. I kept track of my route by imprinting images of passing shops and street signs into my memory. I reached Market Street and boarded the first bus that appeared. Clutching my bag, I slipped past strangers to the empty last row. The bus teetered along steep hills, revealing the vastness of San Francisco. Miles and miles of buildings stretched far into the mist. In the Town, where everyone knew my name and family, I never once considered myself invisible. But in this gigantic sprawl of disconnected lives, without a soul besides my parents who knew who I was, I felt imperceptible to those around me, like a ghost aimlessly floating about. This budding recognition of my insignificance brought about a lingering emptiness, a sense of bewilderment at how trivial my life could be to others.

I got off at an arbitrary intersection. On one side of me was a row of blue, white, and beige townhomes, similar to the streets I'd passed during the bus ride over. But on the other side of the junction was what appeared to be an entrance to an extensive green space. Intrigued, I crossed the road and entered through a dirt walkway surrounded by towering trees. Signposts labeled this lush, natural area as Golden Gate Park. Prior to then, I'd envisioned a park as a small neighborhood trail encircling a rickety play structure. Golden Gate Park couldn't have been more opposite to that idea. It was sprawling and sheltered. The trees blocked out any sight of surrounding buildings, enshrouding me within the peaceful greenery. Since it was a weekday afternoon, I crossed paths with only two or three pedestrians. I walked mostly without another human being in sight, taking in the pleasant humming of insects, the moist smell of mulch, the swaying of the long branches. There were paved walkways, but I left them and meandered through the forest-like parts of the park.

As I ventured deeper in, I temporarily forgot that I was in San Francisco. I felt like I was back on the East Coast, immersed in the forest Sagar and I would run around in. Warm memories washed over me. The park's close resemblance to my childhood sanctuary made me reflect on how much I missed playing in the woods and how lucky I was to have had those pure experiences. I longed, I ached, to leave San Francisco and return to the Town, or to at least have a set date for when my mother and I were going to fly back. But the separation was indefinite, and I wasn't able to do anything to change that. This staggering awareness made me feel utterly helpless. It weakened my legs and clouded my vision, causing me to lose track of my route. I stopped to recalibrate and figure out which direction I'd come from.

I sensed him before I heard his voice, as if a part of me knew he was going to appear. I'd memorized the melody, haunted by it during my incessant dreams. His voice rang loud and clear in my ears. It enveloped me and guided me to its source. I walked up a few steps and arrived at an open area bordered by canopy trees. Three rectangular pools were lined up next to each other. The water within them was still, like a flat sheet, and perfectly reflected the trees and sky above it. Not one ripple disturbed the mirror image. The pool's rendering of the surrounding environment was so faithful that if it hadn't been for my upright orientation, I doubt I would have been able to tell that it was just an illusion.

Sitting cross-legged at the edge of the middle pool, right where the physical environment and its reflection met, was the Singer. His tanpura lay flat on his lap. His head was bowed, his eyes closed. His stomach expanded and contracted with each note. In the leftmost pool, a balding man was casting his fishing line and reeling it back in a rhythmic manner. Cast, wait, reel. Over and over, he repeated this action with meditative grace. The Singer's humming matched the rhythm of the other man's activity. They built a symbiosis with one another, and the space around them listened attentively. Everything seemed to move at a similar pace: the birds, the fisher, the breeze, the Singer's voice.

When my strange dreams had started after the wedding, I'd desperately wanted to find the Singer. But now that he was in front of me, with nothing barring my path to him, I didn't know where to begin with my interrogation. So, I asked the one question that summed up every other one I had.

"Who are you?"

He didn't reply. He continued to sing as if he hadn't heard me. I was irritated. Who did he think he was, appearing and disappearing in my life whenever he pleased? If it hadn't been for him, I wouldn't have left Sagar at the station.

"Hey! I'm talking to you!" I yelled, walking toward his side of the pool. If he wasn't going to talk to me willingly, I would make him. The meditative atmosphere cracked, as though it could sense my aggression. The man by the other pool stopped casting his fishing line, the birds began to croon out of sync, and the Singer's eyes opened. They pierced me, and I was unable to move.

"We meet again," he said.

My body was still frozen.

"Sit."

I obeyed his command. My feet led me to the opposite end of the long pool. I sat exactly like him. He spoke no louder than a whisper. Despite the distance between us, I heard him clearly.

"Why did you disturb me?"

The words tumbled out of my mouth. "Who are you, and what are you doing here? I don't understand why you keep entering my dreams, and why, when I want to find you, I can't, and when I don't … well, here you are! What the heck is going on?"

The Singer raised one eyebrow. "I was meditating, and then you disturbed me. That seems to me all that is going on."

I huffed, annoyed by his unhelpful response. "Why do you appear in my dreams? How do I get them to stop?"

"I can't control what you dream about. They're in your mind."

I wanted to know whether the Singer had actually been on the train platform the day of the opening, but I was terrified of asking him. If he responded that he hadn't been, if I'd left Sagar for a hallucination rather than an actual person, my guilt would have weighed on me even more. So, I asked instead, "Are you real?"

The Singer smiled, amused by my question. "I'm talking to you, aren't I?"

"Then, what are you doing in San Francisco? Did you move here too?"

"Is that where you think we are? San Francisco?"

"Well, obviously."

"Hm," he said, looking around. He closed his eyes once again. "Now if you'll excuse me, I would like to go back to my meditation."

"Wait!"

His eyes shot open again in exasperation.

"Where did you think we were? How could you not know that we're in San Francisco?"

"Listen, child, leave me alone—"

"No!" I exclaimed. "You want to meditate so bad? Well, I will stay here and yell and scream so loudly that you won't be able to. And my name is Akash!"

My heart was pounding with exhilaration. I was channeling Sagar's defiance.

The Singer's nostrils flared. "You wouldn't be able to understand if I explained it to you."

"You said the same thing when I asked you how to meditate. But I still did it."

"That's true," he said, his expression thoughtful. "And you saw something when you were meditating, correct?"

"Yes," I murmured. I had hoped he wouldn't remember. "But it was stupid. I thought that paint was raining down around me."

His eyes narrowed. "That's not stupid. That's not stupid at all. And after the paint rained down, what did you see?"

"You told me to think of a moment I missed. For a second, I felt like I was standing in the same place that I pictured."

The Singer's forehead scrunched up. He began muttering to himself.

"I can't hear you."

He observed me with a fresh curiosity. "It's strange. I've been able to meditate without interruption for a long time. No voice, no sound has disturbed me. Until you. Maybe … just maybe … you and I were meant to meet. I don't know why. But I have a hunch …"

I had no clue what he was rambling about. "So, now will you explain whatever you thought was too advanced for me to know?"

He hesitated. "I have a gift, Akash. When I meditate, I am transported somewhere else. I don't pay attention to where I am in this world, because I spend most of my time in another one."

"What do you mean? Where do you go?"

"I call it the Imagined."

"Never heard of it."

"You wouldn't have. You see, the Imagined comes from a special ability I possess. I wasn't sure if anyone else shared this skill, but if fate has brought us together … I wonder."

"You mean I can go to the Imagined too?"

"Let me ask you this: is there a memory you intensely desire to return to? I'm not talking about one you casually miss every so often. But a moment, or collection of related moments, that make your heart ache because they are now in the past? Some part of your life you long to experience again, because since then, you've felt empty?"

My eyes lowered. "Yes."

"Then let me try to show you. It will be easier to explain what the Imagined is after you've seen it."

He began to pluck the strings of his tanpura. "I want you to do exactly what we did last time. Close your eyes, listen to my voice, and hold on to one image that encapsulates that memory."

He began to sing. I shut my eyes and listened to the sounds of my environment: the chirping birds, the mellow water, the conversations of nearby pedestrians. I concentrated on his voice and the gentle hum of the tanpura. Slowly, the other sounds started to fade. His singing overtook them all. My body felt weightless, untethered, and I was able to float peacefully. I began to think of the carefree days of summer. Oh, how I wished I could go back to when Sagar and I ran through the forest, before I met Mayuran, before my body began to change, before the opening of the station, before I started dreaming of the Singer. Back to when we would lie under the three trees without a care in the world. Back to when life was perfect.

My eyes opened. I was stranded in an endless black vacuum. The Singer's voice echoed around me as I hovered in nothingness. I tried to remain calm, knowing that I had been here before. But the feeling of being stranded filled me with dread. A glimmer of light expanded at the top of this void. Exactly like before, the first meteoric streak of paint shot toward me, this time a shade of mud brown. I watched as it fell right beneath my feet. It spread out and composed a dirt-covered forest floor, stretching as far as my eye could see. Other colors were pouring down as well, morphing into trees, bushes, and fallen leaves. Each drop of paint varied in size, depending on what it transformed into when it landed. As detail was added to the space around me, I realized that these droplets were composing an environment that I recognized all too well. I was standing in the forest beside the Town.

The rain ended. There weren't any traces of paint left around me. The forest looked exactly as I remembered it. The Singer's voice had vanished, replaced by the calls of sparrows and cicadas. But these sounds didn't come from Golden Gate Park—they were distinctly part of the forest back home. I looked up. Between the tops of the trees, I saw a narrow glimpse of blue sky where the speck of white light had been a moment ago. An airplane rumbled past.

I examined my hands, turning them back and forth to make sure my entire body was present. I crouched down and reached hesitantly toward the forest floor, jumping back in shock the second my finger contacted the dirt. What was going on? Was I really back in the Town? The forest seemed too lifelike to be part of a dream.

My right foot stepped forward, then my left. I ambled in the direction of the three trees, a natural choice for my first destination. I continuously touched the surfaces around me, reconfirming to myself that they existed. When I'd lived in the Town, I'd passively accepted the forest for what it was. But as I walked through in this hypnotic state, I finally saw and appreciated the beauty of it. Soft streaks of sunlight nudged their way past the treetops. A mild breeze brushed past me, bringing awareness to the droplets of sweat that formed around my temples. I inhaled a whiff of my humid surroundings, replenishing my nose with the fresh, earthy scent of the soil and plants.

"Hello!" I yelled out, testing if my voice worked.

"Akash Dada?"

I froze. It couldn't be. I couldn't see him, but his voice was unmistakable. Wondering if this was a trick of my imagination, I whispered, "Sagar?"

"What took you so long? I've been waiting forever."

It was undoubtedly him. I sprinted in the direction of his voice. The three trees materialized, and I saw a body lying on the ground among them. My heart was beating fast from anticipation.

"Sagar? Is that really you?"

He sat up, turned toward me, and smiled that mischievous smile of his. His face looked exactly as it had before the incident at the station. Not a single cut or bruise marked him. A streak of daylight lit the top of his hair and cast an angelic glow around him.

"Sagar!"

I ran faster, kicking up a storm of dirt. But an abnormality on my left side caught my eye. Rather than standing straight up, one tree leaned at a freakish diagonal angle, its branches grotesquely curling away in thick loops. Although I wanted my focus to remain on Sagar, my attention was diverted by this deviant tree. I couldn't remember anything like it existing in the forest.

I slowed to a jog, disturbed by what I saw. As if detecting my brief hesitation, my surroundings began to crack. The fine details of the environment were reversed into a collection of thin brushstrokes, rupturing the illusion of the forest. The world around me started to resemble a painted composition rather than an actual physical place. The brushstrokes split back into their original droplet forms and surged upward one by one. The sky shrank into a singular white circle, and the black void prevailed around it.

I tried to look in Sagar's direction, but it was already too late. My body was tugged downward, and I tumbled into darkness. I scrunched my head toward my chest to combat the harsh sensation of freefalling. Suddenly, the plummet ceased.

I opened my eyes and focused my blurry vision on the Singer. I was back in Golden Gate Park.

"What was that?" I asked in a daze.

"What did you see?" he asked with urgency.

"I could ... I could see it all. I was back there. Back in the Town. But ... how?"

"I was right," the Singer murmured. Tears sprang to his eyes. "I've found someone else who understands."

"Was it real?"

"Let me ask you something. Were you able to feel the world around you? Were you able to smell and touch and move freely?"

"Yes," I croaked.

"Then you have your answer."

Sagar. Sagar was there, fully recovered.

I shot up. The nausea hadn't left yet, and I had to steady myself to avoid throwing up. "I have to go."

"Wait!" the Singer called out. "I have more to ask you. We must figure this out!"

I ignored the Singer's desperate calls and raced down the steps toward the walkway. With immense conviction to return to the apartment, I easily figured my way out of the park. I had to tell my mother that Sagar was okay. We could go back to the Town.

I'd misjudged how far I had traveled from the apartment. I impatiently bounced in my seat on the long bus ride back. After I disembarked at Market Street, I sprinted through the crowded streets, weaving my way through pedestrians until I reached the apartment building. I climbed up the stairs, two at a time. When I reached the door, I heard my mother's voice coming from inside. "Varun, I told you, he's not here—"

I knocked, and the door immediately swung open. My mother scowled at me and hung up the phone. "Akash! Get in here!" She grabbed my collar and pulled me into the apartment. "Where the hell were you?"

"I went out to explore. But, Mama, I have something to tell you—"

"You went out by yourself? Akash, I told you specifically not to leave this apartment while I'm gone."

"Mama, listen to me—"

"Do you know how terrified I was when I came home? After everything with Sagar …"

"That's what I need to talk to you about. Sagar is okay!"

My mother shut the door. "What did you say?"

"I saw Sagar, and he's okay! His injuries have healed."

"What do you mean you saw him?" she asked slowly.

"It's hard to explain. I'll tell you later. But you have to call Vaishu Mavshi. This means we can go home!"

She backed away and fell onto one of the folding chairs.

Her face paled. "Akash, why would you say that?" she whispered.

"Why do you look so sad? Everything's going to be okay now!"

"Akash, stop it—"

"You should call her. I'm sure they want to hear from us."

"I said stop it!"

I was exasperated by her lack of action. "Why? Why won't you call?"

"Because he's dead, Akash!" she cried, her eyes blazing.

We stared at each other in silence while I tried to process the words that had just come out of her mouth.

"That's—that's not possible," I choked out.

"The night we left, an hour before I woke you up, Harsh left a voicemail for your Aaji and told her the news. She was asleep, but I heard it. The injuries ... the damage to his lungs ... it was just too much for him." My mother began tearing up.

"He's ... he's really dead?"

"I didn't know how to tell you. I figured I would wait until we settled here."

"Settled here?" I repeated, shocked. "So, we're not going back to the Town?"

"How can we ever face them again?"

I pictured Vaishu Mavshi and Harsh Kaka crying next to Sagar's cold body. My arms were numb, hanging off my heavy shoulders. "Shouldn't we be there with them?"

"You and I are to blame. If he'd recovered, maybe they would have forgiven us. But now ..." She covered her face.

I slowly fell on the couch, astonished by her revelation. I was listening to what my mother was saying, but I wasn't understanding any of it. My brain wasn't able to make sense of how life could reach such an unimaginably horrid state. How could my mother and I live away from the Town? What would the world be like without Sagar in it? And the reigning question, the one holding me hostage in a state of disbelief rather than of grief: if what my mother said was true, then how had I seen Sagar a little over an hour ago? If I hadn't returned to the Town, where on earth had I gone?

CHAPTER 12

FIRST DAY

THERE HAVE BEEN a few moments in my life when I've looked at myself in the mirror completely bemused by the person I saw staring back. After a long stretch of passively glancing at my reflection, I would finally study the structure of my narrow face, the ridges on my bright pink lips, my droopy right eye, the freckles that tickled my cheekbones, surprised that these features were a part of me and not of another person. These moments occurred most often during the period of my adolescence when my physical appearance was rapidly changing. They would wrench me away from myself and make me feel as if there was an Akash that existed within me and an Akash that everyone else saw. I was familiar with one, but the other was a stranger.

On a chilly Monday morning at the end of February, almost two months after I'd left the Town, I experienced one of those out-of-body moments. I stood in the bathroom of my father's apartment, freshly bathed with combed hair. A cream-colored shaft of early morning light shone through the tiny window in the bathroom, landing on the right side of my face. I'd been suspended in front of the cracked mirror for a while, scrutinizing my skinnier appearance. My bones were more pronounced, and my cheeks curved inward. I trembled as I stared at myself, confused as to where I was, who I was, how fast life had derailed, and how unable I was to catch up. I couldn't believe I was in San Francisco. I couldn't believe that Vaishu Mavshi and Harsh Kaka were no longer everyday figures in my life. I couldn't believe that Sagar was …

"Binders, notebooks, pencils—that's all you'll need for today, right?" my mother called out, snapping me out of my daze.

I straightened my T-shirt and exited the bathroom, yawning loudly. She stood by the kitchen counter, packing supplies into a brand-new JanSport backpack. It was my first day back at school. Instead of continuing in elementary, I was set to attend a public middle school that covered sixth to eighth grade.

My mother zipped the backpack and fastened the straps over my shoulders, even though I was more than capable of doing it myself. This whole experience of her fussing over me was bizarre. She'd never taken me back-to-school shopping before then. Whenever I'd needed supplies in the past, Vaishu Mavshi would pick them up in the City after her nursing shifts. But ever since my mother had revealed that our stay in San Francisco was permanent, she'd been incredibly involved in getting me back to school. She pushed the school admin- istration to enroll me even though the semester had already begun. She eagerly took me on a massive shopping trip and bought supplies I didn't even think were necessary. When the cashier rang up the total, my mother paid without hesitation. I knew the amount she spent was more than we could afford, having seen how cautious she was when purchasing groceries or take-out food. We were barely able to make ends meet off my father's small stipend from the startup and my mother's earnings from the salon, so much so that I was able to see where corners were being cut.

My mother's overinvolvement and pampering was evidently aimed at rekindling our tense relationship. After she found out about my solo outing around San Francisco, she installed a combination lock on the outside handle of the front door to ensure that I did not leave the apartment again without her knowledge. She locked it every day before she went to work and took it off when she came home. She told me that it was for my safety, though leaving me jailed in the claustrophobic apartment with little to do but ruminate over the information she'd revealed about Sagar seemed far from my benefit. My distrust in her was evident; I would respond to her mostly in monosyllables.

"You're all set, baby," she said, leaning down to kiss me on the cheek. I dodged her lips.

She straightened out and pouted. "Aku, don't be like that. How long can you go without talking to me?"

"Forever."

She sighed. "I know you're sad. I am too."

"Really?" I snapped. "Because you don't seem to care at all."

The morning after my mother told me the truth about Sagar, she blithely headed off to work as if the previous night hadn't occurred. She was rarely in the apartment and no longer moped around when she was. The salon had become her sanctuary, and she picked up as many shifts as possible, dedicating both weekends and weekdays to the job.

Her eyes widened. "Of course I care, Akash! You don't think I'm affected by this? You don't think it eats at—you know what, forget it. The point is, we have to figure out a way to be happy here. We can't let what happened destroy our lives." She took a deep breath, placing her hand on my arm. "That's why I really need you to try to have a good time today. Please. For me."

"I don't even want to go back to school."

"It'll be good for you. Trust me. Look how much being back in a salon has helped me."

"You're going to make me go either way."

She used her hands to comb through my already brushed hair. "You're right. I'm your mother. And I know what's best for you. You'll thank me one day for doing this."

Although many retorts were swimming through my mind, I shut them away and reluctantly followed her out of the apartment to the bus stop.

When the bus arrived, she held my shoulders tightly. "Come home straight after, okay? I'm taking off the lock today because I have a late shift, but you have to promise me that you won't go anywhere else."

I mumbled an incoherent reply while hopping up the stairs.

"Be safe and have f—"

The doors shut behind me, cutting off the rest of her sentence.

———

I hadn't cried since learning that Sagar was dead. I wanted to cry. I knew that I should have. I'd seen enough television to know that it was the correct response to information like this. But I was unable to process his death. It seemed too unreasonable to me. There was a voice in my head that told me he was still out there somewhere, that his condition was not as absolute as my mother had made it out to be. I could not comprehend the finality of his absence, especially when my mother went about her life as if there had been no disruption to it. Only when I thought of Vaishu Mavshi and Harsh Kaka did I feel a glaring emotional reaction. The rock of guilt burdened me as I visualized how vacant life would be for them without Sagar. I was not equipped to handle such afflicting anxieties at my young age, so I swiftly dispelled these thoughts and focused on my anger toward my mother. It was easier to direct my emotions at a person near me.

I also struggled to accept Sagar's passing because of my mystifying encounter with the Singer in Golden Gate Park. I was prevented from mourning because I was too preoccupied with wondering how I had seen Sagar lying in the forest if he was dead. My dreams had become inexplicably less intense since that day, as if I'd found some sort of release by visiting the forest. Though there were a million questions I wanted to ask the Singer, he was a stranger with unknown intentions. If Sagar really was dead, I was either losing my sanity or seeing ghosts. Neither option was preferable, so I'd decided ignorance was the best path forward. Besides, even if I had wished to return to Golden Gate Park in the previous months, my mother's lock would have prevented me from doing so.

After a twenty-minute commute, I arrived at my new school well before my first class. Tucked away in the corner of a quiet block, the campus consisted of a three-story building as well as a small outdoor patio with a basketball court and benches. The inside of the school was lively. The hallways were overflowing with a diverse array of students speaking over each other in small clumps. Most students towered over me, sporting modern styles and aloof attitudes. Standing in my worn-out sneakers and childish graphic T-shirt, I could sense how little I fit in. I tried to mimic the detached demeanor of the other students, but no one else cared how I came across. They were too preoccupied with maintaining their own social appearances.

After a brief meeting with the school counselor, I was handed my schedule and guided to my first-period class. The teacher made me introduce myself before my peers. I was flustered while trying to come up with a fun fact, so after a painful minute of watching me draw a blank, the teacher asked me to share another time. I skulked to the back of the class and found refuge from my embarrassment in a corner seat. The teacher began her lecture, and the other students lost interest in me.

Adjusting to the unfamiliar curriculum was grueling, but the most difficult change for me was not having any connection to the rest of the student body. I knew each student in the Town so well that I could list the names of their parents and closest friends. Even Mayuran and I had started our friendship with a base understanding of who the other was. This was the first time I would have to become acquainted with someone my age from scratch.

When lunchtime arrived, I bought a hot meal from the cafeteria and scanned the lunch tables. Similar to the separated sixth-grade circles back in the Town, the students here sat in clusters of three to ten people. I contemplated which group I would fit in with best. Despite the diversity of the school, I noticed that students predominantly hung out with those of a similar ethnic background. Though this was not the case for every group, it was the only visibly obvious distinction that I could gauge when knowing nothing about their personalities. I had observed before, especially while walking around Manhattan, how ethnicity grouped people together, but I'd never thought it would be a factor when deciding on potential friends. I rationalized this separation by considering how regional and religious backgrounds affected who was closer to who in the Town. Bilal and Sameer, for instance, had become best friends because their families went to the mosque together every weekend.

Worried that I would seem peculiar if I did not follow the protocol already established in the cafeteria, I scoured for other Indians. I found a few scattered about, but they were already part of well-established groups. Six Indian-looking boys wearing Adidas track pants and Golden State Warriors hoodies energetically passed off a basketball to one another in the far-right corner. Their robust, sporty behavior intimidated me. A group of brown girls in the middle of the cafeteria were huddled over textbooks, anxiously passing sheets of paper among each other as if they were key documents in warfare. They appeared too stressed to accept any new members at their table.

As I peered over at the left side of the room, I noticed an Indian girl who was sitting alone. I recognized her from my third-period yearbook class. She was tall, even with a noticeable hunch in her shoulders. The hood of her dark brown sweatshirt covered most of her head, leaving only a sliver of her violet-streaked hair visible near her forehead. Thick eyeliner encircled her hooded eyes. She had earbuds in, which were connected to an iPod on the lunch table.

Funnily enough, she was looking in the same direction that I'd been looking in only a moment before. Her eyes were focused on the group of frazzled Desi girls at the center table. Her expression was hard to read, but there was a hint of wistfulness in the way she stared at them, almost as if she wished to be sitting there passing homework around as well. I took that as an indication that she wanted company during this lunch period. Though she appeared to be older than me, possibly even in eighth grade, her seclusion made the prospect of approaching her less daunting. I mustered up the courage to walk over.

"Hi," I squeaked.

She jumped at the sound of my voice and looked up at me with bewilderment.

"My name is Ak—" I choked on my name and swallowed the gob of saliva preventing me from finishing my sentence. "Sorry. My name is Akash. What's yours?"

"Uh, Priya," she replied with confusion, pulling one of her earbuds out.

I was only prepared up to this introduction. While scrambling for another conversation topic, I stared at her with my mouth slightly open.

She uncomfortably pulled at the sleeves of her hoodie. "What? Why are you looking at me like that?"

Realizing that my silence was causing her to feel self-conscious, I blurted out, "You're Indian, right?"

She inspected me with suspicion. "Can I help you with something?"

"Um, well actually, I was standing over there and saw that you were sitting alone—"

"Yeah, so what?" she replied, crossing her arms. "You have a problem with that?"

"Not at all! I just thought maybe you'd like a friend to sit with."

She pursed her lips. "I don't."

"H-huh?" I was caught off guard by how straightforward her response was.

"Just because I'm sitting by myself doesn't mean I'm waiting for someone to join me. I'm perfectly okay on my own. I like it better."

Startled by her bluntness, I struggled for an adequate response. "Oh, o-okay."

"Anything else?"

I timidly shook my head no. Priya put her earbud back in, officially ending the conversation. I hurried away, flushed with embarrassment. The curt, unexpected rejection deeply discouraged me from approaching anyone else in the cafeteria and possibly experiencing a similar outcome. Perturbed by Priya's hostility, I dropped off my tray by the trash bin and darted to an adjacent hallway. I wasn't sure where to go, so I continued until I found the entrance to the library. I stepped into the sequestered room, where the boisterous conversations of students were replaced by the hushed sounds of rustling pages and squeaking chairs.

A few of the students studying in the library looked up at me when I walked in. I stiffened, afraid that they were judging me, but they promptly returned to their books, paying me little mind. I went to the end of an arbitrary aisle, where I wasn't visible to anyone. I sat on the floor, hugging my backpack, wishing that I'd saved the burger on the lunch tray instead of throwing it away. With my only company being shelves of dusty books, the longing for the Town crept up once again. I wished for my community, for established friendships, for the warmth of my family, instead of this newfound pit of loneliness that had just split open beneath me.

———

After school ended, I had a choice. Although my mother had instructed me to return to the apartment, I was revolted by the thought of being shut in by myself after spending the day overly conscious of my solitude. During my last two classes, I was overcome with an urge to revisit the strange vision of Sagar I'd had in Golden Gate Park. Walking through the forest and seeing Sagar's smiling face had provided me a staggering sense of hope that I longed for once again. Since the lock to the apartment was off, nothing was barring me from returning to the park except my own trepidation.

While I waited at the stop outside of the middle school, the same bus that had taken me to Golden Gate Park arrived at the opposing curb. Driven by fearless determination and defiance, I ran across the street and stepped aboard. Only as the bus lurched away did I start to consider that the Singer might not be at Golden Gate Park, that our paths had crossed previously only by complete coincidence. Besides, there was no guarantee that I would be able to revisit the dreamlike Town again.

Yet, when I arrived at the casting pools, I found the Singer situated at the edge of the water. The fisher wasn't present, but a few strangers were scattered across surrounding benches, silently observing the beauty of the space.

"I'm back," I said.

The Singer's eyes flung open. "Join me."

I sat at the other end of the middle pool, exactly as I had before. I nervously glanced at the strangers, wondering how they were perceiving me.

As if the Singer could read my thoughts, he said, "Don't let anything else distract you. Focus on me."

I did as he commanded, keeping my gaze steadfast on him. "I want to understand."

"What do you want to know?"

"Last time I was here, I somehow traveled back to my hometown. At first, I thought I was dreaming, but it felt too real for that. I could touch and smell everything around me. You told me that you too are transported somewhere when you meditate. Where do you go?"

"A place known as the Imagined. Based on what you've shared with me, I believe that's where you went as well."

"What does that mean? Where is it?"

"Let me try to explain it in the simplest way possible. Answer me this: what do you think separates us—humans, I mean—from other living things? What makes us uniquely more complex than them?"

I shrugged.

The Singer pointed to his temple. "This. This wonderful, sometimes terrifying, source of power that we each have."

"Our brain?"

"In a sense. You see, other living creatures have brains too. But the human mind is complex beyond measure. It allows us to form intricate thoughts, to experience deep emotion, to see and recognize beauty in the world around us. But most importantly, it blesses us with the ability to imagine.

"Most people experience imagination on a surface level. They read a book and form images in their mind. Or maybe they dream of their future, conjuring up hollow ideas of their desired house or children. But their visions are shallow, and they are too tethered to day-to-day life to sit with these fantasies for long. Then there are those who probe their imagination further. These are the artists of our world. They can conjure up ideas, such as magical abilities or creatures, that do not normally exist. Some of them pour their creativity into books, songs, or visual art, so that they can remain in the physical world while their minds occasionally float to made-up realms. Humankind tells us that this is the extent we are able to engage with our imagination."

The Singer paused, exhaling slowly. "But I have discovered that there is much more we can achieve. The imagination of a select few is so powerful, so immense, that they can use their memories, emotions, and sensory capabilities to construct a world they can immerse themselves in. This is what I refer to as the Imagined."

Though I tried my best to follow his explanation, the concept was too dense for me to grasp. "So, everything I saw last time was just my imagination? The forest, my cousin … none of it was real?"

The Singer smiled. "As you come to better understand the Imagined, you will realize that reality is not as black and white as it may seem. Yes, what you saw was born from your imagination, but the experience was real. Your movement was real. What you might have said was real. You see, a dream is out of your control. You have no say over how you act. Same with a memory. It has already occurred, so the events of it are fixed and inalterable. But in the Imagined, you have autonomy over yourself. You can say what you want. Move how you want. Exactly like you would in the physical world."

"Sorta like a video game."

"Like a what?"

"A video game. Even though you play in a fantasy world, you control your character's actions. It's different from when you watch a movie and can't control what anyone does. The story is already written."

"If that helps you make sense of it, then sure."

As my comprehension of the Imagined developed, I began to get excited with the possibilities of this power. "Does that mean I can create any world I want? Could I travel to a palace? Or a huge spaceship!"

"It's not that simple. As much as I do believe there is more to be discovered in our imaginative abilities, the only being who is able to conceive of any world they wish for is God. There are limitations I have not yet figured out how to overcome."

"So, where can I go then?"

"Last time we met, I asked you to think of a memory that you wished you could return to. Do you remember that?"

The image of Sagar lying in the forest materialized in my mind. "Yes."

"For us to leave this world, we must fully commit to our destination. Memories we have the deepest emotional need to return to tend to be the most powerful, most comprehensive ones we contain. They allow us to detach ourselves from this world. We can touch, smell, and see so vividly in an Imagined based off these memories because we can recollect what it would be like to touch, smell, or see there, rather than having to figure it out from scratch. You cannot conjure up any Imagined you want because you will not be able to form a world as realistic or thorough."

"But when I go to the Imagined, I wouldn't be traveling back in time, right?"

"No. Your Imagined might be informed by one specific moment or a collection of related memories in one place, but the Imagined is a constructed space. It does not have a date or time attached to it."

Bits of what the Singer was saying made sense, but his advanced vocabulary and grasp on the concept obstructed me from gaining a well-rounded sense of the Imagined. What I could gather was that this separate, mystical world would allow me to see and speak to Sagar again. To me, that was all that mattered, especially after the dreadful day I'd had.

"I want to go back to the Imagined," I said with conviction.

"Fully experiencing the Imagined, existing within it for more than a few moments, is a challenging task. I am still figuring out how to master it. But I'm willing to teach you. I want to have someone I can finally share this knowledge with. All I request is your commitment to learn."

"Whatever it takes for me to return."

Satisfied with my answer, the Singer plucked the first string of his tanpura. "Let us begin."

———

As I entered the Imagined, I paid attention to the process with new understanding. I succumbed to the melody that transported me to the black void. I observed in awe as the multitude of colors composed an intricate recreation of the forest. I walked between the trees in wonder, amazed how the simple need to return to Sagar had created this living, breathing world. Exactly as I'd hoped, the familiarity of sounds and smells brought me a sense of euphoria and temporarily erased the desolation I had felt earlier that day. My memories of the forest were fresh, and I was certain that everything looked exactly as it had when I'd lived in the Town. As much as I wanted to study every minute part of my environment, I had only one goal in mind: to find Sagar.

I picked up my pace, racing toward the three trees, grinning as the wind whipped through my hair and stung my eyes. My body felt unfettered and free. I sped up when I saw Sagar's legs sprawled out on the ground. I did not let anything else distract me, not even the misshapen tree that had diverted my attention the previous time.

"Sagar!" I yelled out. He jolted up, right as I tumbled onto him. I immediately grabbed his face, felt his cheeks, ran my hands through his hair. I made sure that every part of him was intact and true to what I remembered.

He tried to wrestle me off. "Aka— Akash Da—"

"Are you really Sagar?"

"What? Of course I am."

He kicked me in the shin. I rolled off him and stretched out, panting heavily. I was unable to look away from his face. I scrutinized every movement of his, fearing I would come across an error that would prove this version of him was inauthentic.

"Say something else to me. Say something Sagar would say."

"You're acting weird."

"When is your birthday?"

"Why are you—"

"Just answer!"

He looked at me questioningly. "June third."

"What's your favorite story that Aaji tells us?"

"There's so many."

My heart dropped. I knew that he was too good to be true. "No, you have one specific story you ask for."

"You mean Arjuna and Karna?"

Tears formed in my eyes. I threw my arms around him and enveloped him in a tight embrace. I had missed him so much. He hesitantly raised his hands and hugged me back.

"Akash Dada, are you okay?"

"I'm just so happy to see you."

"Okay, weirdo. Do you wanna play now?"

It was just like Sagar to prioritize a game over this heartfelt reunion. I grinned. "Of course. What game?"

"Since you brought up Arjuna and Karna, we could play that. I'll be Arjuna and you can be—"

"Karna. That sounds perfect."

He scrambled up and mimicked stringing an imaginary bow. Circling around me, he began retelling the story with emotive expressions. "We are on the bloody battlefield where the epic battle between good and evil is taking place. Many have been slain in this war."

He valiantly raised his fist in the air. I chuckled, causing him to break his narration.

"What's so funny?"

"Nothing. Continue."

He recomposed. "As I was saying, in one of the last efforts to bring victory to the Pandavas, Arjuna decides to face his nemesis, Karna. Although Arjuna is a brilliant archer, will he be able to beat the equally skilled Karna? Will he be able to restore peace to the world?"

I applauded, and Sagar took a mini-bow.

"Are you ready, Karna?" he teased.

I hoisted myself up. "Oh, I'm ready."

He aimed an imaginary arrow at me. "One, Tw— Hey!"

I'd already taken off, gleefully zigzagging between trees, while the reassuring sounds of Sagar's footsteps and battle cries chased after me.

———

"How was it?" asked the Singer.

"Incredible," I replied, still exhilarated from my reunion with Sagar. "I can't believe I have this ability."

"Neither can I. It feels like I can be whole again, like every part of me that was missing can suddenly be found. Tell me, how did you come out of the Imagined?"

I thought back to when Sagar had finally caught up to me. After we'd finished the game, we'd headed back to the three trees and lazed around. When I'd been ready to leave, I'd closed my eyes and felt the world peacefully dissipate around me. "I just knew that it was time to go."

"Good, good. A gradual exit. That's what you want. The Imagined is a strange and fickle thing. If you wish to stay within it, you must fully believe in everything around you. If you start to doubt any aspect of it, then you will be harshly pulled out."

"That happened to me last time! I saw this weird tree and stopped to look at it. But the minute I did that, everything else started coming apart."

"You have to believe wholeheartedly that the world you create is true. That's why this ability requires an immense amount of dedication. The more you visit the Imagined, the less you'll doubt what you see. If you stay away for too long, you'll forget details of the place you're attempting to revisit. Your imagination will fill in those gaps with bizarre peculiarities."

"When I saw the weird tree, I tried to remember what it

looked like back home. But I couldn't figure it out. I never used to pay attention to it before."

"Even if those tiny details seem out of place, do not doubt yourself. Ignore it or accept it as the truth." The Singer gazed at me wistfully. "There is so much I want to teach you. Will you promise me that you'll return often?"

"Why wouldn't I? That was … amazing."

The Singer smiled. Shadows fell across the pool in front of me. I looked up and noticed how low the sun was.

"Shoot!" I exclaimed. "I have to leave."

"Until next time then, Akash."

I rushed out of the park, worried that I would not make it home before my mother returned from her shift. If she found me missing again, she would undoubtedly place the combination lock back on the door. Upon arriving outside the apartment, I pressed my ear against the front door. I couldn't hear any voices. Relief swept over me when I pushed the door open and saw that neither parent was back.

I flopped onto the bed, already replaying every treasured moment I'd had with Sagar in the Imagined. My mother returned an hour later, her shoulders drooping like Vaishu Mavshi's used to after taxing hospital shifts.

She was relieved to see me in the apartment. "How was your day?"

"Awesome!"

She looked pleasantly surprised by my response. "Really? Oh, that's wonderful, Aku! I'm so happy to hear that. Did you make a new friend?"

I contemplated telling her the truth, but she seemed so pleased with my answer that I didn't want to ruin her mood with any mention of Sagar. In any case, I wasn't sure how to explain the Imagined to her when I was still trying to figure it out for myself. "Sort of."

She joined me on the bed and put her arm around me. I did not resist. I was too giddy from seeing my cousin to continue being angry at her.

"I had a great day too. You should come to the salon sometime so you can meet Nabeela Aunty. She is just … larger than life. She calls me one of her most dedicated workers, even though I've only been there for a little while. She said that with a bit more experience, she would let me supervise a couple shifts. That stupid Simran Kaur never let me do anything like that."

"Remember when you threw a box of dye on her?"

"That was pretty funny, wasn't it?"

I nodded, and we both giggled at the memory. It was a soft giggle, hesitant and subdued, not as uncontrolled as our laughter used to be in the Town. But it was the first sign of shared optimism between me and my mother since the move.

My mother kissed the top of my head. "See. Things are starting to look up already."

CHAPTER 13

AN UNCUSTOMARY BIRTHDAY

A THUNDEROUS CRASH jerked me out of my sleep. I groggily lifted my head from the couch and found my mother kneeling by the rusty oven. She muttered indignant curses as she collected scattered pieces of brown mush that had fallen by a metal cupcake pan. My father was fast asleep on the bed, undisturbed by the noise. My mother noticed that I'd risen.

"Shit," she whispered. "You're not supposed to be up yet."

I wiped my eyes. "What's going on?"

"Let's see if I can salvage one." She plucked the most intact cupcake out of the pan and grabbed a candle and matchbox from the kitchen counter. She approached me while lighting the candle.

"Happy birthday, baby," she chirped. "Make a wish."

I blew the flame out, praying for Monday to arrive faster. Four excruciating days had passed since my first proper visit to the Imagined. Although I desperately wished to return, an opportunity hadn't presented itself. My mother had worked early shifts for the remainder of the week, forcing me to head back to the apartment immediately after school. She was fortunately scheduled to work a late shift the following Monday, and my anticipation for my imminent freedom was almost intolerable.

"Mama?"

"Yeah, baby?"

"It feels weird to celebrate without the rest of the family."

"Don't think about it, Aku. It's easier to be happy when you push those thoughts aside. Remember, we have to look ahead." My mother broke off a piece of the cupcake. "I followed an online recipe. I hope it turned out okay."

She expectantly watched my expression as she fed me. I forced the overly salty bite down, but my mother caught sight of my scrunched-up face before I could mask my unpleasant reaction.

She frowned. "Forget it. Don't eat it if it's bad."

"It's not!" I said, reaching out for another bite. My attempt to reassure her was ineffective. My mother marched to the trash bin and dumped the remaining cupcakes inside. She then roughly discarded the cupcake pan in the sink. This time, my father woke up from the harsh reverberations.

"Who's making so much noise?" he said, yawning. He stretched his arms and combed through his messy curls. "I'm trying to sleep in."

"Varun, aren't you forgetting something?" my mother replied.

He regarded her with confusion. "What?"

"Wish your son a happy birthday."

"Birthday? Wait ..." He checked the clock on the bedside table as if it were going to show him the date. "Shit, I've been losing track of the days."

He hastened out of bed and ran to me. He buried me in a hug and sloppily kissed the top of my head. "Happy happy birthday, Aku! You're getting so big, huh? Huh?"

"Dad, stop!" I said, pushing him off with a grin.

"Well, we have to celebrate! I was gonna go to the office and work on a few designs ... but, you know what, forget that! Time for a family outing! What should we do? Mall? Beach? Go-karts?"

My mother eyed me. "Varun, I don't know if that's the best idea. It's our first year celebrating in a new place. Maybe we should do something more low-key. Something in the apartment."

"Hell no! You only turn twelve once. Right, Aku? What do you say?"

His eagerness was resolute. Being out of the apartment was always my preferred option, even under the melancholic circumstances.

"The beach could be fun."

My father jumped up and smacked his palms together. "Beach it is!"

—

Despite the chilly weather, Ocean Beach was brimming with people. My mother and I, bundled in layers of jackets, were anchored on a blanket far removed from the crowded part of the sandy stretch. We hugged our knees to our chests and fought through the shivers. The sky was clear and bright, appearing deceptively balmy. Only a few clouds brushed the blue, and the sun shone down brilliantly on the rolling waves. Large kites teased each other, gliding in and out of the sun's glare.

My father waved at us. His pants were rolled up to his knees, his feet bravely immersed in the icy water. When he'd asked us to join him, my mother and I had responded that we wouldn't go in even if he dragged us.

"You're going to freeze," my mother yelled, beckoning him to return.

My father gestured that he couldn't hear her and blew back a kiss.

"Idiot," she muttered endearingly.

"Mama, are you going to marry Dad?"

My mother turned toward me. "What? I don't kn— why? What made you ask that?"

"If we're staying here, I thought maybe …"

"We're not at that point yet. I don't even know what we're doing right now."

I glanced at her empty ring finger. "Have you talked to Nikhil recently?"

My mother fidgeted with her hair. "No. I haven't."

"I liked him."

"I did too," she said quietly. After a brief silence, she inched toward me and hugged me with one arm. "But you know what? Your dad and I have always had this intense connection. There's so much history between us. The timing has never worked out before, but I really think we've got a shot now. He's grown. We both have."

"And if it doesn't work out? Where will we go?"

She clutched my arm. "It's going to work out."

My father emphatically waved once again.

"You should join him," said my mother.

"Come with me."

"No way."

"It's my birthday. You have to do what I say."

"Not nice, Aku."

I triumphantly stood up and reached my hand out to her. She grabbed it and hoisted herself up. We jogged toward my father, who danced with glee when he saw that we'd caved. I rolled up my pants and dipped my big toe in the ocean.

"Dad, the water is *freeee*-zing."

"It gets better once you stand in it for a while," he said, outstretching his hand to me. He was already knee deep.

I braced myself and plunged my right foot in. After

adjusting to the temperature, I crossed my arms and plodded toward him. My teeth chattered as I fought the waves pushing and pulling my lower half. I sank my feet into the sand to steady myself.

"Come here, bud," he said, embracing me when I finally reached him. He looked at my mother, who was standing at the edge of the water. "Don't be such a wuss, Mahi!"

She retreated a few steps on the sand. "There's no way in hell I'm getting in."

"C-can we p-please go b-back?" I asked.

My father inhaled deeply. "In one minute. Soak it in for one minute."

"I-it's too c-cold."

"But look at how incredible the ocean is right now."

He was right. Though the beach was crowded, few had dared to venture into the water. Nothing obstructed our view of the sublime expanse. From our vantage point, the ocean stretched on infinitely, appearing as a shimmering blanket of crystals.

"When I look at something so vast … so majestic … I feel so unbelievably tiny in comparison," murmured my father. "We're given such a short window to make something of our lives that it feels pointless to even try. Most people give up. They live a meaningless life and die forgotten. But I won't. I want to be as glorious as this ocean. Maybe even more so."

My shivering ceased. The wind stroked my cheeks and fondled my hair. I turned to my father and watched him stare out at everything and nothing. As ripples of light fell across his pensive face, my heart swelled with pride for being able to call him my dad. Regardless of how the rest of the world perceived him, he was and had always been glorious to me.

He mischievously leaned in. "What do you say we annoy your mother?"

I grinned. "How?"

He whispered the plan to me as we trudged back to shore. My mother was eyeing the shallow waves and cautiously dipping a toe in with displeasure. When my father tapped my hand, we both charged toward her, splashing water everywhere around us.

She yelped and covered her face. "Don't you dare!"

I splashed water on her while my father grabbed her by the waist and lifted her off the ground.

"Varun! Put me down!" she squealed.

My father twirled her around and set her back on the sand. "It was all Aku's idea."

"Dad!"

"Okay, fine, it was my idea."

My mother fondly punched his arm. "What are you teaching your son?"

He grinned at me. "To be exactly like his crazy dad."

———

After we dried ourselves and collected our belongings, my parents and I stopped at a pretzel cart on the sidewalk.

My father browsed the menu. "I can't decide between the chocolate or caramel drizzle. Aku, what are you getting?"

"I don't want any toppings."

"Lame. I'm going to get both."

Just as we were about to move to the front of the cart, a woman with an egregious spray tan bolted in front of us.

"Hi, two pretzels with chocolate drizzle," she ordered. "Quickly, please. We're in a bit of a rush."

A little girl, no older than five or six, hopped to the woman's side and shrieked, "White chocolate!"

The woman rolled her eyes. "You heard her. White chocolate on one pretzel."

My father tapped her shoulder. "Excuse me. We were in line."

"Oh, I didn't think you were ready yet."

"Well, we are."

"I've already given my order. It'll take two minutes. We're in a hurry."

The pretzel seller's panicked gaze oscillated between my father and the woman. He held up a pretzel, waiting for a consensus to be made on whose order to take first.

My father's eyes narrowed. "You think you can cut just because you're in a hurry?"

"Mom, why is he getting angry at us?" whimpered the little girl.

"Don't worry, honey." The woman glared at my father. "There's no need to be rude."

My mother tried to tug my father back. "Varun, just let her order."

"Yeah, Dad. I don't mind if she goes first," I added.

"That's the issue!" he responded, pushing my mother off. "We let people like her get away with this sort of stuff all the time. But it's wrong, and I won't stand for it!"

"Varun, you're making this a bigger deal than it is."

"Your wife has more sense than you," muttered the woman. "Kayla, let's get dessert from somewhere else. This man is not being very nice."

My father threw up his hands. "Are you kidding me? You've made such a big fuss about ordering first and now you won't even do it?"

The little girl began to cry, causing the woman to groan in frustration.

"Look what you've done, asshole." She grabbed her daughter and gave my father the middle finger before storming off.

"Fuck you too!" he yelled, kicking the side of the cart.

The timid pretzel seller squeaked, "Sir, please step aw—"

"Yeah, yeah, we're going," snapped my father. He stomped away from the cart. My mother and I chased him to the parking lot.

"I'm calling a cab," he said. "I don't want to ride a fucking bus right now."

"Was that really necessary?" my mother asked.

"Great, now you're gonna give me shit too?"

"You ruined a perfectly good day over an unnecessary argument."

My parents hadn't engaged in one of their explosive arguments since we'd started living together. I'd been waiting for one to erupt, and I feared the time had finally come.

"I'm still having a good day," I said, attempting to defuse the tension.

My father ignored my comment. "That lady was a bitch."

"I don't care," my mother replied. "You can be so stubborn sometimes."

"Then tell me what I should have done! Should I have just let it go? Forgive me for wanting to teach our son better. I mean, can you ever take my side? Is that so much to ask for? You say I'm stubborn. Have you looked at yourself?"

His chest heaved up and down, impassioned by his temper.

My mother clenched her jaw. I anxiously waited for her to commence her own tirade, for their exhaustive, snappy back-and-forth to begin. Instead, she paused for a few seconds and replied, "You're right. I'm sorry."

My father blinked. He'd clearly been gearing up for a fight too. "Huh?"

"I should have taken your side. I'm sorry."

"That's it?"

"Is there something else you want to say?"

"N-no."

"Then give me your phone. I'll call us a cab."

My mother outstretched her hand. My father hesitantly gave his phone to her. She stepped away from us and made the call.

When she returned, my father sheepishly hugged her. "I'm sorry. I overreacted."

"Let's forget about it."

"I love you, Mahi."

He pecked her on the cheek. She impassively received it.

"Family hug!" he said, beckoning me to join.

———

To commemorate the end of my twelfth birthday, my father insisted that we all sleep together on the full-sized bed. When nighttime arrived, I crawled in between my parents. They each draped an arm around me and warmed the top of my head with their breathing. Our chests rose and fell in unison. Though we were squashed against one another, I felt protected by their bodies on either side of me. Ironically, my dream of us uniting under one roof had come true. I hated myself for thinking it, but I knew that if the horrible incident at the station hadn't occurred, I would never have been so intimately intertwined with my parents as I was that night.

The elation I felt was accompanied by an even greater fear that this moment was fleeting, that it would disappear as quickly as it came. I couldn't understand why it had taken us twelve years to find this form of affection for one another. In a way, we clutched each other that night with a hint of desperation, as though if any one of us loosened our grip, someone would slip out, and the hasty image of happiness we'd constructed would vanish, like it had never existed in the first place.

CHAPTER 14

PRIYA

MY LIFE WAS split between tolerating a mundane existence and relishing my extraordinary imagination. My mother volunteered herself to work more late shifts at the salon after confirming on a couple occasions that I returned to the apartment after school. I seized every opportunity afforded by her absence to take the bus to Golden Gate Park and visit the Imagined. My days at school, especially my solitary lunches in the library, were spent itching for the final bell to ring. With the company of Sagar to look forward to, I had no desire to humiliate myself again by attempting to make new friends.

My afternoons spent in the Imagined followed a similar routine to my initial visit in February. I would find Sagar by the three trees, and immediately after, we would commence the game of Arjuna and Karna. We would sprint around the forest, hollering, while ferociously swinging our pretend swords and shooting our make-believe arrows. Sagar's stamina never weakened, so we ended the game only after I exhausted myself beyond the point of continuing. To cool off, we would lounge under the three trees or wade in the stream. This latter part of the visit was the time I most cherished. Sagar and I would rest our voices and enjoy the untroubled sounds of the environment. I would gaze at the fallen bark on the fertile soil, or the ants that crawled in a single file on the damp rocks, or the restless birds that hopped from branch to branch. I had seen all of this when I'd lived in the Town, but I no longer took any of it for granted. Like an infant whose eyes had been pried open for the first time, I stared in incredulous wonder at how pure and delicate life could be. Heeding the Singer's advice, I exited the Imagined gradually, preparing my body for the soft plummet when, and only when, my heart was full and satisfied.

Returning to the Imagined felt like I was resuming a never-ending day. The sun was consistently positioned in the sky as if it was early afternoon, and the weather was always hot and humid. Sagar wore the same outfit (a purple T-shirt and blue cargo shorts) that I'd pictured when I was first tasked to trigger the Imagined with a memory. As the Singer had stated, I was floating in a space unconstrained by time. I did not have to worry about the moment being fleeting. I could return the next day, the day after, and almost every other day for the foreseeable future, just to play with Sagar and lie in the forest. In this endless summer, my life seemed to be halted. I could restrain myself from growing up and remain a naïve, untroubled child for however long I wished.

This awareness was freeing, and I was reminded of it whenever I looked at Sagar's mirthful face. His playful eyes, his broad dimples, his enthusiasm to run and jump and be free, exuded the essence of childhood. When I was with Sagar, loss, grief, longing, and all the other dreadful emotions that I was forced to stomach in San Francisco did not exist. While playing with him, I tried my best to be as ignorant as I'd been the previous summer. I rebuked myself for ever resisting Sagar's wish that we stay kids forever. I wanted to forget the thick spurts of blood I'd seen in Nikhil's video games, to erase the taste of cigarette smoke and the terrifying sound of a gunshot going off in front of me. Though these memories were unfortunately etched in my brain, I could pretend in the Imagined as if they hadn't happened yet. Under the guise of contrived innocence, happiness was possible once again.

I was curious about the basic functions of the Imagined, especially how far this fabricated world could stretch. The Singer cautioned me that I should stay where the Imagined took me and not try to push the boundaries beyond that. Since I was enjoying my time with Sagar, I mostly adhered to this rule. I didn't wish to see the train station again or venture beyond that to the City. But I was occasionally tempted to visit the Town. During an early visit, I inadvertently ran toward Main Street, intending to mislead Sagar in our game. I emerged at the cul-de-sac next to the Mahmoods' tailor shop and was appalled to see how blurry the environment was. Unlike the forest, where the details were sharp and lifelike, the cul-de-sac was melting into a shoddy three-dimensional watercolor painting, where lines were absent and unrestrained colors blended with one another. It felt as if a foggy lens had been inserted over my eyes and was purposefully aimed at distorting my vision. Unable to remove the lens, I watched in discomfort as the grass in the front lawns thawed into green paint and trickled along the flimsy pavement, as the brown from the roofs dripped down the sides of houses, as the blue from the sky drizzled on top of the tailor shop. I attempted to step onto the road, but I immediately met resistance. My breath shortened, and my body felt stretched beyond its limits. Afraid that I too would deform into misshapen streaks of paint, I hurried back into the safety of the forest and doubled over from a splitting headache. When I asked the Singer about this odd occurrence, he responded that I didn't have an immediate need to enter the cul-de-sac.

"But I miss my home too!" I cried. "I want to see Juhi Aunty and Bhaskar Uncle and everyone else. I want to see my family."

"As I said, missing something and having a deep emotional need to return to a specific memory are two separate matters," he explained. "A need is powerful enough that it will choke and beat you until you dismantle it. Your mind creates the Imagined because it has to somehow satisfy this yearning."

"You said that I couldn't go wherever I wanted in the Imagined because I wouldn't know what it looked or smelled like. But I know the Town inside out!"

"Patience. Your mind is leading you to where you need to be, even if you don't fully understand why. Trust in it and enjoy what the Imagined offers you."

The Singer's answer left me dissatisfied, so the next time I returned to the forest, I decided to experiment with my abilities in another way. Sagar and I were dipping our feet in the stream when I said to him, "I can't wait to move back from San Francisco."

Sagar cocked his head in confusion. "What do you mean 'back from San Francisco'?"

"I live there with my parents. You should know that."

Sagar contemplated my statement. "You live with us in the Town. Your father lives in Brooklyn."

"Not since your accident."

"What accident?"

"You seriously don't know what happened at the train station?"

He said resolutely, "I have no clue what you're talking about."

I studied his face to see if there was any hint of dishonesty, but his eyes unflinchingly told me that there wasn't. I regretted having asked him, because the minute I could see that he wasn't aware of the present situation, I had to grapple with the fact that this boy standing in front of me, this outline of Sagar, was only a figment of my imagination. His actions were so realistic otherwise that it was usually easy to suspend my disbelief. As expected, the Imagined heard my doubt and started to unravel. I toppled back to Golden Gate Park disappointed, resolving never to challenge him again. I was thankful he'd answered as he had. The cheerful Sagar, the one I'd been friends with before we'd distanced, was who I wished to return to anyway. Any other depiction of him would have reminded me of our strife and made the Imagined less ideal.

That said, the Imagined did have its imperfections. Like the disfigured tree, other standalone peculiarities in the environment tested my faith. I once encountered a bush on the forest floor with monstrous purple leaves. On another occasion, I stumbled on a pile of sand, similar in quality to the Ocean Beach sand, at the base of a tree. When these deviances emerged, I shut my eyes and fought to recollect how the actual forest appeared. Despite my best efforts, once a detail was forgotten, it was permanently lost from my memory and replaced with whatever altered version my imagination came up with. As the Singer recommended, I had to ignore these oddities, focus on what I knew to be true, and restrain the specks of doubt that wanted to wrench me away.

Even though these errors reminded me that the Imagined was a constructed world, I continued to return. Accepting the illusory renderings of Sagar and the forest was much more favorable than having to cope with the misery of my otherwise alienated life.

———

Early one morning in May, my father left his cereal untouched. He swirled the soggy Lucky Charms around and peered at his bowl like he was about to vomit in it. In an attempt to dress more professionally, my father had styled himself in a navy-blue turtleneck and tan slacks. He'd buzzed his curls off, leaving pointy shards of hair dotting his visible scalp. Instead of providing him an aura of respectability, the haircut made him appear scrawny and a little unwell.

The investor in my father's project had gathered a focus group to evaluate the progress of the team's work. My father and his business partner, Sean, were scheduled to present their concept video later that day. The weeks leading up to the presentation, my father would return to the apartment late at night, cram whatever dinner my mother had thrown together, and continue to draw on the wooden table for hours. We'd traded places in our sleeping arrangement due to his erratic schedule; he slept on the couch, while I slept with my mother on the bed.

My father stood up and emptied his bowl of cereal in the kitchen sink.

"Here we go," he said, grabbing a pile of drawings off the counter and stuffing them into his satchel.

"Good luck, Dad."

"Thanks, buddy."

Once my father left, I frantically reviewed a set of questions I'd drafted on binder paper. Earlier that week, my yearbook teacher, Mr. Sutton, had announced an end-of-the-year project. It was tradition for the yearbook to feature two student profiles from the class. Each of us was supposed to pair with a classmate; interview them about their family, interests, and goals; and compose a brief report on their life. Mr. Sutton would then evaluate the submitted writeups and choose which would be published. He stressed that he wanted moving, poignant stories—a large ask for a class of middle schoolers. After he explained the project and gave us permission to find our partners, the other students raced to their friends. Noticing that I was sitting on my own, Mr. Sutton called out to the class, "Is there anyone else besides Akash that needs to be partnered?"

I shut my eyes in mortification and prayed that when I opened them, a kind, misunderstood student would be raising their hand. Before I had a chance to scan the room myself, Mr. Sutton announced my partner.

"Okay, then! Our last pairing will be Akash Patil and Priya Peterson!"

I peeked in astonishment at Priya, who sat three rows in front of me. We hadn't acknowledged each other since the day I'd approached her in the cafeteria. After learning in class that she was indeed in eighth grade, I assumed she'd reacted as she had because she wanted nothing to do with a sixth grader. Still, I couldn't wrap my head around why her response had been that immediate and antagonistic. After my partnership with Priya was declared, the boy sitting next to me patted my back and whispered, "Good luck." Though I was comforted knowing that I wasn't the only one who had seen Priya's sour side, the boy's sympathetic stare heightened my nerves. I was deathly afraid to speak to her again.

Priya came up to me after class and curtly asked if I could meet Wednesday after school. Her direct tone made it seem like we hadn't spoken before. Though I usually spent Wednesday afternoons in the Imagined, I'd been too nervous to suggest an alternate time and had hurriedly agreed to her proposal.

Sadly, the day Priya and I were scheduled to meet was upon me, and as I packed up my sheet of questions, I realized that I was more tense than I'd originally believed. While at school, I zoned out in every class. My restless legs trembled in nervous anticipation. After my last period, I ran to the school library and secured an empty table in the section where conversations were allowed. I removed the list of questions from my backpack and opened my notebook to a fresh sheet of paper. I tapped on the wooden table as I waited for Priya to arrive.

After fifteen minutes, she plodded in, pulling her earbuds out and wrapping them around her iPod. As was her outfit on most days, she wore a baggy hoodie and sweatpants, with her face being the only visible part of her. Her hands were shoved into her pockets, and she moved with a stiff, guarded posture. Her head was hung low, but I could still make out her fiery eyes flitting about, as if she was trying to catch and frighten anyone notably perceiving her.

She set her backpack down and glanced at the sheet before me. "Were we supposed to write questions down? I was gonna wing it."

"That's okay!" I said. "I wanted to be prepared."

"This is such a bullshit assignment. I'm sure he already has his favorites that he's going to pick for the yearbook. He's only grading us on this because he knows how dumb this class is otherwise."

I nervously chuckled. "Should I start?"

"What type of questions do you have?"

"Nothing much. Just like where you're from, what your parents do—"

She grabbed my paper. Her nose scrunched up in displeasure as she read over my list. "Let's skip this whole interview thing. I know it's part of the assignment, but I can give you a written-up statement about myself to save us time."

"Oh, um, I guess that works. Should I do the same?"

"Yeah, it's easier that way." She stood up and lifted her backpack off the ground.

Worried that she was leaving because of our previous interaction, I blurted out, "I'm sorry!"

She hesitated. "For what?"

"For coming up to you in the cafeteria that one day in February. I'm sorry if I did something that made you mad. I didn't mean to."

She looked away, her cheeks reddening. "You didn't. It was … honestly, I could have been nicer."

I flipped my notebook shut. On the front cover was a Sharpie sketch of Main Street. It was rough and only depicted a few shops, but Priya saw it before I could put the notebook away.

"Did you draw that?" she asked.

"Yeah, but it's nothing really. Just a dumb doodle."

She placed her hand on top of the notebook and examined the drawing. "It's not nothing. It's good. What's it supposed to be?"

"Where I used to live before SF. It's a couple hours away from Manhattan."

She raised her eyebrows. "That's far. Did you move here recently?"

"In January."

"And you miss it back there?"

"So much."

She slowly sat back down. "It's hard to adjust to a new place. Trust me, I would know."

"Did you move here too?"

She pretended not to hear my question. "What do you miss about your old home?"

"The people. The shops. This street," I said, pointing at my drawing. "During holidays like Navratri and Holi, it used to be filled with food and dancing."

She blinked in confusion. "Nava-what?"

"Haven't you been to a Dandiya event before?"

"Remind me what it is again."

"The absolute best night of the year! Everyone dresses up and brings these two short sticks. You learn dance routines where you clap your sticks and move from partner to partner." I smiled, thinking about how Sagar would purposely mess up his steps to disrupt the flow of others. "Aren't you Indian? How do you not know what Dandiya is?"

"I know what it is. I just forgot for a minute," she replied unconvincingly. "So, you were just allowed to do these events on the street?"

"Of course! Most of my neighbors were from India."

Her expression turned wistful. "Really? You probably fit right in with the other brown kids here."

"I guess," I said, not wanting to admit how I hid myself in the library at lunch. I put my notebook inside my backpack and stood up. "I'll give you my essay next week."

"Wait!" she protested. "You're leaving already?"

"I thought you were too."

She hesitated, then withdrew a sheet of binder paper from her folder. "We'll still write our own profiles, but I can help brainstorm some ideas for you. Tell me more about this place you grew up in."

"What about it?"

"How many Indian families were in your neighborhood? What were the other events like?"

"You think this should be in my profile?"

"Obviously. Why else would I ask?"

Though Priya's sudden interest in my life baffled me, I was glad she wasn't hurrying off anymore. I didn't know what I had done to alter her mood, but it was nice to feel like something about me captivated her attention.

I sat back down, placed my backpack aside, and began to unravel my memories of the Town.

———

My mother and I sat on the folding chairs, waiting for my father to return to the apartment. A bag of Mexican fast food drooped on the wooden dining table. Since my parents worked late most days, we resorted to this meal often. I preferred it, given that neither of them knew how to cook and did not have the patience to properly follow a recipe. The meals they attempted themselves turned out disastrous.

As I ate my chicken burrito, I reflected on my conversation with Priya earlier that day. We'd spoken for much longer than expected. She'd devised questions about my previous home with genuine curiosity and had prodded for specificity. For most of the afternoon, I narrated the tale of how my Ajoba founded the Town. As I watched Priya's mouth open in fascination, my desire to hold her interest grew. Toward the end of the story, I became even more dramatic in my retelling than my Aaji used to be. Priya and I reluctantly separated after the library shut at five. Exhausted from two hours of talking, I'd skipped my visit to the Imagined and had headed straight back to the apartment.

My mother and I finished our burritos, and an hour later, the front doorknob rattled. My father slipped in, placed his satchel on the couch, and kicked his shoes off. Unlike most days when he burst through the door with high energy, he carried a disturbed, sullen look. He slumped on the couch. "I'm starving."

My mother ruffled through the fast-food bag. "I got a burrito for you."

"Again? How many times are we gonna eat this shit?"

"I can order something else for you."

"It's fine. Just give me whatever you have."

My mother handed the burrito to him. He tore the foil off and began wolfing it down.

"I know we haven't been eating the healthiest," said my mother. "Maybe we can figure out a schedule to trade off on cooking."

My father spoke with his mouth full. "Mahi, I barely have time to breathe. I don't have time to cook."

"And I do?" she muttered. She waved her hands. "Let's forget about that for now. Why are you in this weird mood?"

"I'm not in a weird mood."

As I watched him devour the burrito, I recalled how stressed he'd been that morning because of his presentation. "Did the focus group not go well?"

My father stopped eating mid-bite. He regarded his burrito with disgust and wrapped it up again. "I can't stomach this shit tonight. I'm just gonna sleep."

"Is Akash right?" my mother inquired. "Did the focus group go badly?"

He lifted his turtleneck off and tossed it to the side. "I don't want to talk about it."

"We're your family. Who else will you talk about it with?"

My father unbuckled his belt and removed his pants. "None of them understand a fucking vision."

"What did they say?"

Stripped down to his underwear, my father leaned against his wall of incompleteness, his eyes vapid. "They didn't get it. What we were trying to do. What the purpose of it was. Apparently, looking at the world through my designs serves no practical use. This fucked-up time we live in only cares about fucking utilization. No one appreciates the value of art anymore."

My mother's voice turned grave. "What did your investor say?"

"That dipshit tried to scold us, as if he wasn't the one that backed the original concept."

"Is he still going to pay you?"

"Why would you even ask me something like that?" snapped my father. "You should be concerned with how I'm feeling."

My mother approached him. "You're right. I'm sorry." She tried to embrace him, but he pushed her hands away.

"No …"

"We're here to support you. Right, Akash?"

I nodded, but my father wasn't looking at either one of us. He climbed onto the bed.

"Varun, talk to us," urged my mother.

He tugged the bedsheet over his face, shutting us off from further conversation. My mother slowly sat back down. She weakly smiled at me as if my father's cold behavior was just a small blip in the evening. Despite her reassuring glance, the two of us were still in our chairs, watching my father while his heavy breathing penetrated the apartment, straining it with the weight of his unreachable disappointment.

CHAPTER 15

A TEACHER AND
HIS STUDENT

"TELL ME MORE."

These words were uttered to me time and time again, coaxing me to unspool my memories and make sense of what I had lived through. Over the three weeks that Priya and I had to complete our assignment, we met about ten times after school for lengthy discussions in the library. By the end of the first week, she had more than enough information on me to brainstorm a stellar profile, and yet, she insisted we continue to connect. Most days, she didn't bother to take notes. She would listen intently, her rigid posture softening as she became engrossed in my narration. When the two of us were secluded in our private corner of the library, her eyes wouldn't dart around with spite as they did the rest of the school day. Instead, they became gentle and curious. These afternoon sessions were a designated time for us to talk under the pretense of a classroom project. Priya was fascinated by my childhood. I couldn't figure out why, but the reason didn't matter much to me. I was pleased that I wasn't completely invisible at school any longer.

At first, I only shared stories about my family. Priya was intrigued by my Aaji and found her remarkable ability to fall asleep at any given moment hilarious. She blushed at my recounting of Suhail Mama and Kiara Mami's romance and expressed admiration for Vaishu Mavshi's fierce, protective nature. I provided her a description of Sagar as well, characterizing him as if he were still alive. I couldn't refer to him as passed away when I still saw him almost every other day in the Imagined. Priya was shocked that a family as humongous as mine could cohabitate in one space. I responded that I was equally shocked other families didn't live like I had; growing up without constant company seemed sorely depressing.

After tackling my family, I shifted to the various characters in the Town. I described Bhaskar Uncle's wisdom, Aneesa Aunty's kindness, and Juhi Aunty's eccentricity. Throughout my anecdotes, I carefully avoided any mention of the train station and reflected solely on the good memories of the Town. When Priya asked why I had moved away, I said that my mother and I wanted to try living with my father for a bit, an answer that wasn't entirely out of the realm of truth.

Determining what parts of my past would captivate Priya was like solving a riddle. Although she was interested in whatever I shared with her, she engaged with certain subjects more than others. She asked the most about topics I would not have usually considered fascinating, such as the Indian events our Town hosted, the traditions my family followed, and the connection my Aaji's generation had to their native countries. Priya would probe so deep into the history and meaning behind some customs that most times I wouldn't know how to answer her.

As I tracked the common thread behind Priya's questions, I realized that she was primarily invested in the aspects of my childhood that were influenced by my heritage. On multiple occasions, she would even remark how fortunate I was to have been brought up in such an Indian way. I didn't understand what she meant, assuming that we were raised in a similar manner. But her line of questioning unlocked a new awareness about my life: these traditions Priya asked about had been an ordinary part of my childhood, as much as going to school or celebrating birthdays were. The attention Priya placed on them made me, for the first time, evaluate them as separate from everything else I did. There was now a distinct "Indian" part of my life, and all that I knew, ate, listened to, partook in, either did or didn't fit under this category. Of course, I had known I was Indian before then, but growing up in a secluded immigrant community had sheltered me from considering that certain aspects of my life were unique and not shared among all. I felt the same way I had on the first day of middle school when I was scouring for other Indians in the cafeteria. A label that hadn't mattered to me before suddenly became an important focus in my life.

After figuring out what Priya wished to know more about, I narrowed my stories to what I believed fell under this "Indian" category. The result was a slew of scattered fragments. I summarized what I could from the Hindu mythology my family had taught me (though plots were often muddled and character names forgotten). I described the songs of Lata Mangeshkar and Asha Bhosle that my Aaji loved to listen to, as well as the iconic performances of Shah Rukh Khan and Amitabh Bachchan that wove themselves into many conversations along Main Street. I illustrated the outfits that my family wore for Diwali and simulated the prayers that we would recite during Aarti. Given the time pressure of the approaching class deadline and the uncertainty of whether our conversations would continue after, I rushed through as many stories as I could. Whether or not this was what Priya wanted when she asked about my Indian upbringing, these were the memories that first came to mind.

Still, my answers always felt like they were missing something vital. Although I could share a surface explanation of these experiences, I wasn't able to convey the true essence of living through them. How could I impart my excitement while rewatching a classic Bollywood movie and giddily dancing along to the songs? How could I capture the familiarity I'd felt hearing conversations spoken in native tongues along Main Street, even when I hadn't always understood what was being said? How could I express the monumental awe Sagar and I experienced when play-acting Arjuna and Karna in our games—how these two characters we hardly had anything in common with connected us to generations of our deceased family that had listened to, loved, and passed down this epic story? The most memorable part of my upbringing was not the meanings or facts or ideologies behind the traditions, but rather, my emotional attachment to these experiences. Emotion, though, was the one feature I was unable to pass on to Priya.

It surprised me how little Priya knew about Indian culture. Unlike the first day when I'd expressed shock that she hadn't heard of Dandiya, I approached each story without questioning what she was aware of. I assumed the role of an informal teacher, like the Singer was in guiding me through the Imagined. I wanted to know more about Priya's background, but each time I tried to pry, she would deflect the conversation back to me. I relayed her confusion about Dandiya to my mother, who said that Priya might have grown up in a household that didn't follow the same traditions we had. She added that Dandiya originated from the state of Gujarat, and my Marathi family only celebrated it because there were quite a few Gujaratis in the Town who took charge of organizing the event. Besides, Dandiya was a Hindu festival, and the Indian diaspora included folks practicing a variety of other religions. My mother said that Priya's name indicated she was Hindu, but names were mixed around all the time in this day and age. Even Suhail Mama's name was customarily Muslim, but my grandparents had loved it so much that they'd decided to use it anyway.

Her answer left me dumbfounded. Not only was I supposed to consider which parts of my upbringing were Indian and which weren't, I now also had to judge how they fit under even more precise subgroups, such as the state my family hailed from and the religion we practiced. This whole business of classifying myself and what I knew was very confusing. I'd always assumed that the inhabitants of the Town were part of one unifying culture, but delving further behind the meaning and history of these traditions made me realize how disparate we actually were.

As a twelve-year-old, I wasn't able to probe deeper into why all of these realizations alarmed me. As an adult, I've come to understand that latching on to memories during this volatile period eased my separation from the Town. It brought me comfort knowing that even if my family and I weren't speaking, I still carried pure pieces of my past with me. Pieces that were firm and steady in my mind, pieces I was sure about. But the unwanted recognition that traditions held meaning—meaning I often wasn't aware of—and that they belonged to distinct groups of people exposed me to how ignorant I was about my heritage and upbringing. Doubt wiggled its way into my stories. If my experiences in the Town stemmed from several Desi cultures, how was I supposed to separate what belonged to my family and what belonged to others? Were there correct customs that I was supposed to know and carry forward? Did I know them all? Talking to Priya certainly made me feel like I didn't. Because of the move, I couldn't fall back on the Town or my extended family to provide me guidance or clarity. I could ask my mother, but she definitely wasn't as informed as my Aaji or Vaishu Mavshi were. And so, with my limitations in knowledge, was I still able to consider myself as Indian as the older, more cognizant generation? Or was that privilege lost along with all the other forgotten or unexplored pieces of my heritage that had quietly dissipated over the course of this separation?

My growing bewilderment in myself, my culture, and my previous community strengthened my need to return to the Imagined. Playing with Sagar was easy and unvarying. Whenever I could find time in the afternoons, I would rush to Golden Gate Park and slip into the Imagined as easily as if I were boarding a train. The process was familiar to me, and for months, I'd gone by obediently following the Singer's instructions. But after my talks with Priya revealed the issue with blindly following custom, I decided to ask the Singer a few questions to better understand our routine.

"Why do I have to hear you sing to be able to enter the Imagined?"

The Singer contemplated my question. "The Imagined requires a trigger. You need something that will allow you to focus on your emotion and summon your imagination."

"Is music the only thing that can trigger the Imagined?"

"I'm not sure. There might be more. I've only ever used this."

"And why this specific thumri? Would I be able to enter on my own without you singing?"

The Singer held up his hand, halting my interrogation. "I am merely teaching you what has worked for me. If you wish to try other methods on your own, be my guest. To me, this thumri evokes a sense of nostalgia, which is exactly what one needs to feel to produce the Imagined."

"How did you learn this thumri? Did your parents teach it to you?"

"My parents … my father did."

"Was he able to go to the Imagined too?"

"I-I don't think so. Maybe." The Singer smiled with unease. "It's all so distant now."

With each additional answer of his, ten new questions formed in my mind. Since we'd begun our journey together, the Singer hadn't shared any details about his life. He'd been a wonderful instructor who'd taught me how to control my abilities. And for a while, I'd been content with him solely being my guide. But no longer.

"Where do you go when you enter the Imagined?" I asked.

The Singer's expression reflected surprise that I was crossing our invisible teacher-student barrier. His eyes grew misty. "I go home."

"Where is that?"

"In a small room. Tucked away amidst a crowded city." He closed his eyes and spoke slowly, savoring each word. "When I'm in that room, I hear the sounds of carts rolling past our building, of fruit sellers yelling their prices of the day. I hear children playing Antakshari outside, as well as their mothers calling after them. And when I return to the Imagined, I don't return as an old man. I assume the form of a young child. The young, timid child that I was."

The Singer opened his shimmering eyes. "Before me sits my father, my guru. He holds a tanpura in his lap, the same way I am now. In that room, he teaches me how to sing, but more importantly, he teaches me why he sings. He believes that when we—meaning all humans—are stripped of our wealth, our possessions, our relationships, everything in life that tethers us to this world, including our bodies, we will be left with the purest version of ourselves. If we commit deeply to music, especially to Indian classical music … if we allow the emotions it evokes to transcend us out of our physical bodies, then we will be one step closer to attaining this purity."

I couldn't fully grasp the philosophy the Singer was preaching, but I gathered enough to be able to jump off his explanation. "That's why the thumri helps me enter the Imagined. Listening to it helps me lose my connection with this world and transport to another one."

He smiled. "You're a fast learner, Akash."

"Was your father a professional musician?"

"Far from it. He wanted to be, but he wasn't able to make a living off his talents. You see, I was very poor growing up. My father was a schoolteacher, and his meager salary barely got us by. Five of us in the family squeezed in that one small room."

"Five of you in one room! How'd you live like that?"

"When you are surrounded by people who shower you with love, the circumstances do not matter much."

"Do your siblings appear in your Imagined as well?" I asked, wondering when I would be able to step out onto Main Street and see other people besides Sagar.

"I assume they are playing outside. Only my father and I are in the room."

"So, you go to the Imagined just to sing with your dad?"

"He will sing a phrase. I'll repeat it. We continue like this throughout each visit, and still I feel like we do not have enough time together."

"That sounds boring."

The Singer chuckled. "Not to me."

"Why did you leave then?"

"Leave?"

"You're here with me. How come you're not still living in that room?"

"I ... well, this was when I was a young child."

"Yeah, so when did you move out? How'd you get from that room to here in San Francisco?"

"I ... I ..."

I was confused by his hesitation. "Do you not remember?"

The Singer clutched his head. "I've spent so long in the Imagined, focused on this memory, that everything beyond my childhood has slipped away."

"What do you mean it's slipped away?"

"I'm certain that I'm older now, and that I need the Imagined to calm some sort of deep longing of mine. But the actual details of my life are hazy."

"Haven't you tried to remember what's happened between then and now?"

"I've never needed to." His expression was pained, as if these questions were stretching his mind beyond capacity. "Even my name is lost. I remember the pet name my father uses for me, but my actual name has ... disappeared. Vanished into the abyss of my mind."

I was foolish not to have questioned the Singer earlier about his life. I'd been so captivated by the Imagined that I'd quickly accepted the Singer's mystical existence as a given. But the more I asked, the less his presence made sense. Hearing about his childhood, realizing that he was as human as I, wiped away all my credulity and made me consider how coincidental it was that the Singer had appeared to me in the Town when I'd lived there, and now appeared to me in San Francisco, almost as if he'd followed me here. I also realized how odd it was that he always lingered at Golden Gate Park, sitting by the same pool, wearing the same outfit. There hadn't been even one instance when I'd come and found him absent. "How can you forget so much of your life? Where do you go when you're not here with me? Where do you eat? Where do you sleep?"

His eyes searched mine for answers he should have known. "I don't know. I don't know. I don't know ..."

———

Priya handed me a writeup on herself the day before the year-book assignment was due. The two-paragraph report was half a page long. Besides mentioning that she used to live in Utah, she included zero information about her personal history.

I handed the paper back to her. "Mr. Sutton will give me a bad grade if I turn this in. There's nothing on it about your family."

She bit her lip. "Look, I don't have a family like yours. I don't have stories like you do."

"Everyone has stories."

"I can email you the doc. You can make up whatever and add it in."

"I've shared so much about myself. Don't you think I should know more about you?"

"Why?" she asked, her eyes narrowing. "Why do you so badly want to know about me?"

Her guard was back up. The progress we'd made was gone.

"Because friends should know things about each other."

"Who said anything about us being friends?" Her sharp voice drew the attention of other students in the library. They glanced at us with concern.

"I thought—"

"You need to get over this weird obsession you have with me."

I clenched my fists. I was fed up with her unfriendliness. Why was I wasting this valuable time with her when I could be spending it in the Imagined? I pushed my chair back and began to zip up my backpack.

Priya's eyes widened. "Where are you going?"

"The assignment's over. We don't need to talk to each other anymore."

"Wait. Akash …"

I stood up. "See you in class tomorrow."

Priya's hand darted across the table. "Can you sit for a minute? Please?"

I remained standing, avoiding eye contact with her.

"It's not easy for me to trust people," she whispered. "Or share with them. A wall just shoots up."

I continued to give her the silent treatment, though I did not make any more effort to leave.

She sighed. "If you want to know the truth about me, I should start by telling you that I didn't grow up in an Indian household."

I glanced at her in surprise. "Aren't you Indian?"

"I guess, but I don't feel that way." She nervously fidgeted with her earbuds. "I-I'm adopted. And I don't know who my birth parents are. I was raised by an Irish couple in a part of Utah without any other brown kids."

"Wow." I was unable to picture a childhood so different from mine. I sat back down and asked, "What was it like growing up?"

"Lonely." Priya tugged at her hoodie. There was a hint of fear in her voice. "I felt like I was being watched all the time, like there was a big sign over my head that labeled me as the odd one out."

"Is that why you moved here?"

She nodded. "Last year, my parents saw how much living there hurt me. They thought being in an area with other Indians would be better. But it's not. It's worse. At least in Utah I knew why I didn't fit in. Here, I've found people that look like me, but I don't get them. I don't get the jokes and comments they make with each other about their culture. And I feel like I'm supposed to."

Priya's voice quivered at the end of her sentence. She quickly looked down and shut her eyes.

"I'm sorry, Priya."

She covered her face. "Stop. I hate pity. I don't want it. I'm better off on my own. I can't be excluded or judged ever again this way."

"Have you talked to your parents about this?"

"They love me so much … but I have such nasty thoughts about them. Like maybe if they hadn't adopted me, I wouldn't be in this mess. Maybe I wouldn't feel so, like, contradicted all the time. Which I know is stupid because I should be happy they even give a crap about me. But I hate being seen with them. I haven't told anyone else here that I'm adopted."

"I don't think people would look at you differently."

She uncovered her face and glared at me. "Easy for you to say. You don't know what it's like not knowing where you come from. Or how it feels to be cut off from something that should be an important part of your life. You were born into a community that taught you how to be Indian."

"Is this why you were asking me questions about the Town? It's because you didn't have a similar experience growing up?"

"I would kill to have what you did. I tried convincing myself that it didn't matter to me, but listening to your stories made me feel like I was connecting to a part of myself that's always been out of reach."

"That's a good thing, right?"

"They're just stories. It's not like I lived through them."

"But I learned what I know about India through my Aaji's stories. And now you know most of those too. That has to count for something."

She was quiet.

"Are you sure you like being alone?"

"I don't have a choice."

"Why not?"

She pulled her hood down until her face was completely covered. Her voice trembled. "Because if I tell people the truth, then they'll see how lost I am. They'll see that I don't have a clue who I'm supposed to be."

I heard her muffled crying, softened by her sleeve. I was reminded of how scary Mayuran used to seem before I'd gotten to know him. Once I'd learned who he was behind the chilling rumors, I'd come to understand that there was absolutely nothing about him to be afraid of.

"I don't think you're lost. Maybe you felt connected to my stories because you want to find that faraway part of yourself. And maybe it's possible to, even if you don't have a family like mine."

She slowly raised her head and looked at me. Her cheeks were pink and bloated. "You think so?"

"I don't know. I'm in sixth grade. I barely understand any of this."

A hint of a smile cracked on Priya's lips. She brushed away her tears and glanced down at her report. "You're right. This is too short. I'll type up a better one and give it to you tomorrow. It's not like I'm going to be chosen for the yearbook anyway."

She stood up and collected her backpack. "Can you please keep this between us?"

"Yeah. Who would I tell?"

Priya nodded, and without any trace of hostility left, murmured, "Thanks, Akash."

———

My mother had booked a restaurant dinner later that evening to celebrate supervising her first shift at the salon. My parents and I hadn't yet dined out together in San Francisco, but my mother was ecstatic with her newly designated responsibility and decided it was time. While dressing up, she gushed about how much she enjoyed her job.

"I feel valued, Akash. Nabeela Aunty makes me feel needed in a way I've never felt before," she said, applying lipstick in our bathroom mirror. I lounged on the couch in a new black button-down shirt and khaki pants. I was growing taller by the day, so most of the clothes I'd brought from the Town were swiftly being replaced with fresh ones in San Francisco.

My mother was wearing a sparkly blue dress. She'd pinned her hair back and applied kohl around her eyes. Her attire was reminiscent of what she would wear back in the Town, but there was a newfound sense of composure in her style. She stood with confident maturity, and the playfulness in her appearance was subdued.

She exited the bathroom and peeked at her watch. "Varun should have been back by now. We're going to be late for our reservation."

My father's stress had been escalating since the day of the focus group. He continued to spend most of his time at the office with his partner, Sean. They rushed to create a new plan for their project, afraid that their investor was steadily losing interest in them. On the rare occasion that my father was home, he would either collapse from exhaustion or sluggishly slump around. I preferred when he was asleep. His temper had become short, and my mother and I had to deal with the brusque end of it. One evening, I moved his towel to the opposite rack in the bathroom so mine could fit, and he snapped at me for being inconsiderate of his routine. Even though I apologized, he muttered passive-aggressive comments for the rest of the night. I learned from my mother how to brush his tantrums off and pretend like I hadn't heard him.

My father's behavior astounded me. He used to act as if seeing me those few weekends of the year was the best gift he could ask for. But now that he was forced to see me every day, he treated me as if I was a nuisance. His initial delight over living with me and my mother was ebbing away. I recalled when Vaishu Mavshi had said that my father showed interest in us only when it was convenient for him. I didn't want to believe he could be that self-centered, but it was becoming harder for me to retain the high respect I had for him when he behaved crabby and terse.

After waiting another twenty minutes, my mother begrudgingly said that we should head to the restaurant without my father. She left him a voicemail to meet us there. We strolled to a cozy restaurant in Little Italy and postponed ordering as long as possible. Every time the door swung open, my mother jerked up, similar to my father the night of *The Book of Mormon* show. Unlike then, my mother and I went through our entire meal without my father appearing. She toyed with her pasta and paid the bill with a defeated face.

"Congrats, Mama," I said encouragingly.

With a weak smile, she replied, "Thanks, baby."

We returned to the apartment and found my father spread out across the bed, munching on a burger and sipping out of a glass bottle of soda. He sat up sheepishly.

My mother's expression hardened. "What are you doing here?"

"Don't be mad," he replied. "I know we were supposed to go out, but I had to stay late. I was starving and picked up some food on the way home."

"You can't call or text telling me that? This night was really important to me, Varun."

"We'll go out again another time."

"I don't care about that! I'm pissed you didn't even bother to tell me you weren't coming."

He stood up and crossed his arms. "I'm sorry I can't be in constant communication with you. In case you haven't noticed, I'm working very long hours to make something of myself."

"I understand. But tonight, I wanted to celebrate my accomplishment."

"You supervised one shift, Mahi. I think you need to read up on what an accomplishment actually is."

My mother stiffened. A fierce, unruly heat exploded within me—a wild anger I hadn't experienced before, directed at someone I'd never imagined would be at the receiving end. I wanted to lash out at my father for treating my mother callously. After seeing firsthand how many hours she worked at the salon, how tired she was upon coming home, I was enraged that he could dismiss her hard work with one comment. I wanted to snap back, but I didn't know how to raise my voice to a man I'd only ever admired.

"You don't have a clue what it's like to believe in something," my father continued. "I'm making sacrifices for *our* future together. I've been taking cuts in my salary to pay the engineers overtime."

My mother sat on the couch and began removing the straps of her heels. "I don't want to fight with you."

Why wasn't she arguing back? Why was she accepting his entitlement? My mother was responding exactly how she had that day at the beach. It was clear that my father was in the wrong, but instead of engaging, my mother was shutting herself off.

"We're having a conversation. You can't just end it because you feel like it," my father fumed. "Are you trying to say that I don't care about you and Akash?"

My mother quietly continued removing her shoes.

My father paced between the bed and the kitchen, pointing the bottle of soda threateningly at my mother. "Who was the one that took you in when you needed it? Who was the one that listened to you when your family shut you out? Who was there for you when you had no one? And now you're trying to blame me?"

My mother's hand was suspended over her ankle.

"There's something wrong with you, Mahi. Like seriously fucked up."

She was silent.

"Say something, goddammit!"

"I don't want to fight with you," repeated my mother.

"It's a fucking conversation!"

My father forcefully waved his hands. In the heat of his emphatic gesture, he lost his grip on the soda bottle, and it flew across the room. The motion was swift enough that I didn't have time to duck. I heard a crash and my mother's high-pitched scream. A warm liquid trickled down my cheek. I touched the affected area and saw a streak of red on my finger. The bottle had shattered against my father's painting of the three of us, and one of the stray glass shards had scratched my cheek. Surprisingly, I wasn't focused on the injury at all. My eyes were glued to the patch of soda that marred the ruined painting.

My mother rushed to the kitchen counter and grabbed a rag. My father was paralyzed. After a moment of blankly staring at me, he approached me, terror-stricken.

My mother pressed the rag against my cut. "Are you okay, baby? Does it hurt?"

Tears gushed out of my father's eyes. He fell on his knees in front of me and cradled my hands. "Aku, I didn't mean to … I'm so stressed out. You know I would never hurt you intentionally, right? I'm not that type of father. Please say you know that, buddy."

He began to sob loudly, theatrically almost, but I felt no compassion. No part of me wanted to console him. I remained frozen while my mother dabbed my face and my father begged for absolution.

———

In the middle of the night, I heard my mother's subdued sniffles emerge from the bathroom. I drowsily knocked on the door.

"Who is it?" my mother whispered.

"Me," I whispered back.

She cracked the door open. I sat on the edge of the bathtub and hugged her.

"How's your cheek?"

"It doesn't hurt," I lied.

She stroked my hair. "I'm sorry that happened to you, baby."

"Why didn't you fight back, Mama?"

"You'll learn when you're an adult that you have to pick your battles carefully. If I won that argument, we'd be the ones to lose in the long run."

She wiped away her tears and hugged me back. In an already claustrophobic apartment, my mother and I found ourselves locked in even tighter quarters, hiding from the one person we'd come to San Francisco in search of.

CHAPTER 16

THE MONEY

AFTER MONTHS OF built-up anticipation, I was finally about to meet my mother's boss. It was early June, close to the end of the school year. Nabeela Aunty had invited my mother over to her apartment for tea, and I was supposed to be an added surprise to the visit.

Before heading over to Nabeela Aunty's, my mother took me to her workplace. The salon was tucked away in a slim unit crammed between a Thai restaurant and a bank. It was older than Simran Aunty's salon and in desperate need of upkeep. Purple paint peeled off the walls, and dark smudges coated the mirrors. But my mother seemed unconcerned with the state of the space. Her station was in the far corner, right below a TV that looped videos of Pakistani singers on Coke Studio. Her counter was decorated with colorful stickers and a photo of me at Ocean Beach. She demonstrated how she would close out a day at the register and introduced me to the rest of her coworkers. They each emphasized how diligent and driven my mother was, two adjectives I'd never heard used to describe her before. Though she waved off their compliments, my mother was grinning from ear to ear when we left.

"Make sure to show a little extra respect," she said as we

climbed the stairs of Nabeela Aunty's apartment building. "She's done a lot for me."

My mother knocked on the front door. The floorboards inside the apartment creaked under the weight of heavy footsteps. Nabeela Aunty opened the door, dressed in a maroon salwar kameez. She wore a gray headscarf and thin, pointy glasses. I couldn't tell whether she was actually frowning or if the sagging skin around her lips made it appear like she was. She was short and stocky, with broad shoulders and a thick neck. Instead of greeting us, she curtly nodded at me.

"This is your son?" She flashed a set of rotten teeth and gold crowns as she spoke.

My mother put one hand on my shoulder. "Surprise! Yes, this is Akash. I thought it would be fun if you two met."

Nabeela Aunty stared me up and down with shrewd blue-gray eyes. I squirmed under her gaze.

"Maybe I should have called you first," added my mother worriedly.

"I was hoping to speak with you only, but no matter, no matter. He's already here." Examining me once more, Nabeela Aunty remarked, "He's too skinny, Mahi. You should feed him more."

My mother chuckled. "I'll try."

"Come, come, don't stand there like fools."

Nabeela Aunty turned around and hobbled down the hallway. We followed after her. Her apartment was compact but not stuffy. Tacked on her walls were photos of the salon from over the years. I stopped in front of a faded film photograph dated October 1990. A wrinkle-free Nabeela Aunty stood outside the building with her hands clasped behind her back. Her salon appeared in much better condition than what I'd seen in person. The exterior was freshly painted, and the windows were clear and shiny.

I strode past the photo-adorned hallway and entered the dining room. Nabeela Aunty had neatly set her dining table with cups on top of saucers and small spoons laid out next to folded napkins. A case of sugar was placed in the center in addition to packets of sugar alternatives. Though Nabeela Aunty's mannerisms were gruff and hurried, her setup revealed that she'd put time and care into preparing for the visit.

Nabeela Aunty was in the kitchen removing an additional cup from a high cabinet.

"Let me help you," said my mother, rushing to Nabeela Aunty's side. She reached for the cup.

"Leave it!" Nabeela Aunty barked. She pivoted away from my mother. "Go sit! You are my guest."

My mother meekly nodded and returned to the dining room with her head hung low, as if she'd been yelled at by a teacher. I humored myself and envisioned what it would be like if Nabeela Aunty met my Aaji. Nabeela Aunty would likely get irritated with my Aaji's dramatic remarks and long, disconnected rambles. My Aaji, unable to handle the most minute criticism, would be scathed by Nabeela Aunty's bluntness. Despite their differences, the presence of an older woman, one who carried wisdom in the folds under her eyes, made me miss my Aaji's wild tales and comforting voice. I felt taken care of under Nabeela Aunty's roof, same as I had back home.

When we all sat down and began drinking our tea, Nabeela Aunty inspected me and asked, "What year are you in, Akash?"

"He's in sixth," replied my mother.

"Let the boy speak."

"Right, sorry. Aku, tell her how you like school."

"It's okay," I murmured.

Nabeela Aunty leaned forward. "I can't hear you."

"It's okay," I repeated, louder this time.

"Any favorite subjects?"

I shrugged.

Nabeela Aunty shook her head. "This boy needs to learn how to speak up for himself."

My mother patted me reassuringly. "She means that in a good way."

"I meant it how I said it," Nabeela Aunty muttered while taking a sip of her tea.

"Aku, you need to hear the story of how Aunty founded the salon. It's so inspiring."

Nabeela Aunty waved her hand. "I don't know about that. My husband passed away shortly after we moved here from Pakistan. I didn't have children or family living near me, but I knew that if I went back, my life as a widow would be miserable. So, I did what I could with the little money I had."

My mother regarded Nabeela Aunty with admiration. "And look at what you've built."

"I had no choice. I had to believe in myself when no one else saw worth in me. This salon has been my pride for many years."

Nabeela Aunty paused and set down her cup. She glanced at me before speaking again. "Mahi, I called you here today for a specific reason."

"Oh?"

"I have some unfortunate news, but I want you to remain calm until I finish."

My mother chuckled uneasily. "You're scaring me."

"I've decided to shut the salon. I've told a few of the other ladies already, but I don't want this news to be discussed until everyone knows."

My mother clutched her cup in shock. "What?"

"I know this is not what you want to hear. But I'm getting older, and it's harder for me to manage the business. That's why I've been having more people supervise for me, you included."

"I thought you asked me to supervise because you saw potential in me."

"I did. I still do."

"When are you closing?"

"At the end of June."

Tears dotted my mother's eyes. "Please don't do this, Aunty."

"Mahi ..."

"You don't understand how much I need this job. I can't afford not to have it. Especially now—"

"Listen to me—"

"I'll help more. Whatever you need—"

Nabeela Aunty waved her hand forcefully. "Enough! I will not have any tears."

My mother sniffed and covered her face. I pictured my mother returning to how she'd been when we first arrived in SF: staying in bed for hours, dejectedly staring off into space.

Nabeela Aunty softened. "I care about my employees deeply. I've always thought of you girls as my daughters. Even though you haven't been with us for long, I consider you a dear part of the family, Mahi. I've admired your commitment to this job. I would not let you go without considering what's best for you."

Nabeela Aunty stood up and shuffled toward an antique cabinet in the corner of the dining room. She took out an envelope and brought it back to the table.

"In addition to an extra month's pay, I have decided to offer a loan, in cash, to those who wish to take it. You are free to use the money however you want, though I would encourage you to build something meaningful, maybe even a business of your own. There is no rush to return it."

Nabeela Aunty handed my mother the envelope. My mother opened it and peeked inside. Her eyes widened. "Aunty ... this is too much. I can't accept such a large amount."

"You are a smart girl. I have no doubt you will use this money wisely."

"Are you sure about this?"

"Absolutely."

My mother set the envelope on the counter and kneeled on the floor before Nabeela Aunty.

"No, Mahi. None of this." Nabeela Aunty tried to hoist my mother off the ground.

"You have changed my life more than you could know," replied my mother. She kissed Nabeela Aunty's hand.

Nabeela Aunty relented and caressed my mother's head with tenderness. "May you have a long and bright future ahead of you, Inshallah."

As my mother gazed at Nabeela Aunty with reverence, I saw a hint of pain in her eyes, a longing for her mother. I could tell she was reminded of my Aaji as much as I was when looking at Nabeela Aunty. Though my mother had found a temporary replacement for a maternal figure, Nabeela Aunty would never fill the void of a missing parent. My mother rarely mentioned the Town or seemed affected by what had happened, but I knew the painful memories still haunted her. I wondered how much she thought about the family, how much she missed them. She didn't have the Imagined like I did to help cope with the separation. She could only hold on to this weak sense of familiarity the salon and Nabeela Aunty provided her of her old life. Once her job ended, I didn't know what she would be able to turn to for support.

When my mother and I were back in the apartment, she opened a drawer on the far-left side of the kitchen and removed a small, unassuming tin box.

"Akash, I need you to keep a secret for me," she said, lifting the lid off the box. There was cash already inside, to which she added the five thousand that Nabeela Aunty loaned her. "I've been saving portions of my salary and tips in here."

"What are you going to do with the money?"

"I haven't decided yet. But it's good that you and I have some financial freedom now."

"Does Dad know about this box?"

"No. That's who I need you to keep this a secret from. I'll tell him someday. I just need to have a more definite plan first."

Feeling loyalty to my mother after my father's insensitivity, I agreed not to say anything to him.

She closed the box and placed it as far back in the drawer as she could. The money was hidden from the naked eye but incredibly present in both of our minds.

———

As promised, Priya handed me a longer version of her student profile the morning our assignment was due. She didn't include her complicated feelings about her background, but she put in enough information about her adoptive parents for me to receive a decent grade. Luckily, neither one of our profiles was selected for the yearbook.

Priya and I didn't speak much after the assignment was over. We would wave to each other in the hallways and say hello before our yearbook class began, but we didn't meet again after school. I would have loved to continue our talks, but Priya seemed nervous whenever we crossed paths. It wasn't in a guarded or hostile way like before. Rather, she would avoid eye contact, and if she did accidentally look in my direction, her cheeks would turn red, and she would shyly make an excuse to leave. I wondered if I'd said something wrong to her in the library. I couldn't figure out what I'd done to make her uneasy.

Nevertheless, I observed Priya from a distance and saw subtle changes in her over the remaining month of the school year. She began to ditch the hood on her sweatshirts, allowing her face to be seen without impediment. In class, instead of remaining quiet and drawing as little attention to herself as possible, she would participate and ask questions. Her posture was less protected, and she didn't stare daggers at people who looked her way.

During lunch one day, I collected my meal from the cafeteria and was about to head to the library. I'd found a small group of sixth-grade outcasts who I spent most lunch periods with. We would hole up at a corner table and quietly work on our own activities. They would play cards or Nintendo DS, and I would bring scratch paper and a kids-sized pan of watercolor paint. I enjoyed the comfortable silence I shared with them.

Before walking over, I peeked at the cafeteria lunch tables, curious whether Priya still sat on her own. She wasn't sitting at the same place she'd sat at in February. I scanned the other tables and caught sight of her settled among the group of Desi girls she'd previously been eyeing from afar. She was chatting with one of them when, suddenly, she covered her mouth to suppress a giggle. She appeared not just comfortable but exuberant as well. We made brief eye contact, and she subtly waved at me, a rare smile glowing on her face.

The only time we said more than a few words to each other again was on the last day of the school year. The hallways were stuffed with proud parents of eighth graders waiting for the promotion ceremony to begin. I was snaking through the crowd after the last bell, heading toward the bus stop outside.

"Akash! Wait up!"

I turned and saw Priya squeezing her way through, holding

the edges of her black promotion dress. She was panting when she caught up to me. "I was hoping to catch you before you left. Can't believe I'm going to high school now."

"Nervous?" I asked.

"Not really. I have a feeling it's going to be way better than middle school was." She looked down and shifted her stance. "Look, I know we lost touch toward the end of the year, and that's my fault. I was kinda embarrassed by how much I shared with you."

"It's okay. Have you told more people since?"

"I've mentioned that I'm adopted, but I haven't said anything about Utah. I did make some friends, though, and we actually get along really well."

"The same ones I saw you with at lunch?"

"Yeah. I thought I wouldn't be able to connect with them at first, but it's not like that at all. They make comments that I don't get sometimes, but I'm honest when there's something I don't know, and they'll just explain it to me. They even invited me to go to Dandiya later this year."

"That's awesome! You'll see how much fun it is."

"It's all thanks to you."

"Me?"

"Those stories you shared in the library stuck with me. I couldn't stop thinking about them after we finished the assignment. I don't have a family like yours that can pass on Indian traditions to me. But after hearing about your childhood, I know that I need to feel connected in some way. I'm always going to feel like something is missing if I don't. You helped me see that."

I smiled. "I'm glad my stories could help."

"I'm opening myself up. It's slow, but it's happening."

An adult voice called Priya's name. A middle-aged white man was waving at her to join him.

"I should get back to my parents," she said to me. "Are you doing anything fun for summer?"

"Not that I know of yet."

"Really? You're not going back to the Town?"

I was caught off guard by her question. Since my mother and I rarely spoke about our old home, and I'd only discussed it with Priya through memories, it was the first time in a while I thought about the Town in terms of the future. I shook my head, disturbed by my own answer. "I don't think that can happen this year."

"When will you go back next?"

"I-I don't know. Not for a while I think."

"That sucks. It would be sad if you lost touch with that place. It sounds like it was special to you."

My voice caught in my throat. "It ... it really was."

"I'll see you around then, Akash. Don't be a stranger when you get to high school."

Priya sprang back to her father. She held his hand as they walked back into a sea of chattering parents and students.

On the way back to the apartment, I agonized over Priya's remark about the Town. I realized then that it had already been half a year since my mother and I bolted in the middle of the night. With the Imagined, I was usually able to stifle my homesickness enough that the harrowing distance did not perpetually haunt me. I could pretend like a short trip to Golden Gate Park was all it took for me to go back. But Priya's question put into perspective how long it had been since I'd seen my extended family, and that there wasn't any assurance I would see them again in the upcoming years, or maybe ever.

I wondered if this was how life was going to be, if no contact was just a permanent state I had to accept. I didn't want to. I couldn't. Even if I was able to leave the forest somehow and meet my family in the Imagined, did that mean the memories I already had with them were all I could latch on to for the rest of my life? Would we never be able to create new ones together? Wheels were churning, spiraling out of control, as I registered with great horror the undying effects of my move to San Francisco. An emptiness, similar to what I'd experienced before I'd found the Imagined, returned with full force. It was like a cavity reopened in my chest, leaving me weak and vulnerable.

I was on the verge of tears while unlocking the door to the apartment, but I quickly sucked it in when I saw that I had company.

"Dad?"

My father was lying face-down on the bed. He sat up and looked at me. His eyes were unfocused. "Aku?"

"Why are you back early today?"

He stood up and faced the window. "It's over."

"What is?"

"The investor pulled out."

"Pulled out?"

"I begged him to give us more time. But that fucker said there were more promising ideas popping up every day. He said that he would rather end this when only petty cash had been spent."

"I'm so sorry, Dad."

"After the focus group, I had a feeling this was going to happen. My first instinct was to leave as early as I could. But then I gave it some more thought and realized … if I quit, what would I do next? I've tried so many different projects already. This was supposed to be my chance at making something memorable. My only goal in life has been to prove myself, to prove my uniqueness, to the world. If I can't do that, then what else do I have to live for?"

I stretched out my hand, wanting him to look at me. But he passed by me and walked to the apartment entrance.

"I'm going out. Don't tell Mahi about this yet."

He shut the door behind him. I crumpled on the couch, burdened with another one of my parents' secrets. I was fatigued by the events of the day. I needed to expel all unhappy thoughts related to my father's confession and my extended family's absence. I was unequipped to handle the surge of hopelessness rising within me, having persistently ignored my own sorrow since leaving the Town.

There was only one place I was certain I could find relief. One place where I could shove these issues aside and pretend like they didn't exist. I needed my refuge, my shelter from my pain, more than ever before.

CHAPTER 17

A FRAGMENTED ILLUSION

BEADS OF SWEAT dripped down my flushed cheeks. My fists were clenched, my teeth gritted, as I tried to force myself back into the Imagined. No matter how much I attempted to focus on the Singer's voice, I was unable to evade the scattered thoughts that obstructed my concentration. I heard Priya's comment about me losing touch with the Town. I saw my father blankly staring out of the apartment window. Then came the other dismal parts of my past, the ones I had pushed aside since discovering the Imagined. The chaos of bodies at the train station, Mayuran glowering at me with his bruised eye, my mother kneeling on the hospital floor. How could I surrender myself to the image of Sagar underneath the three trees when there was so much unhappiness clouding my mind?

"You are not able to focus," said the Singer.

"I know," I snapped. "But I need the Imagined."

"Maybe you should step away, collect your thoughts, and try again later."

"No! I can't wait. I have to go back now."

"Impatience never yields the results we want."

"I don't want your random philosophical statements," I said with irritation. "Are you going to help me or not?"

The Singer sighed. "The Imagined cannot be forced. You need something that will heighten your longing for the past, like my singing has done for me."

I racked my brain for a solution. I needed some other action to substitute my meditation, to evoke as much nostalgia as the thumri did. "I have an idea! I could run like I do in the Imagined. Maybe that will help me focus on my memory."

The Singer contemplated my suggestion. "It might work. But it's risky. I'm wary of anything that is not a gradual transition in and out of the Imagined. An action that stimulating could be harsh on the mind and body."

"What's the worst that could happen? Either it helps me go back or it doesn't."

I checked to make sure no one else was present around us before I began running in place. I squeezed my eyes shut and picked up my pace, matching it to my usual rhythm in the forest. My arms swung forward while my heels kicked back. My muscles were loosened, and my breath shortened. As I'd hoped, the mere action pushed me to feel liberated and youthful.

"Sing for me," I urged.

The Singer reluctantly began his song, and I listened as intently as I could to him. Unlike before, the desire to enter the Imagined was more so induced by a desperate need to leave this world rather than return to Sagar. I could not calm my mind. I slowly started to feel pinches all over my body, as if shards of glass were pressing down on me, deeper and deeper. The skin on my face was stretched back. My heart felt like it was going to explode in my chest. I was being ripped away from the physical world. The pain was biting, but I resisted the urge to quit. I would do whatever it took to return.

When the pain subsided, I knew that I was back in the forest. My eyes opened, and I approached a full stop. I was alarmed by what my Imagined had become. The trees, ground, and sky were not as lifelike as before. The borders around each shape were visible, as if etched in with pencil. The shades of each color were distinct rather than blended seamlessly together. My impatience and lack of concentration had produced a rushed, sloppy, semi-finished world. Though it was challenging to succumb to this unnatural environment, I willed myself to believe that it was real, that this was how the forest looked back home. I just wanted to find Sagar. Once we began playing together, the surroundings wouldn't matter to me.

I sprinted toward the three threes, yelling out his name. I stumbled over fallen branches and almost crashed into a couple of trees. My mobility was sluggish. I was out of sync with the Imagined and with myself. I rushed past the slanted tree, the discolored plants, and all the other abnormalities the Imagined had produced. When I reached the three trees, I was stunned to find the ground empty. Sagar was absent. I whipped around and yelled his name.

Then, I saw something that terminated my search for him. A speck of red blazed on the trunk of one of the three trees. It stretched into a thin curve, commanded by an invisible pen. Slowly, the curve started branching off into lines and spirals of other colors, creating peculiar shapes and uncoordinated patterns. They formed my father's designs, the same ones he had used for his project. Similar to the video he'd shown me, the markings were so deeply embedded in the tree that I could easily believe they were a part of it. Only this time, I was unable to shut the video off. I was compelled to watch his designs infiltrate my Imagined and pull me further and further away from reality.

I turned away, hoping to look at something stable, something I knew to be true to the forest back home. But my father's designs appeared wherever I looked. They snaked up the trees, slithered across the forest floor, covered every inch of the world like overgrown ivy. I tugged at my hair while the beauty of the Imagined slipped away.

As I beheld the defaced forest, I came face to face with my errors. I had used the Imagined as a crutch to avoid dealing with the confusion of my present situation, and it had worked when I could wholeheartedly believe in the illusion. But as the layers of the constructed world were stripped back, I was forced to see the artificiality that hid at its core, and the desolation that dwelled in mine. The Imagined's undoing was pressuring me to recognize that the carefree afternoons with Sagar wouldn't grace my life again in any other form but a memory. In truth, that chapter of my adolescence had been over even before I'd left the Town. I'd been putting off this unassailable fact of loss, and I wasn't prepared for my ignorance to end just yet.

"Go away, go away, go away," I screamed at my father's designs.

"Akash Dada?"

Sagar was standing a few feet in front of me. I was momentarily relieved to have found him, but when I looked closer, I noticed that he wasn't smiling. Rather, he was on the verge of tears. His expression was exactly how it had been on the platform.

"You forgot about me," he whimpered.

"I didn't!" I protested. "I just want to go back to how things were."

"You forgot about me once, and now you're doing it again." His voice was deeper, impeded by a lisp. He was speaking in Mayuran's voice. I blinked, and a scar formed on Sagar's temple. His lips became thicker. The figure before me was transforming into a morphed version of Mayuran and Sagar.

I wanted to bring back Sagar's original face, but in the stress of the moment, I couldn't visualize what it looked like.

"You forgot about me," the distorted boy repeated angrily. He charged toward me, and I stumbled back, falling, falling, falling, until the world came undone, colors flew away from me, and I tumbled through darkness.

My eyes flung open in Golden Gate Park. I was lying flat on the pavement, trembling. The Singer watched me with concern and disappointment.

"It's all messed up," I said weakly. "Nothing looks how it's supposed to."

"I told you not to force it. But you didn't listen."

"Help me go back."

"You are not ready. Your mind is too scattered."

"Please! I need to tell Sagar I haven't forgotten him!"

"Maybe my first instinct about you was right. You do not have the maturity to master something like this."

My blood began to boil. "At least I'm not as pathetic as you! You're an old man who's still obsessed with his childhood. Maybe I can't focus because I don't want to end up like you! I don't want to sit here forever and forget who I am!"

The Singer was stunned. In a grim voice, he replied, "If you sincerely feel that way, then I'm not sure what more I can do to help."

"What does that even mean!" I yelled.

The Singer hesitated. "Until you grow older and learn respect for this gift, I cannot guide you anymore."

I cried out in frustration, but the Singer shut his eyes, tuning me out. Bursting with adrenaline, I shot up and ran to the sidewalk, ran through the park, ran through the streets of San Francisco. I was running without purpose, without destination. Just simply running away.

———

After hours of wandering, I reluctantly headed back to the apartment. Both of my parents were home. My father was shuffling around the kitchen, poking through drawers. He didn't look my way when I entered. My mother, on the other hand, instantly wrapped me in a tight embrace.

"Akash, my God, I was so worried!" She released me and furiously seized my collar. "What did I say about leaving the house on your own? It's too dangerous!"

"Mahi, please," my father moaned. "Don't yell. Your voice is making my head hurt more. Where the hell is the aspirin?"

She frowned at him. "He disobeyed my instructions and went out by himself. Aren't you concerned at all?"

"Look, he's back. Nothing happened to him."

"What if something had? Akash, I don't want to put the lock back on that door, but I might have to."

"Mama, let go," I said, wrestling with her grip.

She held me tighter. "Not until you answer. Why did you disobey me?"

"I don't want to talk right now."

"Well, I don't care. You can't do whatever you want and not face consequences."

"What am I supposed to do in this apartment by myself?" I grumbled. "Neither of you are ever home."

"Don't blame us for your behavior. I want you to apologize and promise you're not going to disobey me again."

I lifted my chin and met her stern gaze. "No."

Her eyes widened. "Why are you acting like this?"

"Mahi …" whispered my father.

"I'll help you find the pills in a sec. Akash, this is unacceptable."

"Mahi."

"Holy shit, can you hold on for one minute!" she snapped, pivoting toward my father. Her grasp on me loosened.

My father was holding the opened tin box.

"Varun …"

"What is this?" he whispered.

"Don't get upset."

He lifted a bundle of cash out of the box, staring at it in a stupor.

My mother inched toward him. "I've been saving some money. That's all."

"Why didn't you tell me?"

"I was going to! This money is meant for us to build a life together. Maybe move out to a bigger apartment."

"How could you keep this from me?"

"Varun, don't make this a big deal. Just hand me the box." She outstretched her hand, but he didn't budge.

"This money could have helped my project."

"I didn't want you making any snap decisions about where to use it."

His eyes narrowed. "You mean, you didn't want me to use it for my work."

"Give me the money, Varun."

He stepped away from her and hid the box behind his back.

My mother lowered her hand. She hesitated, and for a moment, I thought she was going to passively end the fight like she'd been doing since we'd arrived in San Francisco. But she surprised both me and my father by replying, "You're right. I didn't want you to use it for your project."

He looked wounded. "Why not?"

"There's not even ten grand in there! This money would barely cover any of your costs."

"Anything could help us right now."

She rubbed her temples. "Okay, fine, even if it could, you

know better than anyone that you jump from project to project."

"I told you this time is different!"

"How should I know what's going to stick and what isn't? This money needs to be used for more important things."

"What could be more important than my project?"

"Us! Your family! We're not something that you can pick up and drop whenever you have interest in us."

"I'm not going to apologize for having other things going on in my life. Other aspirations."

"You don't think I want anything else? You don't think I have my own dreams?"

"I'm sorry, but until this year, you'd never even thought about moving out of the Town. You've never dreamed as big as me, never experienced the hunger that I do. Besides, if I'm successful, then we all benefit from it."

"But this has always been about you! Every decision that you make is for you. You chase after whatever will make you feel powerful and accomplished, and we're supposed to go along for the ride."

He stepped toward her, enraged. "What do you want then? You want me to give up my dream? Because if so, then you're like the rest of the motherfuckers who doubted me. You're just like my shit parents. There was a point in time when you used to idolize me. You used to worship my art and tell me that I would become huge one day."

"When we were teenagers! We're not kids anymore."

"So, what? You don't believe in me anymore?"

My mother wavered. "No. I don't. You have no clue what you're doing. You came to San Francisco without knowing a thing about tech. You gave up everything for a project that you hadn't even properly thought through. Varun, you're not as special as you think you are."

My father's eyes bulged with fury. "You have no one besides me. Not even your own family will talk to you."

"Last I checked, Akash and I are the only family you have. You're just as alone as I am."

"Fuck you, Mahi!" my father screeched through clenched teeth. He raised a fist in the air with his free hand.

My mother did not flinch. She calmly replied, "What are you going to do? Are you going to hit me?"

He gritted his teeth, as if he was about to. My anger toward him was bursting, the heat erupting even more than it had the previous fight. It was so hot, so irrepressible, that I released it in one powerful yell—

"*Stop!*"

My father's gaze shifted to me. His eyes widened in horror. He stepped back and withdrew his hand.

For a few minutes, the three of us were silent. The sounds from the street traffic and hissing vents carried on, unconcerned with our quarrel. A drunk man screamed nonsense outside of our building. A grating alarm went off in the downstairs apartment. Finally, my father's body slackened, and he placed the box on the kitchen counter.

He spoke in a soft, trembling voice. "We're all tired. None of us are thinking clearly. Let's go to sleep, and we can have a calmer conversation in the morning."

My mother took the box off the counter and placed it back inside the drawer. My father slumped on the couch. He was the first one of us to fall asleep. My mother waited for him to begin snoring before she reclined on the bed. I curled up next to her, shaking, until I too fell asleep.

———

When I woke up the next morning, the couch was empty. I figured my father went to get pastries from the downstairs bakery, like he usually did on Saturday mornings. I shook my mother awake. She squinted, adjusting to the daylight.

"I'm sorry I disobeyed you," I said.

"It's okay, baby," she replied, stroking my face.

"What's going to happen now?"

"Your father isn't in the apartment, right?"

I shook my head no.

My mother sat up and clasped my hands. "We need to move out for a bit. Just you and me. I don't think we should wait any longer. Your father is not thinking clearly. He's too obsessed with his project right now. With the money Nabeela Aunty loaned us, I think we can afford to sublease a place for a few months while I look for other work."

"We're going to leave Dad?"

"I'm sorry this is so sudden, Aku. I know how much you adore Varun. I think time apart will help us."

"It's okay. I'm ready to leave."

She kissed my cheek. "How did I get so lucky with you, huh?"

"Mama!" I groaned, batting her away. She ruffled my hair.

"Hey, Aku?"

"Yeah?"

"I'm scared to live on my own."

"But I'll be with you."

She grinned. "That's true. Don't ever think about leaving me, okay?"

"Okay."

She rose from the bed. "I need some coffee. You want anything?"

"I'll eat whatever Dad brings home."

She opened the drawer for mugs, the same drawer she'd put the tin box in the previous night.

"No …"

"What?"

"It's gone." She stumbled back. "The money … the loan, my savings, all of it … but … he wouldn't …"

I looked over at the wall of incompleteness. Most of the tacked-up artwork was missing. Only a few scrappy drawings were left. How had I not seen the blank wall when I'd woken up? How had I not heard him take it down during the night?

"Mama …"

She was staring at a ripped piece of sketching paper on the table. Her distraught eyes met mine. "I need to find him."

She raced to the door, threw it open, and vanished down the stairs in her pink pajamas.

"Wait! Where are you going?" I asked, frantically stumbling out of bed. I peeked at the paper she'd been looking at.

I can't let go yet. I'm sorry. One day, I hope you'll understand.

I scrambled out of the building and onto the street. It was a bustling morning in Chinatown, swarming with tourists and locals. My mother was pushing her way through the crowd, and I swiftly chased after her. I felt as if I was back at the train station, striving to stay afloat and fight my way through. My mother tripped on the curb. I ran up to her and helped her to her feet.

"Hold on to me!"

I spotted an empty alley and led her to it. My mother stumbled in front of me, her knees buckling. She gazed up at the sky and howled, "Why? Why are you doing this? Haven't I been punished enough?"

I knelt beside her, placing a gentle arm around her shoulder. My mother wept and whimpered deep into the sleeve of my shirt, waiting for answers that didn't arrive then, and still haven't to this day.

PART THREE

CHAPTER 18

SETTLED

THE COLORS INCREASINGLY teased me the longer I fixated on them. Emerald-green leaves swam down tree trunks like fish careening through a rushing creek. Flecks of creamy light leapt across the forest floor in a crisscross motion, playing hopscotch with each other like boisterous children do. Misty gray ripples from the stream became as light as pollen and levitated in the air. The shapes that were supposed to be stationary roamed free, and I was an observant audience to their transgressions.

"Mr. Patil, are you here with us?"

I blinked, and the colors returned to their original form, exactly how I had placed them on the page. I turned my attention to the front of the classroom. Mrs. Suárez was staring at me expectantly. I looked at the other students, who were all either on their phones, dozing off, or gawking at the clock and waiting for the bell to ring. Mrs. Suárez wasn't concerned with any of them. Her focus was only on me.

"Sorry," I muttered.

She smiled, happy to have recaptured my attention. "As I was saying, perspective is key to give any composition depth ..."

Mrs. Suárez was a recent addition to the faculty, replacing the incompetent art teacher before her. Unlike him, Mrs.

Suárez approached each lesson with careful thought and encouragement. Even though I was in her last class of the day, her energy was habitually high. When she lectured or spoke to a student about their work, her round, mouselike face lit up with pleasure, and her large ears twitched with excitement.

Unfortunately for her, most students treated this elective class as a GPA booster and did the bare minimum to pass. I was the only one who responded to her lectures and applied the skills she taught to my work. Art class was a form of release for me. Working on my projects, especially my paintings, helped me detach from the rest of the school day and relax. I felt a sense of accomplishment when I finished a piece, amazed that the once-disconnected shapes and textures had assembled into a coherent scene. Mrs. Suárez had picked up on my aptitude for the subject early on. She would often call on me to exhibit my work to the class. Unless she wanted to show off a piece of mine that I wasn't proud of, I appreciated the special attention. It was nice to be a teacher's favorite.

I glanced down at my painting. It was far from finished, but I could already tell what the end result was going to be. Usually, I planned my compositions beforehand and stuck to still life or portraits. But for this watercolor project, I'd decided to dive in without any preparation. My unshackled pencil had whizzed across the page, liberated from intention. I'd realized only after the rough sketch was completed what I'd been unconsciously drafting. The forest was forming—not the original one Sagar and I had played in as kids, but the reconstructed one from my last visit to the Imagined. It had been five and a half years since then. Five and a half years since I'd witnessed the forest crumbling before me; five and a half years since I'd last seen Sagar. Life had progressed through the awkwardness of middle school and stress of early high school, but the visuals of that evening were still excruciatingly etched in my mind.

I'd attempted to terminate the project. I had set the piece aside for a couple weeks and sketched a hallway in our school instead. But I'd been compelled to revisit my original idea. Thoughts of the incomplete project had haunted me until I'd reluctantly picked it up again. Without a doubt, this surrealist painting flowered like none of my other technically proficient pieces had before. The beauty and sheer chaos of it captivated me. So, I continued to trudge along, curious how the final product would turn out.

My cellphone buzzed. I flipped it over and saw an incoming text from Ravi Desai: *meet at lot.*

I sent back a thumbs-up. The bell rang, and students dashed out of the classroom before Mrs. Suárez could finish explaining our homework assignment. She scrambled to wrap up her address. "Class is over already? Time really does fly when you're having fun, huh? Until we meet next, I hope you stay creative and inspired!"

We shuffled out of the classroom while Mrs. Suárez flashed us encouraging smiles. I walked down the main open-air hallway toward the parking lot. Students were filing out of the classrooms and reconnecting in small groups by the bell tower quad. I heard complaints about gratuitous homework as well as tearful confessions of subpar test scores. I smiled to myself, thinking how dissimilar this Bay Area high school was from what was shown on television. Rather than obsessing about popularity and social status, the students here were fixated on their academic and extracurricular accomplishments, a byproduct of being within the hyper-competitive environment of Silicon Valley.

I headed to the row where Ravi usually parked, sidestepping cars that bolted out of their parking spaces with no regard for those walking around them. The parking lot was crowded with groups of seniors lounging on the hoods of their vehicles. They passed around vapes and bopped to trap music blasting from their car speakers. I spotted Ravi at the very end of the lot, standing by his shiny new Tesla. Although Ravi came from one of the richest families in this already well-to-do neighborhood, he tried to be as inconspicuous as possible. He would park away from the rest of the seniors, hide any fancy gifts his parents gave him, and dress in a nondescript manner. He embraced his title as the school stoner. Other seniors approached him when they wanted joints but tried not to associate with him otherwise, so as not to ruin their studious image.

Ravi waved at me. He was wearing baggy cargo pants and a black sweatshirt. His hood was pulled over his skin-fade haircut, cupping his long, scrawny face. As usual, his shoelaces were untied. His rectangular glasses drooped, and he pushed them up on reflex. I'd told him countless times before to look for frames that fit his face, but he was attached to the gigantic ones he owned.

"Down to hang?" he asked.

"For a bit."

"Can you change up your answer once in a while? Why is it so hard to just say yes without adding some sort of condition to it?"

I opened the front passenger door. "Because I'm only ever available for a bit."

A hoarse voice yelled out, "Y'all better not be leaving without me!"

Eva Tran marched toward us with sharp, rapid steps. Unlike Ravi, who moved in slow motion, Eva walked like she was on a mission. She never lagged and was never late. Her long, pin-straight black hair whipped from side to side behind her. She wore gray leggings and a tight, dark-brown tank top.

Ravi grinned. "We would never."

"Akash, I already called shotgun this morning," said Eva, slipping into the front passenger seat.

"I didn't even know about this plan until five minutes ago," I replied, closing the door for her. Ravi mouthed "wimp" to me as we both got in the car, him in the driver's seat and me in the back.

Eva turned around to face both of us. "Where are we going?"

Ravi shrugged.

"Bitch, I thought you made a plan."

"That's what you're there for," he said, reaching out to her.

She smacked his hand away. "Should we do the usual?"

"I'm down."

I chimed in, "Sure, but—"

"Yeah, yeah, we know. You have to be back by five." Eva rolled her eyes. "You act like we've never hung out before. Why do you always have to set time limits with us?"

Ravi winked at me in the rearview mirror. "What'd I say?"

He reversed the car horribly out of his space and was an inch away from hitting the car behind him.

Eva groaned. "You're the worst driver in the world."

"You wanna drive? Be my guest. Oh wait, who failed their license test again?"

"Shut the fuck up."

I leaned against the window, smiling as their banter continued.

———

"Can we switch? I hate Taro."

"Ravi, you say this every time," I said, chuckling. "Just order something else."

"I like to be consistent."

I took a sip of my milk tea, adjusting the straw so that it could capture the few remaining pieces of boba. The three of us reclined on a grassy hill overlooking the 680 freeway. The sweeping view made the houses below seem like props in an architectural model.

"I'm submitting my last application this weekend," said Eva, clutching her knees and rocking back and forth.

"What the fuck," said Ravi. "I still have to finish half my supplementals."

"I told you I'd help with them."

"Eh, I'll finesse."

"Procrastination's gonna bite you in the ass. Anyways, I'm terrified."

"Of what?" I asked.

"My decisions, of course!"

"You're a genius, Eva. Colleges will beg you to come."

"I hope so. Every conversation in class is about the future. It's stressful. I just want to go to a nice private school that's far, far away."

Ravi patted her on the back. "You worry too much. Be like me. I've already accepted that I'll go to whatever school accepts me and then work some soul-sucking tech job after."

"No offense, but you're not exactly my role model."

He clutched his chest in fake agony.

"What about you, Akash? Have you finished?"

"What?"

"College apps, dumbass."

"Um, not really."

"See, Akash is on my vibe," said Ravi.

"How far along are you?" Eva asked, ignoring him.

I set my drink down and checked my phone. It was at five percent battery. "It's getting late. We should head back."

"Master at avoiding."

I stood up and dusted off my backside. "I'm not avoiding. There's just not much to talk about."

"Bro, don't tell us you're going to community college," said Ravi.

Eva smacked his arm. "Shut up, you elitist motherfucker."

"Maybe," I said. "We'll see. It's complicated."

Eva shook her head. "You're such a mystery, Akash."

"That a bad thing?"

"No. Just an observation."

We cleaned up and trekked back to Ravi's car. Ravi dropped Eva off first and then headed to his house. As always, he offered to take me to my place if I'd tell him where it was, but I politely declined and said I preferred taking the bus. I disembarked from Ravi's car at the base of the steep, winding road that led up to his house. I waited for the bus, anxiously hoping it would arrive on time. I checked my phone for the time, but as soon as I tapped on the lock screen, the phone went black.

"Fuck me."

———

"You're late."

"I know."

"I hate working up front."

"I know."

I stuffed my backpack in a free cubby, strapped on my apron, and took my position behind the register. Luke lingered by the counter and tapped his fingers impatiently against the table. His hazel eyes begged me to entertain him.

I smirked. "You're still here?"

Luke sighed dramatically. "He's in such a bad mood today."

"What'd you do?"

"Nothing!"

"Liar."

"Fine. I may have switched up the order of his sauce bottles."

"Luke! He hates that the most."

"Well then, he needs to relax. I got one good thing out of it, though."

Luke discreetly removed his phone from his jeans pocket and opened up Instagram. A few months earlier, Luke had started an account that featured photos of our boss, Yusuf Uncle, in his rages. Although normally a jolly man, Yusuf Uncle was particular about how work was done at his fast-casual falafel restaurant. If he noticed kitchen items were not where they were supposed to be, his eyes would flare up, and his cheeks would turn bright red. He would get impassioned to the point where proper sentences wouldn't come out of his mouth, just a collection of sputtered words that Luke and I would decipher after. Yusuf Uncle's tantrums had frightened me when I first started working for him, but after seeing how quickly he moved on from them, they began providing me entertainment. Luke purposely provoked Yusuf Uncle whenever there was a slow shift, and the creation of the Instagram account only exacerbated his attempts.

There were about twenty photos uploaded, all sneakily taken by Luke. The page had five followers. Luke would often try to persuade me to create an account and follow it, but I'd tell him that there was no way in hell I was going to be associated with his antics. As much fun as we made of Yusuf Uncle, Luke and I considered him a great boss. He would give us large portions of the tips and abide by our desired shifts. If we were sick and needed time off, he would worriedly interrogate us about our health and offer us free food. He treated us more like sons than employees.

"You're an asshole for this," I said. "He's going to find out one day."

"Can you imagine him on Instagram? He would post the most cringey shit."

"Is Akash here?" yelled Yusuf Uncle from the kitchen.

"Yes, Uncle! Sorry I'm late!" I shoved Luke and whispered, "Now you have to go back."

Luke groaned and pushed himself off the counter. His arm grazed mine. "Don't miss me too much."

I rolled my eyes. Although Luke and I had known each other for only a short time, we'd formed a close friendship. Before Luke, Yusuf Uncle's thirty-year-old son had helped out in the kitchen. He'd avoided interacting with me and would respond in a hushed voice if asked a question. Each shift had dragged on without someone to make conversation with. Once Yusuf Uncle opened up a San José branch of his restaurant, his son left to be the head cook over there. Luke was hired shortly after as his replacement. Even though Luke and I were closer in age (he was only a year older than me), I thought we would have the same relationship I'd had with Yusuf Uncle's son, one based on respectful silence. Luke was unable to, or didn't want to, pick up on the hints that I was unaccustomed to speaking with the assistant cook. He'd hung around the front counter during his breaks, yapping away until I'd finally given in and engaged. I was happy he'd persisted. I eagerly looked forward to my shifts with him.

Customers filtered in and out, never in large quantities. As the shift progressed, my eyes drooped with exhaustion. No matter how many times I had been through this routine, the physical toll of attending a full day of school and working a late shift wore me down. I was relieved when Luke called last orders. After we closed shop, I said goodbye to him and Yusuf Uncle while they both got into their respective cars.

Yawning intermittently, I walked to the bus stop and checked my phone. Still dead.

I chose a window seat on the empty bus and leaned my head against the glass. I usually listened to a playlist of lo-fi music on the ride home, but with my inoperable phone, the only sounds available to me were from the bus rolling through the quiet, wide streets of Fremont. The Bay Area suburbs were much more tranquil than San Francisco. Life moved at a slower, simpler pace. Shops closed by nine, and houses had their lights off by ten or eleven. I preferred living in the sleepy outskirts where space was plentiful. The only downside was the silence. During brief intervals, like on the bus, when I was alone and didn't have an activity to complete, my mind would wander to places I didn't want it to, places where I would mull and chew and puzzle over the tumultuous years that had paved the way to the present ...

After that unforgettable day when my father abandoned us, my mother and I waited a month for him to return to the apartment. My mother called his number from several pay-phones but didn't receive a response other than his voicemail. By taking Nabeela Aunty's money as well as my mother's savings, my father had left us with practically nothing. My mother gave up hope at the end of the month that my father was coming back, and we temporarily moved out to Nabeela Aunty's apartment.

San Francisco, for my mother, was a constant reminder of the promising future she'd attempted to build but hadn't been able to prevent from crashing down. She decided it was best if we distanced ourselves from the urban center but moved somewhere close enough that we didn't have to conform to an entirely new setting. Through a stroke of luck, we found a listing online for a tiny guest house that had been converted from a shed. It was available to rent in Fremont, a suburb an hour out of SF, and was in a price range we were comfortable with. I strongly supported the move. Fremont was known to have a massive Indian population, and even though we wouldn't know anyone there, I believed adjusting to a familiar community would be easier than acclimating ourselves elsewhere.

Once we moved to the suburbs, my mother started working again. Nabeela Aunty encouraged her to find another salon, but my mother said she couldn't handle being somewhere that reminded her of the money she'd lost. She ended up working as a transcriber at a private immigration law office. The work was dull, and she never showed enthusiasm for it. We were barely scraping by on her salary, so when I turned fifteen, I applied for jobs at every restaurant, coffee shop, and clothing store in Fremont. Most places immediately turned me away because of my young age and lack of experience, but Yusuf Uncle hesitated when I stopped by his restaurant. I took his pause and ran with it, begging him until he caved.

Once I was employed, I freed my mother from having to solely provide for us. Yusuf Uncle's hole-in-the-wall restaurant was located at the border of North Fremont and Union City, about twenty minutes by bus from my place. The work was dependable and far enough away from where I lived that the likelihood of running into someone I knew was slim.

Despite being my closest friends, Eva and Ravi didn't know about my job. The three of us had become acquainted freshman year in gym class, and by the end of the semester, we were hanging out every day at lunch. Still, I was cautious with sharing information about myself. I'd told them that I'd grown up in San Francisco and had also vaguely mentioned living on the East Coast, but I was disinclined to share more about the Town. I wanted to push my memories of it as far away as possible. I also hadn't invited the two of them over to the guest house. Though they'd been intensely curious about my life in the first year of our friendship, by senior year, they had given up prodding for information and accepted that I would share when I was ready. The high school we attended was public, but most students, including Ravi and Eva, came from semi-affluent or affluent families. I was embarrassed to tell them that my mother and I lived on someone else's property and were struggling to sustain ourselves. It was easier to keep my life a mystery than be the odd one out.

The bus reached my stop, and I wearily walked down a secluded street. I lived about a mile away from my high school. The main house was owned by a kind, good-natured senior couple. Their kids had long moved out of the Bay Area, so they were happy to have company near them. They showered me and my mother with warm greetings and offered us left-overs whenever they'd cooked more than they could eat. My mother liked them because they respected our privacy and were accommodating if rent needed to be delayed.

I opened the wooden gate on the right side of the house and entered the backyard. The guest house was in the far corner, hidden from cars and pedestrians on the main road. My mother and I lived in anonymity. We didn't have a listed address for our shed. We put our landlords' address on forms, and since we paid in cash, we didn't have any documented rent payments. The only people who knew where we were staying were our landlords. My mother and I had transitioned from living in our family home to a rented apartment in San Francisco to what could hardly pass off as a residence. But we were more or less settled. And I was grateful not to be rootless anymore.

I opened the door to the guest house and dropped my keys on the counter. The setup inside was sparse. We had a kitchenette, a lamp, a couch, and a full bed in the corner, next to the bathroom. Besides these rudimentary furnishings, we hadn't decorated the place at all. Even the walls of a motel room would have been more appealing than our blank ones. Regardless of how long we'd lived there, my mother still viewed the guest house as a temporary arrangement and refused to make it a hospitable environment.

She was sitting on the couch when I walked in. Her hair was spread out over her flowery nightgown. My mother looked more like my Aaji each passing day, mirroring her outfits rather than contradicting them like she used to back in the Town.

She stood up abruptly. "Why are you back so late?"

I took off my backpack and grabbed a cup for water. "I always work the late shift on Tuesdays. You know this."

"But you usually text me when you reach the restaurant."

"My phone died."

She crossed her arms angrily. "How many times have I told you to take a charger with you? I didn't know where you were or if something had happened to you."

"Okay, well, I'm back now."

I took off my shoes. I was eyeing the bed and considering falling into it without changing my clothes.

"Akash!"

Her piercing voice startled me. "Why are you yelling?"

"Because you're not listening to me!"

I rubbed my forehead. It was too late in the night for an argument. "You're making this a bigger deal than it is. It was a one-time mistake."

"What would I have done if you hadn't returned? I'm left here wondering whether you were kidnapped or hurt or ..."

Her voice trembled. I knew what she was thinking. *Or if you'd left?*

I walked toward her. She turned away from me. I pulled her into a hug. She tried to push me off.

"No."

"Mama ..."

She relented, though her arms hung limply at her side. I was much taller than her, so I could feel her tears dampening my chest.

"I was so worried, Aku."

"I'm here," I murmured. "I'm not going anywhere. I promise."

CHAPTER 19

NABEELA'S NEWS

"AKASH, CAN YOU stay a minute, please?"

Mrs. Suárez perched herself on a stool by my desk. The last few students in the classroom made their way out, leaving the two of us alone.

"Sure."

She eyed my watercolor. "This painting of yours is beautiful. I've been admiring it from afar."

"Thank you," I replied meekly.

"The colors, the depth, the style. It all fits seamlessly together. May I ask how you came up with it?"

"Imagination, I guess."

"Well, you have an imagination like no other. Every art teacher's dream is to have a student as talented as you."

I blushed. "Thank you."

"Have you ever considered pursuing art professionally?"

"Not really."

"I think you should. A talent like yours cannot be wasted. I'm not sure where you're applying to college, but there are a lot of schools out there with terrific art programs."

The truth was that I hadn't contemplated my future career, in art or in any other trade. I was so caught up in making ends meet day to day that long-term goals were far beyond my mental bandwidth. Besides, most of my peers were planning to go to college for some sort of science or engineering program, and I had little interest in those subjects.

Just to indulge Mrs. Suárez, I briefly pondered the possibility of what my life could look like as an artist. Being able to work on my paintings every day, dreaming of compositions for the rest of my life, feeling fulfilled with my work—the thought was alluring and would have remained as such if I had not veered off to memories of my father, the only artist I'd known who had tried to pursue his talents professionally. I was immediately filled with such a vile sense of repulsion that the temporary dream vanished.

"I'm sorry. I don't see myself doing this for a living."

Mrs. Suárez smiled, though a hint of disappointment was visible in her expression. "No worries. You should pursue what you want. I just thought I would ask."

She patted my arm and returned to the front of the classroom. I packed the rest of my belongings, waved goodbye, and hurried out.

My mother and I were planning to visit Nabeela Aunty that afternoon. This was one of the first times Nabeela Aunty had insisted we meet. Usually, my mother was the one to suggest a trip to see her. During our get-togethers, the three of us would stay in Nabeela Aunty's apartment to chat and play cards. We would sometimes visit stores, although physical tasks were harder for Nabeela Aunty as she aged. My mother wanted her to move to the suburbs, but Nabeela Aunty would stubbornly respond that she didn't see the point of leaving an area she was comfortable with. I reckoned that my mother's persistence stemmed from her loneliness in Fremont. She said these visits were to keep Nabeela Aunty company, but I believed these visits were more necessary for her.

My mother and I met at the Fremont BART station and

boarded the first northbound train. When we exited at Montgomery Station, I could hear my mother's breath quickening. Even though a significant amount of time had passed since we'd moved out, my mother was still agitated whenever we returned to San Francisco. Because of her unease, we wouldn't linger for long. We would head home right after meeting Nabeela Aunty, never passing Chinatown or our old apartment.

Nabeela Aunty had been a pillar of support for us after my father's desertion. It had taken my mother a week to tell her what had happened, and she would have waited longer if it hadn't been for the encroaching rent deadline. My mother went with her head hung low, embarrassed that the money Nabeela Aunty had so generously given her was gone. She sobbed in broken apologies, but Nabeela Aunty shushed her. Instead of reprimanding my mother, Nabeela Aunty waved her hand in the air and told us to "forget about that bastard." Though she couldn't offer the same amount of money as before (and my mother would have refused it if she had), Nabeela Aunty provided us enough to finish off the last month of the lease. She then offered her living room as a temporary bedroom for the two of us until we found other accommodations.

We were forever indebted to her, and as such, I made sure never to miss a visit to her place. With my father missing, Nabeela Aunty was the closest person we had to family in the Bay Area. But regardless of how much our relationship had developed over the years, she still greeted us with gruffness.

"Finally you're here," Nabeela Aunty huffed, peering at us over her thin glasses. "I was expecting you earlier."

"Sorry, sorry. We took a later train," said my mother. She leaned in for a hug.

Nabeela Aunty ducked and straightened out her blouse. "None of that, please."

Even though my mother was rebuffed each time, she persistently tried to show physical affection to Nabeela Aunty. It was the only expression of endearment she had learned from my Aaji. She was holding on to the hope that one day Nabeela Aunty would receive it.

Nabeela Aunty scrutinized me. "He's getting skinnier, Mahi. Soon all he'll have is bones. You need to feed him more."

"I eat more than I should, Aunty," I said, smiling at the familiar retort.

"Hmph," she grumbled, widening the door and leading us to the dining room. Nabeela Aunty had developed a slight limp in her walk. She supported her right hip as her body swayed from side to side. Although she used to rebuff us if we attempted to help with tasks, she now allowed my mother to set the table and serve her tea. She wouldn't ask for it outright, and if my mother didn't offer, I'm sure Nabeela Aunty would have struggled to do it herself. But my mother was always more than willing to help. Nabeela Aunty would recline on a chair and watch from afar with silent gratitude.

We made small talk about my school and played gin rummy. After the third round, Nabeela Aunty set her cards down and said, "You remember my niece, Sana?"

My mother continued reorganizing her cards without looking up. "The one that lives in Texas?"

"Yes, yes, very sweet girl she is. She recently had twins."

"Good for her."

"One minute, let me show you."

Nabeela Aunty harshly tapped her phone screen. She brought the device an inch away from her face and squinted at it.

"Can I help?" I asked.

She handed me the phone. "I don't know why they have to make all this techno-shmeckno so complicated."

Somehow, Nabeela Aunty had landed up on YouTube. I went to WhatsApp and pulled up her thread with Sana. The last message read: *Can't wait to see you soon, Khala!*

Without glancing at the rest of the conversation, I clicked on the shared media tab and enlarged a photo of a woman cradling two baby boys.

"Is this it?" I asked.

Nabeela Aunty scrunched her nose and peered at the screen. "Yes, that's the one. Show your mom."

My mother glanced at the photo with indifference. "How sweet."

Sana was Nabeela Aunty's sole relative in the United States. She'd emigrated from Pakistan to study medicine and had since become a pediatrician. Her courage, intelligence, and independence elicited the utmost praise from Nabeela Aunty. Sana had visited San Francisco thrice in the previous six years but remained a mysterious figure to me and my mother. All three times, Nabeela Aunty had canceled our scheduled meetings instead of inviting us over to meet her niece. During the visits following Sana's departure, my mother would bring an excessive number of sweets and gifts for Nabeela Aunty. My mother's jealousy of Sana was blatantly obvious. She wanted to be regarded as Sana was, to fill the same spot Sana did in Nabeela Aunty's life. She wanted to earn the title of family.

"Twins are not easy to manage," said Nabeela Aunty. "Even Sana is having difficulty with them."

My mother yawned. "I'm sure."

"She is a strong young lady. I'm very proud of her."

"Mmm."

"But she's worried right now. She has to return to work soon, and her husband also has long hours. She will need someone to watch the kids."

Based on the text I'd read from Sana, I had a strong inkling of where this conversation was heading.

My mother, though, was oblivious. "I'm sure she'll find a good nanny."

"You're not understanding," said Nabeela Aunty. "She asked me to come to Texas."

My mother looked up with suspicion. "To visit?"

"To live."

My mother chuckled. "Poor girl. She must have been upset when you turned her down."

"Mahi, I said yes."

My mother slowly set her cards down. "You're leaving the Bay?"

Nabeela Aunty sighed. "Yes."

"For how long?"

"There's no plan to come back."

"How can you … how can you leave? You said you never wanted to live anywhere but here."

"Don't be upset."

"You spring this on us out of nowhere! Do you think that's fair?"

"Mahi," said Nabeela Aunty sharply.

The two of them stared at each other in stiff silence.

I hesitantly jumped in. "I think what my mom is trying to ask is why now?"

They both turned to me, as if they had forgotten I was there.

Nabeela Aunty responded, only looking at me, "I'm growing old, as much as I try to pretend that I'm not. It will be good for me to have company."

"But you have us here," said my mother.

Nabeela Aunty fidgeted with her teacup. "We should continue this conversation another time."

My mother opened her mouth like she was about to snap back. I swiftly interceded. "When are you leaving?"

"April. Sana is flying here to help me move. Of course, I won't be carrying much with me, and you are more than welcome to take some furniture or kitchen appliances. We can look through and see what you want."

I studied my mother's narrow eyes, inferring her unexpressed feelings. I didn't even consider my own emotions regarding Nabeela Aunty's move. I solely worried what this loss might do to her.

Nabeela Aunty noticed how tuned out we were. "Mahi, we will still call often. This move has nothing to do with either of you."

Although Nabeela Aunty probably intended for her statement to be affirming, I knew these words would confirm to my mother how irrelevant a factor she'd been in Nabeela Aunty's decision to leave San Francisco.

My mother straightened out. "Okay."

Nabeela Aunty pushed her glasses up in surprise. "Okay?"

"Your decision is made. What can I do about it?" She paused and asked, "Should I make some more tea?"

———

"Who kept her company for the past six years? Who accompanied her to doctor visits? Who brought her groceries? Did Sana do any of that? Huh? Sana doesn't know how she likes things made. Sana doesn't know how particular she is about her belongings. Sana doesn't know anything. Just watch, she'll come running back after a few months, wishing she'd never left."

My mother and I were back in the crowded underground Montgomery Street Station. Her tirade prompted curious glances from other people waiting on the platform. Though I was happy my mother was opening up to me, her anger was overwhelming. I wanted to soothe her, but I didn't know what words would do the trick. I listened intently, but I was worried that by not saying anything, I was furthering her outrage.

"Mama, she just wants to live with her family. We aren't related to her."

My mother scowled at me, making me wish I had remained silent.

"So? So what? Do none of my actions matter? Just because they share a bit of blood, it erases everything I've done?"

"I'm not saying that."

"No one appreciates what I do. No one sees my worth. But one day, when I'm gone—"

"Mama, please don't say that."

"Why? No one seems to care whether I live or die."

"Stop, please—"

"Maybe I should die, just so everyone can realize—"

"Mama, stop!" I exclaimed. Frustrated tears sprang to my eyes.

My mother's expression softened. "Akash …"

"You know how much it hurts me when you talk like that."

She stroked my trembling back and ran her fingers through my coarse hair, acting as if I did not tower over her. "What would I do without you, Aku? You're the only one I can trust. The only one who has stuck beside me."

The operator announced that the BART train was approaching. A loud gust of wind enveloped us as the metal tube came to a halt. The doors opened, and a flurry of impatient people pushed past one another to get off or on. My mother and I maneuvered through the horde obstructing the open doors.

I glanced to my right. I don't know why I did. If I hadn't made that slight movement, I might not have seen him. He was dressed in an ironed suit, carrying a shiny briefcase. His hair was cut short, and he had grown a bit of well-groomed facial hair. He'd just exited the train and was walking toward the staircase. I panicked—another mistake—and vigorously rushed my mother to the nearest train car. Given her already unbalanced temper, I feared that seeing him would upset her more.

"Akash, stop pushing me!"

"Hurry up! The doors are about to close."

I don't know whether he heard my voice, or also, like me, made an unfortunately timed glance in our direction. Either way, we met each other's gaze. His eyes refocused in confusion, then shifted over to my oblivious mother, widening in recognition.

In a last-ditch attempt, I elbowed the boy that was blocking me from entering the crowded car.

"Ow." The boy held his shoulder in pain, glaring at me. By then, it was too late for an escape.

"Mahi? Is that you?"

I shut my eyes. My grasp on her loosened, and we both turned in disbelief toward the voice.

There he was—a changed man, and yet, so recognizable. My mother whispered his name as if it carried the weight of a dozen more from our past.

"Nikhil."

CHAPTER 20

A FAMILIAR FACE

WE WERE FASTENED into a standstill, absorbing the changes time had carved out in each other's faces. The train hastened away. We were the only ones on the platform besides a few stragglers. My mother's lips were parted, but sounds weren't escaping. Nikhil was the first to break the silence.

"I can't believe it's you."

Unable to procure a response from my mother, he directed his attention to me. "Wow, Akash, look at you, man. You've grown up so much."

I thanked him, even though he had said it more as a factual statement than a compliment.

Nikhil emitted a slow chuckle of disbelief. "This is ... I mean, what are the chances? Do you, I mean, have you ...?"

"We live near here," I responded hesitantly.

"Your voice is so deep now. I'm sorry, I can't get over how strange this is."

"What ... what are you doing here?" I asked. "Do you—?"

"—live here too? No, no. I'm on a business trip. But I don't live in the Town anymore either."

My mother flinched at the mention of our old home.

"Business trip?" I repeated.

"A lot has changed in my life, as I'm sure it has in yours."

He coughed awkwardly and glanced at my mother. "How are you, Mahi?"

She opened her mouth, but there were still no words that could overcome her astonishment. Nikhil seemed to understand that, so he reached into his pocket and removed his wallet.

"Listen, this is all a bit shocking right now, and I have to run for a dinner meeting. But let's properly sit down and catch up. What do you say?"

He handed me a business card with his name and number printed in professional black lettering.

"My return flight is early tomorrow morning, but I'm in SF often on assignment. Maybe we can get dinner next time I'm here." While only looking at my mother, Nikhil added, "Please call."

He slowly backed away from us before mounting the escalator and disappearing from view. The operator's voice returned, announcing that the next train would arrive in ten minutes. Soon, a new batch of prospective passengers poured in around us. They were all ready to proceed to their next destination, eager to encounter the forthcoming events of their lives. Meanwhile, my mother and I sank deeper into the platform, unable to circumvent the chokehold our resurfaced past put us in.

——

Seeing Nikhil was undoubtedly shocking, but in a way, it felt inevitable. I hadn't known I would run into him specifically, but I'd suspected I would cross paths with a familiar face from the Town at some point in my life. As much as I suppressed thoughts of my old home, I'd secretly hoped for an encounter like this. The years away had made the separation easier, but there would always be a part of me that missed the Town and yearned to know how the beloved characters from my childhood were. I wanted to know if Suhail Mama and Kiara Mami had any kids, if Bhaskar Uncle and Juhi Aunty still ran their shops, who my Aaji was telling stories to instead of me.

Over the years, I'd wondered whether Vaishu Mavshi and Harsh Kaka would consider meeting me and my mother. It seemed ridiculous at times how far we were from each other. We were family after all. But then I would think back to the root of this separation and admonish myself for being heedless. They blamed me for their son's death. They had told my mother they wanted us to leave. Even if they agreed to meet us—the thought of which made me nauseous—what type of relationship would we have? How could I have a conversation with them without being reminded every second of the pain I had caused? I was settled in the Bay, and my life was decent. I could feel happy without Sagar's death constantly weighing on me. It was better to forget and move on.

Still, the sight of Nikhil as a suave businessman rather than the quiet young adult who wore graphic tees and beanies reignited my curiosity for what people in the Town were presently like. Even though my appearance had significantly transformed, I'd foolishly believed that everyone in the Town looked exactly as they had when I'd seen them last. I hadn't considered that they were capable of going through such a stark metamorphosis. It saddened me knowing how much development I'd missed during this prolonged split. Meeting Nikhil for a meal suddenly didn't sound like a horrible idea. It offered a perfect way to connect to the Town without getting too close.

After a quiet journey back to the guest house, I subtly tried to bring up Nikhil's proposition to my mother.

"That was strange," I said. "Running into him like that."

She took off her jacket and placed her purse on the couch.

"Where do you think he lives now?" I continued.

"I don't know."

"Do you think he visits the Town?"

"I don't know, Akash."

"Or keeps in touch with anyone there?"

"Akash! I said I don't know. Why are you asking me this?"

"I just wanted your opinion."

She sighed. "It's been a long day. I need to take a nap."

"What should I do with his card? Are you going to call him?"

"I'm not doing anything right now but sleeping."

"I didn't mean at this exact moment. Will you call him at some point? Should I keep the card?"

She plodded over to our bed. "Keep it. Throw it. I don't care."

"That's it? You don't want to know what he's up to?"

"Akash, now is not the time."

"We can't pretend like we didn't have a life before this, Mama."

She hesitated and tilted her head toward me. Then, instead of responding, she fell onto the duvet.

I exhaled in annoyance. "Whatever. Do what you want. I have to get to work."

I withdrew a wrapped chutney-and-cheese sandwich from the fridge and flung it into my tote bag. When I left, my mother was facing away from me. I couldn't tell whether she had fallen asleep yet.

I spent my shift reminiscing about Nikhil and the video games I used to play in the cluttered back room of Das Electronics. My thoughts eventually drifted to Mayuran and that one frigid afternoon we'd spent outside of Juhi Aunty's store. I remembered how elated I had been when he'd trusted me enough to open up about his late mother, when he'd allowed me to be the first one to see him as more than the Town recluse. Our brief kiss was one of my most cherished memories from my childhood. I'd had my fair share of short-lived crushes throughout high school, but none of them compared to the innocent excitement of the first one. Too much was left unfinished between me and Mayuran. I was well aware that he'd been the basis of my strained relationship with Sagar, and yet, I didn't harbor any resentment toward him. If anything, I hoped that he had left the Town like he'd always wanted. I hoped that he was happy.

Luke and I were the only ones working at the restaurant that evening. Yusuf Uncle was at the San José location assisting his son. Luke indulged in the lack of surveillance. Whenever I wasn't ringing up customers, he would emerge from the kitchen and show me a curated assortment of memes he had saved on his phone. Even with his exuberant commentary, I found myself spacing out. Luke took notice.

"You good?" he asked.

I snapped back to his phone. "Sorry."

"Akash, come on! This is the funniest one!"

"I swear I'm watching."

Luke restarted a short clip of a three-year-old girl sassing her father for not tucking her in. It was hilarious. Luke and I giggled as the girl stormed away from the conversation with a dramatic hair flip.

"Your taste is so random," I said.

"What can I say? I'm a complex person with complex interests."

I grinned. "Uh-huh."

Bright headlights brought my attention to the front door. Through the glass, I saw a familiar car parking in front of the restaurant. A person I hoped I would never see at this job exited the vehicle.

"Luke, I need you to cover the register."

"What? Why?"

"Just take the next order for me. Please."

Before Luke could ask any more questions, I darted behind the curtain that separated the dining area and kitchen. I pulled the curtain back slightly to observe the scene. The door opened, and Ravi entered.

"Man, I am fuckin' hungry," he said, approaching the counter. "Thank God you're open late. Everything else is closed in the 'burbs."

Luke fumbled with the register. "What can I get you?"

"Can I cop one falafel wrap?" Ravi rubbed his stomach. "Actually, make that two."

As Luke entered the order, Ravi's eyes flickered around the restaurant. I realized too late that I was visible to him. Ravi and I made eye contact. I quickly shut the curtain and tightened my fist, praying that he had not been able to recognize me.

"Cash or card?"

Ravi didn't respond, so Luke repeated the question.

"Um, what? Sorry. Cash ... wait no, what am I saying, card? I'm sorry, I thought I saw ... never mind."

My heart was pounding. I considered going out and saying hi but decided against it. That would confirm to Ravi that I had been hiding from him.

Luke slipped through the curtain. I backed away so I was out of Ravi's eyeline. Luke shot me an inquisitive look while he prepared the order. Only after Ravi had taken his food and left the restaurant did I cautiously go back to the register.

"You know him?" asked Luke.

"Know who?" I replied, playing dumb.

Luke hesitated, scrutinizing me. "Never mind."

We finished the rest of the shift in our separate workspaces. Luke came to the front once more to talk to me, but I was too embarrassed to engage in conversation. He took the hint and stayed in the kitchen until Yusuf Uncle popped by to lock up.

After leaving the restaurant, I sat on the curb by the bus stop. I crammed as much of my mushy sandwich as I could into my mouth.

"Waiting for the bus?"

I jolted in surprise. The sandwich flew out of my hand and landed on the pavement. Luke walked up behind me.

"Oh shit, didn't mean to startle you," he said.

"It's all good." I picked up the misshapen, dirt-coated sandwich.

"I would apologize, but that sandwich looks sorry as fuck anyways."

"Hey. I made it with love."

He sat down next to me. "Can I give you a ride home?"

"The bus'll be here soon."

"Driving's faster."

"Don't you live in Union City? My place is in the opposite direction."

"I don't mind."

"Thanks, but I don't want to put you out."

"I can't let you stay out here alone, especially after I just destroyed your dinner. I'll wait with you."

"Luke, you seriously don't need to."

"How about this. My house is close by. Come eat dinner, and then you can take the bus home."

I was surprised. Luke and I hadn't hung out outside of work before. "Luke …"

"Come on. My mom made lasagna tonight. I know you're hungry."

My empty stomach urged me to accept. Having to endure

a long bus ride before I could eat again was a vastly unappeal-
ing thought. "Fuck it. I'm down."

Luke grinned. He shot up and outstretched his hand to me.

———

An impassioned R&B ballad exploded out of the car speakers.
Luke immediately reached for the dial to change the station.
"This is embarrassing."

I leaned back in my seat. "Keep it on."

Luke hesitantly retracted his hand right as the vocalist
reached her climax. He reversed out of his spot and began
humming to the tune. By the time we left the parking lot,
Luke was fully belting along. He scrunched up his face as he
strained to hit the high notes. I couldn't help but laugh. He
was a horrible singer, incredibly pitchy and lacking rhythm,
but his commitment was endearing. We reached his street
by the end of the song, only having to drive past two signals.

"How was my performance?" he asked as the station went
to commercial.

"Whitney Houston would be bowing down to you."

He parked his car in front of a small one-story house
jammed in between two others of a similar style. His front
yard was enclosed by a rusted metal fence. A plastic baseball
bat, a mini trampoline, and three soccer balls decorated the
overgrown grass.

Realizing I knew nothing about Luke's family, I asked,
"Do you have siblings?"

Before he could answer, two girls emerged from the house.
One of them waited by the door while the other ran up to the
car. The latter girl wore a bright-pink T-shirt with rainbows
on it, and her hair was separated into two pigtails held up by
sparkly scrunchies. She couldn't have been older than six or

seven. Although her T-shirt was radiant and cheerful, her expression was far from pleasant. She put her hands on her hips and examined me with a harsh glare. The other girl by the door was much more bashful. She appeared to be older— maybe around twelve or thirteen.

"Who are you?" the girl with pigtails asked when I exited the car.

"Uh, hi. I'm Akash. What's your name?"

"I'm not telling you yet."

Luke surfaced next to me. "Jada, be nice. Akash is a friend from work."

"Is he the handsome, mysterious one?"

"Jada!"

The girl by the door broke out in giggles. "You talk too much."

"Shut up, Chloe!" Jada screamed before chasing her into the house.

I nudged Luke. "So, tell me more about this handsome, mysterious guy."

"Talking about Yusuf, of course."

"Of course."

"Prepare yourself for my family," he whispered, leading me inside.

The living room was bursting with energy. A laugh-track sitcom was playing on the TV, even though no one was paying attention to it. Jada was tickling her sister on a long L-shaped couch. Two boys on opposing sides of the room passed a foam football to one another, shouting taunts and cheers. They seemed to be close in age, although slightly younger than Luke. The jubilant, contrasting energy of the siblings was reflected in every surface of the house. Framed family photos hung on the walls, in addition to drawings and awards from Luke and his siblings over the years. Jackets, books, and toys were dispersed across the couch and coffee table. The extensive collection of keepsakes made the house feel as if it were another member of the family, not just a place for them to reside. It reminded me of my house in the Town. Back there, the walls displayed our history, especially from the years that my mother, Suhail Mama, and Vaishu Mavshi were growing up.

Luke cupped his hands around his mouth to combat the noise. "Everyone, this is Akash."

The boys nodded in my direction, but the girls were too embroiled in their tickle fight to even look up.

"Lots of siblings," I whispered to Luke. "Got any more?"

Luke chuckled. "Not unless my parents have hidden them from me."

The overlap of yelling and hearty laughter brought me back to my childhood, to the meals around the living room table filled with bickering and merriment and disconnected tangents, all while a Marathi serial boomed in the background. I missed it dearly as I observed the turbulent dynamics of Luke's family.

"Ready for some food?" asked Luke.

I nodded. He led me down a carpeted hallway to a square kitchen. A curly-haired woman in a baggy sweatshirt and leggings was washing dishes in the sink. She had earbuds in and was singing along way better than Luke had been in the car.

Luke tapped her on the shoulder. "Mom?"

She jumped up and yanked the earbuds out. "You scared the crap out of me."

"I seem to be doing that a lot tonight."

She kissed him on the cheek. "Hungry, sweetie?"

"Starving."

"And who's our guest?" she asked, eyeing me curiously.

"This is Akash. He's a friend from work. Could he have some lasagna too?"

"Thank you," I said. "I don't mean to be an imposition."

"Oh, please. You're more than welcome. Let me warm up some slices for you boys. I'm Michelle, by the way."

She cut off four slices of lasagna from a baking dish and split it onto two plates. She began warming one of the plates in the microwave.

"I apologize for the mess," she added. "If I'd known we were having a guest over, I would have cleaned up."

"Your house is perfect as is."

Michelle chuckled. "I like you already. Did Luke's siblings overwhelm you yet?"

Luke smirked. "Jada definitely did."

"I don't know what to do with that child," Michelle sighed. "They're such a handful. Luckily, Luke is there to help me whip them into shape."

"As if they listen to me."

"Of course they do! You're the best older brother they could ask for."

Luke rolled his eyes, although his slight smile exposed how pleased he was by her statement.

The timer beeped. Luke opened the microwave and switched the plates.

"Are you in school?" Michelle asked me.

"Yes," I replied. "Last year of high school."

"College is coming up soon, huh? Any plans for where you want to go?"

"Still looking around."

"Any idea what you want to do in the future?"

"Mom, stop interrogating him," interrupted Luke.

"I'm not interrogating anybody," she said defensively. "My baby is going off to college soon, so forgive me if it's on my mind."

"We'll see. Decisions are still a ways away."

"You applied this cycle?" I asked in surprise. When Luke had started at the restaurant, he'd mentioned that he was going to work part time for a few years to save up for college. He hadn't told me he'd changed his plans since then.

"Yeah, but we'll see where I get in."

"They'd all be lucky to have you," gushed Michelle. "One day, they can proudly claim that Luke Morrison, star pediatrician, went to their school."

The microwave beeped, and Luke took out the other plate. "And with that, we're going to my room."

"Thank you for the food," I said.

Michelle waved her hand. "Don't mention it. Friends are welcome anytime."

I followed Luke into the hallway. He opened one of the doors and said, "Welcome to my cave."

Upon entering the room, I was pleasantly taken aback to see interests of Luke's that I hadn't known about. A train-themed duvet covered his double-sized bed. His walls were bedecked with string lights and an eclectic collection of posters, ranging from SZA and Rihanna album covers to obscure anime characters. A substantial number of manga books were neatly arranged on a bookshelf by his bedside table. I walked over and ran my hand across the spines. "Okay, nerd."

"Don't judge until you try it."

"I'm not judging. I'm just surprised."

He sat on his bed and patted the spot next to him. "In a good or bad way?"

I joined him. "Neither. There's just a lot I'm learning about you tonight. Pediatrician?"

He handed me my plate of lasagna. "It's been a dream for a minute. I've always loved kids and taking care of people."

"How come you've never told me that?" I took a bite of the lasagna. "This is delicious, by the way."

Luke chuckled as he watched me devour the rest. "Slow down, you're gonna give yourself a stomachache. And, I don't know, it didn't come up. You never want to talk about the future."

I paused mid-bite. "That's not true."

"See, even now. The mention of it makes you tense up."

"It's complicated. My future is dependent on more than just me."

"Meaning what?"

"Meaning there are other considerations, other people, I have to factor in."

"But if you could choose any path you wanted, what would it be? What would your dream life look like?"

"It's … not that easy."

Luke set his plate down. "I don't know enough about your situation, but can I offer some input?"

"Go for it."

"As you can see, my family is humongous. My dad is in the military, so he has to travel a lot. My mom works full time in insurance claims, so she can't look after us as much as she wants to. Most of my teen years were spent as a third parent to my siblings. They've always been my first priority. When I graduated high school, I set aside my goal of being a doctor, yes, to save up money, but also because I couldn't imagine leaving them.

"But Jada, that little know-it-all, asked me one day when I was going to start working in a hospital. I told her I didn't know yet and that I was gonna stay home for a little while. I thought she would be overjoyed that I had more time to play with her. Boy, was I wrong. She said she'd already told all of her friends that I was a doctor, and it would be embarrassing for her if I wasn't gonna be one anymore."

I laughed. "She really said that?"

"I swear. Can you imagine this small-ass kid checking me like that?"

"I want to be her best friend."

"Good luck. Anyways, when she said that, I realized that my siblings were more independent than I gave them credit for. They're more than capable of figuring their lives out on their own. Honestly, the best thing I could do for them is pursue what I want. I would be depressed if I continued to stay home for years, and that's not really role model–worthy. So, I applied this year, and I don't regret it one bit."

"I see your point, but your situation is different than mine."

"I'm sure it is. But this is your life. This is your one chance to be who you want to be and pursue whatever it is you want to pursue."

"Life's too much of a burden to do that."

"Well, that's fucking depressing."

"It's true."

He shifted toward me. His hazel eyes peered into mine with intense concentration. "It doesn't have to be. Life can be full of opportunities if you open yourself up to it."

"How are you so positive all the time?"

"Because I have to balance you out." He put one hand on my right knee. "I hope one day you start living for yourself, Akash."

My breath was shallow. Our faces were close enough to each other that I could see the stubble growing above his upper lip. His brown skin was luminescent under the glow of the string lights. We were unwittingly moving closer to each other.

A vibration in my right pocket interrupted us. Luke cleared his throat and looked away. I pulled my phone out and saw that my mother was calling.

"I should go."

"Oh, okay," said Luke with a hint of disappointment. "Are you sure you don't want me to drop you home?"

"Yeah. I'm good with the bus."

Luke nodded. He took my plate and straightened out the duvet cover.

"Hey, Luke?"

"Mm-hmm?"

"Thanks for tonight. I had a really good time."

He replied with soft sincerity, "Me too."

CHAPTER 21

A LATE-NIGHT ADVENTURE

A WEEK LATER, Mrs. Suárez stopped me again after class. She handed me three glossy pamphlets with photos of smiling students strolling across manicured lawns.

"In case you change your mind about pursuing visual art, I would love for you to take a look at these schools," she said. "All of them have stellar programs. Two are theory heavy, but the third one has a more flexible curriculum."

"Isn't application season almost over?" I asked. "It's already January."

"For most schools, yes. You'll have to wait until next year for the theory-based ones. However, the one in Florida accepts applications until the end of Feb. You'll have to get a portfolio together, but you should have enough work from this class to do that."

"I appreciate it, but the cost—"

"—is steep. That's for sure. But if you look at the back ..." she said, turning the red pamphlet over to show a detailed set of notes in her handwriting. "I've laid out all of the scholarships and grants the school offers or accepts, so if you have enough from that, work-study, and financial aid, the amount left over should be minimal."

I skimmed through her markings, amazed at how helpful

they were. For each scholarship, she'd noted the deadline, the associated website, the amount they could provide, and materials needed to apply. She'd ranked them by which she believed I had the best shot at.

"You really did this for me?"

Mrs. Suárez smiled. "Of course, Akash. I told you that the greatest joy for a teacher is to find talent. You have it. There's no doubt about it."

"I-I don't know what to say," I said, choked up.

"You don't need to say anything. Just think it over. If you still decide this is not for you, there's absolutely no hard feelings. This is your decision, and I am proud of the work you've done in this class either way."

"If I decide to study this, what would I be able to do after?"

"So much! Continuing in fine arts might be tough, but the skills you learn will be applicable to many other fields. Graphic design is growing. Animation is huge now. Illustrators are needed in many companies."

"I knew someone—someone who used to be very close to me—that pursued art and failed miserably. I don't want to end up like him."

"I won't lie and say this is the easiest path. There will certainly be bumps in the road, but that's true for every field. Layoffs and job insecurity exist across all professions. If everyone chose a major based on what they thought was safe, we would have no more art in this world. Can you imagine how horrible that would be?"

"I see your point."

"You don't have to follow the same trajectory as that artist you knew if you don't want to. Learn from his mistakes and be strategic with your career. This is your one chance at life."

I chuckled. "Someone else said the same thing to me recently."

"Then it has to be true," said Mrs. Suárez, clasping my hands.

Her words rang through my head long after I left the classroom. Mrs. Suárez's optimism helped me unlock the self-made door that prevented me from considering the various paths my life could take. Pursuing a career that I loved, one that brought excitement rather than obligation, made the future seem less dull than I'd always thought it would be. My hands trembled from the thrill of these unfamiliar ideas. Energized with newfound confidence, I decided I wanted to do something out of pocket, something that was purely for my enjoyment. As Luke had said, I needed to start prioritizing myself.

I opened the group chat with Ravi and Eva and impulsively sent them the following message: *Let's go on an adventure tonight.* Ravi responded instantly that he was down. Eva texted soon after: *Where is Akash, and what have you done with him?*

When I arrived at the guest house, my mother was heating up leftovers in the microwave. She adhered to a strict routine during the weekdays. She would wake up at six thirty sharp and make herself tea and toast. Then, she would take the bus to her law office, where she worked from eight to three. She would return home, eat a snack, complete whatever chores were pressing, and go for a walk at six. Rain or shine, this walk was a necessity for her. She would finish by seven, read as much as she could, and then sleep at ten. We didn't have a television in the guest house, so reading had become an important hobby for both of us. I picked up novels across several genres, but my mother exclusively read poetry or nonfiction related to spirituality.

Her interest in this subject was a recent development. Back in the Town, my mother would yawn and mumble through prayers, showing little initiative to practice outside of what we'd do together as a family. But since our move to Fremont, my mother visited the nearby temple every Saturday morning. She would kneel before each idol for an elongated stretch and squeeze her hands together with profound emotion. Sometimes, a tear or two would slip through her closed eyelids. I was unable to discern whether her prayers were built on awe or anguish. Her obscure expressions could have either indicated that she was begging or admonishing God. I never asked her to clarify.

The fabric of my mother's personality had transformed over the course of our time in Fremont. Her talkative, attention-loving side had pretty much disappeared. She preferred to sit in silence, and her rare smiles were restrained. She used to love dressing up and experimenting with makeup, but in the Bay Area, she recycled the same three sweatshirts and jeans. Even for her job, she threw on a loose cardigan and flats five minutes before leaving.

Most shockingly, she had lost her affinity for social interactions. I doubted that my mother had anyone else in her life besides me and Nabeela Aunty. She never talked about any of her coworkers or mentioned other friends. I didn't even think she had interest in making any.

Once, we were at the grocery store, and an Indian woman approached my mother to compliment her naturally striking features. She pressed the conversation forward, and my mother engaged. The woman gave my mother her phone number and said that she should join her and her friends for a walk sometime. I was excited for my mother, remembering how chatty she could get with Aneesa Aunty and the other workers in Simran Aunty's salon. A month after this interaction, I asked my mother if she'd ever reached out to that woman. She replied saying that she had no idea who I was talking about.

My father's disappearance marked a turning point for my mother, though it took me some time to figure out why. With Nabeela Aunty's assistance, the financial ramifications of his actions hadn't been dire. My mother found the transcribing job soon after, and we were never without a roof over our heads. We pretty much had the life she'd hoped for when she'd planned to leave him. As I matured, I understood how much emotional value my mother had placed on the stolen money. The hope for a better life, one that was far removed from her pain, had been stored in that tin box. If her life was devoid of family, at least she'd had this goal that could numb her. But after the results of her hard work were taken from her, my mother was unwilling to dream again. She no longer nurtured a passion, believing that if she did, it was bound to crash and burn all over again. Life for her became about existing, nothing more.

Because of her lack of interest in other activities and people, our bond was stronger than it had ever been. Our weekends were spent entirely with each other. In addition to our temple visits, we would run errands together, browse through stores, or simply read at home. During the week, I hung out with Ravi and Eva for short periods after school. If I wasn't working, the rest of the afternoon and evening was spent with my mother.

For this reason, I was nervous to tell her that I wanted to go out with Ravi and Eva later that night. I had a nagging feeling that I was abandoning her by doing so. I considered saying that I'd picked up a shift, but hiding the truth seemed silly. I decided the more nonchalant I was in my approach, the less of an issue it would be.

I dropped my backpack by the bed and said, "I'm going to be gone for a bit in the evening."

"Aren't you off today?" said my mother.

"Yeah, but I'm hanging out with some friends."

"Tonight?" she asked, removing her food from the microwave. "Why?"

"Just. For fun."

"Why all this hassle? It's a school night. Go another time."

"It's just Ravi and Eva. I've told you about them. We're all free, so I thought—"

"How long will you be gone for?"

"Not sure. But I'll hang out with you until it's time to leave. We can go for a walk."

"Why don't you see them at school? I don't want to stay up waiting for you to get back."

"You don't have to stay up."

"Of course I have to stay up!" she said, exasperated. "You think I'm going to sleep without you home?"

"Mama, I'm almost eighteen."

"That doesn't mean you can stay out all night."

"I didn't say I was going to!"

"Don't yell."

"I'm not yelling!"

"Akash, don't yell at me."

I clenched my fists. "I'm a senior. I'm supposed to be spending time with friends. Just because you don't have any doesn't mean I shouldn't as well."

Her eyes lowered. Immediate regret washed over me.

"I'm sorry. I didn't mean that."

She toyed with her food. "No, you're right. We should have lives outside of each other." She paused. "I've changed my mind. I'll let you go tonight."

"I was already planning on it," I replied, annoyed that she'd needed to exert the final say. I removed my jacket from the coat hook. "I'm going to head to Ravi's now, actually."

She shrugged. "Why are you telling me? You'll do what you want anyways."

I bitterly shoved my hands into my jacket pockets and felt a stiff piece of cardstock. I took it out and saw that it was Nikhil's business card. My mother and I hadn't discussed our encounter with him again, so I'd forgotten his information was still with me. I tossed the card on the counter. My mother continued eating, pretending to ignore me. I shut the door firmly on my way out.

———

Ravi's house was palatial, to put it lightly. An engraved mahogany door and marble columns graced the entrance. Tile floors, picture windows, and minimalist art enhanced the spacious indoors. I asked Ravi once what his parents did for work, and he replied, "Bro, who knows? My dad runs some tech company, and my mom works in education something."

Ravi wasn't stingy or arrogant with his money. If anything, he was generous almost to a fault. He would try to cover the cost of meals whenever he, Eva, and I went out for lunch. Once, he let me borrow his expensive, temperature-controlled water bottle, but I lost it on the bus ride after. Though I apologetically asked for the vendor's name so that I could order him another one, he chuckled and said not to worry; he had three more just like it at home. He had a big heart, but he could be oblivious to how privileged his actions came across. Though Ravi's family was an extreme example of wealth in the area, many of my peers enjoyed comfortable lifestyles as well. They had the luxury to solely focus on grades and extracurriculars instead of financial stress.

I hadn't disclosed much about my life to my friends, or anyone else in Fremont, because of this disparity between me and them. I'd been afraid my secrets would catch up with me after Ravi stumbled into the restaurant, but he didn't mention seeing me the following day at school. I believed I was safe for the time being.

Ravi and I watched hours of trippy cartoons before Eva arrived at sundown. Ravi's mom hugged each of us and handed Ravi a packed bag of snacks. She told us to have loads of fun without inquiring where we were going. As Ravi, Eva, and I walked down the driveway, Ravi quickly removed a Ziploc from his pocket and thrust it in the snack bag. His action was so discreet that I couldn't make out what was inside. Soon enough, we were sailing on the freeway to an unknown destination. Eva was sitting shotgun, and I was settled in the back.

"Ravi, where are you driving us to?" I asked.

"It's a surprise, bro," he said, winking at me in the rearview mirror. "You wanted an adventure, so you have to be game for wherever I take you."

"Bet."

"Akash, I was shocked when you asked us to hang," said Eva. "What came over you?"

"Damn. I don't know. I missed you."

"And me?" Ravi asked.

"Eh."

Ravi flipped me off. "Guys, I can't believe we're almost adults. Remember ninth-grade gym class?"

"Yeah, and how you would come up with a new fake injury every Tuesday to get out of running the mile? Eva, what were his excuses again?"

Eva chuckled. "Leg injury, sore throat, migraine …"

"I think he said heart palpitations one time too."

"Mr. K hated you."

"Hey, I still passed, didn't I?" replied Ravi. "Y'all are haters."

"But why the mile?" I asked.

"It's hard, okay. You try it."

"We did! Every week that you were sitting on the bench!"

Eva burst into uncontrollable giggles. She wheezed as she struggled to catch her breath.

"You good?" asked Ravi, chuckling.

"I-I haven't … I haven't laughed like this in a long time," she said, wiping a tear away. "I'm so glad I came out. The wait for college decisions has been soul crushing."

"Just think how irrelevant this will be in ten years. You'll be a lawyer—"

"—Ugh, please."

"—living in a penthouse in New York—"

"—I'll be good with any high floor."

"—Married."

"Yuck. I hate all guys except for you two."

"Let's lock it down then," teased Ravi.

"I would rather die."

Ravi began making loud, obnoxious kissing noises. Eva punched his arm.

"Eva, I'm driving!" Ravi exclaimed, swerving slightly.

"Can you turn up the music?" I asked, hearing SZA's distinctive voice slip through the front speakers. I smiled, thinking of Luke's humongous poster of her. Eva increased the volume, and the three of us rocked to the beat. I reached over to the snack bag on the car floor. The topmost item was Ravi's Ziploc bag, which contained three home-baked cookies. I took one out and popped it in my mouth.

"Whatcha eating? Can you give me some?" asked Ravi, reaching one hand back without taking his eyes off the road. I handed him the Ziploc.

"Holy shit." Ravi's tone turned grave. "Did you eat this already?"

"Was I not supposed to?"

"How much did you have?"

"One cookie."

Ravi howled with laughter. "Ah, fuck."

"Is that bad?"

"I brought edibles for the two of you, but you weren't supposed to eat more than half a cookie. You're gonna get *sooooo* high."

"I've never seen Akash on an edible," squealed Eva.

"That's because I haven't had one before," I replied. I was already starting to feel woozy in anticipation of the forthcoming effects.

Eva broke off a piece of the cookie for herself. "Senior year! Woooo!"

Ravi pumped his fist against the roof of the car, yelling, "Best night ever!"

———

"Where the hell are we?"

The three of us stood on a relatively empty street. Brooding trees towered before us, shapeshifting under the faint glow of the streetlights. The wind swooped through the shivering branches and stirred an eerie tune.

"Golden Gate Park," I murmured. "Why here?"

"It's perfect," Ravi beamed. "We have a tonna space to fuck around."

I wanted to run back to the car and lock myself inside, but my body was incapable of independent movement. The edible had taken effect on the Bay Bridge. Since then, my mind had been working in slow motion, as if it had removed itself from my body and was levitating slightly above. I knew I hadn't lost consciousness, but the distance between my mind and body weakened my ability to formulate proper thoughts and speak coherently. My eyes felt as if they were bulging out and sinking back into my head. My mouth was dry, even though I had asked for water on five separate occasions in the car. Ravi said that I was "greening out," and that the worst part of the high would pass soon.

As if he were guiding his two vulnerable children, Ravi held my and Eva's hands and led us into the park. We strolled slowly, silently, our mouths hanging open. I felt like I was trudging through a distant dream. I couldn't believe I was walking through this familiar setting with Ravi and Eva. Two very separate parts of my life were intersecting whether I liked it or not.

By the time I'd entered high school, the concept of the Imagined had become humorous to me, especially when I envisioned how I would explain it to someone else. In a nutshell, I'd met a random stranger who had appeared wherever I'd gone, and with his help, I'd been able to return to my childhood home. Not the actual home, though, but a reconstructed version made from acrylic paint that rained down from a small hole above me. The whole experience sounded ridiculous when I tried to make sense of it. I had written those afternoons off as the product of a child's wild creativity. Given how desperately I'd wished to reunite with Sagar and escape my bleak life in San Francisco, I could have convinced myself of anything.

"What are you thinking about, Akash? You have the craziest expression right now."

"Do I really?" I concentrated on bringing my face back to a neutral position. "Is it gone?"

Ravi laughed. "You're so silly."

Eva abruptly dropped her hand from Ravi's and ceased walking. She covered her face and began to sniffle.

"Eva? What's wrong?" Ravi asked with concern.

She shook her head, unwilling to respond. Ravi wrapped her in a hug and stroked her hair, but I did not budge. I was in no condition to offer sympathy, especially when I couldn't understand why she was crying.

"I shouldn't be this stressed about college, but … but I'm really fucking worried. I feel like my entire life is riding on this decision."

"It's not, Eva," soothed Ravi. "You're gonna be a bomb-ass lawyer no matter where you go."

"What if I go to one of my safety schools and decide I don't want to do law anymore? All the work I've put in throughout high school will have gone to waste."

Ravi comforted her, but I was less inclined to join him the more Eva cried. The edible was heightening my emotions, swinging them out of control. Bitterness clawed its way to my head and pounded against my temples. I was sick of her constantly wallowing in self-pity.

"You should be grateful you have parents that are willing to send you to college," I snapped, sounding harsher than I intended.

Ravi's eyes widened. He motioned for me to tone it down.

"I feel like I'm a burden to them," whispered Eva. "They're so sweet and supportive, and I have no idea what I'm doing."

"None of us do," insisted Ravi.

My balance was unstable. I took a step back without being aware that I wanted to. What did Eva have to be stressed about? Her entire life had been handed to her.

"Akash, you good?" asked Ravi. "Where are you going?"

I realized I was backpedaling away from them. "I'm not comforting her."

"What did you say? You're mumbling."

"Why is she crying right now? It's bullshit!"

Eva lifted her face up from Ravi's chest in shock. Her cheeks were red and blotchy.

Ravi held Eva supportively and glared at me. "That was hella uncalled for."

"You have nothing to complain about!" I fumed. "You have parents that love you and would do anything for you. If you want to change paths, then change paths. If you don't get into your dream school, who the fuck cares?"

"I care!" Eva exclaimed. "I already told you I'm stressed. Some compassion would be nice."

"Compassion for what? People have to go through much worse than this."

"So, what? I'm not allowed to have issues?"

"I need to take a walk." I turned around and bolted in the other direction. My feet had a mind of their own. They were shuffling so fast that I couldn't tell which one was in front of the other.

"Where are you going?" cried Ravi.

"I need some space."

"How will we find you!"

"I have my phone. I'll text you."

"Akash, we know you have a different life than us!" yelled Eva.

I froze.

"Ravi told me how he saw you at the restaurant. We drove by the next day to confirm that you were working there."

My hands were shaking uncontrollably.

"Eva—"

"No, Ravi, he can't just say that shit and take off. Akash, you never share anything with us. You don't tell us about your past or family or any other personal shit. You don't even let us see your house. We respect that you're private, but you can't be angry at us for what we don't know. You can't be mad when you don't let us in."

A hush fell over the group. After a moment's hesitation, I continued to walk away.

"Bro, stay with us!"

"Akash!"

Their voices petered out. Leaving Ravi and Eva in the middle of the park was wrong of me, but I had such an intense desire to be alone that I couldn't bear to be with them. I needed the high to wear off so I wouldn't say anything more that I was incapable of controlling. I rushed down a path that led me deeper into the park. My awareness was dipping in and out, stringing together snapshots of what I was able to see. My heart thumped against my chest, especially after I noticed how thick the mist around me was. I could see a few feet in front of me, but the rest of the path was hazy. Occasionally, a friend group or a couple would walk by. I was overly aware of their perception. When their eyes passed me, the hair on my arms would stand erect with trepidation.

I paused briefly and caught my breath. I was disoriented as to where I was in the park. Tears fell out of my eyes, battling the harsh wind. I went off the designated path and accidentally tripped on a fallen branch. My head slammed on the ground, knocking the air out of my lungs. Dancing black spots impaired my vision. A jungle of bleeding scrapes had formed on my throbbing elbow. I shut my eyes in panic, momentarily forgetting that my phone was safely tucked away in my pocket. I felt so lost, so alone, within the dark web of trees that reminded me of the Town's forest. I cried into my palms and tasted a mixture of blood and dirt. The more I tried to calm myself, the more uninhibited my hopelessness became.

A soft rustle caught my attention. I lifted my face out of my hands and saw movement around one of the faraway trees.

"Hello?" I asked cautiously.

Due to the lack of light, I couldn't properly see what had caused the noise. I speculated that it was an animal, but I needed to get closer to confirm. I heaved myself off the ground. My arms were caked in small twigs and mushy soil.

I slogged toward the unknown shape, my breathing shallow and strained. The trees were pillars of physical support for me. As I neared, the shape slyly darted in the opposite direction. It appeared to be running on two legs, confirming that it was indeed a human and not a forest animal. I stumbled a few feet forward and leaned against the firm bark of a tree. Unable to regain my sense of stability, I vomited on a prickly bush. My abdomen pushed in again and again, expelling more undigested food each time. The third and final wave was so intense that I dropped to my knees. Saliva dripped down the side of my mouth.

My spinning head lolled up, and even though my vision was distorted, I was convinced that the dark, faceless, moving shape was Sagar. There wasn't any evidence to prove my conjecture, but I still felt certain it was him. I wanted to believe that I had left him behind in my childhood, but there I was, an adult, still haunted by the same visions. In that moment, my memories of the Imagined did not humor me at all. I knew exactly where the outline of Sagar was running to and sensed that I was supposed to join. Trembling with unease, I reluctantly picked myself off the ground and followed his trail.

When I arrived at the casting pools, the dense fog mystically separated around the water. The subtle ripples shimmered under the glow of the silver moon. At the end of the middle pool—sitting in the same cross-legged position, wearing the same white kurta—was the Singer.

"Why am I back here?" I whispered.

"You are much taller … and your face has matured," he said, examining me with softness, even pride, in his gaze.

"And you haven't aged at all. I would ask how that's possible, but I know it's just another question about you that won't get answered."

"I've lost track of time, Akash. Tell me … how many years have passed?"

"This isn't happening. The edible is making me see things."

I shut my eyes, hoping the Singer would disappear by the time I opened them. My feeble attempt was useless. The only difference from before was that his expression had soured significantly.

"Are you aware that you've ruined my Imagined?" he said bitterly.

"What?" I asked, surprised by his sharp shift in tone.

"When you were young, you asked me why I was not living with my father. Remember?"

"Sort of. It was a long time ago."

"Your question consumed me. Instilled doubt in me. No matter how much I tried to recollect the forgotten years, it was as if a collection of pages from my life had been torn out and tossed in the dustbin. I lost conviction in my created world. My concentration during my father's lessons wavered, and I did not hold on to details as tightly as I should have. My father's face is slipping away, and it's all because of your inability to accept a gift given to you. My Imagined was perfect before you challenged it."

"I'm not sorry I did. Don't you find it scary how much it's taken over your life? I was too young to understand it back then, but the Imagined is a trap. It doesn't let you move on."

"Say what you will, but it seems like you still need it as much as I do."

"You think I want to go back?" I muttered angrily.

"You've returned to me, haven't you?"

I was silent.

"You've always had a choice. You could walk away right now."

The Singer was right. When I'd accepted that the moving shape was Sagar, why had I chosen to follow him? Why hadn't I run in the other direction?

"See, as much as you think you do not need the Imagined, there's a reason you keep returning," he continued. "Like me, you still have an emotional urge to go back."

"I am nothing like you," I spat.

"Answer me this then: are you happy? Or since happiness is fleeting, I should ask: are you fulfilled?"

"That's too broad a question."

"It's a simple yes or no. Are you fulfilled with your life as is? Or is there something still missing? Something deep down you are still searching for?"

Buried flashes from my childhood, memories I tried to pretend meant nothing to me, erupted from their tight encasement. Sagar's sweaty purple shirt on a hot day, Harsh Kaka's fragrant cooking, Suhail Mama tossing a ball in his bedroom, my Aaji brushing her long hair, Vaishu Mavshi stroking my mother's face.

The Singer smiled smugly at my hesitation. "I thought so. I will forgive you for what you said the last time we met. You are older now, so I'm willing to take you back as a pupil. Take a seat, and we can enter the Imagined together."

I heard faint voices calling out my name. Ravi and Eva were close, but they sounded like they were passing the casting pools.

"You're wrong about me," I forced out.

"Answer my question then. Are you fulfilled?"

I thought about laughing with Ravi and Eva on our hill, the intimacy I'd shared with Luke in his bedroom, the courage I'd felt when Mrs. Suárez told me she believed in my talent. These were moments in my present life that rooted me. I didn't want to be haunted by the Town forever when I had enough to propel my life forward. I had to let go once and for all.

"I am. I don't need the Imagined anymore."

The Singer grimaced. "Even if you leave now, I guarantee that you will be back."

I retreated as the mist folded in front of me and enshroud-ed the Singer. I sprinted in the direction of my friends' voices and burst out onto an open pathway. I saw the two of them cupping their mouths and yelling my name.

"I'm here!" I shouted.

They turned around and ran toward me. Ravi crushed me in a hug. "Dude, don't scare us like that!"

"I'm sorry," Eva sniffled, joining our embrace. "What I said was horrible."

"You have nothing to apologize for," I replied. "I'm the one who's sorry. I can't believe I took off like that."

"I'm just glad you're safe. I'm never taking Ravi's edibles again."

My head rested between theirs. "I don't want to be any-where else but here."

———

During the drive back to Fremont, I was the closest I'd ever been to telling Ravi and Eva about Sagar. I decided to start with a smaller step toward honesty by giving Ravi my real address. When Ravi parked on my street, he and Eva exited the car and embraced me once again.

"We love you, bro."

"Seriously."

I ambled toward the guest house with a wide grin until I remembered the argument I'd had with my mother earlier that night. As annoyed as I was, I felt guilty for having left her on a tense note. There were other ways I could have expressed a desire to be independent without having shoved her loneli-ness in her face. I should have been grateful she even wanted to spend time with me.

I slowly opened the door, ready to apologize, but the lights were off. I assumed she was sleeping, but when I tiptoed inside, I noticed the bed was empty. A thin strip of yellow light emerged from the bottom crack of our bathroom door. My mother's muffled voice seeped out in short, nervous fragments. I wondered who she was speaking to, especially at such a late hour.

I placed my keys and wallet down on the empty counter. I hesitated for a moment. Something felt amiss.

Nikhil's business card. I'd tossed it on the counter before leaving. Where had it gone? I bent down to the floor to see if it had fallen, but it wasn't there either. A mellow, airy giggle emerged from the bathroom. I rose slowly and pieced together who was on the other end of the line. Half of me wanted to pull at my hair in exasperation, while the other half wanted to laugh at the irony of the role reversal. The night I resolved to progress past our dark past, my mother plunged herself right back into it.

CHAPTER 22

DINNER WITH NIKHIL

THE PHONE CALL didn't last much longer. By the time my mother surfaced from the bathroom, I'd just managed to slip under the bed covers. She curled up beside me and whispered my name, but I pretended to be asleep. The next morning, neither of us acknowledged the evening spent apart. We carried on with our usual dialogue as if we hadn't argued. I anticipated my mother would bring up the call eventually. It wasn't normal for her to keep secrets from me. I didn't want to be the first to bring Nikhil's name up, since I wasn't even sure she'd spoken to him. Besides, after that night, I didn't stumble in on any more private calls. I reassured myself that I had jumped to conclusions too quickly. My mother could have disposed of the business card or tucked it away somewhere I hadn't seen. The call could have been with anyone else.

I would have continued believing these alternate theories, but a few weeks later, in early February, my mother confirmed my suspicions. We were lounging on the couch, reading. I was immersed in a manga comic Luke had lent me.

"Aku, I want to ask you something," my mother said, setting her book down.

"Hm?"

"You know how you suggested that I call Nikhil? I thought about what you said and decided it was a good idea. I spoke to him briefly, and well, he wants us to meet him for dinner."

"What? When?"

"This Friday. You don't have a shift then, right?"

"No, but—"

"He's already found a restaurant in SF."

"Mama, are you sure you want to do this?"

"You were the one that suggested we meet," she said pointedly.

"I'm not sure it's a good idea anymore. Do you really want to bring everything up again?"

"I appreciate your concern, but I'm an adult. I can handle seeing him. So much time has passed, and didn't he mention he doesn't stay in the Town anymore? This dinner would just be three old friends catching up."

"If you say so."

"Should I tell him we're coming?"

After my pledge to myself on the edible, I wanted to advise her to forget about Nikhil and close that chapter of our lives. But this was the first time in Fremont my mother was taking initiative to meet someone besides Nabeela Aunty. She was expectantly waiting for my answer, and I couldn't bring myself to let her down. It was only one dinner after all.

I shrugged, and my mother affectionately squeezed my arm.

The night of the dinner, my mother spent an hour trying on dresses and curling her hair. Nikhil was taking us out to a trendy Japanese fusion restaurant. My mother instructed me to wear my most formal attire, but the best I could do was a maroon button-up and khakis. As calm and confident as my mother appeared, I was certain she was as tense as I was to meet Nikhil. He was irrevocably connected to the incident at the station. We'd run away from him as much as we'd run away from everyone else in our family. I hoped seeing him wouldn't reopen old wounds, especially for my mother. I could figure out a way to navigate through my own feelings, but seeing my mother crushed would be much tougher to handle.

On the train ride to San Francisco, my mother and I were huddled together in the last row of our empty compartment. The solemn, dark blues of dusk hovered over the passing houses.

"Doesn't this remind you of when we used to go to Manhattan?" my mother asked.

"A bit," I replied, surprised that she was bringing up a memory from our time in the Town, and even more shocking, a memory that involved my father.

"You were so tiny back then. It's cliché, I know, but you've grown up in the blink of an eye, Aku. Looking at you now makes me feel ancient."

"You're only thirty-six, Mama."

"I know, but I feel older than that."

I yawned and rubbed my eyes.

"Tired, baby?"

"Yeah. I had a late shift yesterday."

"You shouldn't work such long hours. It's not good for you."

I didn't want to rehash an argument we'd already had many times. My mother refused to admit that I needed to work, but my additional earnings ensured that we were not just scraping by paycheck to paycheck. Nevertheless, this wasn't the night to engage.

"I'll ask Yusuf Uncle to reduce my hours."

I yawned again, and my mother patted her shoulder. "Take some rest. I'll wake you up when we reach."

I leaned my head against her shoulder. She wrapped an arm around me and kissed my forehead. Only in my mother's embrace did I feel completely at ease, like I could surrender every worry and affliction that had troubled me over my lifetime. It didn't matter how old or tall I'd become. Her touch would always feel familiar. The scent of her perfume—daisies and lavender and fresh-cut grass—filled my nose, and I relaxed into a light slumber as the train rumbled on.

———

The restaurant was a block away from Market Street. The ambience was upscale, with echoes of smooth jazz trickling in from hidden speakers, and lighting so sparse that I had to squint to find the hostess's table. The other restaurant-goers were wearing fancy cocktail attire: blazers, glittering dresses, stilettos, etc. My mother and I, even in our best attempt to spruce up, were underdressed among this crowd.

The hostess led us to our table in the back corner. Nikhil was already there, browsing through his phone. His sleeves were rolled up, and his jacket hung on the back of his chair. He shot up when he saw us.

"Hi, Mahi. Akash."

"Hello," my mother replied softly.

Nikhil pecked my mother's cheek and gave me a handshake. We sat down and awkwardly smiled at each other.

"Should we figure out what to order?" he asked, handing us menus. "I've heard their corn fritters are good."

We silently scanned the starters, though I doubt any of us were processing what was listed. We stole glances at each other when it seemed the other two weren't looking. When the waiter came by to take our order, my mother and I said that we would have whatever Nikhil was having. Nikhil ordered for the table, and the waiter left with our menus. Without any more excuses to delay conversation, Nikhil dove forward with the first question.

"So … the Bay Area? How did you end up here?"

I'd assumed he and my mother had discussed our move on their call, but I realized then that the truth would have required her to reveal how she'd abandoned him for my father. Sensing that my mother was unwilling to answer, I jumped in and said, "It's a long story."

"I'm sure. Maybe for another time."

"And you? How did you end up …?"

"Looking like this?" he said, glancing down at his corporate attire. "It surprised me too."

"What do you do for work?"

"Consulting. I'm going on three years now. Do you know anything about it?"

"Not really."

"Basically, companies hire us if they're having an issue they want to outsource. We work with them for a bit, propose a strategy, and then move on to the next client. It's nice not having any long-term commitments," he said, glancing at my mother. "There's a lot of late nights, and the travel isn't great, but so far it's proven to be good work."

I was still wrapping my head around how the demure young adult who was content working at his father's electronics shop for the rest of his life had become this polished man in a suit. But watching Nikhil's eyes continuously drift over to my mother, I understood that the answer was simple: a broken heart could force even the steadiest person to seek out a new identity.

"When did you move out of the Town?" I asked, prompting my mother to flinch.

"Soon after you … um … left. Business wasn't going well for my father, so he closed the store. We moved out to Philadelphia, where my older sister lives. I reenrolled in community college, transferred to Penn State, and finished in two-and-a-half years. Been based in Philly ever since."

"Have you been back to the Town?" I was simultaneously hoping and dreading that he would mention the rest of our family.

"Akash …" my mother said warily.

Nikhil grimaced. "I've never had a reason to. I wasn't close to that many people. I stayed in the Town after high school primarily to help my father, and then later for … So, no, I haven't been back. Mahi mentioned on the phone that you haven't either?"

"Nope."

"That's a shame."

We were dancing around the subjects we wanted to address. My mother was absently staring at the adjacent table as if she was tuning out our conversation, but I could tell she was listening intently. The waiter brought out our starters. Nikhil waited for him to leave before speaking again. His eyes were now unabashedly fixed on my mother.

"Mahi."

My mother blinked, surprised to be directly addressed. "Yes?"

"You look beautiful tonight."

She blushed. "Thank you."

"I need to say something that I couldn't bring myself to on the phone. I'm afraid I won't have the courage later tonight, and if we don't see each other again, then I'll always regret not telling you."

"O-okay. What do you want to say?"

"You asked on our call if I hated you. I have to confess that I would have answered yes a few years ago."

"Maybe this isn't the best—"

"No, please, let me finish. I was very angry when you disappeared. I buried myself in work because it was the only way for me not to constantly sit in resentment. You know I don't usually have intense emotions."

My mother paled. "Nikhil, I—"

Nikhil shook his head. "I'm not saying this to get you to apologize. It took me some time to understand why you left without telling me, but once I came to terms with it, I wasn't angry anymore. I thought about my mom and what she must have been going through when she decided to elope with another man. It was probably one of the hardest decisions she'd had to make. But running away was the only option she saw to preserve her own happiness. She wouldn't have been able to move on from a life she felt trapped in unless she cut off contact.

"And just like my mom, you did what you needed to do to free yourself. I was the reason you left Sagar on that platform. I will be a reminder of that horrible day for the rest of your life, and the last thing I want to do is cause you any more pain. So, I want to tell you that I understand. I understand completely."

My mother sprang out of her chair. "I have to use the restroom."

"Mahi, I didn't mean to upset you. I won't talk about it anymore if you don't want me to."

She wavered.

"Can I say one last thing? And then we can forget about this topic?"

My mother didn't reply, but she didn't move either.

"No one was able to see them after he passed. There was no funeral, and they never seemed to leave the house. I'm not sure how they were getting food or anything. Obviously, I don't know what's happened to them since, but my father is still in touch with a couple people from the Town. If you want, I can try to find out more."

My mother was silent.

"That's it, then. That's all I have to say."

"I'll be back in a few minutes," my mother mumbled. She turned the corner and headed toward the restrooms.

Once she left, Nikhil motioned for me to begin eating. I started scooping out the garlic edamame.

"What grade are you in, Akash?"

"Twelfth."

"Time really flies by, huh? Does that mean you're applying to college now?"

I was about to answer with my usual vague response that I was still figuring it out, but the truth was that I'd been considering the colleges Mrs. Suárez had suggested, specifically the one in Florida. I'd brainstormed what I would write my personal statement on, though I hadn't actually begun the application. Since I had a prospect in mind, I wanted to avoid another infuriating conversation where I was prodded on my next steps if not college.

"Actually, I'm considering one school."

"That's fantastic! Which one?"

"It's an art college in Florida."

"Art, huh? Following in your father's footsteps?"

"God, I hope not."

Nikhil looked over at the hallway leading to the restrooms, then leaned forward to me. "Can I ask you something? Did you guys come to the Bay for him? I remember that he moved here all those years ago. Is it connected, or am I just crazy?"

I didn't want to interfere in his and my mother's business, and I doubted the truth would have provided him solace. "I can tell you that he's not involved in our lives now. The rest, you should probably discuss with my mom."

"Discuss what with me?" my mother asked as she slipped back into her seat.

Nikhil leaned back, studying my expression. "Nothing, nothing. Just talking about Akash's Florida college."

I stiffened, regretting my thoughtlessness. I shouldn't have mentioned the college to Nikhil when my mother and I hadn't even discussed it yet.

My mother's bewilderment was written all over her face. "Akash's what?"

"I'm thinking about applying to a school in Florida," I said hesitantly.

"Florida? Why? I thought you wanted to stay here after high school."

"It'll be good for him," said Nikhil. "College changed my life."

My mother ignored his remarks and addressed me directly. "Why didn't you tell me? We should have discussed it."

"It's not that big a deal," I muttered, even though I knew it would be for her. She was the main reason why I hadn't started my application yet. Me leaving for Florida either meant that she'd have to stay in the Bay Area by herself or move once again to an unfamiliar place. Neither option would please her. On multiple occasions, I'd been close to letting go of the idea entirely. But then, Luke's voice would pop into my head and remind me that she was an adult who was responsible for herself. I had to live my life the way I wanted to.

Still, I feared my mother's response. Fortunately, all she said was, "We'll talk more about it later."

Nikhil reached for the serving spoon. "Here. Let me serve you."

When Nikhil started scooping out the edamame, I saw a glint of something shiny on his finger. I tried to make out what it was, but the lighting was too dim. Nikhil caught me staring.

"Oh. I probably should have mentioned this earlier," he said, holding his hand up. As I suspected, he was wearing a silver wedding band on his ring finger.

"You're …"

"Married, yes. For about a year now. Her name is Sarah. We work at the same firm."

My mother tucked her hair behind her ear. "That's, wow, I'm happy for you, Nikhil."

"Thanks. It's nice that we're in the same field. We understand each other's crazy schedules, so we don't get mad when we have to spend time apart."

"Was it love at first sight?" asked my mother, forcing a smile.

"Don't know about that," said Nikhil sheepishly. "We worked on a few cases together. She asked me out early on, but I was a bit reluctant."

"Why?"

"I, um, hadn't been with anyone in a while. My dad actually convinced me to go on a date with her. He was worried that I wasn't putting myself out there enough. He even tried to get me on dating websites, but this seemed like a better option."

"What's she like?"

"She's … she's nice."

My mother nodded. "That's great."

Nikhil took a bite of his food. "This is good. It reminds me of—"

"—that sushi bistro in the City, right? I was thinking the same thing. Although that place was a dump compared to this."

"Do you remember the one time we went there and almost ran into the Mahmoods?"

"How could I forget? Of course that had to be the one time they left the Town for a meal."

"I don't know why we thought we were safe going on dates in the City," said Nikhil, grinning.

My mother chuckled. "You had a car too. We could have driven anywhere out of a five-mile radius."

"The sneaking around seems kind of ridiculous, looking back. What were we afraid of?"

"Lots of things I did back then seem silly now," said my mother, her expression softening.

"But we had fun together, didn't we? I hope that Mahi isn't completely gone."

"We did have fun."

They stared at each other, thin smiles on their lips, remembering moments that I wasn't included in. They searched each other's faces for the good times they'd left behind, for the names and places and experiences they'd cut themselves off from. Nikhil brought the Town back to my mother without her having to return, and she did the same for him. We continued to eat, but the awkwardness between them disappeared. They chatted openly for the remainder of the evening. Before we left, Nikhil said that he would be in San Francisco every two to three weeks for the case he was on. He stressed that he wanted to see us again.

My mother tried to suppress a huge grin the entire ride home. Her dimples, which I'd forgotten she had, flared up with delight. She complimented Nikhil at various instances throughout the ride, noting how well he cleaned up and how gracious it was for him to have treated us to dinner. When we returned home, my mother was in such a good mood that she completely forgot to address the college issue. She took off her makeup, changed, and slept soundly.

Meanwhile, I opened up my secondhand laptop and clicked on the application portal. I'm not entirely sure what convinced me to start my essay. It could have been the relief of seeing my mother revive a friendship on her own, or my admiration of how far Nikhil had progressed in his career. His trajectory motivated me to dream beyond my stagnant life. I didn't want to stay working at my restaurant job and living in the tiny guest house forever. I too could leave and begin a new chapter. So, with a burst of excitement, I took a chance on my future.

CHAPTER 23

THE FIGHT

IT WAS UNDENIABLY my fault. I shouldn't have hung out with Ravi and Eva as long as I did, nor should I have tucked my phone away in my pocket. I didn't realize how low the sun was until it was too late. I panicked and asked Ravi to drop me off as quickly as he could at the Fremont BART station. I rushed out of his car and ran up the steps to the platform.

My mother was waiting on a bench, tapping her foot impatiently. "I called you a million times."

"I'm an idiot. I forgot to switch my phone off of silent after school, so none of my alarms went off. Will we make it in time?"

"I don't know. I asked Sana to stall as long as possible."

April had rolled around faster than my mother and I had expected. We'd rarely addressed the topic of Nabeela Aunty's upcoming move in the past months. The date of her departure had seemed far enough away that we'd treated the remaining visits as if there were still many more to be had. My mother had been worse than I in terms of processing the news. Even when Nabeela Aunty had told us the date and time of her flight, my mother hadn't been the least bit fazed. She'd convinced herself that Nabeela Aunty would realize how much effort uprooting her life would be and back out at the last minute.

But the high possibility that we might miss Nabeela Aunty before she boarded her flight finally compelled my mother to accept the imminent change. She was visibly stressed while standing near the edge of the tracks, scouring for an approaching train.

The next steps of our journey were a blur. Somehow, we made it on a train, navigated our way through the enormous airport, and arrived at a crowded security line that snaked through a maze of stanchions. We were on the outskirts of the line, frantically skipping from side to side, looking for any sight of the aunt-niece duo.

"Do you see her?" my mother asked, standing on the tips of her toes. "Sana texted me fifteen minutes ago that they were still waiting in security."

"No," I replied, straining my neck to see past the rows closest to us.

My mother pressed her cellphone against her ear. "Shit. She's not picking up."

I spotted a headscarf near the front of the line and hopped to my left to get a better view. "Wait! There they are!"

Nabeela Aunty and Sana were facing away from us and placing their bags on the conveyer belt. My mother and I frantically waved and shouted their names, but they didn't notice. The countless side conversations of people in line prevented our screams from reaching their ears.

In desperation, my mother attempted to enter the security line. She was immediately stopped by an airport employee standing guard.

"Boarding pass, ma'am."

"I don't have one, but—"

"We require a boarding pass to enter this line."

"I know, but I just need to say goodbye to someone. It'll take one minute."

"I'm sorry. It's against policy."

"Fuck your policy." My mother tried to maneuver past the employee, but he stood his ground.

"Ma'am, I'm going to need you to take a step back unless you want me to call security."

"She's literally right there, you idiot!"

The employee reached for his radio. In order to deescalate the situation, I tugged my mother's arm.

"Mama, just step out of the line," I urged. "He's not going to let us through."

"Don't touch me," she snarled, aggressively pushing me away. She screamed Nabeela Aunty's name once more, but her voice was hoarse and inaudible over the rows of people separating us from them.

Nabeela Aunty and Sana collected their bags on the other end of the belt. Sana outstretched an arm for Nabeela Aunty to hold on to, and they shuffled out of security and away from our line of sight. We'd failed to say goodbye in time.

My mother blankly stared at the spot where Nabeela Aunty had been a moment ago.

"Mama, I'm so, so sorry. I feel horrible."

Her expression was unreadable. I anxiously prepared myself for a violent, incensed reaction. I was ready for her to blow up at me. I deserved it.

"Mama, please say something."

"Doesn't matter. It's over now," she said reticently. "Let's go."

She turned around and strolled out of the airport terminal. I hesitantly followed her, unnerved by her lack of emotion. I was torn as to whether I should continue apologizing, offer support, or do something else entirely. She'd always been vocal with me, sometimes to the point where her honesty had brought me great discomfort. As difficult as it was to hear my mother's pain and pessimism, I preferred her communicating with me over silence. I studied every inch of her face for an indication of her inner feelings, but there wasn't a single clue to grasp on to. No line or curve indicated anger, sorrow, or any other emotion. Nabeela Aunty's departure had tipped her into a state of complete apathy.

Rather than returning to Fremont, my mother and I took a cab to Union Square. We were supposed to meet Nikhil again for dinner. Since the first meal at the Japanese restaurant, we'd seen him every subsequent time he'd been in SF. It was becoming a bimonthly tradition as we headed toward our fifth dinner with him.

"Are you sure you still want to meet up tonight?" I asked. "I'm sure he'll understand if we cancel."

"It's fine," said my mother. "We're here already."

We exited the cab and waited to cross the street. I glanced at my phone and saw that Yusuf Uncle was calling me. I stepped away from my mother and answered.

"Hello? Hello!" screamed Yusuf Uncle. Rowdy voices flooded around him. I had to hold the phone slightly away from my ear to preserve my hearing.

"What's up, Uncle?"

"Akash! Can you hear me!"

I rolled my eyes. "Yes, Uncle, I can hear you."

"Akash, son, please come! It's madness over here!"

"I'm off today."

"I know, but I have to help out at the other location! Luke is the only one here."

I bit my lip. My mother motioned for me to cross with her.

"It's a little tough for me to come right now."

"Please, son! I'm begging you! I will double your pay for tonight, and you can eat whatever you want from the back after."

I wavered, but finally said, "Okay, I'll come. It's going to take me about an hour to get there."

"Thank you, son, thank you! Luke will be very happy to hear. I'm leaving my keys with him to lock up."

Before I could respond, Yusuf Uncle cut the call. I chuckled, picturing a distressed Luke managing the packed restaurant by himself.

A few weeks earlier, a teen influencer had discovered Luke's Instagram account of Yusuf Uncle. He'd reposted a few of the photos, and within two nights, the page had gained over five thousand followers. Within a week, Yusuf Uncle amassed a loyal fanbase who named his flushed, wide-eyed expression as #theuncleface. One follower commented that they recognized Yusuf Uncle and knew where he was based. The fate of the restaurant transformed instantly. What once used to be a low-profile establishment now had lines crawling out of the building. Yusuf Uncle wasn't aware that he was a social media sensation. Although he was perplexed when customers asked for selfies, he relished the sudden burst of business.

I headed back to my mother. "Slight change of plans. We need to go back. Yusuf Uncle asked me to come in today."

"Didn't you call out?"

"Yeah, but it's an emergency."

"That's his issue to figure out. We've already committed to dinner."

"Mama, he really needs the help. I promised him I would go."

"I don't care. It's rude to cancel on Nikhil last minute."

"We'll see him next time he comes."

She gazed at the crosswalk, contemplating for a moment. "Another option is that we split up. You could head back, and I'll stay here."

"Wouldn't it be better if we just rescheduled? Today's already been a rollercoaster."

"I told you I'm fine. The more I think about it, splitting up seems like the best thing for us to do. You'll be fine getting back by yourself?"

"Yeah, but—"

She kissed my cheek. "Great. Text me when you get to Fremont."

"What time are you going to be back?" I asked, but my mother was already scampering across the crosswalk, out of earshot.

I wondered if I'd made a mistake by agreeing to her plan. My mother had been getting more comfortable with Nikhil each progressive dinner. They would plunge themselves deep within their private memories, often to the point where they'd entirely forget that I was present. She was more open to talking about the Town with Nikhil than she'd ever been with me. Since he was unaware of our lives after the move, she could drift back to her previous self without confronting any of the aftermath. Her eyes were bright while speaking to him, and she would laugh vivaciously. On occasion, she and Nikhil would lean so close toward each other that their arms would be only inches away from touching. I suspected that their feelings for each other were reviving, but since I'd been a pseudo-chaperone at each dinner, nothing had been able to progress even if they'd wanted it to.

Since my father's disappearance, my mother's trust in men had significantly waned. She'd ceased entertaining passing flirtations. If a man tried to talk to her, she would politely end the conversation and walk away before he could ask her anything else. But the situation with Nikhil was different. Their trust in each other had been solidified years before. Rather than start with someone from scratch, which I knew she wasn't willing to do, my mother simply had to conjure up established feelings.

Even so, I reassured myself on the way to Fremont that I had nothing to be worried about. My mother knew that Nikhil was married. She had seen the ring the same time I had. She'd become so cautious about allowing people into her life that I couldn't picture her making any rash decisions just because I wasn't there. The person she'd been in the Town would have done what she wanted without regard for consequences, but the person she was in Fremont would never act impulsively. I surrendered my mistrust and relaxed into my seat.

The time I had to unwind was brief. My mouth opened in disbelief when I saw the enormous line outside Yusuf Uncle's restaurant. I hurried off the bus, swerved past the waiting customers, and bolted toward the register, where a frenzied Luke was punching in orders.

"Let me take over," I said, grabbing my apron from under the counter.

He collected scattered order receipts and bounced over to the kitchen. "You're my hero."

The shift whisked by without a second of rest. I was taking orders, passing notes to the kitchen, handing out to-go boxes, and denying requests to see Yusuf Uncle all at the same time. I didn't realize how exhausted I was until Luke shooed out the last customer and changed the sign from open to closed. He made us each a burger and put the leftover fries on a large platter. We collapsed on the same side of a corner booth and scarfed down the food.

"What a day," he groaned, stretching his legs to the opposite bench.

"Seriously," I said.

"I swear I'm aboutta quit. Panera should be hiring, right?"

"If you leave me, I'll show Yusuf Uncle the account that started this."

"You want me murdered?"

I giggled, continued giggling, and before long, began howling with delirious laughter, convulsing until my side hurt. The fatigue was making me feel deranged, like I was high on Ravi's edible all over again.

Luke grinned. "What's so funny?"

"This … this is … all your fault."

Luke was chuckling alongside me, although he was thrown off by my intense reaction. "What the hell are you saying? I can't understand you."

"Why … did you make that … that goddamn account?" I was coughing from how much laughter was pouring out of me. "You … you set us up for disaster."

"I didn't know this was going to happen! You know, a frickin' child got so mad when he realized that Yusuf Uncle wasn't here. He threatened to throw his drink at me if I didn't bring him out!"

"Stop, stop." I clutched my stomach and used my other hand to throw fries at Luke. "I can't laugh anymore. It hurts too much."

Luke threw a handful of fries back at me. "Bitch!"

"Okay, truce, truce. We're gonna have to clean this up."

"Can't handle what you throw, huh?"

His exhilarated eyes sparkled. Even under the painfully ugly overhead lighting, his baby face shone with a handsome radiance.

"I'm glad I'm doing this job with you, Luke. Seriously. You make it ten million times better."

Luke blushed and looked down at his hands. "Damn."

I picked up my plate and used a couple of napkins to clean the crumbs off the table. I turned back to Luke. "Hey, so—"

He kissed me gently. His lips were soft and warm, exactly like his tender personality. Surprisingly, I didn't feel shy. The kiss was comfortable, like the familiar embrace of a relative.

And yet, I pulled away. My inhibition was stronger than my desire to succumb.

Luke touched his lips in embarrassment. "Shit."

"I'm sorry."

"No. I should apologize. I misinterpreted."

"You didn't. I was just … a little caught off guard."

"If I'm being honest, I've been wanting to do that for a while."

"Luke, I don't want you to think … it's just, my life is messy. I don't know if I'm ready to bring someone into it like that yet."

His face drooped. "Gotcha."

"I value you so much."

He stood up and cleared his throat. "We should probably clean up."

"Uh, sure. We can do that."

Without looking at me, he said in a shaky voice, "And could we just forget about this?"

I wanted to reach up and pull him back to me, but instead, I replied, "Yeah, okay."

—

I thought about Luke the entire bus ride home, imagining what could have happened if I'd leaned into the kiss. I asked myself what was holding me back, why I was this afraid of intimacy. No one was preventing me from letting Luke or anyone else in; the only one inhibiting me was me. I was conflicted on how to proceed, especially since I didn't want to lose him as a friend. Luke would not act spiteful—I was sure of that—but the failed kiss would hang around us as we joked and laughed in the future.

When I returned to the guest house, I was surprised to find it empty. I had been so preoccupied with Luke that I'd forgotten about my mother's dinner with Nikhil. The clock showed that it was eleven thirty. When the two of us went for dinner together, we would arrive home by ten thirty latest. I reassured myself that she must have lost track of time. I tried calling her, but my ineffective attempts went straight to voicemail. I sat on the bed in darkness, waiting for her return.

One hour passed. Then two. I left her a dozen voicemails and texts but heard nothing back. Horrible situations formed in my mind, becoming more gruesome and violent with each passing hour. What if someone had harmed her on the ride home? What if an unruly car had hit her while she'd been walking? Even though I was exhausted, worry kept me wide awake. I searched for Nikhil's business card, but I couldn't find it anywhere. My mother would usually coordinate the dinners with him, so I didn't have his number saved. I dialed the number of the restaurant they'd met at, but it was closed by the time I called. There weren't any friends of hers that I could get in touch with for help. This was solely my issue to deal with. I considered going to the police station, debating if it was too drastic a measure to take. I entered 9-1-1 into my phone a few times. My finger hovered over the call button but never pressed down.

It was 3:07 a.m. when the doorknob rattled. I shot up from the bed right as my mother stumbled in.

"Mama! What the hell happened?"

I switched on the light. My mother squinted and shielded her eyes with one hand. Her hair was tousled, her makeup faded. She shifted uncomfortably and straightened her top. Her hand lowered, revealing her guilty expression. I knew instantly what had occurred when I saw her appearance.

"Dinner went late," she mumbled.

My voice was frighteningly low. "No text. No call. Nothing."

"My phone was off. Just like yours seems to be all the time now." She walked to the bathroom. I followed her. She was about to close the door, but I used my palm to keep it open.

"What's that supposed to mean?"

"I stayed out late one night. You do this constantly. It's not a big deal."

After the trip Ravi, Eva, and I had made to Golden Gate Park, the three of us had been spending more time with each other. Some of our hangouts had gone late, but in my mind, these were two incomparable situations. I was a teenager, spending time with my friends. My mother was an adult, staying out late with a married man.

"I was terrified something had happened to you," I said.

She began to wipe her makeup off. "I'm tired, Akash. It's been a long day."

"So, that's your answer? Dinner went late?"

"Yes. Can you leave the bathroom now?"

"Last I checked, the restaurant closed at eleven."

Her hand froze. "Akash …"

"Mama, he's married."

"It's none of your business."

"He's married."

"I'm an adult, Akash. Don't forget that. I shouldn't have to explain myself to you."

"He's married."

"It's Nikhil!"

"Who is now married."

Her eyes narrowed. "Akash, I'm telling you to stay out of it. I'm your mother. That's it. I don't want to talk about this anymore."

She attempted to shut the door again, but I kept my hand firm.

"Just because you say it's over doesn't mean that it is. If this is about Nabeela Aunty leaving—"

She threw the makeup wipe down and pushed past me into the bedroom. "This has nothing to do with that."

"I understand if you're sad. I am too."

She spun toward me. "For one night, I felt like myself again! I haven't felt this way in years. Why can't you be happy for me?"

"Because, Mama, he's committed to another woman."

"What we have is different. It's a deeper connection."

"Doesn't matter. He's moved on. Unless he told you he's getting a divorce, he's eventually going to get up one day and leave. Just like Dad. You're setting yourself up to get hurt, and I'll have to be the one to pick up the pieces."

"How dare you."

"It's the truth."

"How dare you! I've never asked for any emotional support from you."

I laughed in disbelief. "Are you kidding me? Mama, since we've moved here, I've had to listen to every single depressed thought of yours, and I've done it because I know I'm the only one you have."

She held up a finger. "Akash, you are crossing a line."

"No, I'm not," I replied, impassioned. "These are things I should have said a long time ago. For years, I felt guilty spending time away from you because I knew that meant you would be alone."

She sat on the couch and rubbed her temples. "Enough."

"I'm eighteen now, and I'm still afraid to tell you when I'm hanging out with my friends. Isn't that messed up?"

"You want to leave? Fine! Go do whatever you want, Akash!"

"Who else will you have then? Dad left. Nabeela Aunty left. I'm the only one that stayed. I couldn't even picture myself going away to college because I was scared of abandoning you. But you know what? I've applied to the one in Florida, and I hope to God I get in so I can leave this shithole," I said, waving at the bare, stuffy room we shared.

"I've tried to provide you the best life I possibly can," said my mother. "Don't you know how horrible it makes me feel knowing that these are the conditions we live in? Everything I've done has been for you. Moving here was for you."

"Don't even start with that."

"Do I have to remind you why we came here? What happened at the station?"

"Mama—"

"I don't want to bring it up, but you're giving me no choice. We moved to protect you."

"Stop saying that! It's not true!"

"You left him alone on that platform."

"No, Mama, you left him!"

"I told you to stay with him. I told you to watch each other."

"I was a child!" I screamed, tears streaming down my face. "He was your responsibility! You should have been looking after him. You should have been grown enough to know not to leave two kids in a crowd."

My mother kept shaking her head. "I'm not saying I'm innocent. But we both share fault."

"For years, I believed you. I was young enough to trust anything you said. I blamed myself because you told me to. But I finally know that his death was not my doing. Our family did not split up because of me. You manipulated me into sharing your guilt because it made it easier for you. If you had someone who felt as ashamed as you did, you would feel less alone. But I finally see the truth now. I see you for what you are. You're a sick, sick, selfish person!"

My legs trembled from the repressed emotions that were pouring out.

My mother was stunned. Her mouth hung open limply.

"How … how can you say something so cruel? Haven't I proven enough how much I love you?"

"I don't even know if I believe that Vaishu Mavshi and Harsh Kaka said they wanted us gone. I think you were just too much of a coward to face them."

"What happened to my sweet boy? My Aku?" my mother whispered. "Where did he go?"

"I'm going to sleep at a friend's tonight," I muttered. I texted Ravi, the only person I knew who would be awake at a late hour. He responded immediately that I could stay with him. I packed a bag of clothes and toiletries while my mother silently watched me. Without saying goodbye, I stepped outside, slammed the door behind me, and savored the bittersweet taste of fresh air.

CHAPTER 24

MOVING ON

I RECEIVED THE notification during art class. An email message appeared on my phone, informing me that there was an update on my application portal. I excused myself to the restroom and hurried out of the classroom. My fists were blood red from how hard I was squeezing them. After I locked myself inside a stall, I took my phone out again. I nervously pressed the link to the portal. Eva had committed to Georgetown in the past week, and Ravi was deciding between UC Riverside and San Diego State. Hearing them discuss their college decisions had made me more anxious for my own. I was surprised by how desperately I wanted to get in, when less than a year ago, I hadn't planned on applying anywhere.

The sluggish school Wi-Fi was delaying the site from loading. I tugged at my hair in anticipation.

"Come on, come on."

The portal finally appeared. The top of the page had a large yellow banner that read: *Click here to see application update.*

I muttered a quick prayer and opened the decision.

After the last remaining student exited the classroom, I approached Mrs. Suárez's desk. "I have something to tell you."

"Everything okay?" she asked.

"The school in Florida got back to me."

"And?"

I smiled.

She cheered and threw her fists up in the air.

"They gave me a hefty scholarship too. I still have to see if I can manage the rest of the tuition through work-study and loans, but ..."

She clutched my arm. "You don't know how happy this makes me."

"Thank you for believing in me. I wouldn't have applied without your help."

"Oh, please. It's my pleasure. You observe the world in a unique way, Akash. No one can replicate the talent you have. Don't forget that."

I smiled, trying my best to hold back tears.

"Go now before I start crying," she said, shooing me away.

On my way to the bus stop, I wobbled with exaltation. Seeing the decision letter had been even more exhilarating than I'd dreamed it would be. Triumph was a peculiar but affirming emotion, and I recognized that this was the first time since I'd left the Town that I felt proud of myself. It was a liberating feeling. After the years of criticizing and doubting every decision I'd made, I felt fearless. I felt empowered to attack everything else in my life that I previously didn't have the courage to do.

I pulled out my phone and opened my text thread with Luke. I messaged him: *Where you at?*

He responded: *At home. What's up?*

I messaged again: *Can I come over?*

The typing bubble vanished. I feared that my adrenaline had gotten the best of me. A minute later, a new text from him appeared: *For sure.*

I grinned widely and shut my phone off. I decided to drop my backpack off at the guest house before heading over to Luke's. It was on the way, and plus, I figured that I should tell my mother about my admissions result earlier rather than later. A week had passed since our fight. I was still sleeping over at Ravi's and had only returned to the guest house once to gather more clothes. I'd made the visit as brief as possible, procuring what I'd needed and leaving immediately after. My mother hadn't acknowledged me while I'd been there, which angered me further since it seemed like she was waiting for me to apologize first. I refused to give in.

When I neared the entrance to our place, I heard a slow, romantic ghazal coming from inside. The song was old, and the vocalist's voice was grainy and distorted. I opened the door to find my mother lying on the couch, staring vacantly at the ceiling, dressed in the nightgown that looked exactly like my Aaji's. The song was playing from her phone.

I dropped my backpack off at the base of the bed and went to wash my hands in the bathroom. My mother lowered the volume of her music.

"Today is your Ajoba's birthday," she said in a hollow voice. "This was one of his favorite songs. He used to play it to the three of us to help us fall asleep. There was another one he loved, but I can't remember now what it was called."

I fixed my hair in the mirror, pretending not to listen.

"Did I ever tell you how he passed away? The truth, I mean?"

I stiffened.

"It was the middle of winter, and he'd been missing for two weeks. It wasn't odd for him to disappear, but he usually came back within a day or two. The whole community searched tirelessly for him. Bhaskar Uncle was the one who found him deep within the forest, dead from hypothermia."

"Why are you telling me this?"

"I'm not sure. I've been thinking about him a lot today. You know, Vaishu wasn't fond of him. She hated that he would vanish without telling us where he was going. It didn't bother me, though, because he always returned a renewed man. Maybe it was naïve of me not to question where he went, but I loved how he doted on me after he returned. No matter what horrible things I said or did, no matter how bratty I was, he would never discipline me. Everything was forgiven in his eyes … or, at least, that's what I believed."

I exited the bathroom. "Mama, I still don't understand why you're talking about this now."

"People thought he'd lost his way, but he knew the forest even better than you did. The strangest thing about his death was that he was found sitting in a relaxed position, slumped against a tree. His face was calm. His eyes were closed. His lips even had a hint of a smile on them. From afar, he looked like he'd just dozed off. And I wonder now … he couldn't have been in such a peaceful state unless he knew exactly what was going to happen to him. Unless he finally realized that he would be happiest if he was permanently away from us. Away from me."

"I got into college today. The one in Florida. I haven't accepted it yet, but I'm thinking about it."

My mother nodded. "I want you to be happy more than anything in the world, Aku. I really do."

"Great," I said sarcastically, heading to the front door.

"I called Nikhil and told him that we shouldn't see each other anymore. That our night together was a mistake."

My hand hovered above the doorknob. "What did he say?"

"He didn't try to fight it," she said, confusion plastered on her face. "Not even a little. He said he'd already known deep down I was going to run away again."

I opened the door.

"Aku, baby," she murmured. "Stay with me. Please."

If she'd made this same request a few months ago, I would have immediately canceled my plans, run to the couch, and spent the rest of the afternoon comforting her. But I couldn't give in as easily anymore. I was tired of the constant suffocation that came from being her emotional crutch. In that moment, I was standing at a crossroads, forced to choose between her needs and my own.

In order not to be swayed in my decision, I left the guest house without glancing again in her direction.

———

Jada examined me with a suspicious stare. I nervously smiled and tried to see if Luke was somewhere behind her, but she'd cracked the door open ever so slightly, making room only for her head to poke out.

"Don't you remember me?" I asked.

She raised one eyebrow. "Maybe. Maybe not."

Luke's voice rang from inside. "Jada, let him in!"

Jada huffed and opened the door. She used two of her fingers to gesture that she was keeping an eye on me. I nodded very seriously before walking down the corridor to Luke's room.

He was sprawled out on his bed in a tank top and shorts. He sat up when he saw me. "Yo."

"I want to tell you something."

"Actually, me too."

"Oh, really?"

"Yeah, but you go first."

"O-okay," I stammered, unsure where to begin. "Could I sit down?"

He motioned to the bed and moved over to his desk chair. I sat down on his covers. Soft light shined on Luke through the shutters of his bedroom window, gleaming against his broad shoulders.

"You're scaring me," he said.

"I know we promised not to talk about that night in the restaurant—"

"I'm sorry again about that."

"No, no, don't be. What I'm trying to say is that … I mean …" I was losing my words. I took a deep breath in. "Luke, I keep people at a distance because I'm afraid of revealing certain parts of myself and my past. But when I'm with you, I don't want to be scared anymore. You bring hope into my life, something I've been missing for years. And, well, I guess, what I'm trying to say is …"

He smirked. "Oh, so, now *you* wanna kiss *me*, huh?"

"Yeah. I really do."

He rolled his chair close to me. We slowly leaned into each other until our lips touched. He broke away momentarily. "I was scared for a sec you were going to reject me all over again."

I pulled him back and ran my hands through his hair. My heart was pounding in my chest as I lifted his shirt and he lifted mine, as he pushed me down on his train-themed covers and looked into my eyes. The bed was cramped, and we were awkwardly pressed against each other in order to fit. But neither of us cared. I wrapped my arms around his back, he draped his leg over mine, and we fervidly discovered the parts of each other we hadn't seen before. I was as carefree as a teenager should be, relishing the thrill and clumsiness of inexperienced intimacy.

And after we finally put our clothes back on and kissed each other goodbye, I walked out of his house to a golden sky. The sun was about to set, casting brilliant light on the roofs along his street. A gentle wind ruffled my hair. I closed my eyes and rocked back and forth, remembering Luke's touch. His street was quiet except for the melodious hum of a sprinkler. I couldn't stop smiling while walking to the bus stop. I felt grateful to be alive, to be free, to experience desire and be desired by someone I trusted. For a moment, the world was at peace, and so was I.

———

I went back to the guest house instead of to Ravi's place. Being with Luke had marginally dissipated my anger toward my mother. I realized how harsh I was being, and though I needed to set strict emotional boundaries with her, I did not want to continue this dreadful separation of ours forever. Our relationship was complicated, but she'd been the only constant in my life, the only one who knew my life inside out—both the good and ugly parts of it. I was ready to begin making amends, even if at a small capacity.

I entered to darkness, which startled me since the evening was young. It was too early for my mother to have fallen asleep. My eyes were adjusting to the absence of light when I heard a quiet whimper. I pivoted toward the sound and saw her lying on the floor next to the kitchenette.

Her body was limp. In her hand was a thin razor, glinting from the last streaks of dusk that entered through the window. A pool of blood had formed around her wrists and stained her nightgown.

I was paralyzed. I don't know whether I screamed or whether I was silent. I can't remember if my knees buckled or I gradually fell. I do not know how I ended up next to her—I don't even remember moving. I lost control of my senses. My hands were active, but I swear that I was not commanding them.

"What have you done?" I moaned.

Her eyes rolled back, and she mumbled something incoherent. She was barely conscious. I grabbed onto her arms—right where the long gashes were—and pressed down to stop the blood from pouring out. My touch only made the flow more aggressive.

"Mama, hold on. Please, hold on."

I reached into my pocket and took out my cellphone. I was trying to navigate to the dial pad, but my bloodstained hands were hindering my visibility of the screen and causing me to press the wrong numbers.

I wish I could remember what I said to the 9-1-1 operator, or how the next few minutes progressed, but I can't. My vision was blurred, my head pounding from fear. I don't even recall telling the operator our address. All I'm certain of is that I held my mother the exact same way she used to hold me. I cradled her in my arms as she neared her end.

Her lips moved, and I pushed my ears closer to make out what she was saying.

"Mama, hold on, the ambulance is on their way," I pleaded, stroking her hair.

Her mouth moved again, and this time, I understood what she was saying.

"Baba …"

"Mama, it's me. Aku. Stay with me." I wanted her to repeat my name. I wanted it to ground her in this world.

"Baba …" she repeated, softer this time.

"No, it's Aku. Your son," I cried, weeping like a baby.

Each breath was becoming more difficult for her, and yet she didn't appear to be fighting it. I grasped her tightly, hoping that if I didn't let go of her, she wouldn't let go of me.

She whispered her final words, using the force of her breath to enunciate each syllable.

"Baba, I'm sorry."

PART FOUR

CHAPTER 25

THE ASHES

WHENEVER THE WORLD felt like it was weighing down on my sore shoulders, a state I found myself in more often than not, I would enter the first bus I could find and let it carry me away. I would choose a seat in the back, far removed from the other passengers. As people shuffled in and out at each stop, their eyes occasionally passed over me but never lingered. I was completely anonymous on this vehicle.

I would travel for as long as I needed to. Usually, this meant progressing beyond the recognizable streets and shops of Fremont. Out in the unknown, there wasn't a risk that my ride of anonymity would be interrupted. I was a free man, floating without any ties to emotion, to people, to places and things and memories that suffocated me. Nothing restrained me on the bus. Nothing forced me to confront the absolute mess of reality I was in. I was invigorated by the possibility that if I continued transferring from bus to bus long enough, I could run away from my current life. I could leave the turmoil behind and begin a new existence in a distant, secluded place where not even one resident knew my name or history. I had done it once before; there was no saying that it couldn't be done again.

But at some point along the ride, panic would prevent me from journeying further. Unrest would reverse the comfort I'd previously found in my unfamiliar surroundings. The thought of running away, once an alluring idea, would seem like a fool's dream. I'd leap off the bus and stabilize myself on solid ground. Sometimes, when I wasn't ready to head back just yet, I would look up the nearest Indian restaurant on my phone. It didn't matter if the food was badly reviewed or the restaurant was farther than a couple blocks. I would walk as much as needed to reach it. If the restaurant was empty, I would immediately turn around and leave. The bleakness of those places depressed me right from my entry. I sought out the places that were congested with people, where the tables were pressed tightly against each other and the noise levels were so high that you needed to cover your ears to prevent hearing loss. The waiter would seat me in the back corner, away from the other families. My solitary dining would elicit a few concerned stares from other customers, but after five minutes or so, they would redirect their attention elsewhere.

I would eat a large meal, even though I barely had the money to afford it. I drank sweet lassi and ate oily, fried snacks. I crammed chaat down my throat and drowned myself in a thali. Every bite softened me, every sip provided me momentary comfort. I would not stop until queasiness prevented me from eating more. At that point, my gaze would lift from the emptied dishes and scan the other brown faces in the establishment. I watched mothers dab their toddlers' faces and fathers slap phones out of their teenagers' hands. I observed grannies fixing their saris and uncles rubbing their bellies with satisfaction. I listened to the familiar mix of Hindi, Tamil, Telugu, and other Indian languages I could not identify. The longer I examined the lively restaurant, the more I could convince myself that I had never left the Town. This scene was familiar, one I had been a part of time and time again in my youth. Seeing Indian families of all shapes and sizes, from various backgrounds and histories, come together for a meal eased the cumbersome weight on my shoulders. I felt like I had found the destination of my search. I had finally arrived at a place where I belonged.

The waiter would inevitably pull me out of my transfixed state by bringing over the check. After this interruption, I would look around once more, this time with fresh eyes, and realize that I knew not even one person in this restaurant, and no one knew me. No one knew that I had run away from the Town or that my mother had killed herself. No one cared if I lived or died. Even though I was surrounded by people who looked like me and easily resembled the community I'd grown up with, I would feel the true severity of my loneliness sitting in that far-removed booth. Nauseated by my anguish, I would quickly pay and depart.

My only option from there was to return to where my journey began. So, I reluctantly boarded the bus again, recognizing that I had nowhere else to go. And though I always ended these rides the same way, I was unable to stay immobile for long. These aimless, cyclical trips repeated relentlessly, providing me no solace or objective, only perpetual disquietude.

———

Ravi's family was incredibly accommodating after my mother's death. I moved in with them shortly after and slept in their guest room. His parents cared for me as if I were their own child. Ravi's father was integral in helping me navigate the processes and paperwork of handling a death. He paid for my mother's cremation and stowed the urn in a cupboard, promising me that her ashes were ready whenever I wanted to let them go. Ravi's mother brought meals directly to the guest room and wouldn't question when I left most of the food untouched. Even Ravi's little sister made tiny origami flowers and placed them outside my door each morning. The whole family would eagerly greet me when I exited the room but granted me privacy when I was shut inside.

Even though his parents did not mention a move-out date, I was overly conscious that I was taking up space in someone else's house. Feeling like an imposition was an unnerving position to be in, especially since I'd become mostly self-reliant in the previous years. The longer I stayed cooped up in Ravi's house, the more unsettled I was. I tried to leave whenever possible, but my excuses to do so were slim. I couldn't bring myself to return to school, as much as Ravi urged me to. At the beginning of June, the school informed me that my chances of graduating that year were near impossible. Too many of my assignments were incomplete. Mrs. Suárez said she would pass me regardless of whether I finished my final project. My other teachers were accommodating and permitted me to complete tests at home, but even then, I couldn't focus on meaningless multiple-choice questions when much of my day was spent ruminating over the image of my mother's lifeless body. My aimless wanderings across the Bay Area were my only escape. Roaming around by bus was mind-numbing and gave me something to do outside of Ravi's house. When I returned from these trips, no one in the family would ask where I had been, and I didn't offer to tell them.

Ravi and Eva showed support in dissimilar ways. Whenever I exited the guest room, Ravi would drop whatever he was doing in order to keep me company. We didn't do much besides watch TV and pick up food, but even these simple activities were appreciated. Ravi was terrible at bringing up sensitive subjects, so he rarely mentioned my mother. Eva, on the other hand, doused me in tearful hugs and words of affirmation. Though she did not push me to discuss the death, she continuously reminded me that she was available to talk whenever I wanted to.

The question I was asked most often was whether I had contacted my other family. In truth, I had thought about reaching out to my father, even though I didn't particularly want to see him again. However, I didn't have a way of contacting him. I searched his full name, Varun Iyengar, on the internet and scrolled through the countless results this fairly common name produced. I couldn't find anything related to him—no social media, no website, nothing. For someone whose primary goal in life was to have his name on the tip of people's tongues, it was laughable how invisible my father ended up. For all I knew, he could have been dead as well.

I still had the phone number for my childhood home committed to memory. I could have easily picked up the phone, dialed those ten numbers, and waited until someone answered. But I couldn't bring myself to. Part of it was fear. How would I deliver this news to people I hadn't seen in years? How could I explain my mother's suicide when I hadn't fully processed what had happened myself? Besides, what would their response be? If they did not receive my phone call well, my lingering anxiety that I was completely cut off from my family, that I was truly and utterly alone, would become an indubitable truth.

Even if they responded with forgiveness, I didn't feel like I deserved family again in my life. My solitude was punishment for my selfishness. At a time when my mother had needed me the most, I'd left her. Worse, I'd screamed horrible things at her. She'd asked me to stay that day, and I hadn't listened. I'd heard her pain, and I'd still chosen to ignore it. I wanted to be angry at her for leaving me alone in this world, but I could only muster up rage that was self-directed. This nightmare could have easily been prevented if I hadn't been so heartless.

Just like Sagar, she had needed me. I had pushed them away, and now they were both gone. How could I ask for my family's forgiveness when history had repeated itself? How could I, even for a second, think I deserved people who had done nothing but love me? I deserved to rot in misery, and even then, it would not feel equitable to the pain I had inflicted. Anyway, my family in the Town had probably made peace with the fact that my mother and I were out of their lives forever. There wasn't a compelling enough reason for them to know she had passed away when it would only cause more heartbreak. Keeping them ignorant seemed like the most considerate option.

So, when Ravi's parents asked about contacting my other family, I told them that my father was out of the picture and that the rest of my family was estranged. I kept my explanation as vague as possible while still maintaining the truth. When they first asked, I thought it was because they wanted me out of their house. I promised them that I could look for other accommodations, but they assured me that I was more than welcome to stay for as long as I needed. As an eighteen-year-old, I was beyond the age for any required government intervention. I was considered an adult and had to navigate my future as one.

Memory was the cruelest, most inescapable aspect of the aftermath. My dreams were often violent and filled with viscous, cherry-red blood—exactly like what had pooled out of my mother. If I shut my eyes during the day, instead of darkness, I saw flashes of her stiff expression and unfocused eyes. The night of her death, time had slipped through my fingertips faster than I could grasp. Since then, each second of that night was dragged out in my mind. Memory detained me to that kitchen floor, but the primary difference between living in that moment and recalling it later was that I could no longer do anything to alter the course of the night. Time mercilessly pushed me forward.

Fed up with my inability to think about anything else but her, I got up one afternoon with a desperate urge to dispose of her ashes. I sprinted downstairs to the cupboard where Ravi's father kept my mother's urn. The cupboard was near the front entrance. Whenever I'd passed it previously, I would hesitate for a few moments in front of the tiny door and imagine what the urn looked like behind the barrier. The image I'd conceived was so disturbing that opening the cupboard had seemed too daunting a task. But I'd pushed the deed off long enough. Letting go of her ashes was necessary in order to ease my suffocation.

The living room was empty. I cautiously approached the cupboard, as if it were an animal about to leap at me. My palms were sweaty. In a swift motion, I threw open the door. The urn was black, unassuming, and barely larger than a beer mug. It was stuffed in the corner, along with random papers, old photos, keys, and other knick-knacks. My hands shook while pulling the urn out, but once I could properly examine it, I realized that my anxiety had been in vain. The body of the urn was stale and lifeless, holding absolutely no resemblance or connection to my mother. Discarding the contents inside did not feel as scary anymore.

"Whatcha doing?"

I spun around. Ravi stood at the opposite end of the living room. His eyes shifted down to the urn.

"Oh," he said uncomfortably. "Are you …?"

"Feels like it's time."

"I guess. Hasn't even been two months, though."

I shrugged. "It's just ash."

"Where are you gonna do it?"

"I don't know." In my impulsive rush, I hadn't considered what to do after securing the urn. Looking at Ravi's expectant gaze, I knew I needed a better answer. I thought of pretty parks that were walking distance from his house. "Maybe Lake Elizabeth?"

"Lake Liz! Are you serious?"

"Ravi, it's not that big a deal. I just need to get it over with."

"Please don't do it at Lake Liz. Everyone goes there to smoke."

"Where else then?"

"There has to be at least one place that's more meaningful. What about the guest house you were staying at?"

"Absolutely not." I shuddered at the thought of returning there.

"Okay … well, were there any spots that made her happy? Anywhere she would want to remain forever?"

I racked my brain. It was tough to think of a spot my mother had connected to in the Bay Area. After a minute, I came up with an idea. "There might be one place."

Ravi perked up. "Really? Great!"

"It's a bit far, though."

"Bro, as if I'm doing anything important. Wait two minutes. I'll get my keys."

———

"Are you sure this is the right address?"

Ravi and I stood gaping at a hipster coffee shop. The establishment had floor-to-ceiling windows and a polished white interior. Matching sets of wooden tables and chairs surrounded the sectioned-off area in the center where the baristas worked with stainless steel espresso machines. A large menu was neatly framed behind the register, with prices for lattes averaging around seven dollars. The shop balanced trendy decor well; succulents and hanging plants beautified the space but did not overwhelm it.

"Yes," I whispered, remembering when my mother had brought me for the first time. Of course, the interior had looked very different back then. The finishings had been old and rusty, the walls had been shedding themselves of purple paint, and the space had been enlivened with chattering customers and Pakistani songs. I'd hoped the next business that took over the lease would modify the space only slightly, but the coffee shop had wiped away any existence of Nabeela Aunty's salon. It saddened me how much the salon had meant to my mother, and how it had vanished, just like her.

"You sure you want to do it here?" asked Ravi.

I shook my head. "This place would mean nothing to my mom now."

"Is there anywhere else you can think of?"

"Let's just go back to Fremont. I'll do it at the lake."

"Dude, no. Even if we don't go somewhere that was important to her, we can still choose a better place, right?"

"I'm tired. I don't want to keep moving around."

"I'll pick somewhere close by! You don't have to do anything."

I sighed. "Fine. But after that—"

"We'll go home. I promise."

The two of us climbed back into his illegally parked car. Ravi drove us through the steep hills of San Francisco, cursing each time he approached an incline. At some point along the journey, he handed me his phone and asked if I could play music.

"What do you want me to queue up?"

"No, no. This isn't about me. What music do *you* want?"

I subtly rolled my eyes and checked Ravi's library. The only albums he had were by mumble rappers. Listening to hip-hop while holding the urn felt grossly disrespectful.

"Actually, could we not play anything?"

"Of course, dude. Whatever you feel like."

I vowed to deposit the ashes wherever Ravi took us next. The refurbished salon-turned-coffee shop wasn't the right place, but any other location would do. I just wanted the deed to be over with.

After another twenty minutes of driving, Ravi turned onto a highway bordering the ocean. The sun was setting over the turbulent tide. I instantly recognized where we were. Ravi had brought us to Ocean Beach, the same place my parents and I had spent my twelfth birthday. Although my initial feeling was to steer Ravi away, I convinced myself that this memory meant nothing to me. I had promised myself that I would discard the ashes wherever we went next, and I planned on sticking to it.

Ravi pulled into a sandy parking lot. "Whatcha think? Pretty nice, huh?"

We both disembarked from his car. The tempestuous wind tore at my hair. I clutched the urn tightly as we trudged through the dense sand.

"Do you want to do it in the ocean?"

"That seems appropriate, right?"

"Up to you, dude. I'll wait back here."

I carefully set the urn on the sand before rolling up my pants. I picked the urn back up, and with an encouraging nod from Ravi, started toward the ocean. The other people on the beach were distancing themselves from the mighty waves, but I powered on with my trek. Goosebumps crawled up my stiff arms after I reached the chilly water. I gritted my teeth, held my ground, and looked out at the horizon.

As much as I wanted to expel any thoughts of my twelfth birthday, I couldn't relinquish the memory. My father and I had stood in this water together. I'd looked at him that day with adoration. Little had I known that his promises were empty and that his failures would leave me broken. I was convinced that if I ever saw him again, I would kill him. I would do it without hesitation, and it still wouldn't be enough to avenge the suffering he'd put me and my mother through.

My grip on the urn loosened. I was too consumed by anger to let go. Even though the ash did not resemble my mother in any way, I could not emotionally detach myself from the person it used to be. I wasn't ready to say goodbye. I couldn't understand why I needed to. If this urn was all that was left of her, then why wouldn't I hold on to it for as long as possible?

I slogged back to the shore and collapsed in front of Ravi. I hugged my knees, safeguarding the urn in the crevice between my chest and thighs. My tears crashed against the lid.

Ravi sat beside me. "Bro …"

"We should have gone back to Fremont. Why the hell did you make me come here?"

"I just wanted to help."

"You didn't. I feel even more like shit now, thanks to you."

He put one hand on my shoulder. "What can I do to make this better?"

"Ravi, my mother died."

"I know."

"Meaning she's gone forever. She's never coming back."

"I know, dude. I know."

"Then what the fuck do you think you're going to do to help me? Can you bring her back? Can you go back in time and prevent her from killing herself?"

"Why are you getting angry at me?" he whispered.

"Because, Ravi! I'm trying to let go of my mother's ashes, and you want to make a fun little day trip out of it."

"I'm sorry. I didn't mean for it to come across like that."

"Of course you didn't! You have no clue what it feels like to watch your mother die in your arms. You don't understand the pain I face every single day. Don't you get that I have to deal with this on my own?"

Ravi was flustered. "Yes, but—"

"You really want to help? Then leave me the fuck alone."

"Let's go home. We can talk about this later."

"No, I mean it. I want you to leave."

"Like right now? How will you get back to Fremont?"

"I'll figure it out."

"Bro, I can't leave you here."

"Then I'll go."

I stood up and marched away from him. He scrambled after me.

"Hey, come on. Don't be like this," he said, grabbing my wrist.

"Let go." I tried to wrangle my arm out of his grasp.

"Not until you stop walking away."

I pushed him back, snapping our hands apart. He lost his balance and fell on the sand.

"Fuck," he muttered, rubbing his right elbow.

He reached up to me, but I turned away and said, "I told you to leave me alone."

I walked away without checking to see if he was following. When I felt like I'd created enough distance between us, I looked back and surveyed the area where he had been. I couldn't locate him. Even though I'd told him to leave, I was mildly upset that he'd listened and given up. I found a new spot to sit and continued to hug the urn. The sky bled with anguish. Orange faded into crimson, and crimson dissolved into dark amber. The haunting colors of dusk lingered until darkness sucked them away. I remained in the same place, shivering, as the rest of the visitors cleared the beach.

I needed to hug her again. I needed to tell her how much I loved her and how sorry I was for leaving that night. I needed to feel her warm, living body, her hair falling on top of my face, her kiss on my cheek.

There was only one place where I could find her again. My need to go back was immense. I had to see her, even if she could only exist as a figment of my imagination. I picked myself off the sand and plodded through the empty beach. The bitter wind ferociously whipped around me. I kept my eyes focused on the trees bordering the other side of the highway. I knew that behind them was an entrance to Golden Gate Park. I steadied my breath and braced myself to revisit a place I'd firmly believed I would never have to see again.

Before long, I was in front of the casting pools. The Singer was sitting by the water, waiting for me, as I'd suspected he would be. He opened his eyes. "Are you ready to return?"

"I am."

CHAPTER 26

RETURN TO THE IMAGINED

I EMERGED IN the Imagined with my face tilted up toward the circle of light. Heavy pellets of green and brown paint showered around me, softening into splotchy puddles beneath my feet. I was initially disappointed when I saw the forest forming. The memory I'd wished to return to was in the master bedroom of my childhood home, with me burrowed between my mother's arms. But I was soon grateful that I had landed at my old entry point. The familiarity of the woodland setting allowed me to stabilize myself after years of disengaging from this unusual skill of mine. When the colors had settled, I knelt down and dug my hands into the earth. I removed a clump of the moist soil and sifted it through my tiny fingers. My body was transformed back to the way it appeared at eleven years of age. My face was soft, my figure delicate. My sensitive ears could pick up even the faintest buzzing of insects flitting about. I was a teenager stuck in a child's body.

The sensory influx was staggering. Sadness consumed me, and I began to weep. I wept because of how much I had missed the sights, sounds, and smells of the Imagined. And I wept because of how much I loathed myself for coming back. Why did I have to regress to find solace? Why was it so difficult for me to move on from this forest?

Remembering how harshly I'd left the Imagined during my previous visit, I hesitantly glanced around at the trees, hoping not to catch a detail amiss. Copious time away made me uncertain about how well I could recollect the forest. Unless the deviance was glaring, I could have easily accepted it as the truth. Thankfully, from what I could see, the environment around me appeared genuine.

My intent for reentering the Imagined did not require me to look for Sagar, but I was still curious about his condition. The last time I'd seen him, his face had been marred with irregularities, including Mayuran's scar and a furious expression I'd never seen on him prior to then. I knew this image wasn't faithful to what he'd looked like when he was alive, but whenever I tried to recall his unadulterated face, I could only conjure up the warped version. The Imagined had torn me away from my authentic memories, but I hoped that the lapse of time would be a good reset. I expected the Imagined to hand back what it had stolen.

While walking toward the spot where Sagar resided, I came across the malformed, tilted tree, one of the first deviances I'd ever seen in the Imagined. My eyes did not waver while gazing at it. Shockingly, this tree, even with its curly branches and odd angle, felt as naturally a part of the forest as any other upright tree. I'd seen this tree during countless visits and had convinced myself of its existence to the point where it no longer felt abnormal. My lack of unease worried me. I needed to question all other anomalies I came across until they reverted back to how they used to be.

My path toward the three trees cleared, and I spotted a body lying face up among them. My heartbeat quickened. Years later, and I still felt the same confusing mess of comfort, nostalgia, guilt, and sorrow upon seeing Sagar. A speck of red caught my eye, and I glanced up at the tree trunk directly behind him. Swirling, multicolored lines snaked up the bark, forming untamed, asymmetrical patterns. My father's designs were still intact from my tumultuous last visit. I couldn't reclaim the unsullied form of the tree when this freakish visual was carved into my memory. I quickly looked down and shielded my eyes. Maybe Sagar would be different. That's all I cared about. Even if the rest of the forest was distorted, all I wanted was to see his pure, innocent face, exactly as it used to be.

"Sagar," I whispered.

He lifted his head up. I should have turned away the second I saw the scar. When I looked into his eyes, the soft, wide, brown eyes—the one part of him that I would always be sure about—I was almost able to convince myself that this was Sagar, that this was what he had looked like. But the abnormalities on the rest of his face, especially the addition of Mayuran's features, were too jarring to grapple with. An invisible suction began underneath me, pulling me down, as the forest unraveled into distinct colors. With immense mental strength, I turned my face away from Sagar and looked in the opposite direction. The suction ceased, and the forest settled back to a stable form.

"Akash Dada? Do you want to play with me?"

"Not now, Sagar." He wasn't the reason I had come to the Imagined, and he wasn't going to deter me from my actual goal. I walked in the direction of the Town, careful not to let my gaze wander back to him.

"Where are you going?" he asked.

I could hear his feet shuffling, following me.

"Main Street," I mumbled.

"Let's play. It's such a nice day."

"I'm not in the mood."

Sagar ran in front of me and barred me from walking further. I averted my eyes.

"Come on. It'll be fun. Arjuna and Karna? Or something else?"

"Sagar, please, move out of my way."

"You're acting strange." His voice deepened into an unusual growl. I was afraid of angering him again and falling out of the Imagined. I needed to create distance between us. After a momentary pause, I sidestepped Sagar and ran as fast as I could toward Main.

"Wait! Don't leave!" he called out.

I swerved around trees, attempting to disrupt my route so that it was harder for Sagar to follow me. In the back of my head, I wondered why I was trying to outsmart him. Since he was a product of my mind, I should have been able to control his actions. But the more credence I gave this thought, the angrier the Imagined became. I sensed that it was on the cusp of expelling me, so I flushed away any doubt that Sagar wasn't real. I had to believe that every part of the Imagined was authentic, including him. That was the only way I was going to find my mother again—the human version of her, not the shapeless ash.

New peculiarities surfaced along my route. None were particularly large or concerning on their own, but when compounded together, it was obvious how weak my memory of the forest had become. I remembered the gist of my surroundings, but many minute details had escaped me, more so than when I'd visited as a twelve-year-old. Some leaves were discolored, sporting a spectrum of hues from mahogany to turquoise. Select branches were gargantuan compared to the trunks they extended from. The forest floor contained a collection of odd lumps, almost like it had sprouted warts, that ranged from the size of a bowl to a sled. Some of the deviations were so ridiculous and inconceivable that it almost felt like the Imagined was poking fun at me for not being able to recapture the forest in its entirety. I was being tested to see how long I could persuade myself to believe in my surroundings before I finally gave up. My imagination was controlling me, and if I wanted to stay within this illusory world, I had to allow it.

When I reached the cul-de-sac where the Mahmoods' tailor shop stood, I once again saw that the environment beyond the forest wasn't fully formed. The blurred colors swished, swirled, and melted into one another, rather than organizing into concrete shapes. Sagar was catching up to me, but I blocked out his voice and closed my eyes. Maybe if I could recall as many details about Main Street as possible, I would be able to stretch the limits of the Imagined and incorporate more of the Town into it. I pictured the thin road and the worn-out shops. I visualized inhabitants of the Town chatting with each other on the sidewalks, smoking cigarettes and drinking steaming cups of tea.

After I felt like I had concocted a decent enough image in my head, I opened my eyes. The colors had formed a clearer, but still vague, outline of the path before me. The cul-de-sac appeared like a blotchy watercolor painting where structure was fluid and abstract.

"Come back to the forest," said Sagar from behind me.

"I can't, Sagar. I'm sorry."

I took a leap of faith and rushed toward the half-formed street, mustering up my strength so that I was not as brutally rejected this time around. But the second I left the forest, my body felt like it had run into a brick wall. An invisible resistance pushed against me, and I squinted my eyes, trying to see through the jumble of colors. I waded through the cul-de-sac as if I were wading through the deepest part of an ocean. My movement was slow, and I could only focus on one limb at a time. In order to gauge my progress, I glanced at the wall of the tailor shop. My vision was blurry and prevented me from staring too long, but from what I could see, the pliable bricks of the shop were tangled, and the viscous roof was sliding down. Despite the building's absurd state, I used it to ground me as I continued to push forward.

The mental strain far outweighed the physical. I had to keep my mind unwaveringly focused on the goal of reaching my house in order to move forward. But this was challenging to execute when the Imagined relentlessly hindered me. It was tiresome to control my thoughts when my mind and body were rejected with each step. It felt like I was being pressed against a thinly stretched rubber band that was eager to shoot me back to the forest.

When I reached the corner of the tailor shop and was about to turn onto Main Street, the mental strain became too excruciating to power through. Two parts of my brain, representing what I wanted and what the Imagined wanted, were sparring with each other. I screamed out in pain—a silent scream that even I was unable to hear—and plummeted down.

I awoke on the pavement of Golden Gate Park with a broken, drained body. My breathing was uneven and my limbs weary. I tried to focus my eyes on the Singer, but in my dazed state, multiple versions of him were popping up and floating around.

"What happened?" he asked. "What did you do?"

"I needed to leave the forest," I coughed out.

His eyes narrowed. "Are you trying to stretch your Imagined again? I told you not to do that."

"But these are my memories! I should be able to control where I can go."

"The mind acts in ways beyond our understanding. We think we can control it, but in truth, it behaves as its own independent entity."

"I need to find someone. It's urgent, and I know I have a deep emotional need to see them. Why won't the Imagined let me go directly to them?"

The Singer thought for a moment. "Your mind could be telling you that your need to access this other memory is not as strong as the one you are currently returning to. Subconsciously, you still desire the original setting more."

"Nothing is more important right now than seeing my mother."

"Why are you not able to see her otherwise?"

"It doesn't matter."

"Has she passed away?" whispered the Singer.

I didn't respond.

The Singer regarded me with sympathy. "I'm sorry, Akash. Truly, I am. I'm certain that I've experienced loss at some point in my life, though when and for whom, I cannot recall. But the despair lingers."

"Can you help me find her or not?"

The Singer sighed. "This might not end up the way you hope. The Imagined is supposed to help you find comfort, but this ... this could lead to further frustration. As I said before, I have never tried to exit the room where my father and I practice music. That's the only place I want to be, and I've been content without leaving it. Doing this ... stretching the bounds ... it's unfamiliar territory."

"But it might be possible, right?"

"It's hard to say."

"I have to give it a shot then."

"Please reconsider, Akash. Look at the toll this visit has taken on you." The Singer's tone was soft, and he spoke with the tenderness of a concerned parent. The affection in his voice sparked a twinge of abashment within me.

"I'm going to do this with or without you," I said. "After all these years, I still don't know what or who you are. But one thing I'm certain of is that you're my ticket into the Imagined. It would be easier to navigate this with your help, but if you're not willing to offer it, I will figure out another way to get there, no matter what it takes."

His eyes begged me one final time, but I held my ground. Reluctantly, he said, "Fine. I will help you. But promise me that you will approach this with caution."

I nodded and stood up, carrying the urn with me. Unlike before, the Singer did not immediately close his eyes and return to his meditation. Instead, he watched me leave with a protective yet worried gaze.

———

It was past midnight when I reached Ravi's house. After my harrowing experience in the Imagined, I hoped that I could sneak into the house and deal with the fallout of our fight the following morning. I slowly unlocked the front door and tiptoed inside. The lights were off in the foyer. I breathed a sigh of relief, walked to the cupboard where Ravi's dad had kept the urn previously, and placed my mother's ashes back inside.

As I headed upstairs, I heard loud blasts coming from the media room. The door was wide open, and I had to pass by it in order to reach the guest room. I prayed that if I crossed quickly enough, whoever was inside wouldn't notice me.

Just as I stepped in view of the room, Ravi's father called out my name. "Akash, you're back?"

I turned toward his voice. Ravi and his family were sitting together on the reclining couch. Ravi's sister had fallen asleep, but the other three were wide awake. Ravi did not look in my direction.

"Uh, yes," I replied.

Ravi's father paused the movie. "Ravi said you were staying at Eva's place tonight."

"Decided to come back a little early."

"Want to join us? We're watching *Star Wars*."

"I'm a little wiped, but thank you." I glanced at Ravi, but he didn't meet my eye.

"See you in the morning then."

I shuffled away to the guest room. Once inside, I immediately shut the door and collapsed on the bed. As exhausted as I was, sleep did not come easy to me. My head still felt like it was splitting in two, and no amount of steady breathing or lo-fi music could calm it down.

The next morning, I clomped down to the kitchen, bedraggled and weary. Ravi was sitting by the counter, eating cereal. He nodded at me as I sat on the chair next to him.

"Wanna watch some *Rick and Morty* later?" he asked, passing me the box of Cheerios.

"Sure," I said.

We finished the rest of our breakfast in silence. Neither of us was brave enough to confront the events of the previous day. For the time being, our fight was slipped under the rug, but the toll it had taken on our friendship was felt in the words unspoken.

I hadn't returned to Yusuf Uncle's restaurant since my mother's death. I'd sent him a text soon after the incident, informing him that I had to quit immediately due to some personal issues. He tried calling me several times, but I didn't answer. On his last attempt, he left me a voicemail saying that he was sorry to see me go, that he thought of me as a son, and that he hoped whatever was happening in my life would be resolved soon. His message made me regret leaving my job the way I had. I'd expected Yusuf Uncle to get angry at me for not giving him more notice. I wished that he had. His understanding and compassion, despite not knowing what was happening in my life, brought me further shame.

More than Yusuf Uncle, I couldn't bring myself to tell Luke the truth about my mother. I hadn't spoken to him since the afternoon we'd spent together in his bedroom. It was taxing for me to break the news to anyone, but it was uniquely painful to contact Luke again knowing that if I hadn't gone to his place that day, that if I had just stayed back at the guest house, my mother would still be alive. I knew it was unfair to accuse Luke of something he didn't know about, but resentment was easier than accountability. Pinning some of the blame on him lightened my load. I deleted all of his texts and missed call notifications with spite. After a few weeks of us not speaking, he sent me a long paragraph. Like with the other texts, I deleted it without reading. But before it vanished completely, I caught a glimpse of the last line. He said that he would not reach out anymore. And he stayed true to his word.

Yusuf Uncle mentioned in one of his voicemails that he would leave the payment from my last few shifts in an envelope by the counter and that I could pick it up whenever I wished. Although I considered forfeiting the check, I did not want to be dependent on Ravi's parents for money. I reluctantly accepted food and other life necessities from them, but I felt too guilty taking cash. Since I was planning on making more trips to San Francisco, I needed a way to pay for the BART tickets. Between asking Ravi's parents for money and picking up the rest of my payment, the latter seemed like the less humiliating option of the two.

I planned my visit so that it would not conflict with one of Luke's shifts, but when I reached the restaurant and opened the front door, I found him standing at the register.

He caught sight of me before I could turn around. "H-hey."

"Thought you didn't work afternoons," I muttered.

"Wanted some extra cash."

"And you're working register?"

"Well, you're not here to cover it."

I coughed uncomfortably. "Yusuf Uncle said that my payment ..."

"Oh. Right." Luke removed an envelope from behind the counter and handed it to me.

"Thanks."

We awkwardly stood there for a few seconds, waiting for the other person to break the silence. Finally, I turned around and walked out of the restaurant, exhaling loudly on my way to the bus stop. Though our conversation had been anticlimactic, I was thankful it was over.

"Hey, wait up!" Luke exited the restaurant and ran up to me. His eyes searched mine frantically. "Where have you been? Please tell me what I did wrong."

"Luke, no, you didn't do anything wrong."

"Really? Because I can't seem to find any other explanation for why you would quit your job and stop responding to me."

"It's just not a good time."

"Please tell me what's going on. I won't take it personally if you don't like me anymore."

The desperation in his face was heartbreaking to see. Knowing that I had caused him pain made me want to flee as fast as possible.

"What happened between us ... it meant something to me," continued Luke.

Unable to formulate a good response, I turned away and quietly whispered, "I'm sorry."

"Why are you doing this?" he asked, his voice quivering. "Why are you hurting me like this?"

The bus rolled up next to the curb.

"I've gotta go," I muttered.

Luke's eyes began to water, but he shifted his gaze to the ground so I couldn't see. "That day you came over, I was gonna tell you that I got into UC San Diego. It was one of my top schools."

"That's great, Luke. Congrats."

"My family convinced me to accept the decision. I paid the deposit and everything, but I'm still not a hundred percent set on going. There are some things I want to consider first."

"Like what?"

"Distance mostly. I have some other options closer to here." He glanced back up at me.

"You should go," I murmured.

His expression was laced with disappointment. "You really think so?"

"Yeah."

Luke shoved his hands into his pockets. "Well, I guess that's it then."

I stepped on the bus and watched Luke walk back to the restaurant. The only other passenger inside the vehicle was an old Korean man. He smiled warmly at me, seemingly happy for a companion on this lonely ride. I covered my face with my jacket and hid myself from him. I understood then why my mother hadn't cried after Nabeela Aunty's departure. The emptiness had ravaged me to the point where I had nothing left to feel. It's strange how much I despised my loneliness, and yet, I couldn't see my life progressing in any other way.

When I returned to Ravi's house, I shut myself in the guest bedroom and began to sketch Main Street on scratch paper. I combed my brain for every possible detail that was locked away, feverishly preparing for my next visit to the Imagined.

CHAPTER 27

PURGATORY

TIME NO LONGER progressed as it once had. With more waking hours spent in the Imagined than in the physical world, I lost track of days first, and weeks soon after. Graduation for my high school class came and went without my knowledge. I only found out that it had occurred after I returned from San Francisco the day of and saw Ravi's parents cutting him a cake. Mrs. Suárez left me a voicemail encouraging me to take summer school classes and finish my outstanding credits. She said that if I explained my situation to the arts college in Florida, they might be willing to defer my admission rather than rescind it. But I didn't care about my education anymore. Nothing mattered except for my objective to find my mother.

Over the course of many visits, I was exposed to the sheer magnificence and horror of what the Imagined could be. Sketching out what I remembered of the Town helped me construct the imaginary version of it, but during each trip, I was only able to take around five to ten steps down Main Street. Like the first time I tried to leave the forest, I would have to fight through amorphous globs of multicolored paint. Once I did, they would crystallize into shapes that resembled the shops I'd known. But pushing myself forward and commanding these colors to arrange into recognizable figures required immense mental strength and concentration. The task never got easier. In fact, with each step further away from the forest, I faced even more resistance to continue.

Before entering the Imagined, I would brood over the image of my mother's bedroom so I could go there directly and avoid this taxing walk down Main Street. Despite my best efforts, my point of entry remained the middle of the forest. I recalled the afternoon before Suhail Mama's wedding reception when I first tapped into my Imagined. During that brief visit, I'd started to generate Suhail Mama's room before Kalpana Aaji interrupted me. Because of this occurrence, I figured it was possible to reproduce other places in my Imagined besides the forest, but for whatever reason, an unknown mental hurdle was presently obstructing me from doing so. I was at a loss trying to reason how my emotional need for Sagar and the forest could be deeper than my need to be with my mother. This might have been the case if I was still twelve years old, but at eighteen, I didn't have a strong desire to see him at all.

Another obstacle I had to face before and after each visit was the hour-and-a-half commute from Fremont to Golden Gate Park. I tried to access the Imagined on my own in Ravi's house, since all I really needed was a quiet place to meditate. I would sit in the guest room with the door shut, close my eyes, hum the thumri, and concentrate on my memories of childhood. I would sit in this position for hours, sweating as time slinked by. Without the sounds of the natural environment, without the visuals that brought back memories of the forest, it was impossible for me to summon my nostalgia in the guest room the same way I was able to in the park. In order to focus and rid myself of the horrible, distracting thoughts related to my mother's death, I needed to immerse myself in an environment that brought forth sentimentality with minimal effort.

In my Imagined, no people appeared on Main Street. I was only able to conjure up buildings and other inanimate objects. I understood why I only saw Sagar in the forest; no one else from the Town went there. But on Main, I expected to see old neighbors like Bhaskar Uncle or Mariam Aunty having conversations outside of the shops. I even tried to sketch them out in preparation. Still, the street remained deserted. The only person I could hear was Sagar, his far-off voice begging me to return and play with him.

Unlike the forest, which took shape the minute I entered, the rest of the Town had to be composed. I was the painter, and my mind was the brush. There was more room for error, and accordingly, a broader range of surreal characteristics. Colors would not always land where I wanted them to. The sky had become a light shade of lavender, and the trees behind the shops were tinted silver.

Even the basic shapes of shops were warped based on what I associated them with. Das Electronics, where I'd spent many afternoons with Mayuran, was crumbling into heaps of rubble, just like the simulated buildings would in our war-themed video games. Simran Aunty's salon, which jogged my memory of Nabeela Aunty's salon, was transformed into a towering, multistory San Francisco apartment building. Additionally, my father's drawings snaked across the pavement, throbbing exactly like they had on the three trees. The Imagined Town was an intersection of the various places I had lived, the virtual worlds I had partaken in, and the engineered lenses that had manipulated my vision. There was no telling where reality ended and imagination began, especially since years of distance from the Town curtailed confidence in my fractured mind. Memory was the only tool I had to gauge what was authentic and what wasn't, but its fickleness made it an unreliable source.

I felt a deep sense of despair in my inability to control my environment. I couldn't look anywhere for long on Main Street, because if I did, the Imagined would unravel. I tried to overwrite these distortions and focus on making sure the Imagined came out the way I'd drawn it, but my mental energy was already consumed by pushing forward toward the house. I had to make a choice whether I wanted to reach my mother or focus on building the Town out properly. I was distressed knowing that my recollection of my birthplace, the foundation of who I was, was faltering. However, I wasn't able to do anything about it if I wanted to proceed with my goal.

Upon returning to the physical world, my body was racked with fatigue. I felt winded, like my lungs were about to collapse at any given moment. A searing pain would shoot through my head and cause my eyes to water. My weak muscles were incapable of immediately pushing my body off the pavement. I would have to lie down for about five minutes, catch my breath, and reorient myself to Golden Gate Park before I could even think about standing up.

The Singer's concern multiplied the more I returned wounded and weakened. He begged me to abandon the search for my mother and stay where my mind wanted me to be. He expressed that I should either enjoy the Imagined as is or not visit at all. The first time we'd met, the Singer had been so preoccupied with his own Imagined that he'd barely even looked at me. But his attention had shifted in recent months. From the moment I arrived at the casting pools to the moment I left, he observantly watched me. He did not offer any more advice about how to maneuver through the Imagined, nor did he rush me away so that he could return to his meditation. Instead, he would worriedly ask me questions about my physical state while I recovered. Seeing the discernable care in his eyes made me want to hide myself from him. I couldn't stand his attentiveness. There wasn't anything about me I believed he should be fond of.

After I was able to lift myself off the ground, I would go on a much-needed stroll. Walking helped defuse the nausea and reorient my mind outside of the Imagined. I would wander around for however long I needed to feel stable. San Francisco was a sleepy place, so even though I was in the middle of an urban area, I often found myself walking on sidewalks without anyone around me. The same bouts of loneliness I'd experienced when I first moved to SF were reignited with greater intensity, eating away at me like I was a carcass. I still felt like a child, lost without guidance, trying to claw my way up to adulthood but incapable of finding the correct path toward it. My thoughts would plummet to dangerous places, where the disgust I held for myself was mulled over and reaffirmed.

I didn't need my mother to tell me that Sagar's death was my fault. I knew it well enough. His death, my mother's death. These events were consequences of my selfishness. And since then, I'd continued to push people away. My relationship with Ravi had been strained ever since the day I'd shoved him on the beach. Not to mention Luke—oh, poor Luke. His wounded voice during our last conversation still rang clear in my ears. I was the reason for my revolting loneliness, for my prolonged isolation from twelve years of age to now. I had no one to blame but myself. I was the product of two opposites: a mother who'd seen no value in her life and a father who'd seen too much in his. For the time being, I was caught between the two, drifting aimlessly through barren, foggy streets.

Sometimes on these walks, especially as I amassed more visits to the Imagined, I would catch a glimpse of a tree from the Town's forest standing proudly at an intersection. On other occasions, I would see distorted shops from the Town in place of San Francisco storefronts. These frightening exchanges between the physical and imaginary worlds would appear in the corner of my eye. I would immediately stop walking, close my eyes, and concentrate on grounding myself, whether it was by focusing on my breath or how my feet were planted on the pavement. I would open my eyes once my body was calm, and by then, the jarring piece of the Imagined would have vanished. These experiences disturbed me greatly. I needed the Imagined and the real world to stay separate, because if they didn't, I would have to accept that I was losing my sanity. And if I didn't have control over my mental faculties, what else did I have left?

I was especially aggravated one evening after seeing a flash of Sagar running around the corner of a townhouse. I walked for an abnormally long stretch after to clear my head. I did not pay attention to where I was until my surroundings became unusually familiar. I'd ended up in Chinatown, less than three blocks away from my father's old apartment. Though I considered walking away, my curiosity steered me toward the building. Little had changed. The bakery we used to pick up breakfast from was still running on the bottom floor. The neighborhood hadn't undergone any discernable renovations. Even so, I felt impassive. There was nothing left for me there, no person or physical structure that held sentimental value. I turned around and left Chinatown for good.

Shortly after that unplanned visit, a strange anxiety clouded my walks. I began to develop a growing suspicion that I was being watched. I emerged from the Imagined one day and found a red blanket draped around me. It was thin and devoid of distinguishable logos or patterns. I scanned the area to see who my mysterious benefactor was. The Singer confirmed that it wasn't him, which I believed since I hadn't ever seen him rise from a seated position in the park. I wrote it off as an act of goodwill. Pedestrians occasionally strolled around the pools. One might have felt compelled to keep me warm without disturbing my meditation.

If this had been my only experience with a mysterious presence, I wouldn't have let it bother me. But every subsequent time I exited the Imagined, there was another blanket around me, and sometimes, a small plate of takeout food on my lap as well. I would circle the pools to see if anyone I knew was hiding behind the surrounding trees. After ten or so instances of waking up to these simple gifts, I obtained a nagging itch at the back of my neck. I was certain someone was watching me, even though I hadn't been able to find a lurker. This feeling of unease would continue throughout my walks, on the BART ride home, all the way to Ravi's house. Whenever I would whip around and attempt to catch the culprit, the only people I saw were disinterested strangers, none of whom would have had any motive to stalk me. My paranoia was reaching an all-time high. I would dart my eyes left and right and shift my clothing uncomfortably. I was always on edge, always perturbed.

Once, however, I was ambling along a crowded, restaurant-filled street and sensed the stalker behind me. I spun around and glimpsed a nondescript person in baggy, hooded clothing pivoting away from me. They pushed their way past a group of standing teens and vanished. I only got a brief peek, and I wasn't even sure that this person was the one following me. But it was the only lead I had. I hastily started in their direction, breaking into a fast jog, only to arrive at an intersection without any clue as to which direction they had disappeared down. I traipsed to the BART station, holding my heavy head in doubt.

That same night, I locked myself in the guest room and spent copious effort perfecting one final sketch. I was so close to reaching my old house. I needed to get each detail right so that there would be no issues with finding my mother in her bedroom. Draft after half-finished draft was crumpled and thrown on the floor. No matter how much I concentrated on recollecting every feature of my old cul-de-sac, I wasn't satisfied with what ended up on paper. I doubted my memory too much to trust any of my sketches.

Frustrated by my lack of progress, I angrily ripped up what felt like my hundredth drawing. As the scraps tumbled to the floor, I looked around at the guest room. It was in complete disarray. My previous drawings were scattered all over. Some were messily tacked up, but others were strewn on the ground or bed. Most of them were of poor quality, ruined by agitated scribbles and fragmented ideas. I realized with horror how much my collection of drawings resembled my father's wall of incompleteness. I was further dismayed to see that the clothes I had on—a stained sweater and oversized sweatpants—looked exactly like what my father used to wear.

I stumbled to the bed in shock. I was turning into someone I despised. Was I really as directionless as he had been? Ever since he'd left, I tried to distance as much of myself as possible from him. Whenever I was conscious that I was acting in a way that mirrored him, I would immediately counteract my behavior and vow never to carry myself that way again. I hated him, thought terrible things about him, but there I was, finding out that we weren't that different after all.

I was more than ready to give up. Why was I holding on to the joy from my childhood or the subsequent guilt when I couldn't even reclaim details of the place where these emotions had formed? Where was the truth in my memories when they were all susceptible to manipulation? If the past could be as easily rearranged as paint on a canvas, then why did I continue to be affected by it? Even that very moment in the guest room was already being reduced to a memory. So, what was the point of persisting when the future would ultimately become the present, and the present would just as rapidly turn into the past, and the past would disintegrate into ashes, just like my mother, only to be let go and forgotten? What was the point of having ambition, striving for a better life, searching for meaning, when none of what I accomplished or gained mattered after my short, fleeting life vanished into a vacuum? Then, I asked myself the scariest but most necessary question I had been avoiding: if all of this was true, then what was the point of continuing to live? I could end it all as easily as my mother had. Ravi's house had sharp enough knives, and it would only take two quick cuts along each wrist. I didn't expect the entire affair to last longer than an hour. I checked the time. It was around five p.m. By six, I could be dead, and the torturous amount of loneliness and desolation I had contained inside of me would mean nothing anymore. I closed my wet eyes and turned my face upward. Please, show me the way. If there is any meaning to this, then, please, tell me. I cannot find the correct path. I'm pleading like never before to be pulled out of this misery and allowed solace. Please guide me. I don't trust myself enough to do this on my own. I'm being severed into opposing parts that are all battling with each other. If death is the only way I can find release, then please grant it to me. End this bloody war within my mind. I beg of you.

———

"I cannot help you anymore," said the Singer sullenly.

"What do you mean you can't help me?" I snapped.

"I won't sing for you again."

"But I have to go back!"

"Look at yourself. You are filled with anger. You've relentlessly abused the Imagined. I can see the toll this is taking on you, and I refuse to be a part of it. I'm sorry."

"So, that's it?" I snarled. "You introduce me to the Imagined, watch it take apart my life, and then refuse to help me when I need it the most? I should have known you would abandon me again."

"This is not like when you were a child. Please understand that I'm doing this now for your benefit. I thought it would make me happy to have someone else who shared this skill, but I was sorely wrong. It hurts me to see you torturing yourself."

"You're a hypocrite, you know that? You act like you have so much wisdom about life, but you don't. You don't know anything."

The Singer was silent.

"Fine, don't sing for me. I'll still find a way to get there."

"Please," the Singer begged. "Do not do this. Whatever you are searching for is not as important as your well-being. Let go of the Imagined. It's not worth it."

"I never would have expected you to say this."

"I've come to care a great deal about you, Akash. Especially after learning about your mother's passing, I do not want you to be in pain."

"Well, it's too late for that."

I shut my eyes and thought back to the one time as a twelve-year-old I'd had to force my way back in. I needed a trigger that would bring my physical state as close as possible to how it had been as a child. I shot up with determination and began to run in place. It took a few seconds to build up sweat and stretch my legs out. I hummed the thumri to myself, and even though I wasn't able to sound exactly like the Singer, the tune still evoked a much-needed feeling of longing. I inhaled the fresh, crisp smell of the park, grasping desperately on to anything that could trigger my nostalgia. Soon, sharp pinches began all over my body. They pushed deeper, down to the root of my muscles, as I tore myself away from Golden Gate Park. The physical and mental pain were beyond anything I'd ever experienced, but I continued running, knowing how close I was to being in my mother's arms again.

The already deformed Imagined appeared even more haphazard due to my hasty entrance. The sky was a dark shade of purple, and red clouds hung like clots of blood. I sped toward the same spot I'd made it to the previous time—at the corner of my cul-de-sac, only a few steps away from the house. Neon rose bushes lined the walkway toward the front door. The house, although generally representative of what I recalled, looked two-dimensional, as if it had been scribbled in. The door was short and white, and with increasing revulsion, I realized that it was exactly like the entrance to the Fremont guest house my mother and I had lived in. With enough concentration, I might have been able to recall the correct door shape, but I didn't want to waste my energy recapturing this forgotten detail when I still had to work my way up the stairs. I pushed through the entrance without staring too long at it.

Each step felt like I was trudging through a windy, cheek-biting hurricane. My memory of the home's interior was thankfully unflinching. The details were vivid, down to the exact color of the TV stand. The couch, the living room table that we would sit around, the family photos—they were all there. I could even smell chopped onions and slightly burnt chapatis. Like the rest of the Imagined Town, no one was visibly present, and yet, the house still felt alive and inhabited. I tightly held on to the conviction that my mother was in her room. I was sure she would appear if I believed strongly enough. She had passed away, just like Sagar. If I were to find anyone else in the Imagined, it would make the most sense if it were her.

I panted heavily as I climbed to the upper floor. The stairs were shifting underneath me as if they were steps on an escalator. Ripples passed through the unstable walls. The inside of the house was melting into watered-down paint and trickling to the floor. While the Imagined was collapsing around me, I reached the closed door of my mother's room. I tried the handle, but it did not budge.

"No, no, no, come on," I muttered, jiggling the knob even though it felt like liquid in my hands. The plummeting sensation commenced.

"Come on! Let me in!" I screamed. Using my remaining power, I kicked the door. Once, twice, three times. The roof of the house was separating into tiny droplets that rocketed toward the sky. I rammed my entire body against the door, but it still did not splinter like wood should. It was shutting me out.

I paused, recognizing that further physical actions were not going to help. I concentrated on the image of my mother lying in her bed. I thought about her arms around me. Her sweet-smelling hair falling on me. The warmth of her skin. I released one final kick. The door exploded, dividing into gigantic droplets that sprang away from each other. Behind it, where the room was supposed to be, was a blinding white light. I only had a second to see it before my body catapulted back from an intense blast. I plummeted through darkness with my arms outstretched, trying to salvage the remains of my fabricated world.

"No!" I howled. My torso slammed against the pavement of Golden Gate Park. "No!"

I hit the concrete with my hands, even though I didn't have any strength left in me. The Singer was gone. Night had fallen in the park, and I was completely alone. I stood up and let out a blood-curdling scream. I screamed until my voice was hoarse, and then I crumpled to my knees. "What more do you want from me? How much more are you going to take away?"

Tears gurgled out of me, produced from a sorrow so enormous that it couldn't remain within my weak body. Nothing was tethering me to this world anymore. Nothing was motivating me enough to exist. I could feel my grief in every heavy heartbeat, every strained exhale. I couldn't do life on my own. I couldn't exist without her. I needed her to hold me, to caress me, to kiss my forehead, and if that wasn't possible, then I couldn't live. I just couldn't.

A slight rustle sounded. I caught a glimpse of someone hiding behind one of the nearby trees. Only then did I notice that a blanket and small takeout box of Chinese food were sitting on the ground next to me.

"Who are you?" I yelled, wiping away my tears. "Show yourself!"

The park was quiet.

I was fed up. Someone was clearly following me, and I needed to know who it was. I rose, steadied myself, and stormed in the direction that I had seen movement. I wondered if I was imagining Sagar again like I had when high on an edible. But this person felt different. They seemed larger, more real. They did not feel like a hallucination.

I reached the other side of the tree and was irritated to find no one there. A distant crackle of leaves diverted my gaze once again. I followed the noise like a hound until I ended up on the main path. A hooded figure around my height was walking a few yards in front of me. Their hands were shoved into their pockets.

"Hey!" I cried out.

The figure quickened their pace away from me. My suspicions were confirmed. Someone was stalking me. I tailed them out of Golden Gate Park and onto a regular street. They turned a corner and began to run. I chased after them, even though I felt like I was about to collapse. My mind was splitting apart to the point where I was hallucinating innumerable pieces of the Imagined in San Francisco. Oak trees were popping up in between buildings. The sky color was morphing into a haunting purple. The figure turned another corner, and I followed after them.

All of a sudden, I was back in the forest, right by the three trees. All the townhouses, all the street signs, all the hills of San Francisco had vanished. I was fully immersed in the Imagined again, even though I'd made no attempt to be.

"What is going on?" I muttered. I hobbled forward and weaved in between trees. The Imagined and the physical world were merging. I couldn't distinguish anymore what my mind was inventing and what was tangibly there.

Through a pocket of visibility, I saw the hooded figure running to my left. I changed my direction, careened around a forest tree, and ended up back on a sidewalk in San Francisco. I clutched my abdomen, nauseated at how easily I was switching between what used to be two separate worlds.

I stumbled forward and realized that I was in the middle of a road. A car horn blared. Bright headlights sped toward me. The hooded figure, who was on the opposite sidewalk, halted and pivoted my way. Their hood was pulled so far forward that I still couldn't see their face.

I lurched back out of the car's path. My feet lost sensation, causing me to teeter. I slipped and collapsed on the sidewalk. My vision was blurry, but I was beyond the point of pain. I couldn't move a single limb.

Someone lifted my head off the ground and cradled my

neck. I blinked a few times and made out that my stalker was hovering above me.

"Who are you?" I whispered.

They lifted their hood off.

I did not trust myself. My grasp on reality was too far ruptured for me to be confident in any one of my senses.

"Dad?"

My eyes rolled back, and the world went dark.

CHAPTER 28

VARUN'S TALE

I WOKE UP in the guest room under the protection of clean sheets. They were tightly wrapped around me, like I was a toddler who'd been tucked in. The morning sunlight leisurely strayed in through the shutters. The tinkling windchime in Ravi's backyard and the crooning birds outside my window created a soothing song. I scanned the rest of the room. My drawings of the Imagined were collected and neatly piled on the desk. I stretched out and yawned, pleased with the coziness of my surroundings. I wanted to laze in that comfortable bed forever.

Flashes of the previous night interrupted my serenity. They materialized in rapid visual bursts: the erratic state of the Imagined, the blast of light, the hooded figure. As I spread out under the soft, cloudlike covers, these images seemed implausibly intense and downright inconceivable. They felt more like a bad dream than actual events I'd experienced. If what I remembered of the previous day had occurred, then how had I gotten back to Ravi's house? How did I end up swaddled under these sheets? Even the reveal that my father was the hooded figure seemed highly unlikely upon further reflection. I shook my head and chuckled at how far the fantasy had run.

A knock at the door forced me to lift myself out of bed.

"Bro, you up?" whispered Ravi from outside.

"Yeah, come in."

Ravi cautiously opened the door. He regarded me with concern and pointed to my forehead. "Fuck, dude. How does it feel?"

I couldn't figure out what he was referencing, so I slowly raised a hand to my face. My finger contacted gauze, and as I pressed harder, I felt a burning pain underneath. I turned toward the wall-mounted mirror and almost gasped at my sickening appearance. My bloodshot eyes were sunken into my gaunt face. Thin, veinlike scrapes tickled my left cheek. Plastered on my forehead was a lump of gauze that had turned maroon from all the blood that had seeped through. I slowly removed it, wincing as the adhesive ripped off my skin. A deep cut ran from the top of my forehead down to the corner of my eyebrow. Flakes of dried blood coated the surrounding skin.

"What ... what the hell?" I murmured. "What happened?"

"You tell me. The doorbell rang hella late at night. Thank God my parents didn't hear. There was a man on our porch holding you up. Bro, you looked fucking out of it. I thought you were dead."

"This man. Did he say his name?"

"Nah, he just said he was a friend. He handed you over to me, and I helped you walk the rest of the way here. By the time I got back to the front door, he was gone."

"What did he look like? What was he wearing?"

"He was your height. Had curly hair. Lowkey, he looked like an older version of you. But forget about him for a minute. What happened to you? Are you okay?"

I sat back down on the edge of the bed in a daze. "I can't remember."

"Scary shit. I was up all night thinking of what we could say to my parents. My mom's been worried sick about you ever since she came in here yesterday and saw the mess. She cleaned up a bit. I tried to tell her not to."

"No, it's okay. I should have kept this room in better condition."

"We'll tell them that we were playing basketball. You tripped and fell and then ... Bro, you good?"

My throat was closing. The previous night hadn't just been a bad dream. My father was the one who'd found me and brought me back. I saw his face even more clearly now that Ravi had confirmed it.

"Ravi, I think I need a minute."

"Oh. Sure. Come down when you're ready. We're just eating breakfast." He turned to the door and hesitated. "Also ... Eva wanted me to tell you that she misses you."

"What do you mean? I see her when she comes over."

He fidgeted with his shirt. "She feels like you don't really want her around. Again, her words, not mine."

I sighed. "Can we talk about this later?"

"Yeah, for sure. I'll see you downstairs."

Once Ravi left the room, my mind flooded with questions. Why was my father following me? How long had he been watching me? How did he know where I was staying? The hairs on my arm stood up as I circled back to the most important conclusion: my father had found me. I was conflicted on how I felt. To go from a complete lack of awareness about his whereabouts to learning that I'd seen his face less than twenty-four hours ago was an unbelievably jolting recognition to grapple with.

As I stood up and became more aware of my aching body, I detected a slight bulge in the left pocket of my jeans. Even though I'd slept on a clean bed, I still had on the same filthy clothes as the previous day. I appreciated that Ravi hadn't undressed me; I would have felt much worse than I already did. I slipped my hand into my pocket and pulled out a crumpled piece of cartridge paper. I smoothed it out and saw a short written message. The handwriting, with curvy *a*'s and lazy dots on top of the *i*'s, was easily recognizable as my father's penmanship. Incapable of following a straight line, he wrote with a slant, causing his sentences to dip midway through.

> *Akash,*
> *I hope you are feeling better. I know you're probably surprised to see this message. I'm not sure if you realized it was me. Anyways, I want to see you. My number is below. I'll be in the area for the rest of the day. I hope you contact me. ~~There is a lot I need to say~~ I understand if you don't.*
> *Varun (Dad)*

The message was so brief that I had to read it over five times to make sure I hadn't missed any hidden meaning. I was livid. After years apart, this was all he gave me? There was no sign of an apology. There wasn't even the slightest bit of remorse. I wanted to burn the note and forget about it, but there was too much I needed to say. My courage was stronger than it had ever been. After my last visit to the Imagined, I felt like I had nothing left to lose anymore.

I was ready to show my father the extent of my rage.

———

It was a beautiful day at the park. The lake in the center was shimmering, and the pathway around it was buzzing with Fremont residents and visitors. Small children were romping around with summertime fever while their parents kept an eye on them from afar. Dogs dutifully scampered alongside their owners, despite the occasional attempt to chase the numerous geese lazing around the edge of the water. The weather was pleasantly warm. I wore one of Ravi's light sweaters—a blue, knitted crew neck.

I'd texted my father to meet me at Lake Elizabeth twenty minutes or so after reading his note. The park was close enough to Ravi's house that I could leave at any point. Like my father, I had kept my message brief. Though we'd decided on a time, I realized upon arriving that we hadn't discussed where exactly in the park we would meet. I wouldn't have been surprised if he'd abandoned the plan without telling me. In fact, I would have been glad. He was selfish, and his absence would have further confirmed it. My fury was becoming exponentially more untamed with each passing minute.

I rounded a bend in the path and saw him. He was sitting by himself on a park bench near the edge of the lake. The secluded bench was a short distance away from the main walkway and partially enclosed by a thicket of tall reeds. He was hunched over, and his hands were shoved into his pants pockets. His thinning hair was peppered with whites, though cleanly cut and brushed. His face was not completely visible from my vantage point, but I could make out from his broad shoulders and thick neck that he was stockier than he used to be. From afar, he looked much older than thirty-seven.

I walked over to the bench. He noticed me and shot up. His face, like the rest of his body, had aged. His mouth was downturned, and his eyes did not shine with the same vitality. He seemed more stoic—a shock to see. A part of me mourned the loss of his boyish excitement and restiveness.

After a period of silent examination, he motioned for me to sit. We took our places on opposite sides of the bench, facing the lake instead of each other. I fixed my gaze on the family of ducks wading in front of us.

"I forgot," said my father, removing a wrapped jam sandwich from a small paper bag at the base of his feet. "I brought you something to eat in case you're hungry."

I shook my head to indicate that I wasn't.

He nodded and placed the sandwich back in the bag. He glanced at my face, and I averted my eyes so that they would not meet his.

"Your … how is it?" he asked, pointing to his forehead. I mirrored him and touched the bandage covering my cut. I winced, having forgotten it was there.

"It's fine," I muttered.

He rested his hand on his lap and recommenced looking out at the lake. "Nice park."

Squeals of an excited child surfaced behind us. On the pathway, only a little farther down from where we were, a middle-aged man was pushing his young son on a bike. The son had on a Mickey Mouse shirt and was smiling as widely as the character on his tee. His dad pushed the bike with an enthusiastic cheer. They traveled a short distance before the dad slowed the bike down to a stop. His son begged him to continue pushing.

"You've grown up so much," said my father softly. He'd stopped watching the bike-riding duo and was now brazenly staring at me.

"That's typically what happens over six years," I said.

"Akash—"

"How did you find me? How did you figure out where I'm staying?"

He sighed. "It's a long story."

"Are you serious? You brought me out here, and that's all you're going to say to me?"

"I can explain more, but I don't know if you want to hear it."

"How long have you been following me?"

"Not long."

"Meaning what?"

"Few weeks. Maybe a month."

"A month! You've known where I was for a month, and you didn't say anything? You didn't approach me? I thought I was going crazy thinking someone was following me."

"I'm sorry. That's not what I was trying to do. It was wrong of me to hide."

I was taken aback. Where was his defensive behavior? Where were his snappy remarks? I knew they were still there, buried underneath this solemn demeanor. I wanted to rile him up enough to prove to myself that he had not changed.

"She's dead, by the way. Did you figure that out while following me?" I stared at him, wanting to see how he would react to the news. He tensed up and furrowed his brow.

"How?" he whispered.

"She killed herself."

He closed his eyes. His lips quivered. I wanted to push him harder, see him break and splinter.

"She slit her wrists, if I'm going to be accurate."

He winced, providing me a taste of accomplishment.

"And I was the one that found her. Held her as she died."

"Akash …" my father groaned.

"You know the funny thing, though? I wasn't surprised that it happened. It almost felt inevitable. And I realized that it's because she already died the day you took everything from us. From then on, she wasn't able to trust again. She was wary of everyone, even me. Until yesterday, I thought I was responsible for her death …"

My father's eyes were still closed. I wanted him to open them. I wanted to look directly at him as I said what I was about to.

"… But it's really you who I should blame," I spat. This was the moment I had been dreaming about. This was the moment I would crush him, make him feel miserable and small. "You're the reason our lives were so screwed up. You're the reason why she no longer wanted to try and build a future. You convinced us to trust you, and then left us to rot. You're the reason she's gone."

I paused, waiting for his response. I was so enraged that I felt like my heart was going to explode. How dare he sit there in silence? How dare he not look at me!

"One thing you got right though," I continued, my voice growing in volume. "I don't want to hear about where you've been or what you've been doing, because I don't care about you. You were a pathetic excuse for a father, and I can't believe you even had the courage to show your face to me again. You should be the one dead, not her."

A tear escaped from the corner of his closed eye. He swiftly brushed it away and turned his face so I wouldn't notice. But it was too late. I'd already seen it.

I should have been happy. I should have felt proud of myself. I'd received the exact response I'd wished for. I'd wanted him to feel pain from my words, and the tear confirmed that he did. But at my core, I only felt sorrow, despite my best efforts to conceal it with anger.

How do I describe what one experiences when watching their father cry for the first time? This isn't to say that I hadn't seen tears of his before. They would make a noticeable appearance when he and my mother used to have their useless squabbles in New York, and then again, when his project in San Francisco began to go downhill. But every prior occurrence had felt artificial. He would throw a full-fledged production aimed at garnering our sympathy. He would scream, wail, and hurl things so that he could be acknowledged as the victim.

Unlike back then, this tear slipped out inconspicuously, and if I hadn't been staring directly at his face, I wouldn't have even known it had surfaced. It was the first time I saw emotion from him without the purpose of manipulation, of positioning his needs in the center of the conversation. This was the first time I saw my father cry with sincerity.

I thought back to the point in my life when I could only look at him with admiration. Those short weekend trips into Manhattan used to elicit a sense of excitement I'd never felt otherwise. I savored every moment with him, studied every movement of his, assumed every opinion he had. When we were apart, I would eagerly await the next time we would reunite. I wanted to dream as big as him, to one day have as much talent as he did. He stood on the highest pedestal in my mind.

And then, after he abandoned us, I built him up to be this monster, this overarching shadow in my life. I thought of him with such hatred that, in my mind, he swung to the complete other end of the spectrum, to the absolute bottom of my moral regard. Once again, he took the shape of a staggering presence. I regarded him as a devil of sorts, more so than a human being.

But with that one tear, the once-imposing figure was reduced to flesh and bones. I saw his graying hair, loose skin, jacket stain, sagging shoulders, and faced the mundanity of his existence. He was one out of billions on this planet that would live as long as he was destined to, continue to exist in the memories of those that had known him, and then eventually be forgotten and effaced from human history. What really caught me by surprise was that he knew it too. His quiet tear showed me that he was aware of the finitude and irrelevance of his life. He no longer carried himself with the same confidence he once had. He wasn't chasing a colossal ideal that he would never be able to attain. Once I saw the human before me, and not the towering presence I remembered from my childhood, I no longer yearned for his suffering. My anger seemed inconsequential. If our lives were as insignificant as I knew them to be, then any revenge I sought to inflict on him was just as meaningless. Why was I letting my anger eat me inside out when there would never be a substantial gain from it? Even if I properly expressed my bitterness, what would I obtain? What would he?

"How dare you cry," I whispered, fighting for my anger, even though I knew it was a losing battle.

His face was still turned away from me.

"Say something!"

"I'm sorry," he whispered.

"Fuck you."

"I'm sorry for what you've had to see and for what I've put you through. I'm sorry that you've had to live without a mother or father, Akash. You don't deserve any of this."

"You're such a piece of shit."

He faced me. Though I'd hoped to look into his eyes with spite, I was unable to. I turned to the lake and scrunched up my nose. I would not let him see me cry.

"I don't want to hurt you any more than I already have, Akash. If you want me to go, if that will make you happier, then I'll leave immediately. And if that's the case, then I'm very sorry for ever making contact."

I remembered the nights right after he'd left when I'd waited for him to return. I'd prayed to God that his disappearance had just been a big misunderstanding and that he would come back to the apartment with a reasonable explanation for why he had taken the money. I had held on to that hope so tightly.

"Do you want me to leave?" he asked.

After a brief pause, I replied, "I want to know how you found me."

"As I said, it's a long story."

"I know."

"You sure you want to hear it all?"

"Can you just start already before I change my mind!"

He hesitated, studying me. "I'll tell it from the beginning, then. From when I left you and your mom." After clearing his throat and settling into the bench, my father peered out at the bounded lake and began his tale ....

The events of that day, that horrible day, are still fresh in my mind. Looking back, though ... man, it feels like a goddamn lifetime ago ...

I left with one goal in mind: to prove everyone—your mother, the investor, my parents—completely wrong. My plan made perfect sense in my head. The money I'd taken would be used to pay the engineers while Sean and I searched for another investor. I was confident that we just needed a bit of time to decide how to correctly package the project. Every angel investor in Silicon Valley would fall in line at our door once we were able to land on a solid idea. We would start selling our product, and in no time, we'd have a huge hit on our hands ... Jeez, my fuckin' arrogance ... It was never about the money. I couldn't have cared less if I was a millionaire, as long as my work was recognized. I was convinced success was just a short distance away, so I didn't feel any regret when I wrote that note to you and your mom. I know you'll never believe me—it's hard for me to now—but I left with the goal of reuniting one day. I could see that things in the apartment were tense, but I was too blind to understand that the issue began with me. I thought launching this product was a necessary step for the three of us to be happy together. If I was able to make something of myself, you both would understand why I had to take the money and willingly accept me back.

The first night away, I slept at the office. Rumors had already spread that the investor was pulling out. Some employees didn't show up the next day for work. The ones that did were furiously editing their resumés. Even Sean, who'd been my partner in crime from the start, was already figuring out how to sell off our equipment. I was pissed. I felt like everyone had secretly ganged up on me. So what if the investor had left? We still had my designs. That was all we needed.

Sean pushed back. He said that he understood why the investor wanted out. He admitted that when we began brainstorming together, he was so eager to dive into the fast-paced world of tech that he overlooked the insane number of issues that came with our project. Like the investor, Sean said that no one would buy a product unless it served some sort of use in their lives. When I showed him the money I took, he roared with laughter. I'm not kidding—he couldn't stop for the next five minutes. He said that what I had would barely pay for a week in the office. I was shocked as hell. Since he'd been in charge of the finances, I hadn't bothered to learn how much everything cost. I wasn't able to wrap my head around how lucky we were with our first investor, and how impossible it would be to find another idiot willing to pay this high a price for us again.

So, I ignored him. Convinced myself that he was a traitor. Even though the team was falling apart, I wasn't gonna give up. I found a cheap motel to stay at, and when I say cheap, I mean the shittiest place you could ever imagine. The room was made up of a piss-stained twin bed and a tiny wooden desk marked up with dick drawings. The toilet flushed only when it wanted to, and the bedsheets reeked of alcohol and grocery-store sushi. I worked, day and night, tearing my hair out, trying to come up with some sort of marketable utility for our project. The issue was ... well, the issue was that I couldn't see what the issue was. Ever since I'd run away from my parents, I thought so highly of myself that I knew—not just hoped, I knew—I was going to produce something great, something monumental, in my lifetime. The possibilities of augmented reality seemed like exactly what I'd been waiting for. This project would allow my designs to be superimposed on the world. To me, that was the most fascinating shit ever. I was so laser focused on reaching this—what word can I use—triumphant, yes, triumphant version of myself that I couldn't understand what other value Sean and the investor wanted. Who cared if there wasn't any practical use to the AR glasses? What more could anyone ask for when they had my art?

But as I continued to work without anyone else's support or confidence, I started to doubt myself. The money was running out. I had nowhere else to go. Night after night, I was cooped up in the room, drawing a blank on what the purpose of the project could be. How much longer could I hold on to my dream when no one else saw worth in it? I examined my drawings again and, for the first time ever, saw through the delusion ... saw them how others did. The lines and curves were nothing but scribbles. I wasn't creating anything that other artists weren't able to. There wasn't any deeper meaning hidden behind my designs. No divine purpose. Shit, there was nothing extraordinary about them at all. I tried to push past the doubt, but it skyrocketed each passing day.

The money was cleaned out a couple months after I left the apartment. I waited until the very last day, until I had not even a cent left, to leave the motel. I didn't have any friends that I could call for help. No couch that I could crash on. The only people I really knew in SF were you and Mahi. I went back to the Chinatown apartment—desperate, hungry, and tired. But the studio was occupied by a new tenant. He had no idea where you guys had moved to. I vaguely remembered the name of the salon your mother worked at, so I found the address online and checked it out. I was just as shocked to find that the space was being renovated into an entirely different business. I couldn't understand how so much had changed over such a short period.

Of course, I'm thankful now that I didn't find you and your mom at that point. I would have returned as self-involved, as shitty a father and partner, as when I'd left. Probably worse, if that was even possible. The only reason I came back was because I had nowhere else to go, not because I felt any remorse. I'm not sure what would have happened if I'd found you, but I don't think it would have led to any positive change for either of us.

As night approached, I took what few belongings I had and camped out at a tiny neighborhood park. I curled up on a hidden bench and shamefully hid my face with a spare sweater. Finding sleep wasn't easy. Even the tiniest footstep would wake me up in panic. Throughout the night, other homeless people roamed through the park. I was worried at first that they would take something of mine, but I realized soon enough that I had nothing to offer them. I obviously didn't have the staples like cash or food, but I also didn't have any recognizable face value. They had no clue who I was, and they frankly couldn't give a shit. My pride had always been important to me because I'd believed that one day, my name would be known to everyone. Lying on that bench—man—my eyes were finally opened to how invisible I was. I hadn't achieved a single one of my goals. I didn't have any material possessions. And the worst part of it was that I'd sacrificed every relationship in the process.

The next morning, I begged a shopkeeper to let me use his phone. I dialed a number I never thought I would again, at least not willingly. The call was picked up by an unknown woman. I mentioned my father's name and asked if this was still his home phone. She said that it was, so I asked to speak with him or my mother. She was surprised by my request and asked when the last time I'd spoken to either of them was. I told her that I was their son and explained that we'd distanced a while ago. She paused for a minute and then introduced herself as Julia, my father's full-time nurse. A few years earlier, my parents had been involved in a terrible car accident. My mother was killed, and my father was left paralyzed waist down. Julia was originally hired to provide medical assistance, but she'd grown attached to my father and took it upon herself to help out around the house and keep him company. But no matter how much she tried making conversation with him, he would only speak back in short sentences, if at all. She said that he was silent and gloomy most of the time, even when his friends from around the Illinois area came to visit.

Julia told me to wait on the line while she let my father know that I was calling. She said that early photos of me were up every-where around the house and that she'd always been curious where I ended up. She left, and I tried to digest this fuckin' insane news that had just been dumped on me by this stranger. I'd always stupidly thought my parents would be in the same condition as when I'd left them. But hearing about my mother's death was just ... well ... I don't know how to put it into words ... it just made me think of how many years were wasted without us speaking.

When Julia returned to the phone, she told me that my father wanted the phone to be brought to him. Knowing the state of his health, I was even more tense than when I originally dialed the number. His ragged breathing was soon audible on the line. I took that as my cue to begin speaking. I tried to ask him how he was. He didn't respond. Without confessing much, I said that I desperately needed a place to stay. Absolute silence from him. After a minute or so, I heard whispering. Julia returned to the phone and said that my father asked her to book a flight for me. She said that she would e-transfer $200 and send the itinerary to my email. If I needed to, I could print it out at the local library. I thanked her and asked her to thank my father for me too. Later that day, I boarded a flight to Illinois with all the grime of the city park bench still on me.

Julia picked me up from the airport and took me back to the house—the same one I'd run away from years before. I was immediately hit with the smell of my parents. Sort of like ... brewed black tea and dusty books. Yeah. That's it. Strong tea and old books. Julia helped me move into my old room. It looked exactly like how I'd left it. Even though I only lived there for a short while after you were born, Akash, that house holds a shit ton of memories for me. My parents and I had been strangers in that neighborhood, and we'd spent most of our time indoors. I was thinking back to all those crazy fights we had—all the screaming and yelling that happened in the hallways—as well as the nights I used to lock myself in my room, just chewin' over my hatred for them. Unlike back then, the house was still. Quiet. Like all the frustration packed inside it had been removed in my absence.

Julia took me to my father next. I can't find the proper words to describe my shock when I saw him. Forget the hair he'd lost and the wrinkles that were on his face and arms—forget all of that. The accident had left him bedridden. His eyes were unfocused, and he struggled with every breath. He looked half alive. Like he was waiting for death, waiting for the release it would give him. What a horrible, horrible sight it was, Akash.

You've never met my father, so believe me when I tell you that he was a tough man. One of the toughest I've ever known. When I was young, I used to see him as a tyrant. He was incredibly strict and needed his rules to be followed. He would dictate which academic subjects I could pursue, when I would study, what activities I would partake in, when I could go out, who I could associate with, and on and on. He would try his hardest to control me. Yell a lot. Smack the shit out of me if he felt it was needed. Seeing him weak was like seeing a different human being altogether. I couldn't accept that the man before me was my father. The most fundamental part of him had been snatched away. He was unable to move, eat, or function without the help of another. He'd lost his ability to hold authority over others ... over himself too.

*My goddamn guilt in that moment. Whew. It was like a fuckin'
torch had been lit underneath me. I blamed myself for not being
present after my mother's death, and for him needing a stranger to
care for him instead of his own kin. I came back as a failure, both
as an artist and son. I fell at his bedside and cried for all the years
I would never get back. I saw the disgusting person I'd become,
and all the people, including you and your mother, that I'd failed.
My father was quiet the entire time I sobbed. I held on to his limp
hand, hoping for, I don't know, pity or reconciliation or something
like that, but he didn't even flinch. Eventually, I left and went
back to my room.*

*We hadn't discussed how long I was staying for or what I
would be doing in Illinois. To fill my time, I helped Julia around
the house. I cooked, cleaned, mowed the lawn, changed the sheets,
washed clothes, took out the trash. All mundane tasks. I also started
working part time as a check-out clerk at a nearby grocery store.
It was boring work, but hey, I was getting paid something. In
the evenings, I sat by my father's bedside. The first few days were
spent in silence. I needed something, anything, to break the ice, so
I started reading to him. My father was a former engineer, so he
loved sci-fi novels. His shelves were filled with authors like H.G.
Wells and Michael Crichton. When I wanted a break from these
books, I told him stories about my life. I told him about my time
in New York. I told him about you. I told him a lot about you,
actually. He always perked up at the mention of your name. But
I avoided telling him about the move to San Francisco. He didn't
ask, even though the flight Julia had booked for me was from SFO.
Although he was quiet during these sessions, I could tell from subtle
cues on his face that he was listening closely. This weird, one-sided
conversation continued for a year or so. I spent every evening with
him, and to be honest, this was the easiest I'd ever been able to
communicate with him. His silence gave me the freedom to speak
without having to argue.*

Finally, the night of your fourteenth birthday, I revealed the truth about San Francisco. I started with the journey of my project and told him about the money I'd stolen. I glanced at him, expecting to see disgust. I thought he might throw me out once he realized how hideous I was. But his eyes were blank. I pleaded with him to say something, to say anything. I sat with him until Julia interrupted and said that he needed to sleep. I went to my room, anxious as a motherfucker. For half an hour, I stared up at the ceiling, debating whether to leave Illinois on my own in the morning. I didn't know how I was supposed to look at my father again after what I'd shared.

Then, I heard a hoarse croak. He was calling out my name from his room. I jumped out of bed and ran to his side. He reached out to my hand and spoke for the first time since my arrival.

"V-Varun ..." he said, his voice slow and gruff. "I ... I am near the end of my life."

"Appa, stop," I pleaded.

He coughed, a dry, hacking cough. "It's the ... truth ... I know ... Time is almost out ... but I have a f- ... few things to say. First ... you need to know ... know that I never sto- ... stopped loving ... y-you."

I was stunned. "What? Why are you telling me this?"

"You ... you think I r- ... resent you for ... for leaving ... but I n-never did ... I always wanted the b- ... best for you."

"Appa ..."

He coughed again, wheezing this time. "M-my father ... my father ... made me earn ... his love ... I thought I could ... could do the s-same ... b- ... b-but it pushed you ... f-further away ... made you think ... love is cond- ... condition- ... conditional."

"Appa, don't strain yourself. It's okay. You don't need to explain."

He held up his hand, breathing slowly into his handkerchief. "Taking ... taking you f-from your son ... b-biggest mistake ... I made ... you were ... t-too ... young ... your w-whole c-career was … ahead of you … but a-after you left … and your mother passed … nothing … n-nothing mattered … I blame myself … made you believe … your son was l-less … important than … than your vo- … vocation."

"Please don't say that. You can't hold yourself responsible for my mistakes."

"Y-you … are … s-selfish … No deny- … denying … what you have … d-done to M-Mahi and son … h-horrific."

My head fell to his bedside in shame.

"But … you were the c-center … center of my world … Varun … so I made you think … t-that you should be … center of yours … f-for that … I am s-sorry."

I started to cry. "I don't know what to do anymore, Appa. I've failed everyone."

"Are … are they still … a-alive? M-Mahi and … A-Akash?"

"I think so. I don't know. I tried to find them."

"How h-hard … did you … you s-search?"

I did not reply.

"Your life is … n-not over … if you s-see them … a-again … will you … a-atone for … m-mistakes? … Can you … put … put aside … a-ambition?"

"Yes."

"M-must be sh- … sure … Varun …"

"I am sure."

"Then c-continue … search until your d-dying … breath … G-God has g-given you time … one thing I d-do not … do not have much … l-left of."

"I understand."

"Good … go sl- … sleep … I am t-tired … your path will be … clear tomo- … tomorrow."

"Thank you, Appa." I kissed his hand and walked to the doorway. Right as I was about to leave, I felt this strong itch. No, itch isn't the right word. This deep, deep need to say the words I'd never been *able to say to him before. The same words I'd longed for him to say throughout my childhood instead of all the constant shouting. I looked at him wheezing in his bed, saw the same face that I'd hated, that I'd hated so much, and finally said to my father, "Appa, I ... I love you."*

The next morning, I woke up to Julia's screams. My father had peacefully passed away in his sleep.

I dealt with the routine proceedings for his death. He'd left everything to me, and the will was dated long before I'd returned to his house. Two years before then, I would have used the inheritance to invest in a project of mine. It would have been flushed down the drain immediately.

But time with my father had changed my perspective on what I wanted to do. I paid Julia a generous amount, sold the house, and moved back to SF. I found a place in Chinatown, close to where we used to live. Once I was settled, I started looking again for you and your mother. I combed through pages of internet search results and social media accounts. I visited nearby salons to see if your mother was working there. I contacted local high schools to ask if you were enrolled. I didn't get a single lead. You guys were so far off the grid, it felt like you were on a different planet. As kind of a last resort, I started hanging out in the bakery below our old apartment. I'd wait for an hour or two every day, hoping you would eventually return.

Meantime, I started online classes in UI/UX design. It's a pretty neat subject. I found a way to combine my artistic skills with a trade that's hot right now. After earning a few certificates, I landed a full-time role at a midsize company. The job's good. Stable. Exactly what my father wanted for me. I do my best on the projects they assign, but I log off at the end of the workday and leave my professional life behind. I still sometimes work on my art over the weekend, but I don't have any goals to commercialize it ever again. It brings me personal enjoyment. Nothing more. This job got me to finally understand what my father had been trying to teach me.

I'd hated him for wanting me to chase after mediocrity, but it was freeing not to run after this insane idea of having to make a name for myself before I die. I could let go of this belief that I had to be better than everyone else. That my work had to be a record of my existence. I could live peacefully while enjoying a good income. At my job, I'm no different than any of my colleagues. I'm one out of hundred other forgettable faces in the company. Feels weird to say, but I'm okay with that. I really am.

Anyways. Getting sidetracked. Did I already mention the bakery? Yeah, so, I'd sit there most days after work. Lots of times I would stay there until they closed. This went on for years. And then, one random day earlier this summer, I saw you. You were standing outside, staring up at the apartment building. You were much taller than before, and your face had matured. But I knew it was you, Akash. I knew it. You didn't notice me, and as much as I wanted to run out and hug you, I was terrified of making myself known.

So many questions raced through my mind: What was your life like? Where were you staying? Would meeting me only hurt you more? I decided not to rush it. I wanted to have some of these questions answered before approaching you. So, I followed you on the BART back to that gigantic house you're staying at. I returned the day after and waited outside until you came out. I trailed you to Golden Gate Park and watched you meditate by the edge of the casting pools. I thought following you would help me understand what had happened to you. But it honestly left me more confused. I couldn't figure out how you'd ended up in that house, staying with this unknown family, or what the hell you were doing during these park visits. I would watch you sit there for hours, shivering and twitching, sweating so much to the point of fainting. I wanted to understand, but I couldn't. I still don't. You came out of your meditation each time with such intense frustration that I thought if you found me then, it would only add to your anger. I hid behind the trees like a coward until you finally caught on.

Maybe it was wrong for me to worry about timing. Maybe it was wrong for me to follow you at all. But what's done is done. We're sitting in this park now. This is my story, Akash. The whole of it. And I leave it in your hands where to take it from here.

I stood up from the bench and stumbled to the edge of the lake, sorting through the racing bits of my father's narration.

The bike lesson was ongoing on the paved path. The overenthusiastic dad roared jubilantly as his son rode a short distance without his help. He lifted his son off the saddle and lovingly kissed him on the cheek. My heart ached for all the base adolescent experiences I'd never had with my father because of his absence.

"Were you hoping to tell this story and have a great reunion like you and your dad did?" I said, storming back. "If you're looking for forgiveness, you can forget about it right now."

"I would be lying if I said that a part of me didn't wish for it," answered my father. "But I expect nothing from you, Akash. I didn't even expect you to show up today."

"Then, what do you want from me?" I demanded, towering over him.

"I want you to be happy," he whispered. "Whatever brings you that. Even if it means that we never speak again."

I shook my head and, once again, suppressed tears from forming.

"I left out a part of the story," he continued. "After my father passed away, I looked for you in one place other than SF. I went back to the Town."

I slowly sat down on the other end of the bench. "What? How … what did it …?"

"It's very different than how I remember it. But also, it's been around nineteen years since I left."

"What did you do there? Did you see …?"

"I saw Harsh. I went to your old house, and he happened to be the one that answered. We had a very short conversation. I told him that I was looking for you and your mom, and he said that neither of you'd returned to the Town. I thanked him and was about to leave, but he asked me to wait. He grabbed a small envelope from inside and asked if I could pass it on if I ever found you guys."

My father reached into the sandwich bag and removed what I assumed to be that same envelope. "I realized looking at that house who your true family has always been. They were the ones that raised you. Harsh was the father I failed to be."

I took the envelope from him, my hands shaking.

"I have something else I want to give you, in case this is the last time we see each other."

My father produced a pouch from his pocket and handed it to me. It had cash inside, lots of it.

I forcefully placed the pouch down on the bench. "I don't want it. If this is some form of repayment for what you stole—"

"Don't think of it as attached to me. It's just money. You can use it however you want. As I said, I expect nothing. All I ask is that you figure out a way to move forward and be happy."

"What if I don't want to? What if I want this to be it? To be the end?"

My father furrowed his brow. "Is that really what you want?"

"I've been trying to figure out why I'm powering through this pain day after day when at some point my life will be over anyway. Maybe Mama had it figured out. Why struggle when I can let go so easily?"

My father hesitated. "I think I've lost my license to tell you what to do. If that's what will give you peace, then who am I to stop you?"

I looked away. It wasn't the response I'd been hoping for.

"Aku, look at me."

My eyes met his.

"If you're asking me to tell you what the purpose of life is, then I'm sorry to disappoint you. I've given up looking for it. If humans haven't been able to agree on what the fuck we're supposed to be doing here since the beginning of time, then how should I know the correct answer?"

"That's not very comforting."

"But just because we can't find one specific purpose doesn't mean that there isn't any value to life. When I saw you as an adult in Chinatown, I felt shame, yes, but I also felt so much goddamn love for you. It was one of the most incredible feelings in the world, knowing that you were alive and that God had led me back to you. It was the exact same emotion I experienced when I held my father's hand after years of separation. I'd been searching for something larger than the ocean, larger than this universe and the one beyond it, and I finally found it."

He reached out hesitantly and stroked my hair. I don't know why, but I let him.

"You're afraid that the future will fail you, and honestly, it might. But I'm telling you that meaning exists in this world. Not in the way that we've been brought up to understand it. Names will fade. Accomplishments will fade. We'll all be goners one day. But the ability to experience this type of love ... shit, I think it's enough to keep us going. I guess then, if I had to suggest a purpose, it would be to search for love. Do whatever you can to find it."

"But how do I know if I'm meant to experience it? How do I know if it will bring me happiness? What if life only leads to more pain? Then I'll have wasted years searching for something I'm not meant to find."

"I know you've been happy before. Otherwise, you wouldn't be able to measure the pain you're in now. And if it was possible once, then I'm almost certain it is again. But Aku, it can only exist if you look for it. If you wish to find it."

"Have you been able to? Find happiness?"

He squinted, tilting his chin up to the sky. "Not yet, but I'm working on it."

My head was spinning from the effects of the previous day. "I need to lie down."

He stood up. "I won't keep you."

"Is this it then? Are we going back to pretending like we don't exist in each other's lives?"

My father did not look as tiny standing up, nor did he look as old. As I gazed up at him, I wished that I could forget his flaws and return to how I saw him as a child.

"Aku, I would welcome you back into my life with open arms. But the decision is yours."

He stepped away.

"Wait," I murmured.

He paused.

"Stay. Just for a few more minutes."

Without wavering, he sat back down in his previous spot. We stared out at the calm lake in silence. To any passing stranger, my father and I were two unassuming bodies sitting in a trivial park at an inconsequential moment in time. But between us lay the intangible, profuse weight of my mother's sorrow, of memory and regret, of life's onerous mysteries— and as much as I tried to forsake it—of love.

After I felt like enough time had passed, I stood up, took the pouch of money from the bench, and began my walk back to Ravi's house.

CHAPTER 29

MEMORY LANE

WHEN I REACHED the guest room, I first opened my father's pouch and counted the exact amount of money inside. In complete disbelief, I realized that I was holding on to twenty grand. I tried to estimate how many shifts at the restaurant it would have taken me to earn that much, but the calculation was too cumbersome. The irony was not lost on me that my father, who could barely afford dinner at one point in time, was handing me such a large sum of money.

I set the pouch aside and directed my attention to Harsh Kaka's envelope. My hands trembled as I lifted it up. Whatever was inside would be an acknowledgment of the time that had elapsed since I'd lived in the Town, an affirmation that my entire teenage life had been spent apart from my extended family. There was a strong possibility that the contents of the envelope might even bring me up to date on those in the Town my mother and I had left behind. Was I ready to let go of my ignorance and face the present state of my estranged kin?

Curiosity bested my inhibition. I ripped the seal off and removed the notecard inside. On it was a succinct, but carefully written message: *I never blamed you.* I turned the card over, trying to see if there was an additional part of the note that I'd missed. Nothing else was written. There wasn't even a printed name or signature. I reread the note, this time in Harsh Kaka's voice. I said it out loud, wondering if playing with the intonation would help uncover another meaning. The words danced through my mind over and over again, but the message had a singular goal. It didn't waste time trying to hide what it wanted to convey. Why wasn't there more to it? I wanted to toss the note, hold it close, rip it apart, kiss it. I tried to reject the words, convince myself that they weren't for me. Harsh Kaka, the purest soul, had touched pen to paper with no hint of anger, bitterness, or even sympathy, for that matter. His statement was phrased as a fact, not an opinion. How, after everything he'd endured, could he write this? How could he forgive me when I could not forgive myself?

Guilt was so deeply ingrained in me that I couldn't make sense of my life without it. Since I'd laid eyes on Sagar's injuries, since my mother had asserted that I was to blame for his death, my guilt had only ever multiplied. Every opportunity I found to further convince myself of my faults, I took. I believed that I was at the center of each untoward event, that somehow my being harmed the lives of others. Guilt was a wall, preventing me from pining after a future that was healthy and prosperous. The Imagined had briefly allowed me to forget my afflictions by returning to the form of a child unburdened by complex thoughts and consequences. It had been freeing for the short period it lasted, but the Imagined's unraveling had diminished my hope of ever finding innocence or solace again.

Holding Harsh Kaka's note, I knew that I had to make a conscious choice for my future. Growing up, I'd heeded the influence of others, especially that of Sagar, Mayuran, my mother, my father, and Luke. I'd gladly accepted their approaches and values because it had taken the pressure off deciding for myself. But they were no longer around to guide me. I was completely on my own. As my father had hinted, no one could chase after my future but me. No one could search for value in my life but me. There were numerous possibilities as to how I could proceed, and the only way forward, the only way for me to end this misery, was to figure it out for myself. So, I finally confronted the principal question that lay at the center of it all: what did I want from life, if I even still wanted to live?

My first option, the one that required no adjustment in routine, was to keep visiting the Imagined and persist in this struggle to reach my mother. However, the repercussions of my last visit, including the disorienting unification of the Town and San Francisco, made me cautious. I was afraid that my body and mind would not be able to handle another forced visit. Also, even if I did find my mother, how long would I be able to hold on to her, given how rapidly the Imagined was deteriorating? Eventually her face—like Sagar's—would be distorted, her touch would be forgotten, and I would be consumed by doubt as to whether anything about her was as it had been when she was alive. Continued efforts to recapture her would only lead to further frustration.

Instead of returning to the Imagined, I had the option of using my father's money to move out of Ravi's house. I could find another job, sustain myself, maybe even graduate and go to college if I really felt up to it. This option, though, would provide only a temporary solution. The unaddressed guilt would continue to fester. After I adjusted to the routine of working again, I would feel just as lost and astray, just as alone, as I did in the present moment.

As I'd mentioned to my father, following in my mother's footsteps was something I considered often. The fear of rotting indefinitely, of never finding peace again, was enough to convince me to give up. Who would be affected by my death? My dad would assume I didn't want to meet with him again. The family back home would probably not find out, given our distance. Ravi and Eva would move on to college and make new friends. If my own parent, who had been my moral guide since birth, found death to be more desirable, then what was stopping me from mirroring her?

For the first time since my mother's death, I felt concrete resistance to this thought. Something my father had suggested stuck with me: since I'd experienced happiness before, shouldn't I be able to again? If I'd truly found no value in life, I would have followed my mother ages ago. But, as evidenced by the Imagined, I still yearned for hope. I'd encountered pure, prodigious love in my childhood. The torturous emotions that had developed over adulthood, primarily the merciless advancement of guilt and grief, had swayed me into believing that life could not be benevolent. If I took my life, the pain would be terminated, but so would the wonderful moments I knew I had experienced. It would invalidate everything I had lived through and write it all off as worthless. I could not accept that.

My memory of the Town was unreliable, but enough of it was there to assure me that I'd previously recognized the value of existing. As my father had stated, pondering a higher purpose was pointless. I would never be able to figure out why life progresses the way it does, why we get attached to people and places and things only for time to take them away, or why we have to undergo pain and struggle through it. I had to surrender my desire for answers, as well as my frustration at not being able to get them. It was a simple change. Instead of asking myself, "Why am I alive?", I had to accept that life was given to me for whatever reason it was. If I was meant to be dead, I wouldn't have been born in the first place, nor would I continue to survive.

The question I then needed to ask myself was, "How can I find value again while I'm still here?" My father's advice instilled in me an optimism that if I did find happiness again, I wouldn't care that it was fleeting, or that life was fleeting, or that all of this would be forgotten once I eventually passed away. The strength of the emotion would be enough to assure me that persisting was worthwhile.

Harsh Kaka's note was a sobering reminder that the events of the past were definitive. No matter how much I tried to avoid them, move past them, ignore them, and numb them, they had occurred. Sagar was dead. My mother was dead. I was fundamentally a different human being than I had been when living in the Town. The news of my paternal grandfather's death forced me to reflect on the changes that might have transpired in my extended family. I wasn't even sure if my Aaji was still alive. The last time I'd seen her, her health had been declining.

Roused by my father's story of reconciliation, I recognized that I would always be held back without a connection to my extended family. I would never find peace if I didn't attempt to reunite with them. The unresolved friction would linger for the rest of my life, a mark of my cowardice preventing me from ever finding genuine happiness again. Knowing that they weren't aware of my mother's death was suddenly a revolting thought. After reading the note, withholding that information seemed worse than taking my own life. She had been their family too, and time apart had not erased that fact. They deserved to know the truth. Since I was the one who had kept them in the dark for months, I felt strongly that I had to be the one to tell them.

I impulsively picked up the phone and dialed the old house number. I hadn't called it since my first night in San Francisco. An automated voice message announced that the line was disconnected. If my father had gone back to the Town shortly after his own father passed away, after my fourteenth birthday, then it would have been around four years back when he'd seen Harsh Kaka. My family could have moved away during that period. I wanted the smooth resolution my father had experienced with his dad, but it was impossible to predict if my trajectory would imitate his.

The note and money stared at me earnestly. I couldn't give up because of a disconnected phone line. If I wanted this, which I believed I did, then I would try my best to find them, however long it took. I did not know what I was going to say, nor what I was going to accomplish. But this note, and the flicker of hope contained within it, urged me to persevere. I had made my decision.

———

I deposited the money and booked a ticket for a red-eye flight later that night. I told Ravi and his family that I was going to visit some distant relatives. They offered to pay for the flight costs, but I refused. Ravi's mother assured me that whenever I was ready to return, I had a home waiting for me. Ravi dropped me off at the airport. Before leaving the car, I told him that I was sorry.

"For what?" he answered with surprise.

"Being an asshole. You and your family have done so much for me, and I know I haven't been the easiest person to get along with recently."

"Stop this senti shit."

"I'm not being senti. I just want you to know how grateful I am for you."

Ravi smiled. "You don't need to do this, dude. You're my best friend."

I thanked him again for driving me, took my suitcase and urn (which was packed into a sealed, compact crate) and headed into the airport. Nerves kept me awake the entire flight. I realized during takeoff that it was my first time in the air since my mother and I flew to San Francisco. Despite my lack of sleep, I was alert as I entered JFK Airport and boarded the train bound for Penn Station. I had the option to go on the direct train from Penn to the station in the Town, but I decided to follow the long route my mother and I used to take. This would require two trains to a neighboring county, then a bus to the City, and finally a short walk to the Town. I didn't care if the journey took twice as long. I would not step on the platform that had ruptured my family.

The rumbling of the train and the familiar sights outside compelled me to reminisce about the times my mother and I would travel to and from Manhattan. Fragments were appearing, blurry in some parts, but clear in others ....

... While riding the train back home, a man around Suhail Mama's age was intently watching my mother with a sly grin. His eyes were wide set, and he had a gaping dimple in between his eyebrows. His shaggy, shoulder-length hair rested on top of his blue bomber jacket. My mother squirmed in discomfort. Our carriage had been crowded when we'd departed Manhattan, but it had emptied out with each progressive stop until only the shaggy-haired man was left inside.

In a loud, nasal voice, he jeered at my mother. What he said exactly has slipped from my mind, but I'm certain that it was a crude comment. My mother jolted in her seat and clutched my arm tightly. The shaggy-haired man leaned back and began rubbing his crotch. He flicked his tongue out repeatedly, producing a sound midway between a slurp and a hiss. Though I could not fully understand the implications of his actions, I was aware that he was making my mother extremely uncomfortable. My mother leaned forward and covered my ears so that I could not see or hear him. I was confused and a bit vexed with my mother's choice to stay seated when the partition to the other carriage was only a few feet away.

After an excruciating five minutes, the train rolled into its next stop. A couple of other passengers entered. As soon as another person was within our vicinity, my mother tugged my arm and pulled me up. I didn't even have time to see whether the man was still engaging in the same vulgar actions. We sped out onto the platform and entered another carriage that was far, far away from the one we'd just been in.

After years of maturing, I learned to reflect on this event with a better appreciation for why my mother waited to make our exit. The way the carriage was structured put me specifically at a disadvantage for a potential escape. The shaggy-haired man was sitting one row away from us in the direction of the partition. If my mother had been on her own, she could have easily darted past him. But since I was with her, it would have taken more time for me to scoot out of the window seat, potentially giving the man enough time to block our path.

My mother endured his insulting catcalling so that I would not be put at risk of any danger. Before she passed away, I only focused on her wrongdoings in order to convince myself of her selfishness. And although she hadn't been without her faults, I couldn't ever consider her an inadequate mother. Her love had seeped into seemingly insignificant instances, taking shape quietly so that I only saw the true extent of it once it was missing from my life ....

I exited the bus and started down the connecting passage between the City and the Town. What used to be a detached, uninhabited, badly paved road had unsurprisingly undergone a transformation. New houses had been built on one side of the renovated road, opposite the train tracks. I could not make out what was farther ahead due to the dense greenery, but the Town did not seem to be as private anymore. The forest in the middle used to act as a stark geographic separation between the City and the Town. Based on what I could see of the recent development, I assumed that the two locales were more unified than before. I felt oddly connected to my Ajoba in that moment. Just like when he first discovered the Town, I was wandering into unknown territory, not knowing what I was about to find.

The day was still early. A couple of unrecognizable faces were walking their dogs, but the road was empty otherwise. Along the walk, I inevitably came across the train station. There were a few modifications to the signage outside but no other observable changes in structure. It was as imposing as ever, its glass windows glinting with sharp morning sunlight. The parking lot was moderately filled with cars, and stressed commuters rushed inside the building. Like all inanimate places, the station wasn't lingering on previous tragedies that had occurred inside. It continued to serve its purpose with impassivity.

Unable to look at it for long, I strayed from the path and entered the forest. I stood for a moment, turning my face up and observing the pieces of blue sky that appeared between the treetops. I reached out and felt the bark of a tree. I curved my fingertips around its rough edges and embraced the splinters that pierced through my skin. I rooted myself in a place that had been manipulated and reinterpreted many times in my mind. It was emancipating to observe the forest for what it was and not what I remembered.

Still, my confidence wavered. My sensory capabilities were all I could hold on to in order to gauge what was real and what wasn't. But they had previously been used to convince me of the Imagined's authenticity. I'd seen the misshapen tree and multicolored leaves with my own eyes, not someone else's. I wasn't able to trust my perception at that exact moment because I didn't trust my perception of the past. A part of me still doubted if I was standing in the actual forest or if my memory was constructing the environment around me. That same part of me wondered if this whole trip was just a prolonged dream. I treaded forward with fear that I would spot flashes of surreal irregularities. I thought I spotted a couple in the corner of my eye, but it could have just been the product of my own anxiety. Luckily, Sagar was nowhere to be found. If he'd appeared, I would have known with certainty that I was back in the Imagined.

I jumped over the small stream and hurriedly jogged toward the forest exit. Once I reached the back of the Mahmoods' tailor shop, I slowed down to a walk and placed my hand on the outer wall. Unlike in the Imagined, I didn't face any resistance when leaving the forest. I no longer felt like I would be flung back in or that the world was going to break apart if I took another step forward.

As I approached the very edge of the cul-de-sac and was about to pivot onto Main Street, I looked through the side window of the Mahmoods' shop and saw that the business was different. The tailor shop had been converted into a women's boutique; neat clothing racks and chic mannequins in Western wear replaced the cluttered heaps of ethnic fabrics.

I hesitated, worried that other businesses on Main would also be different from what I remembered. I was not ready to see a completely unrecognizable street. Redirecting my attention to the other side of Main, I caught sight of Accelerated Academy, the tiny elementary school Sagar and I had attended. From what I could see, it was the same white building with painted red stripes and an eagle mascot flag hanging at the front. I smiled, happy to know that not all had changed ....

... The morning of my first day of sixth grade was even more hectic than usual. Still on his summer sleep schedule, Sagar refused to haul himself out of bed. Vaishu Mavshi would shake him awake, but he would just collapse back into his pillow the second she left the room. This happened three times before she practically dragged him to the bathroom so that he would brush his teeth.

Vaishu Mavshi wanted to make us omelets or pancakes or some sort of breakfast food requiring eggs—I can't really remember now—but when she went downstairs, she found that Harsh Kaka had already boiled the remaining eggs for his breakfast throughout the week. He sheepishly offered them to us, even though he knew Sagar and I hated eggs cooked that way. After spotting Vaishu Mavshi's murderous glare, he said that he would run to Juhi Aunty's store and pick up another carton.

One issue followed the other. I was supposed to take a shower while Harsh Kaka ran the errand, but Sagar was using the upstairs shower, and my mother was taking her sweet time in the downstairs bathroom.

Vaishu Mavshi knocked ferociously on the door. "Mahi, hurry up!"

"Don't rush me!" my mother yelled back.

"I will if we're going to be late!"

"You're so dramatic. We have plenty of time."

Vaishu Mavshi raised her hands in exasperation. "I can't. I just can't."

Meanwhile, my Aaji, unfazed by Vaishu Mavshi's agitation, was ten minutes into an outlandishly convoluted tale that had started with her first day of sixth standard and was now pure gossip about Amitabh Bachchan. I tuned her out for the most part but would occasionally smile and nod to appear like I was listening.

Harsh Kaka returned with the eggs, but as he was passing them to Vaishu Mavshi, he lost his grip on the carton. The eggs splattered all over the floor. Runny yolk dripped off my shorts and Vaishu Mavshi's jeans (or was she wearing scrubs?). We all stood in shock for a moment.

"What happened?" my mother asked, strolling out of the bathroom, drying her wet hair with a towel. She stopped when she saw the mess and Vaishu Mavshi's panic-stricken expression. Her laugh reverberated through the kitchen. She was the only one brave enough to make a sound. Vaishu Mavshi recovered from her paralysis and launched into action. She ordered my mother and Aaji to clean up the fallen eggs while she and I changed. Meanwhile, Harsh Kaka was tasked to pack us toast to take to school. The next fifteen minutes were rushed and disorderly, opposite of the morning we'd planned to have.

Somehow, Sagar and I ended up at the school's entrance before the first bell rang. My mother, my Aaji, Vaishu Mavshi, and Harsh Kaka were standing in a single row behind the front fence. They waved in unison, beaming with pride. The chaos of the morning was forgotten, and all the attention was redirected to this precious farewell. My mother leaned against my Aaji, and Vaishu Mavshi swiftly wiped a tear away from her own cheek. Even though my father wasn't present for most of my childhood, moments like this made up for it. I had three other surrogate parents who ensured I never felt unloved. Sagar and I rolled our eyes and hurriedly entered the school, but I'm almost positive our family remained standing outside for a while after we'd left ....

Main Street was an unlikely intersection between the old and new. I'd assumed that it would either remain as I remembered or it would be completely uprooted. It ended up being neither. Some of the shops from my childhood stood without any changes, such as Juhi's Groceries and the pharmacy that Harsh Kaka had worked at. Other shops had been remodeled or added upon. For instance, Simran Aunty's storefront still appeared to be a salon, but from what I could see of the inside, it was notably refurbished. The chairs were sleeker, the decor was updated, and the sign outside indicated that it had been renamed.

In addition, the open oval space used for Suhail Mama's wedding was now paved. Other businesses filled out the circumference, and there was a small roundabout for cars that wanted to circle back on Main. Street signs for each cul-de-sac were updated on sturdier posts. I noticed, while walking past the cul-de-sacs, that a few of them were redeveloped. The houses had been torn down and rebuilt to look bigger, more contemporary, and identical to one another. One of the cul-de-sacs was under construction with the same intent. The general structure of the Town was there, but the essence had changed. It wasn't so drastic to the point where I was devastated over what I saw, but the expansion and advancement in the area was still tough to ignore.

Granted, I couldn't gauge the extent of the changes given how early it was in the morning. I was the only one out on the sidewalk. The shops on Main weren't even open yet. Solitude allowed me to reckon with the fact that I'd finally made it to the place I'd been dreaming about for years. Waves of nostalgia hit me with every step, and I fondly reminisced on the times I'd run up and down this street. How comfortable I'd felt then, how safe I'd been ….

… The Town was hosting an open-air Diwali event, and many Indians from around the New Jersey and lower New England area were in attendance. Main Street was lined with electric candles and colorful streamers. Fusion Kathak dancers performed in the oval area, and merry dhol players accompanied them. Sagar and I cheered them on and whistled with gusto. When the performances ended, we played a game of hide-and-seek with some of the other kids in the Town. Sagar and I teamed up and sought out a hiding spot at the edge of the forest. We crouched behind a wide tree and scanned for any approaching players. A rustle farther in the dark forest caused us to jump in fright.

We grabbed on to each other and cautiously went to check out the source of the noise. Though the area was dim, I could make out a young couple pressed against a tree. The taller of the two was Suhail Mama. The other person was an unrecognizable girl around his age. Suhail Mama bent down and whispered something in her ear before proceeding to kiss her on the lips. Sagar gasped.

Suhail Mama whipped around before we could escape. "Who's there!"

He marched toward us, his eyes widening once he realized who the culprits were. "Akash? Sagar? Why are you spying on me?"

"We didn't mean to," responded Sagar timidly.

"Who is it, Suhail?" asked the girl.

"No one," he replied. To me and Sagar, he growled, "If either of you say anything about this to your moms, I will be very mad. Got it?"

"Suhail, stop scaring them." His date moseyed toward us, lifting her lehenga so as not to trip. Her face was round and her dimples prominent. Her curly hair bounced each time she took a step forward.

She bent down so that she was eye level with me and Sagar. "Hi, boys."

"Hi," we meekly replied in unison.

Suhail Mama tried to cut in. "You don't need to talk to them."

She ignored him and keenly gazed at us. "Nice to meet you both. My name is Kiara."

After a brief introduction only made less awkward by Kiara Mami's affability, Sagar and I ran away, promising not to reveal their relationship to the rest of the family. This proved to be immediately challenging given what our mothers were discussing when we found them.

"He's being shady," said my mother as she lounged across two plastic chairs. "I know it's about a girl." (I should note that I'm not entirely certain this is what she said. My recollection of this conversation is very spotty, so I'm going to do my best to fill in the gaps based on how we all spoke otherwise.)

"But who?" inquired Vaishu Mavshi. "Someone from the Town?"

"No way. He's already broken all the hearts here."

"Why isn't he telling us? I need to know who it is."

Sagar and I glanced at each other. Our silent communication did not go unnoticed.

"What, Aku?" asked my mother jokingly. "You know who it is?"

I rocked back and forth.

My mother shot forward, almost knocking over one of the plastic chairs. "Do you actually know who it is?"

"I can't tell you," I replied.

"Vaishu, he knows!" my mother exclaimed, excitedly seizing Vaishu Mavshi's hand. "Tell us. You can trust us."

"I'm sorry. I promised."

"Aku, please, for your poor, sweet mother."

"Her name is Kiara," blurted Sagar. He immediately covered his mouth in mortification. I scowled at him. Why did he tell them? We were sworn to secrecy!

Vaishu Mavshi squealed. "Sagar knows too! Oh my God, Mahi, our kids have become too smart for us."

With the truth already partially uncovered, Sagar and I described in entirety how we found them in the forest. When Suhail Mama returned, combing his hair back into a faux-hawk, my mother gave him an obvious smile and said, "How's it going, Suhail?"

Suhail Mama groaned. "You know."

"Kiara? Isn't she your friend from college?"

He shot daggers at me and Sagar. We both shrank into our seats.

"We've been dating for a while," he said. "I just didn't want you to make it a thing."

"Make it a thing? What thing? We wouldn't do that. We're so chill."

Vaishu Mavshi nodded seriously, but once she and my mother made eye contact, their giggles ran free.

Suhail Mama shook his head. "See!"

"We'll stop, we'll stop," chuckled Vaishu Mavshi, wiping tears of laughter from her eyes. "Listen, Suhail, if you're happy, then we're happy."

"Wait, do you love her?" asked my mother.

Suhail Mama blushed. "I think she might be the one."

"Awwwww," both women cried out. They stood up and buried Suhail Mama in a hug. My mother planted a kiss on Suhail Mama's cheek, making him blush even more.

"I hate you both," he muttered.

"Better get your grades up, Suhail," said Vaishu Mavshi. "You have to get a proper job before thinking of proposing."

"Yeah, yeah, don't need the lecture. She's not the type to care how much I'm earning. She said she would live in a basement if it meant we were together."

"And you'd be okay with that?"

"If I'm with her, nothing else matters. Money, house, cars ... they're all secondary."

"Such a romantic, our baby brother," my mother swooned. "Can you please forgive these boys? Look at Aku's face. He looks like he's going to throw up."

"I'm sorry, Suhail Mama," I whispered.

His face melted into a tender smile. He pulled me into a headlock and ruffled my hair. "Of course I forgive you, Aku."

"I don't think this family knows how to stay mad at each other," declared my mother. "Now that this bombshell has been dropped, let's go find our new sister-in-law—"

"This is exactly why I didn't—"

"Okay, okay! Let's go find the girl you're smooching and daaaance!" ...

Even though details were foggy, even though I couldn't recapture what had been lost, these fragments were beautiful as I remembered them. The details were trivial when I was certain of the emotions that remained with me. The love, joy, intimacy, and endearment I felt all these years later granted the memories importance. And though a part of me would have loved to travel back in time and relive them, I had no desire to alter these moments, because doing so might alter the emotions associated with them. I was a product of these lived experiences, even if they felt distant. They were my foundation—the main reason I was on this journey back home.

The paint was worn out, and yet, the house remained intact. It had evolved just as much as I had. The brick and wood displayed the scars the abode had suffered over years of weathering and maturing. But these wounds didn't spoil the exterior; they made it appear glorious. I felt, even more so than while walking through the Town, a sense of reunification.

I set down my suitcase and slowly walked up to the door. My heart was pounding. I lifted my trembling hand until my knuckles were less than an inch away from altering my life. As I knocked, my doubt soared. What if they weren't in the house? What if they turned me away? I had impulsively flown across the country without any assurance or prior research.

I heard someone shuffling inside. After a minute, a voice called out, "Who is it?"

I uttered my name.

Locks were undone, and the door swung open. His skin sagged, and his hair had thinned out to a few lasting pieces of gray. His belly was smaller, though it still hid behind a tucked checkered shirt. He wore narrow glasses, making his face appear slimmer than before.

"Akash." He said my name as if he had expected me all along, as if it was of no surprise that I was standing in front of him at that very moment.

"Hi, Harsh Kaka."

CHAPTER 30

A DIVIDED HOUSE

THE INSIDE OF the house was exactly as it had been in my childhood. None of the furniture had been moved, replaced, or removed. Great care was evidently exercised in maintaining the house's condition. The floors looked recently swept and mopped. The table surfaces lacked even the standard sparse specks of dust. I was overcome with nostalgia after entering and refrained from properly observing any one part of the living room. Fortunately, we didn't linger for long. Harsh Kaka suggested tea, so the two of us went straight to the kitchen. I offered to help, but he insisted I make myself comfortable at the dining table.

After he joined me with two steaming mugs, he asked me to recount my years away. I began to summarize my time in San Francisco, but before even reaching my father's disappearance, I blurted out the news of my mother's death. I'd been hoping to scope out the right time to mention it, but keeping the information hidden had proven to be excruciating. Harsh Kaka's eyes watered and, like my father, he struggled to respond. He asked how it happened, and I answered bluntly.

"That is … I don't know what to say," murmured Harsh Kaka.

"I'm sorry. I didn't mean to reveal it so abruptly."

"I appreciate that you told me. It's just heartbreaking to hear." He leaned in toward me. "How are you doing?"

"Me? I … I'm not sure."

He nodded understandingly. "We don't have to talk about her right now. I'm horrified that you've had to endure this on your own."

I cleared my throat and took a sip of the tea. Harsh Kaka's signature addition of fresh ginger was unmistakable. The taste used to be too strong for me as a child, but I didn't mind it as much anymore. It was refreshing after the long journey.

"Is Aaji sleeping?" I asked, noticing how quiet the house was. "Vaishu Mavshi is probably at work already, right?"

Harsh Kaka shifted in his seat. "Yes, well, there is a bit I need to update you on as well."

"Are they okay?"

"I hope so. I think I would have heard if something happened. After you and your mother disappeared, and well, after everything else …"

I nervously glanced down at my cup. We'd been avoiding Sagar's name since the beginning of the conversation.

"Vaishu became very closed off," continued Harsh Kaka. "She stopped going to work, and she refused to speak to anyone who tried to visit. Every day was progressively worse than the last one. It got to the point where she would lie in bed for weeks without opening the blinds. Then, one morning, she finally got up, packed her things, and said that she needed to leave for an indefinite period of time. Your Aaji went with her, though I'm not sure how much she understood what was happening. I haven't heard from them since."

I was aghast. "Where did they go?"

"I didn't ask. She made it clear that she didn't want any contact. She said it would be easier for the both of us if I didn't know where she was."

"And you accepted that?"

"It's what she wanted."

"But- that- I'm—" I sputtered. "This doesn't sound like her at all. She wasn't the type to just take off without explanation."

"Grief changes people, Akash. I don't have to tell you that." He paused and took a sip of his tea. "You never knew your Ajoba, but he was not a vulnerable man. He would hide himself whenever he was upset, as if his emotions were something to be ashamed of. During trying times, he avoided facing the people he loved. Your mother and Vaishu followed the example he set."

"When did she leave?"

"About five years ago."

"Holy shit!" I exclaimed. "I'm sorry, I shouldn't curse. I'm just in shock. Did you ever try to look for her?"

"She'll return if and when she wants to. I've kept this house ready for her in the event that she does."

"This is crazy, Harsh Kaka! How can you two not be together?" Harsh Kaka and Vaishu Mavshi's relationship had been a testament of unfaltering love for me throughout my youth. Their relationship was what I'd wished my parents could have had. They used to perfectly balance each other's idiosyncrasies and work as a uniform team to care for our family. I couldn't even picture them separated for such an extensive period.

"I can't force her to be here."

"But it's so unfair. You didn't do anything wrong."

"I stopped chasing fairness a long time ago. If the world was fair, Sagar would still be here."

I flinched, but Harsh Kaka calmly sipped from his mug. I couldn't understand how he could be so rational and controlled when the world had continuously wronged him. "Aren't you angry, Harsh Kaka? We all left you."

"Anger is not going to solve anything."

"How can you forgive so easily? How can you hug me and make me tea and act like all is forgotten?"

"How did you expect me to act?"

"I don't know. Different than this. I've hurt you so much."

Harsh Kaka reached out to my hand. "None of this is your fault."

"But it is! I left him on the station and then abandoned you."

"You were eleven."

"I've grown up since then. I could have reached out to you earlier. I should have."

"You're here now."

"I know, but it's been so long. It feels too late."

"It never is. Even if you had come twenty years from now, it still wouldn't have been."

"What about my mother? You must feel some anger toward her."

"She didn't know what was going to happen at that station. You may have trouble believing me, but I understand why she ran away. She feared that she was the reason for our pain." He sighed. "I wish I could have spoken to her again while she was alive. If only I had figured out how to reach the two of you …"

I shook my head. "How can you be so good, Harsh Kaka? It doesn't make sense to me."

He grimaced. "I have ugly emotions within me too, Akash."

"I doubt that."

"I'm human, just like you." He set his mug down, and his eyes grew foggy. "Before I met your aunt, I was a very different person. Greedy and envious and filled with enmity. I don't think I've ever shared with you that I'm the youngest of three boys."

"You haven't," I replied. Harsh Kaka had been so integrated within our household that, until then, it hadn't even crossed my mind that he would have relatives outside of us.

"Yes, well, my elder brothers and I don't speak anymore. They were cold, cutthroat people. They instilled in me a need to compete for everything—didn't matter what the prize was. Falling in love with Vaishu helped me let go of my jealousy. I was moved by her unwavering dedication to her siblings. After we began dating, I felt like I'd been given a chance to better myself, though at first, fighting my previous tendencies proved to be very taxing. I didn't know who I was if my primary aim wasn't to subvert others."

"One morning we sat at this table, and you told me that the child and adult versions of yourself had once clashed with each other. Is this what you meant?" I asked.

Harsh Kaka nodded. "Maturing is a battle that we all have to face. But the respect and affection I saw within this household kept me committed to the right path. You all love each other unconditionally, even if you don't always know how to express it. You care for each other in ways my brothers never could. That's why I can't be angry. I've seen how evil people can be. I know for a fact that within all of you, the good exceedingly outweighs the bad."

"That's not true. Even recently, I've hurt people and pushed them away. I said horrible things to my mother before she died. I haven't become a better person over time like you have."

Harsh Kaka hesitated. "Akash, if I'm being honest, I don't think it's my forgiveness you are looking for. I don't carry any blame. The most important question is whether or not you're able to forgive yourself."

I peered into my mug. "How did you have the will to continue while you were alone?"

"Preserving this house for you and the rest of the family kept me going."

"But what if we never returned? Wouldn't it have felt like a waste?"

"It wouldn't have mattered. I would still know that I lived my life in service of something worthwhile. You've all filled my life with love. It's a gift I often don't feel worthy of. This is the only way I know how to repay the favor."

I wanted to collapse at his feet and beg him to tell me how horrible I was. I couldn't look in the face of such righteousness and integrity when my heart was tainted by ugliness. Sensing my discomfort, Harsh Kaka offered a warm smile. "Now that you're here, I know it definitely didn't go to waste."

"I'm sorry I arrived unannounced. I tried calling."

"Vaishu changed our number soon after the incident at the station. Too many reporters wanted to interview us about Sagar."

I drank the last bit of tea in my mug. "I came because I wanted to share the news about my mother and see how the family was doing. I guess I've done both now."

"This is your home. You should stay however long you want. Anyways, you haven't told the entire family the news yet. Vaishu should know."

"I thought you said she didn't want any contact."

"This news ... your return ... it changes things. She should know."

"How do I find her? Does anyone know where she is?"

"One person might," said Harsh Kaka uneasily.

"Who?"

"Your other uncle."

"Of course!" I exclaimed. "If Aaji is with Vaishu Mavshi, Suhail Mama would have to know where they are. But wouldn't you have discussed this with him already?"

"Suhail isn't exactly speaking to me."

"What! How is that possible?"

"I have to warn you—he's changed a lot since you knew him. He's the reason for a lot of the residential redevelopment that's been happening in the Town. He left his previous company to form his own, and since then, he's been focused on tearing down homes in this area. I don't know if you've been able to see, but the Town has become quite a desirable place to live because of the station."

"What does that have to do with you and him?"

"He's been trying to buy out this whole cul-de-sac to build more luxurious homes. He hasn't been able to touch it for a while, mostly because of my influence. But over the years, the neighbors have caved. The only house left not to agree is—"

"This one."

Harsh Kaka nodded. "He doesn't just want to buy out select houses. In order to build a cohesive set of larger homes, he'll need to own every single property on this street."

"I don't understand. Why would he even consider demolishing this place? He has emotional attachment to it as well."

Harsh Kaka shrugged. "Greed blinds us."

"This has to be a misunderstanding. I'm sure if I talk to him, he'll move past this disagreement."

"I better not be present when you two meet. There's a possibility he won't say anything if he sees me." Harsh Kaka stood up and took the mugs to the sink. "You should rest for a bit. I'm sure you're exhausted."

The lack of sleep from the flight was catching up to me. "Maybe just for a couple hours."

"Head on upstairs. I'll bring fresh towels for you."

This time while walking through the house, I keenly soaked in my surroundings. I beheld the worn-out couch where we would watch TV and the creaky stairs Sagar would trip on. The Imagined had conditioned me to anticipate dissolution, so I observed the house like it was about to fall apart at any minute. I paid attention to every little scuff mark on the walls and discernable crack in the wooden floor.

Once I reached the upstairs hallway, I slowly turned toward my mother's bedroom, the same one I'd been trying to enter in the Imagined. I grasped the handle and gently turned the knob, preparing for the white light that had blasted me back to Golden Gate Park. But the door opened with little resistance, and I remained unscathed.

The king bed appeared freshly made. Shadows of the trees outside were scattered across the navy-blue comforter. I sat on the left side, where my mother used to insist that she sleep. I picked up her pillow and pressed it against my face. The cotton cover was cool to the touch, just like it had been on those nights I was squeezed in between her and my Aaji. It was probably just delusion, but I felt like I could smell traces of her old shampoo still lingering on the pillow. I pictured us locked in an embrace. My face was resting at the top of her chest, where the skin was smooth and soft. Each exhale of hers warmed the top of my head.

I sobbed, holding that pillow, as I recognized why reaching my mother in the Imagined had been so strenuous. The Imagined could only work if I had unwavering belief that the constructed world was real. I hadn't seen Sagar pass away; I'd only heard about his death through my mother. With a little bit of doubt, I could still conceive of a reality where he was alive. But I'd witnessed my mother take her last breath. I'd held her as her body became motionless. Seeing her alive again would have opposed the truth that my mind was assured in. It would have been impossible to believe.

The room was so empty, so quiet. The house itself was no different. Harsh Kaka's recount of the remaining family's estrangement troubled me greatly. I hadn't expected any conflict to have occurred among those left behind. I wasn't able to go back in time and fix the mistakes made or prevent either death, but I did have the opportunity to bring what was left of this family back together. Partly in a quest to find meaning again, partly in an effort to rectify my and my mother's wrongs, I resolved that this had to be my objective going forward. I craved hope again more than I dreaded failure.

———

Harsh Kaka gave me Suhail Mama's contact information and warned me once again not to be disappointed if his personality was dissimilar to what I remembered. Even after learning that Suhail Mama had attempted to purchase the house, I could not draw a connection between the abrasive real estate tycoon that Harsh Kaka described and the amiable, easygoing uncle he used to be. I called the number, and after a few rings, Kiara Mami answered. Her exuberant, fast-paced speech pattern was instantly recognizable. She gasped loudly after I introduced myself and mentioned that I was back in the Town. Without asking me how or why I was calling her, she invited me over to her and Suhail Mama's place later that day. Since I'd last seen them, they had moved out of their previous apartment to a house in the suburbs of Connecticut. She ended the call by chirping, "*Soooooooo* excited to see you, Aku sweetie! Talk soon, love!"

I chuckled, having barely spoken two sentences in the conversation. Kiara Mami's chatty nature was reassuring to hear. I'd been worried about the call based on Harsh Kaka's words of caution, but Kiara Mami sounded far from cold or standoffish. I took the towel Harsh Kaka left me and headed to the shower, slightly relieved and eager to wash off the hours of travel before meeting with my aunt and uncle.

A couple of hours later, I was in a taxi, en route to Greenwich. As the car neared the address Kiara Mami had provided, I rolled down the window and gazed out at the surrounding affluent neighborhood. Sprawling, manicured lawns and long driveways bedecked the front of each property. The roads were wide and clean, with almost no cars parked on the curb. We passed country clubs as if they were the corner coffee shop.

Suhail Mama and Kiara Mami's place was a two story, Georgian-style residence with a lovely rustic brick exterior. Ivy delicately traced the spine of the house. A wide, spiked gate guarded the horseshoe driveway. I exited the car with my mouth agape. I knew that Kiara Mami's parents were well off and had helped the couple out in the past, but I was still shocked that Kiara Mami and Suhail Mama had amassed enough wealth to move into this gigantic of a house. I walked from the driveway to the front door on a cobblestone pathway bordered by purple hydrangeas.

Before I could knock, Kiara Mami swung the front door open. Her curly hair was longer than it used to be and colored with a caramel balayage. She wore a comfy black sweater and yoga pants. Even though her clothes were loose, I could still make out her pregnant, protruding belly. She leaned back from the weight of the bump and used one hand to protectively support it. Based on her stance, it seemed like the baby was about to pop out at any minute.

"OhmyGodlookhowtallandhandsomesoooocutewow," she squealed, outstretching her arms to me. I walked into her embrace, mindful of not pressing too hard against her stomach. She didn't seem to care and squeezed me tightly. I was smushed, struggling to breathe, and silently praying that the fetus would not be harmed. She pulled away and held my face in her palms. "You've become so big!"

I smiled, unable to take my eyes off the baby bump.

"Silly me! Completely forgot to mention this on the phone," she said, rubbing her belly excitedly. "We're expecting her to come soon, but who knows at this point. I've been in hell for an eternity."

"Is she …?"

"The first? Oh my God, yes. Trust me, I would not look this good if I had any other rascals to look after."

"That's so exciting, Kiara Mami. Congratulations."

"And to you too! You're going to be a big brother very soon."

I lowered my gaze, thinking of Sagar. Kiara Mami's smile wavered as she realized her error. She quickly recomposed and said, "Right, well, why don't you come in? Let's get you something to eat!"

She ushered me to the living room before fetching a decorated plate of frilly biscuits. The couch we sat on faced a picture window overlooking the lush garden outside. A stone fountain of cherubs was centered with the window and surrounded by four white patio chairs. The interior of the house was just as lavish. Ornate glass and gold trinkets lined the shelves. The stale art from their old apartment had been replaced with extravagant and showy pieces.

"Have some more," urged Kiara Mami, motioning to the plate of biscuits lying on the glass table.

"I'm okay, really. I'm full."

"Don't be silly! How can you be full? You've barely eaten anything." She reached toward the plate with great effort. Not wanting to cause her any strain, I swiftly picked up another biscuit and bit into it. Kiara Mami settled back into her seat, content.

"Suhail should be back from work any minute," she said. "I told him that you were coming."

"Harsh Kaka said that he has his own company now."

Kiara Mami's eyes flickered with unease. It was subtle, almost imperceptible. "Yes, he's had it for a while. My dad encouraged him to start it."

I thought back to how much Kiara Mami's father, Manav Ajoba, used to repulse me with his crude commentary and self-important behavior. I was happy he wasn't present.

"Harsh Kaka also told me that Suhail Mama's redeveloped many of the houses in the Town."

Kiara Mami replied hesitantly, "We don't discuss his business much."

"What about you? Where do you work again?"

"Oh gosh, I used to work at a PR firm, but I'm currently on maternity leave. Let's see what happens after the baby's born. Suhail's work schedule is crazy hectic, so I'm sure child duty will fall on me. But now that you're back, maybe you could take her off my hands for a bit. Joking! Well, kind of."

"I'm not sure how long I'm staying for. It's all a bit … up in the air."

"I hope you stay for a while, hon! Where's Mahi, by the way? You mentioned that you were in San Francisco, right? Is she still there? I was hoping to see her. We were all really shocked when you two left. That whole time was crazy, but I always liked your mother. I was *sooo* depressed when Suhail first told me."

"About that …"

A muffled rumbling interrupted me. Kiara Mami perked up. "That's the garage! Oh, Suhail's going to be thrilled to see you!"

Shortly after, Suhail Mama entered through the garage door. He wore a black sport coat, a patterned scarf, and navy-blue pants. He'd abandoned the fauxhawk for a longer, slicked-back hairstyle. He strutted in with suave steps, his chest puffed out. His resemblance to Manav Ajoba was uncanny. The last time I'd seen him, Suhail Mama had seemed to be gravitating toward the influence of his father-in-law, but the current confidence and pretentious style was almost an overt imitation.

He placed his briefcase down on the side table and grinned. "Look who it is. Damn, Kiara, he's all grown up."

"That's exactly what I said," she cheerfully concurred.

I stood up and hugged him. He ruffled my hair and said, "I can't believe you're really here. We searched like crazy for you guys. Reached out to every connection we had, didn't we, Kiara? Where'd you guys go?"

"We sort of moved in with my dad for a bit."

"Ah. Thought as much. I wish one of us had his number or knew where he stayed. Your mom was the only one in contact with him."

"Well, we didn't end up living with him for long."

Suhail Mama nodded. "All in the past now. We've missed you."

Harsh Kaka had to be mistaken. Suhail Mama's style and living arrangement might have changed, but the warmth in his voice was still present. Both he and Kiara Mami had welcomed me graciously and without hesitation. I refused to believe that Suhail Mama would cut Harsh Kaka off over a property dispute. He valued family too much.

Suhail Mama lifted a bottle of scotch from the liquor cart and poured himself a drink. He winked at me. "Want some?"

"Suhail …" groaned Kiara Mami, shaking her head.

"I'm kidding!"

He sat in a standalone armchair perpendicular to Kiara Mami. He leaned back, spreading his legs and sinking comfortably into his seat. Suddenly, he looked around with confusion. "Where's Mahi? I thought she would be coming as well."

"I was just asking him that," said Kiara Mami.

Their eyes were fixed on me as they waited for an answer. The news had naturally flowed out with Harsh Kaka, but something about the unrecognizable, impersonal environment was impeding me. Still, the truth had to be disclosed, even if it felt forced to do so.

"That's mostly what I came to talk to you about," I said. "She passed away."

Kiara Mami's hand shot up to her mouth. Suhail Mama's expression was blank.

"How?" whispered Kiara Mami.

"She took her life."

"Dear God," muttered Suhail Mama. He stood up and walked to the window, facing his back to me.

Kiara Mami shifted closer to me and wrapped an arm around my shoulder. "Honey, that's horrible. I'm so sorry."

I patted her hand and watched Suhail Mama. I was hoping for him to say something, but he was closed off from the two of us. The room was silent for a few minutes.

"Suhail, sweetie," murmured Kiara Mami. "How are you feeling?"

Suhail Mama turned around. His eyes were dry. "I'm okay. Just thinking through things."

"I'm really sorry," I said. "I wish I didn't have to bring you this news."

He walked over and knelt in front of me. "Hey, you have nothing to be sorry about, okay? If I'm being honest, it just makes me so pissed at her. First, she runs off without considering any of us. Then, she leaves you by taking her life? She's always been selfish … but this … this is unbelievable. Does Varun know?"

"Yes, but we've only met once since."

"That bastard! Can't even be there for his own kid!"

"Suhail," whispered Kiara Mami, "I don't think Akash needs to be hearing this right now."

I was surprisingly unemotional. Seeing Harsh Kaka tear up had reminded me of my own devastation regarding my mother's death, but Suhail Mama's frustration made me want to move past the conversation more than anything else.

Suhail Mama sighed and went back to his original seat. "Have you been living alone?"

"Not exactly," I replied. "I've been staying with a friend in the Bay Area."

"Oh, poor baby." Kiara Mami placed her head on my shoulder. "You're more than welcome to stay with us if you want."

Suhail Mama nodded. "Please. Stay as long as you need. Who else knows besides us and your dad?"

"Harsh Kaka."

Kiara Mami's arms stiffened around me.

"Harsh knows?" asked Suhail Mama.

"I'm staying with him in the Town," I said. "I came back to tell the whole family—Vaishu Mavshi too—but he doesn't know where she is. I wanted to see if you did."

Suhail Mama ran a hand through his hair and took a slow sip of his drink. "You're staying with Harsh, huh? Interesting. Maybe you'll be the one to finally get through to him ..."

"What?"

"Nothing, nothing. Forget that for now. You were asking where Vaishu Tai is, right?"

"Yes. Do you know?"

Suhail Mama set his glass down. "My sister's a strange woman. She's never had a problem looking after others. In fact, I think she enjoys it. But when it comes to herself, she would rather shut down than be taken care of."

"That's why I want to find her. I think I can convince her to come back."

"Where? To the Town? I don't see that happening."

"Why not?"

"It holds too many painful memories. She'd constantly be

reminded of what happened to Sagar. And now with this news about our sister … it would crush her to go back."

"But do you know where she is?"

"I do."

"Then let me at least try talking to her. What's her address?"

"Akash, I'm sorry, but she made me promise to keep it secret. She told me that she doesn't want to see anyone from the Town. If our mom wasn't staying with her, I doubt she would have even told me."

Kiara Mami lifted her head from my shoulder and shifted back to the other end of the couch. I glanced over at her for support, but she was vacantly staring at the garden outside.

"I'm family," I insisted. "Why can't you call and ask her? Maybe she'll change her mind once she hears I'm back."

"No, that won't work. She won't even see us when we go over. She asks for advance notice so that she can leave her place. Isn't that right, Kiara? If she can't handle seeing me, there's no way she'll be able to handle seeing you."

I was confused why Suhail Mama was resisting such a simple request. He was denying the call without even properly considering it. "But this is important. If you don't want to get involved, you can just give me her address, and I'll go talk to her directly."

"Suhail, come on," murmured Kiara Mami. She still wasn't looking at either of us, but her tone indicated that she was intently listening.

He sighed. "Fine."

"Thank you," I replied with relief.

"I'm not quite finished. By sharing her address, I would be risking her trust in me. If she gets angry and closes herself off even more, I'll have to do something to earn back that lost trust."

"Like what?"

"I don't know if you've heard, but I'm redeveloping properties in the Town."

I tensed up. "Harsh Kaka mentioned it."

Suhail Mama's eyebrows twitched. "I'm not too sure what he's told you—"

"He said that you're trying to tear down all the houses on our street."

"That's only half the truth."

"I don't understand. Why would you want to destroy the place you grew up in?"

"It's not about destroying. It's about making it better. Better housing will attract more people and businesses to the area."

"But why touch the Town? Couldn't you redevelop in other places?"

"I do on a smaller scale. I've found that I have the most success in the Town because people know and trust me. It's easier to get them to sell."

"Okay. Fine. It's your business. How is all of this related to Vaishu Mavshi?"

"As I said, she doesn't want to stay in the old house because it carries a lot of pain. If we build another house in its place, one that doesn't bring up any bad memories, we could be offering her a fresh start. The Town would be a place she can visit and maybe live in once again. If I break her trust, I would like to gift her this."

It dawned on me what Suhail Mama's aim was. "You want me to convince Harsh Kaka to sell the house to you."

"More or less. Think of it as family doing small favors for each other. You talk to Harsh. I give you the address. Easy-peasy."

"I told you that your sister died, and you're thinking about how you can make a profit?"

Suhail Mama put his hand on his chest. "I'm obviously devastated to hear about Mahi. But it just further proves my point that this family carries too much baggage. We need to figure out a way to move forward. This sale would help all of us. Harsh can live in a better house. Vaishu Tai can let go of the place that has been haunting her. And yes, I'll make good money down the line, but it'll be used to make sure that our entire family is taken care of. Including you. I'm not just going to keep all of it to myself."

"I don't care about the money. That house means so much more to our family than a check. I thought it would to you too."

"I also used to be naïve about these things, Akash. But then my father-in-law taught me how to think strategically. I've learned from him how necessary it is in this country, especially for immigrant families like ours, to be smart about elevating our wealth." He nodded to Kiara Mami's stomach. "With my child on the way, it's very important for me now to focus on this goal. This redevelopment project would be huge for my company. We're so close—we only need one more signature from the whole street—but Harsh's emotions are preventing him from seeing how much this deal will benefit everyone."

"You keep saying that, but the primary person this deal benefits is you." I stood up in frustration. "I don't know who you are anymore, Suhail Mama."

"We can return to this subject again when you're ready to maturely discuss it."

"I'm not helping you tear the house down. I'll find Vaishu Mavshi some other way."

"You're painting me to be a bad guy, but trust me when I tell you I'm not."

"Please stay, Akash," Kiara Mami urged.

"How can you sit by while he does this?" I snapped.

"Akash." Suhail Mama's voice grew stern. "I understand that it's been a troubling time, but you are crossing a line."

"Whatever. I'm leaving anyway." I stormed to the entrance.

"We can drop you back! Or call you a cab at least!" Kiara Mami cried out.

The last thing I heard my uncle say before I banged the heavy, cherry wood door shut was, "Let him go."

CHAPTER 31

THE HUNT FOR VAISHU MAVSHI

I WAS BITTER the entire Uber ride back. Suhail Mama's cunning behavior was a betrayal to my sweet-natured memories of him. Harsh Kaka comforted me after I relayed the catastrophic conversation. Not even once did he mention that he had warned me beforehand. He offered to make me a cup of tea, but I said that I needed fresh air. I left the house and roamed down Main Street. The door to Bhaskar Uncle's shop, Ghosh Goods, was propped open. Eager to see the inside of an enduring shop and rid myself of my dejection, I crossed the street and entered.

Once inside, I wavered with brief bewilderment, adjusting to the updated layout. Bhaskar Uncle's shop used to have a small selection of general appliances such as microwaves and handheld vacuum cleaners, but it had primarily been known for its large collection of puja items, ranging from flower garlands, wooden mandirs, brass diyas, urli bowls, kumkum, and much more of the like. Paintings and idols of Hindu deities used to be hung up or displayed along the walls, and the air had always carried a heavy smell of sandalwood incense.

The current arrangement of the store narrowed the limited puja items to one measly corner. The rest of the shelves were overtaken by kitchen appliances and other home goods. The area where Bhaskar Uncle used to hold town halls was still sectioned off, but it appeared stale and gloomy, like it hadn't been used in a while. The aisles were neat, tidy, and cohesive, which was surprising given how cluttered and stocked they used to be. I'd expected that Bhaskar Uncle would have become more jumbled with age, but the well-ordered configuration told a different story. It might have been because I was the only customer present, but the store felt drabber, as if the decluttering had made the space lose a bit of its anarchic character.

Bhaskar Uncle wasn't at the front desk, so I called out, "Hello? Anyone there?"

No response. I rang the bell on the counter, more insistently the second time around.

"Yeah, yeah, I'm coming," yelled a young, gravelly voice from the back storeroom. Knowing how protective Bhaskar Uncle was of his office space, I immediately became suspicious of the voice that responded to me. Back when I'd lived in the Town, Bhaskar Uncle wouldn't let anyone enter the back, even if they were a friend. I sneaked around the counter and opened the storeroom door.

Another body slammed into mine, and we both tumbled to the floor. Startled by the impact, I realized only after a few seconds that my front side was drenched in burning hot liquid. I pulled my shirt away from my chest and yelped in pain.

"What the hell! I said I was coming out," fumed the gravelly voice.

I looked over at the other fallen figure. Once we made eye contact, my taut heart skipped a beat. He wore an oversized AC/DC T-shirt, a gold chain, and ripped black jeans. Most of his wavy hair was swept back, though a bit of it had tumbled down over his forehead. Two diamond studs were set in either ear. His bottom eyelids were marked with black pencil, which made the white in his eyes pop even more. He'd become brawny, as visible in his sturdier chest and arms. His face was chiseled and his jawbone prominent. In the dim light, his scar shone like a sliver of silver against his walnut-colored skin.

"Hey," I said.

Mayuran's eyes widened with astonishment. "Hey …?"

"W-what are you doing here?"

"I could ask you the same thing." He stood up and towered over me. He looked to be around six feet, maybe even taller. He dusted himself off, picked up his emptied coffee cup, and outstretched a hand to me. "You're soaked."

My T-shirt, which had become lukewarm, was uncomfortably sticking to my chest and stomach.

I waved it off. "It's fine. Wait, you work here?"

He chuckled. "You've been missing for like six fucking years, and you're tripping over the fact that I'm employed?"

"No, no, that's not what I meant," I said, smiling nervously. "I just wasn't expecting you here."

"Relax. I'm screwing with you. I work here part time. Bhaskar Uncle can't man this place on his own anymore."

"And you're the one he hired to help?"

He smirked. "I'm really trying not to take this personally."

"I'm sorry. This is all just a little …"

"Wild. I feel you."

I whispered his name, needing to hear it out loud. I instantly regretted it. A string of jarring images materialized: his bruised face, the kiss, the cigarettes … the gun. I could hear the screams at the station. I could see his terror as he processed what he'd done.

"I, um, should go change out of this shirt," I said, turning away.

"I have some spare ones in the back. I typically go for a run before coming to work."

"It's all good. I'm close anyway."

"Don't leave," he protested. "It's been a solid minute since we've seen each other. Let me get you a shirt, and you can tell me where the hell you've been."

His pleading eyes were hard to refuse. I yielded and said, "Let's see what you have."

———

All of Mayuran's available T-shirts either had a heavy metal band logo or an explicit message printed on the front. I faced away from him and changed into the mildest of the bunch. We awkwardly caught each other's eyes when I turned back around.

"I can't pull this off," I said, adjusting the huge, drooping collar.

"I think it's a look."

"Yeah, right." I pointed to the closet where Mayuran neatly kept some of his belongings, including shoes, spare clothes, and Tupperware. "You're quite settled."

"Been working here for a bit. Had to get my act together at some point."

"You still living at home?"

"Unfortunately."

"Dad still a dick?"

His grin faltered. "It's funny. When we were kids, I was the one that wanted to leave the Town, and you were the one that wanted to stay."

"I'm back now, though."

"Yeah? For how long?"

"Not sure."

He looked like he was about to ask a follow-up question, but he stopped himself and said, "Well, it's good to see you, man."

I appreciated that he didn't probe further. Even though we were both curious about each other's time apart, it was obvious neither of us wanted to share more at the moment.

"I always hoped that I would see you again," he said softly.

My palms became sweaty. "Really? Why?"

"I … um … I made a lot of mistakes when I was younger, and I know some of them impacted your family in ways I'm not even fully aware of. I've spent a lot of time thinking about how if I didn't bring that fucking gun …"

"Mayuran, you don't need to—"

"But that's why you left, isn't it? It had something to do with your cousin's death."

My hesitation was enough to confirm his conjecture.

"Fuck, man." He rubbed his forehead. "I always thought … How are you even talking to me right now? Don't you hate me?"

"No. Not at all."

"How? I fucking killed your cousin."

"You didn't."

"I basically did. The gunshot is what caused everyone to go berserk."

"Mayuran, there are a lot of people who can assume blame for what happened to Sagar."

"Why didn't you tell someone? You had every right to. You saw the gun. You were the only one who did."

"I didn't want to see you suffer over a mistake."

He groaned, falling back onto a stool.

"You haven't told anyone since, have you?"

He shook his head no. "That station still haunts me every day. I thought I could … I don't know … hide it, especially since no one else knew, but talking about this with you, I realize how stuck I've been."

I wanted to reach out and hold his hand, but if he was anything like how he'd been when we were kids, physical reassurance would have been rebuffed immediately. I could hear in his voice the prolonged strife and torture that was reminiscent of my own guilt. I wanted to tell him that he'd only been a child when it had happened, but I could barely apply that understanding to myself.

"Mayuran, you can't beat yourself up," I insisted. "You just can't. That day has eaten up too many people in my life already. I can't watch it do the same to you too."

Mayuran looked up at me with red eyes. "This is way too late, and it's never going to make up for the shit I've put you all through, but if I can ever do anything for you or your family, please let me know. Whatever it is."

"You don't need to say that."

"Please. Even if it's something small, it'll help me more than you could know."

I considered his proposition. "There actually might be something."

Mayuran perked up. "Tell me."

"Sagar's mom, Vaishnavi, has been MIA for a while. Do you have any idea where she could be? I'm trying to find her."

His face fell. "I'm sorry. I wish I did."

"It's all right. Worth a shot."

"But others might. Lots of people have moved away, but I can take you to whoever's still here in the Town. One of them has to know."

With no other leads to follow, I asked, "Are you working tomorrow?"

———

Mayuran decided that Bhaskar Uncle was a good starting point for information. We went straight to his house early the next morning so we could catch him before he left for the store. Mayuran pulled out a key from his pocket and unlocked the front door.

"You have a key?" I asked.

"It's easier if I just enter myself."

I was impressed. Bhaskar Uncle, although beloved by Townsfolk, was one of the most cautious people I'd ever known. Granting a house key to someone outside his family sounded very unusual for him. Mayuran must have had to put in sustained effort to pierce through his distrust.

We removed our shoes at the doorway and walked into the living room. Like the old arrangement of his shop, Bhaskar Uncle's house was decorated with classic Indian art and pungent with a strong smell of antiquity. Sandstone sculptures of Hindu deities as well as copies of Ravi Varma paintings graced each corner of the room. Books written mostly in Bengali were packed underneath side tables or stacked on top of cabinets.

A Zee TV serial was playing in the adjacent room. Bhaskar Uncle's voice rang out, "Mayuran, is that you?"

"Yep, but I brought someone else with me. You're gonna be shocked when you see who it is."

Bhaskar Uncle was sitting on the family room couch. He turned toward us and adjusted his gigantic square frames. He had grown a thick, white mustache, which made his countenance appear stern. Once he recognized me, the hostility in his expression vanished, and a wide smile broke out on his face.

"What a surprise indeed!" he beamed. He tried to lift himself off the couch, using the cane beside him for support.

Mayuran rushed to assist him. "Uncle, don't strain yourself."

It was a relationship I'd encountered numerous times before: Vaishu Mavshi with my Aaji, my mother with Nabeela Aunty, the young assisting the old. But I would have never expected to observe Mayuran—the once reserved and troubled kid—in this context. It was touching to be a witness to his maturation. With this one interaction, I could already imagine how sensitive and compassionate he was with Bhaskar Uncle otherwise.

"You look so much like your Ajoba, Akash," said Bhaskar Uncle, holding my face in his hands. "You should know that he was very dashing."

I blushed. "Thank you, Uncle."

"I always wondered if I was going to see you or your mother again. Where did you both disappear to?"

Sensing my hesitancy to answer, Mayuran interrupted, "I'm sure we can all catch up another time. Akash and I came over because there's a pressing matter at hand that we need your help with."

"Oh?" Bhaskar Uncle motioned for us to sit on the couch. "Do tell."

As I took my seat, I said, "Uncle, I need to find Vaishu Mavshi. Do you know where she is?"

Bhaskar Uncle shook his head regretfully. "I apologize. I do not. What a terrible tragedy she has endured."

"Is there anyone in the Town who might know?"

Bhaskar Uncle thought for a moment. "Someone her age might. Perhaps Simran? She works at the same location. The issue is, Akash, I'm not sure who keeps in touch with who. I've lost track over the years."

"I find that hard to believe. You used to be the pillar of this community."

Bhaskar Uncle's tone became grim. "The Town isn't as it once was."

"Not this again," protested Mayuran. "You'll give yourself a stroke if you get worked up."

"I'm allowed to share my views, aren't I?"

Mayuran grimaced but did not say anything further.

"As I was saying …" continued Bhaskar Uncle, "after the opening of the station, the doors to our Town were unlocked. Since then, many dear friends have moved away."

"Why would they willingly leave?" I asked, bemused.

"Almost everyone in this area was offered a great deal to sell their residence for redevelopment. Quite a few took it and used the money to look for bigger homes or better jobs elsewhere."

"But don't they miss the community here?"

Bhaskar Uncle chuckled. "How refreshing it is to hear someone say that."

"That's why everyone lived in the Town, isn't it? To be near other immigrants, especially other Desi immigrants?"

"At one point in time. But once new people moved in, and new shops opened, the will to preserve the community was lost. For the past few years, I haven't hosted a town hall or planned any events."

"Why not? You were such an integral part in keeping everyone together."

"Oh, believe me, I attempted to for a while. But I don't have the energy to carry it forward on my own. Long ago, your Ajoba built this Town because he was able to gather a group of lonely immigrants who desperately missed their old homes. The original group that moved here have either passed away, grown old, or integrated themselves within this country and don't have the same yearning they once did. And, of course, the succeeding generations don't have enough of a connection to the homeland to care.

"Take my grandchildren for example. They barely return to the Town. They've forgotten the Bengali I taught them and don't want to practice with me. They can't cook any traditional food, nor do they continue any of the customs they were brought up with. They don't want to visit India or learn about the history that is an essential part of their heritage. They show up once a year for Diwali, take a few photos of themselves posing in their ethnic clothes, and leave. How can you preserve a community like ours when the majority are indifferent to our culture?"

"Not everyone is like that, though, Uncle," interrupted Mayuran. "Like I've said before, you only focus on the people that have left. But there are still those that have stayed."

Bhaskar Uncle waved his hand bitterly. "Pah! So much is lost already. They'll follow soon too."

"You're ignoring the fact that those who have moved away still do visit and try to keep in touch with you. You're the one who shuns them."

"And why shouldn't I! They've neglected their roots. If they've decided that leading an American way of life is more important than protecting our heritage and community, then I have no wish to associate with them."

"They might not be invested in the same way they once were, but that doesn't mean the Town means nothing to them. Look. Akash came back, didn't he?"

Bhaskar Uncle's face relaxed. "That he did. That he did." He sighed. "What would I do without Mayuran? He's often the only one who can calm my growing cynicism."

Mayuran grinned. "Someone has to, Uncle."

"Once Mariam and Musa closed their store, and Uma shut her restaurant, I had very little resolve to keep my business open. I still don't. Every day I consider shutting it down, but Mayuran encourages me, almost bullies me, into keeping it open."

"You can't let go yet."

"Doesn't it make you sad, Uncle?" I asked. "How much has changed?"

"But of course! It makes me angry more than anything else. I'm glad your Ajoba is not here to see what rubbish this Town has become. It would depress him to see the purity of our values and customs forgotten, or in the process of being forgotten. Maybe I should have gone to the lengths Ratnam did to stop the station from opening."

Mayuran looked down uncomfortably, his eyes wavering in shame.

"Then why not fight for it?" I asked. "We can bring everyone back together again. I'm sure the people who've moved away will return if there's good reason to."

"It's never going to be how it was," said Bhaskar Uncle ruefully. "And I don't have the strength to force something that can never be. I wish I knew when moving to this country how much I would be giving up. Only old age will give you that perspective. I would return to India in a heartbeat now if my children weren't settled here."

Bhaskar Uncle's hopelessness filled me with frustration. Like him, I wanted the Town to exist as it once had. However, his lack of motivation to try to correct it, to try to bring the Town back together, was even more disheartening to me than the actual disbanding of the community.

"We'll let you be," said Mayuran. "Akash, you want to go ask Simran about your aunt?"

I nodded. Bhaskar Uncle clasped my hands. "Please visit more. It's wonderful to have your company again."

Mayuran stood up. "I'll come check in on you later."

"Don't worry about me," reassured Bhaskar Uncle. "You boys go find her."

Mayuran and I left Bhaskar Uncle's house and walked back to Main. I gazed at him with newfound appreciation.

He smirked. "Why are you looking at me like that?"

"Nothing. It's just nice to see you with him."

"Surprised?"

"Lil' bit. Long way from torturing snails."

"What?" said Mayuran, chuckling. "I never did that."

"That's what the other sixth graders said about you."

Mayuran shook his head. "The rumors about me were fucking ridiculous. Bhaskar Uncle is one of the only people who didn't care about them."

"I'm happy you guys have each other. It seems like he needs you too."

"Yeah. He can be bitter sometimes, but he's just stuck in his ways."

We reached Simran Aunty's storefront. With a closer look, I noticed that her salon was stripped of everything distinguishing it as an Indian-owned business. The framed photos of Desi women with arched eyebrows and bridal makeup had been taken down. The inside was much brighter, airier, and more contemporary than Bhaskar Uncle's decaying store. Moreover, Simran Aunty's salon was crowded with customers—almost every chair was filled.

Simran Aunty joined us outside. She hugged me and asked how my mother was. I told her the truth, recognizing that I had to eventually be comfortable with explaining my situation. Out of the corner of my eye, I saw Mayuran's expression flicker with shock. This was the first he was hearing of my mother's death. Still, he remained quiet and did not interrupt the conversation.

"That's really sad to hear," said Simran Aunty as she offered me a sympathetic pat on my shoulder. "Your mother and I had our differences ... but I cared for her. The salon wasn't the same without her starting drama every day."

I wanted to chuckle, knowing that if my mother could hear this, she would be rolling her eyes as widely as she could. I asked Simran Aunty if she knew where Vaishu Mavshi was, but she responded that she didn't.

"I've been so busy with this business," she sighed. "I haven't been able to keep up with anyone that doesn't come directly to the salon."

"Your place looks different from what I remember."

"That's because I sold it. A chain company offered to buy it from me and keep me as the manager of this location. I don't have to worry about a lot of the back-end stuff now, and I've attracted more business than ever before."

"But didn't you want to keep it as your own?"

Simran Aunty shrugged. "I don't know how much longer it would have lasted. Let's be honest—once the Town started attracting more attention, independent businesses like mine had no chance."

"I can't imagine Main Street crowded with a bunch of chain stores."

"Things evolve. You can either choose to stay stuck or figure out how to profit from it. Once the ownership of this place was transferred over, I was able to afford a bigger house in the City and private school for my daughters."

"But doesn't it upset you that other businesses along Main were replaced?"

"Not at all. I think it's a good thing the Town is expanding and diversifying. We live in America, for God's sake. It's about time we accepted that we couldn't stay in a bubble forever. We had to integrate ourselves at some point."

"Maybe being a part of this community didn't matter much to you, but growing up here was meaningful to me," I replied hotly. Echoing Bhaskar Uncle, I said, "If everyone spreads out, traditions will be forgotten."

Simran Aunty smirked. "And which traditions are you talking about? Hindu traditions? Muslim traditions? Parsi traditions? Or are you referring to Punjabi traditions? Gujarati traditions? Or—"

"What's your point?"

"That the Town lumped many different people together. When you have immigrants from all over India, Pakistan, Bangladesh, and Sri Lanka forming a singular community, traditions get mixed up more than they get preserved. Take me, for example. Even though my parents and grandparents were Sikh, most of my friends growing up here were Hindu. Because of them, I know more about Hindu holidays and customs than the ones that are aligned with my supposed lineage. So, what are the correct traditions that I should be passing down when this is what living in the Town has taught me? What should I carry forward when my understanding of culture is based off which Desis I surrounded myself with, not where my family came from?"

"But Bhaskar Uncle said—"

"Don't get me started on Bhaskar Uncle. He loves to go on and on about how the Town maintained the purity of our culture. But what does 'our' culture even mean? How is what he preaches possible when the first immigrants that moved here came from distinct parts of the subcontinent? And had differing understandings of culture to begin with?"

I was speechless.

"Anyways, it's silly for everyone to get bogged down with the ways of another time and place," continued Simran. "It limits us. I would rather my daughters feel comfortable in this country than worry about the one their great-grandparents came from."

"That's ridiculous," I muttered, my cheeks burning up. "Even if culture can't be preserved perfectly, it doesn't mean that we forget about it entirely."

Observing the heightened tension, Mayuran jumped in. "Hey, maybe we're getting a little sidetracked. We just came to find out info about Akash's aunt."

Simran Aunty fixed her gaze on Mayuran. "I'm sorry. I really don't know where she is. I think I remember Juhi Aunty mentioning that Vaishnavi visited her store shortly before leaving the Town. She might know something."

"Thanks for your help," I muttered sharply.

"Look, Akash, everyone is going to have a different opinion about the Town. You're entitled to have your own too. But I'm happy with the way things are. I seriously believe this is for the better."

"Yep. Thanks again."

I stormed away from Simran Aunty's salon. Was what she had said right? Were the people in the Town as disparate as she'd made us out to be? And if so, how had I still felt such a strong connection with everyone around me, one that had kept me grounded and tied to what I'd believed was my heritage? Were cultures already being mixed up and modified before the Town split apart? I had grown up with the belief that the Town protected my heritage in its purest form. That was, after all, what my Ajoba had intended when creating this secluded community. But was that even possible? Or had the Town been built on a false concept of preservation, like Simran Aunty believed it was?

"Where to next?" asked Mayuran.

"You really don't need to accompany me. Taking me to Bhaskar Uncle was enough."

"I want to. If it weren't for this, I would be listening to him grumble for the rest of the day."

I smiled. "Okay. Only because you want to. I guess we could go ask Juhi Aunty."

"Great!" Mayuran raced in front of me, leading the way to Juhi Aunty's shop, even though I was well aware of where it was. I dutifully followed him, not wanting to ruin the delight he got from helping out.

As we neared the store, I reminisced on the last time we were there together. I wondered if he remembered our kiss as vividly as I did, if that moment was as special to him as it was to me. As much as we'd grown, I could only regard him with the utmost fondness. He was the first boy that I'd ever had feelings for. Though time apart should have reduced them, I still felt the same excitement looking at him as I had back then. It was different than what I felt for Luke. With Mayuran, there was a sense of knowing, of familiarity and vulnerability, that only comes from connecting with someone at an early stage of life. Despite us being adults, Mayuran could still see through to the most central, unrefined part of me, and I could do the same for him. I was grateful he was accompanying me on this depressing journey through the Town. His presence made it somewhat easier.

Unlike Simran Aunty and Bhaskar Uncle's stores, Juhi's Groceries hadn't been modified even in the slightest. The same Indian and Pakistani grocery items were stocked and organized exactly as before. The space was as clean and well maintained as it used to be. I almost felt like I had entered a time portal when I saw the propped-up newspaper at the front counter, covering Juhi Aunty's face. She set it down and peered at me through her circular spectacles. From the beginning of our conversation, I could tell that she was as nutty as ever. She acted as if we had seen each other only recently, making no comments on how long I'd been missing. After vaguely getting her up to speed on my return to the Town, I asked her about when she'd last seen Vaishu Mavshi.

"Very mysterious, that one," replied Juhi Aunty, speaking with a dreamy intonation. "She came in to buy huge packets of dal and other long-lasting food items. She hasn't returned since."

My mind was turning. I was stumped as to why Vaishu Mavshi would have needed to purchase such large quantities of food, unless she'd planned on hibernating.

"I miss your Aaji dearly," continued Juhi Aunty, sighing. "She was a great friend."

"Where could they have gone?" I muttered. I looked around once more at the aisles. "Aunty, I have to ask, how have you been able to maintain this store so well? Nothing's changed since I last saw it."

"Nothing needed to be, dear. Quite a few people in the area still come to purchase Indian groceries. I offer something they can't buy at a regular market."

"It's refreshing that at least one store is the same. Seeing the other changes in the Town has been really upsetting."

"I feel fortunate that my shop's been open for as long as it has, but I too will have to close it someday."

"Why? You shouldn't."

"I will either become too old to maintain it, or there won't be enough customers to keep it open."

"Maybe someone else could take over."

"I would love it if someone does, but I'm not going to seek them out."

"If this store shuts, then I don't even know what would be left of the Town."

"That's the natural course of life, dear. Things have to turn over at some point."

"I don't believe that. If it weren't for that stupid train station, the Town wouldn't have transformed like this."

"Maybe, but changes would have still happened. The older generation would have passed away. Other residents would have moved. Businesses would have closed."

"What does that mean? That we just watch the Town fall apart? Don't you want to fight for this community?"

Juhi Aunty chuckled. "Why would I have to fight for something that already exists?"

"Everyone's spread out. If these stores go, people will eventually forget that the Town existed. They'll forget about my Ajoba, and the other immigrants that first moved here. They won't know anything about the culture or values that were so crucial in building this community."

"I understand what you're saying, dear, but I disagree. Of course, the stores that originally opened here have value. If they didn't, I wouldn't have kept mine open for this long. But this building is just a container that was going to empty out and be refilled by some other business sooner or later. What's more meaningful to me than this shop is the friendships I've formed here. It's true that many old friends have moved out of the Town, but if we used to have a close relationship, they will still come back and visit. We'll laugh and chat like we've always done. If they bring their young ones, we'll share stories about our lives with them, both from the Town and from India. This will continue even once the store shuts, I am sure of it. In this way, I don't feel like the Town is lost at all."

It would have been futile to try to argue back. Juhi Aunty was staunch in her acceptance of the status quo.

"Thanks for the information about Vaishu Mavshi," I said, wearily turning to the door.

"Also, to answer your question, you will find happiness again."

I slowly turned back to her. "What did you say? What question?"

"You were wondering if you would ever find happiness again. I assure you that you will," she replied, her eyes twinkling.

I stared at her in shock. Unsure how to respond, I retreated to the exit with Mayuran. Juhi Aunty picked up her paper again and continued reading.

Shaken up by Juhi Aunty's clairvoyant statement, I hurried down Main Street back toward my family's house. Mayuran struggled to keep up.

"Where to next?" he asked.

"Nowhere. I'm going home."

"We can still ask more people!"

"It's pointless. No one knows where she is." I pivoted onto the cul-de-sac where the house was.

Mayuran grabbed my arm. "Hold on. We don't know that for sure."

"You heard them. Everyone's moved on."

Mayuran hesitated. "This isn't just about your aunt, is it?"

"How has everyone given up? Am I the only one that still cares about the Town?"

"You've been gone a long time. It's different when you've watched this place slowly change for six years. You become numb to it."

"This is exactly what I was afraid of when I returned. I hate seeing the Town like this. I hate how disconnected everyone is."

An intense pain shot through my head, and I suddenly felt weightless. The cul-de-sac was starting to morph into the bizarre, oddly colored version of it that was contained within my Imagined. My emotional distress was causing the separate worlds to blend again.

"Hey, Akash. What's happening? Look at me," insisted Mayuran. He grabbed both of my arms and steadied me. "I can imagine it's hard seeing so much gone. But you've got to open your eyes to what's lasted. Like me."

Staring directly at Mayuran's unwavering gaze, I began to regain stability in my legs. The surrounding environment reverted back to normal. Our faces were unbelievably close to each other.

The sudden squeal of car tires prompted us both to pull away from each other. A taxi rolled down the cul-de-sac and came to a full stop before us. The back door opened, and a bubbly voice cascaded out.

"Aw, honey, I hope you figure things out with your daughter! Keep the change, love. No need to thank me."

The source of the voice heaved herself out of the car, clutching on to the roof for balance.

"Kiara Mami?"

She turned toward me and pursed her lips. "Hi, Akash."

"What are you doing here?"

She shut the back door and the taxi drove away. "I need to talk to you." She glanced at Mayuran. "Privately."

"I don't have anything else I want to say to you or Suhail Mama," I replied coldly, holding Mayuran's arm so that he could not leave.

"I'm sorry about yesterday. It didn't go the way I wanted it to. Suhail listens to my dad way more than he should."

"You sat there quietly and said nothing. You're just as bad as he is."

"I know, and I want to make up for it. I remember how close your family was. One day, Suhail is going to regret that he shut you out like that."

"What are you saying?" I asked cautiously.

She took a breath. "I can take you to Vaishu Tai."

I crossed my arms. "I'm not persuading Harsh Kaka to sign over the house."

"I'm not asking you to."

"What's the catch?"

"There's no catch, Akash. I'm just trying to help you."

I looked her up and down, trying to figure out if she was telling the truth. Kiara Mami sounded genuine, but I was still hesitant to trust her. "I'm assuming Suhail Mama doesn't know."

"No, and he's not going to find out."

"Okay. What's the address?"

"I could give it to you, but it's very easy to get lost using a smartphone map. It's better if I take you there myself."

"When?"

She nervously chuckled. "I was thinking we could go now. We're under a bit of time pressure."

"What do you mean?"

"Well, the house is not actually under Harsh's name. It's owned by your Aaji. Suhail has tried to get her to sell, but Vaishu Tai will not allow it as long as Harsh is still living inside. That's why Suhail needed Harsh's approval so badly."

"Needed?"

"He's hoping the news about your mother changes Vaishu Tai's mind. She's going to be devastated when she learns about it. He thinks he can finally convince her that the house carries too much pain to keep, and that it'll be better to just let it go once and for all."

"That's horrible."

"I know. Which is why we need to leave immediately. Maybe if we can get to her first, we can make sure the house isn't signed over. Suhail will realize his mistake eventually. Right now, he's not even properly processing your mom's death. He's too hyper-focused on this deal."

"Are you sure you're able to travel?" I asked, looking down at her belly.

"I'll be fine. The only issue is that we need a car to get there. No taxi in their right mind would take us."

"Hm. Harsh Kaka doesn't have a car."

Mayuran stepped forward. "Sorry to overhear, but I have one. Akash, you can drive it if you want."

"Come with us," I said. He had been such a comforting presence throughout the day. I didn't want him to leave yet.

"Are you sure?" he asked softly. "It's a private moment for your family."

"I'm a thousand percent sure. Besides, I don't know how to drive."

Kiara Mami jumped in. "Wonderful, wonderful. We should go now so that I can get home before Suhail does. Also, if I don't sit down in the next two minutes, my back is going to break in half."

I glanced at the house, wondering if Harsh Kaka was inside. I decided I would inform him after I returned.

"All right, then. Let's go."

CHAPTER 32

ISOLATION

MAYURAN LED US to his secluded, rotting home. Green moss joined the coiling vines and climbed up along the siding. The panels were frayed and discolored from old age. A battered black pickup truck was parked out front among overgrown weeds.

Kiara Mami was wheezing from the walk over. "Th-thank G-god."

"One problem," said Mayuran. "I have to get the keys from my dad."

"All right, then get them," I replied.

"It's not that simple. He doesn't let me drive the truck on my own. He's afraid that I might take off one day."

"Why would he think that?"

Mayuran lowered his head. "'Cause I've told him that I would."

"What if you asked him to come?"

"You don't want that, trust me. Plus, he would never agree. In case you forgot, my dad is not a generous person."

Kiara Mami groaned. "Couldn't we have discussed this before walking over?"

"What's the plan then?" I asked.

"I can steal the keys," said Mayuran. "I've done it before and taken short trips. He's usually passed out from drinking until early afternoon, so as long as we return before he wakes up, we'll be good."

"Are you sure you want to do this? What if we don't get back in time?"

Kiara Mami nodded in agreement. "Vaishu Tai's place is far. It'll take a few hours."

Mayuran hesitated, then met my eyes. "I had no clue about your mom, Akash. Coming back to the Town and searching for your aunt … it must have taken a lot of courage after everything you've been through."

"That's nice, but—"

"I'm tired of being a fucking coward. If he wakes up and finds me gone, then it is what it is. I'll deal with him later."

He strode toward the front door. I left Kiara Mami by the truck and hurried after him.

"Mayuran," I said earnestly, "you really don't need to. We'll figure out another way."

He inserted his key into the lock. "Wait out here."

The front door creaked as Mayuran stealthily pushed it open. As anticipated, Ratnam was asleep and slumped over on a reclining chair. An empty bottle of liquor sat in his lap. He wore a stained ribbed tank top that barely covered his bulbous stomach. His booming snores echoed through the seedy living room.

"Where are the keys?" I whispered.

"In his pocket."

"Fuck. How are you going to get them?"

Mayuran smiled at me. "Don't worry. I got this."

He cautiously tiptoed toward Ratnam, inching one step at a time. I held my breath as Mayuran neared him. Suddenly, Ratnam murmured something incoherent and adjusted his sleeping position. Mayuran did not budge until Ratnam settled into place and resumed his snores. He reached into Ratnam's pocket and slowly, ever so slowly, drew out the keys.

When he finally secured them, he turned back to me and grinned. I returned his enthusiasm with a thumbs-up and a beckoning wave.

Mayuran's first step back was too eager. The floorboards squeaked loudly under the weight of his leg. Mayuran's smile vanished right as Ratnam's eyes fluttered open. The latter sat up and yawned, assessing the scene with a dazed expression.

"Mayuran?" he slurred. He noticed the keys in Mayuran's hands and felt around his own pocket to confirm that they had been stolen. He scowled. "What the bloody hell do you think you're doing?"

Mayuran's head shrank into his shoulders. He timidly replied, "I'm going out with a friend."

"Like hell you are."

"I'll be back by the end of the day. I promise—"

"Mayuran," Ratnam growled. His hardened face was terrifying. "Give me the keys. Now."

Mayuran was quiet.

"Are you deaf?" bellowed Ratnam.

"I'm not giving them back."

Ratnam squinted in disbelief. "What did you just say? Stupid son of a bitch thinks he can talk back to me. Do not test me, Mayuran."

The room was still, as father and son intensely stared at each other. Then, Mayuran pivoted and raced toward me, yelling, "Get in the truck!"

I heeded Mayuran's instructions and ran toward Kiara Mami. She was leaning on the truck, fanning herself with her hands. When she saw my frantic state, she pushed herself off and worriedly asked, "What happened?"

"We need to get in!"

I tugged the back passenger door open and helped lift Kiara Mami onto the seat. By that point, Ratnam had caught up to Mayuran near the shack's entrance and pulled him to the ground. Ratnam's arms were tightly wrapped around Mayuran's chest, while Mayuran struggled to break free.

"Where do you think you're going?" spat Ratnam.

"L-let go of m-me!" coughed Mayuran, his face turning red from Ratnam's tight hold.

"Bloody idiot worthless piece of shit you disobey me and you just wait you just bloody wait you won't survive one day without me …"

Mayuran's flailing arms were losing power. Tears dripped out of his eyes as he withdrew back to the frightened child who'd stood on that platform. I was about to run out and help him, but before I could, Mayuran's leg shot up and kneed Ratnam in the stomach. Ratnam groaned, clutching his belly. With the advantage of his momentary victory, Mayuran scrambled up and gasped for air.

Once he recovered, he towered over a wounded Ratnam, looking down at him with anguish. "I can't do this anymore. I can't live like this."

Ratnam attempted to grab Mayuran's ankle, but Mayuran swiftly stepped back. Fear darkened Ratnam's face.

"Wait, wait. I got angry, I'm sorry. Don't go," pleaded Ratnam. "I don't have anyone but you, Mayuran. I love you."

Mayuran paused momentarily, gazing at Ratnam with pity. He then shook his head and walked toward me and Kiara Mami. "This isn't love. This is some fucked-up shit."

Tangled among the tall weeds, Ratnam quietly sobbed as he watched Mayuran enter the truck, start the engine, and drive us away. When we were safely cruising along Main Street, I grazed Mayuran's hand.

"Are you good?" I asked.

Mayuran nodded. "Took me eighteen years to say that."

"I'm proud of you."

"Thanks," he replied softly. "Where to now?"

I rotated and found a trembling Kiara Mami in recovery from having witnessed the brawl. Her eyes were so wide that I feared they would pop out of her head. "Kiara Mami? You know the way?"

She blinked rapidly, brought back to our mission. "Yes. Yes. Off we go."

———

A man once wandered into an unknown forest, burdened by the loneliness of his present condition. He walked without any understanding of what he would find, praying that God would show him his path, that somewhere between the trees, there would be an answer to his desolation. He drifted further into the forest, even after he had lost sight of the paved road. He thought about his family—his beautiful wife and daughter— so far removed. He reminded himself that his struggle was for their benefit, but these thoughts did not stifle the insatiable yearning he had for his motherland. He craved the call of morning prayer as well as the crass, raucous yells of street vendors. He missed the foods, the smells, the clothes, and the people. He yearned for a home again, not just the physical manifestation of it, but the sense of completeness, of comfort and intimacy, that came with it. Burdened by memories of another place, his devastation grew, and he found himself further entrenched within the lonely forest.

Forty years later, his daughter followed a similar course and left her familiar life behind. Overcome with the most unbearable pain a human can possibly endure, she withdrew herself from her beloved home and husband, hoping the farther away she was from physical reminders of her suffering, the more likely she was to be relinquished from the ocean of sorrow she had been drowning in. Like her father, the daughter sought out uncharted territory, shrouding herself until she vanished from those that she knew.

There seems to come a point in each one of our lives where we struggle to comprehend our existence. When we reach this state, many of us are separated from the comfort of our home and submerged within a perplexing expanse: a sort of wild, untamed forest of our own creation. At first, we try to make it a refuge from our turmoil, but we're left only further disoriented by this baffling maze. So, we search through the labyrinth of trees, trying to find answers that will never come. We run, we scream, we plead for a sign, any sign, but our calls remain unanswered. Trapped by our emotional distress, we wander in bewilderment, doubting if the path toward understanding, happiness, or whatever we originally sought out in the forest, even exists.

As Mayuran drove us through winding, disconnected roads, segregated from the rest of civilization, I recognized that the maddening search for answers repeats itself endlessly across lands and generations. I used to believe that isolation was the most natural state for me to exist in, and from what I could see, my aunt's pain chained her to a similar opinion of herself. By returning to the Town, I had mercifully navigated my way out of the deepest part of my agony. And yet, when I thought about the distress that had been experienced and replicated throughout my family's history—first with my grandfather, then my aunt, and finally with myself, I wondered if I could ever truly find an exit to the forest imprisoning me, or if this confusion with the self and the world, this inability to find my way home again, would endure for the rest of my life.

Kiara Mami guided us with the map on her phone, but during intervals when we lost service, the route was worked out from her memory and instinct. Unfortunately, neither was reliable. There were multiple instances along the drive when we approached a fork in the road and Kiara Mami told Mayuran to proceed in one direction. About five minutes down the chosen path, she would hit her head and declare that the other road must have been correct since nothing looked familiar. Mayuran would dutifully turn back, and I silently prayed that we were progressing in the right direction. We made frequent stops along the journey for Kiara Mami's capricious bladder. She would waddle behind a nearby tree, and Mayuran and I would awkwardly pretend to ignore the roaring gush of her stream. I'd try to make conversation with Mayuran, but he was quiet and distant, still reeling from the confrontation with his dad.

Forty minutes into our drive, Kiara Mami's phone rang. She gasped when she saw the name on the screen. "It's Suhail!"

"Don't answer," I said.

"I have to. I've been unresponsive all day. He's going to be concerned if I don't pick up."

"Should I pull over?" asked Mayuran.

I shook my head. "Not yet. Kiara Mami, say you're sitting in the backyard. As long as you're calm, he won't suspect a thing."

She nodded and answered the phone. "Hello? ... Yes, all good ... Yes, just in the backyard ... Oh, really? What time? ... Fine. See you then." She hung up the phone and bit her lip. "He's coming home early. His last meeting of the day got canceled."

"Shoot! Why did you say you would see him?"

"Look how pregnant I am. Do you think he would buy it if I told him I was going somewhere else?"

Mayuran slowed to the shoulder of the road. "What should I do?"

"I don't know," whispered a panic-stricken Kiara Mami.

"We can turn back around," I said. "But you have to tell me that's what you want."

She scrunched her face. "I don't know, I don't know."

"Can I ask you something? Why are you still with him?"

Her head rose in shock. "What?"

"I know he's my uncle, but he's changed so much. I'm not married or anything, but I don't think it's good to be this afraid of your spouse."

"I'm not afraid of him," she said defensively. "We've been together for a long time. I-I still believe there's good inside of him. I know there is."

"I don't want to cause any issues for you. If you want us to turn around, we can turn around."

She wavered in indecision.

"Let's go back," I said to Mayuran. He started to rotate the steering wheel.

"Stop," said Kiara Mami resolutely. "Go forward."

"Are you sure?"

She clutched her belly and repeated, "Go forward."

At her behest, Mayuran jerked the truck back into the driving lane and continued on. About an hour later, Kiara Mami announced that we were nearing Vaishu Mavshi's place. The truck rocked on a narrow, unpaved path surrounded by tall, skeletal trees. Nestled at the end of the road was a quaint eggshell-white cottage with a brick chimney. Blue-purple wildflowers blossomed around the base of the house. There wasn't a neighboring residence in sight.

Mayuran parked, and the three of us slowly exited the vehicle. I started toward the front door, my pulse racing even more than when I'd initially returned to the Town. Kiara Mami and Mayuran anxiously wavered behind me, allowing me the space to approach the cottage on my own. Similar to when I'd reached the entrance of our family house, I inhaled deeply, knowing that this action could very well mark another turning point in my life.

I knocked and soon heard hurried footsteps advancing inside. They were light and uneven, unlike the sound of Vaishu Mavshi's precise and rhythmic pace. The door flung open to reveal a short, stout, middle-aged woman with frizzy hair.

She examined me warily. "Can I help you?"

"I'm sorry …" I replied, equally bemused by her presence. I turned to Kiara Mami for assistance.

The woman in the house must have followed my gaze, because she suddenly burst out in an animated voice. "Why, Kiara! I didn't know you were coming. Oh my, look at that bump!" She rushed to Kiara Mami and patted her belly. "You're so far along!"

Kiara Mami sighed dramatically. "It's been such a journey, Marissa, I can't even begin to tell you. More deets another time."

I peered in through the open door to see if anyone else was inside, but all I could make out was an empty hallway.

"Akash, this is Marissa," said Kiara Mami. "She's your grandmother's stay-at-home nurse."

"Grandmother?" echoed Marissa with fascination. She came up to me and shook my hand, using both of her palms to cover mine.

"Akash is here to see Vaishnavi. Is she inside?"

"She's away right now. She should be home in a bit, but …" Marissa bit her lip. "I don't know how she'll feel about this. She doesn't like visitors."

"I'm her nephew," I countered.

"I know, but she's a very private person. She's insisted many times before that I not let anyone in except for Suhail and Kiara. Even when they come over, she likes to know in advance so that she can leave."

"So I've heard."

"Why don't I talk to her this evening, and if she agrees, you can come back another day?"

"Please, this is urgent," I begged.

Marissa nervously wrung her hand around her neck. "I can't lose this job. She already has such a short temper."

"What if you just tell me where she is? I can look for her myself."

"I'm not sure where she goes. She leaves in the morning, returns at night. I don't ask any questions."

"Can you call her?"

"I would, but her phone is switched off when she's away. I have an emergency pager, but that's only to be used if something serious happens to your grandma."

A startling alarm sounded from Marissa's watch. She silenced it and said, "Speaking of, I need to check on her. Give me a moment."

She went back into the cottage, leaving the front door ajar. I realized then that my Aaji was less than ten feet away from me. Though permission to follow hadn't been granted, my feet moved of their own accord, trailing Marissa down the hallway to an open bedroom.

My Aaji was placidly napping on a reclining hospital bed in the far corner. Marissa was adjusting her sheets, unaware of my presence until I materialized by the bedframe.

"How long has it been?" she whispered.

"Six-and-a-half years," I replied.

Marissa rubbed my back. "I'll give you two some privacy. But I'll have to ask you to leave before Mrs. Khare comes back home. I promise I'll ask her tonight, and if she says yes, you can return again tomorrow."

She left and shut the door behind her. I shifted to the head of the bed and keenly observed my Aaji. Her long hair was thin and gray. Her cheeks were hollow, and crow's feet extended around the corners of her eyelids. As she snored, her mouth hung open, and a string of saliva trickled down to her jaw. I smiled, unsurprised to find her in this state of deep slumber. I softly placed my hand on hers and felt the dry, wrinkled skin that proudly evidenced a life well lived.

The bedroom was snug. A large, rectangular window next to the bed allowed in soft light and presented a spectacular view of the blooming wildflowers outside. The rest of the walls were covered with an expansive collage of framed photographs, leaving very little open space. Photos of me and Sagar playing on the cul-de-sac, of Suhail Mama at his graduation, of my pregnant mother rushing to the hospital, and many other key moments in our family's history were exhibited around me.

My gaze finally rested on a faded, black-and-white photo that sat atop my Aaji's bedside table. Captured on it were two people, a suited man and a sari-clad woman, standing stiffly beside each other. Garlands of flowers were hung around both their necks. I recognized my Aaji; she was young, maybe in her mid-twenties or so, but she still had the same defining facial features. On the border of the frame, printed in tiny lettering, was a note, "Nitin and Gayatri Patil."

My Aaji's wedding photo. I eagerly picked it up and examined the man standing beside her. In the other house, Vaishu Mavshi had locked away pictures of my Ajoba so that my Aaji could not dwell on his death. But if my Aaji's dementia had progressed like I assumed it had, my Ajoba's face no longer needed to be concealed. All that used to be hidden to cultivate a jovial household had finally been brought out in this room, showing life for what it was, both the good and painful parts of it. I brought the frame even closer. I was certain I hadn't seen a picture of his prior to the one I was holding, but still, something about him looked eerily familiar. I racked my memory for a time when I might have stumbled on a hidden stash of photos, but I couldn't think of any such instance. How did I know his face?

The digital clock on my Aaji's bedside table reached the hour mark, and a grainy melody began floating out of its speakers. The haunting, lilting, nostalgia-inducing tune was one that I was all too familiar with. It was the same thumri that had been used to summon my Imagined. A tune that had been passed from father to son, and then, as I aptly realized, from grandfather to grandson. A tune which, like the photos, like all other reminders of my family's grief, had been shut away from me during my childhood. I set the photo down and backed out of the room in shock.

Once I was in the hallway, I looked to the front yard where Mayuran and Kiara Mami were standing. No part of me wanted to face them. I noticed a back exit at the other end of the corridor and wildly stumbled toward it, dazed and unbalanced. My eyes clouded as I careened between the frail, slender trees. I ran so fast, I felt like I was about to vomit. Colors shifted, and flew, and seeped from surface to surface as my mind tried to wrap itself around this critical connection that altered my understanding of reality. I wanted to find him, and I knew that if I willed him, he would appear. He was with me wherever I went. Just then, I could hear a deep, low hum in the distance. I ran toward it, entering a sprawling, open meadow.

The Singer sat in a pool of sunlight. Tall grass and yellow daisies swayed around him. His eyes were open, intently gazing at me.

I fell on my knees before him. "It's you. You're my Ajoba."

His face scrunched up in confusion, but slowly, repressed memories filtered through his mind, and the knots obstructing him from the truth were undone.

His forehead smoothed out in recognition, and his shoulders drooped in understanding. "I-I remember everything now. I remember the Town. I remember my family. I remember the ugly and the beautiful."

"H-how is this ... how are you here?" I stammered. "You're supposed to be dead."

"Am I?" he asked sorrowfully. "Tell me, how did I die?"

"You were found slumped over in the forest. It was the middle of winter. No one knew why you were there."

"I remember the moments before ... wandering among the trees ... if what you are saying is true, then I must have passed away while in the Imagined."

"You knew about the Imagined back then?"

"I visited it many times. When I first moved to America, I was beset by homesickness. My initial solution to stifle this was to find other lonely immigrants like myself and form the Town. I thought that if I had a community that felt as familiar to what I remembered of Bombay, the yearning for home would disappear. But it did not take long for me to recognize that the Town was its own creation, and that it could never replace what I had left behind.

"Then, one day, while on a walk through the forest, I had a sudden urge to sit and meditate. The privacy of my surroundings allowed me to reflect on my life, especially on the early days. For the first time since my youth, I sang a thumri I learned from my father—the same one I taught you. Memories of the tiny flat I grew up in rushed back. I thought about my loving siblings who I used to consider inferior due to their lack of financial aspiration. And I thought about my penniless yet pure-hearted father, whom I disowned in shame after I was admitted to engineering college.

"Sitting in that forest, I regretted how thankless I had been toward them and my upbringing in India. I had distanced myself from my family, land, and culture in order to chase after a fictitious higher status in a foreign country. I longed to return to the way things were, and so, my mind constructed and thrust me into the Imagined. I returned as a young boy to that tiny flat in Bombay and sang with my father once again."

"Why didn't you move back if you missed India that much?"

"When I was thirteen, I vowed to make a better life for myself. I envied those with money, those without the struggles I had. With hard work, the opportunities to financially climb in the West were undeniably more abundant and attainable than if I had remained in Bombay. I dedicated my life to this dream, and I could not allow myself to let go of it. I feared that if I moved back, I would consider myself a failure for the rest of my life. Besides, I did not think I could ever belong in India again. Because of my arrogance at being one of the few who made it to America, I had lost touch with most people from my old life."

"So, that's where you would go when you disappeared from the house," I said, piecing together his story with what I'd gathered from my family. "You would go to the forest and enter the Imagined."

The Singer nodded. "I was lost without it. It satiated my longing for home and allowed me to return to the Town free of sorrow. I came across it by accident, but as I continued to visit, I became obsessed. Hours would fly by. Sometimes even days. I would wake up in the forest, dehydrated, hungry, and shaking from the experience of having been out of the physical world for such an extended period. And, as it seems, I died while in the Imagined. I lost everything except for this one pure memory I clung on to. I remained there, presumably floating through nothingness ... until the day you disturbed me—"

"—at Suhail Mama's wedding," I interrupted. "Each time you appeared to me in my childhood ... at the wedding, at the station, after I moved to San Francisco ... these were all times when I was dealing with huge changes in my life. Somehow, my emotional confusion brought you back to this world. I needed a guide. I needed you to teach me about the Imagined."

"I'm not so sure whether that last statement is true. At first, I too believed we'd met because I was meant to share my knowledge with you. But then, I watched what the Imagined did to you. I saw you struggle in a way that made me question if this skill was as wonderful as I used to think it was."

I looked down in shame. "That only happened because I abused it."

"Perhaps. Either way, thinking about your well-being directed my focus away from my father's lessons. I started to care for something, for someone, even more than this memory." He paused and furrowed his brow. "Knowing what I know now, I wonder if we were brought together not for me to teach you, but for me to understand what I had been missing throughout the latter half of my life. In my obsession with trying to recapture the past, I lost precious moments with my wife and children. Instead of cherishing time with them, I would eagerly await my next visit to the Imagined, convinced that I could not find the same degree of happiness in the Town that I'd previously experienced in my homeland. But looking at you now, my grandson, I realize how much I missed, how much love was in front of me that I could not appreciate. It makes me sad to see how flawed I was. I wish I could have been a better father and husband."

"But you were still a great man. Your family loves you."

A tear slid down his face. "Really?"

"Everyone in the Town thinks of you as a hero. Aaji missed you so much that she couldn't even look at your photos without crying. All I had to grow up on was stories, and that was enough to feel connected to you. Your life wasn't wasted."

He smiled. "Thank you. You have no idea what that means to me. If I've learned anything from this experience, Akash, it's that life slips away faster than you realize. Enjoy what time you have left."

"Does this mean that the Imagined was worthless? Was it just a test to see how well I could resist the urge to visit?"

"Do you sincerely believe that it held no value?"

"I don't know anymore. Seeing you as a ghost, visiting the Imagined—it's all too much for me. I don't understand what matters and what doesn't in this chaos."

"Let's consider it for a moment. The Imagined is nothing more than a manifestation of our emotional needs, correct? We only discovered it because we had to pacify our anguish."

"I guess."

"When we feel lost, we crave happiness. Our minds took that craving and searched furiously for what could appease it. The closest thing we could rely on was the past. Our memories were available, and we believed that we could trust them. Trying to find joy in the present is scary—it's unknown, and we do not know what form it exists in. The Imagined was created as a temporary solution. But if you look closer, you will see that the root of your search this entire time was not a need to relive your past, but rather, a search for contentment, for completeness, once again."

"So, what should I do?" I asked. "Ignore the past?"

"No, never," insisted the Singer. "The past is the foundation of who we are."

"But my memories are escaping me. Details are altered so easily within them. I don't know which parts I can trust anymore. How can I figure out who I'm supposed to be if I can't even pinpoint who I was?"

"Unfortunately, our perception of the past will never be as stable as we want. Within our tumultuous mind, the life we've lived is neither fully real nor imagined, but some sort of combination of the two. Once we recognize this, it's inevitable that we will feel a sense of bewilderment with our previous selves. But what we can hold on to in spite of the volatility is our emotional truth. What you felt in those moments you recall, that is what you, as a human, can uniquely claim as evidence that you have lived. Our emotions are only up to us to interpret. Use them to guide your decisions in the present when the rest is lost or forgotten."

"What's the point, though? What if I work for years, like you did with building the Town, to search for this vague idea of happiness and end up as depressed as you were?" I thought back to the weeks before my mother passed away and continued, "The Imagined took me to a period of my childhood before I knew what guilt or grief was. Each time I think I've found the possibility for happiness since, a new obstacle blocks me."

"For guilt, there is forgiveness. For grief, there are new forms of joy. Both can be balanced out. You see, Akash, happiness is not constant. We evolve over time, so our understanding of happiness has to as well. What made you happy when you were young will not bring you the same joy now. What I failed to understand was that life would never look the same in America as it did in India, but that did not mean that I could not adapt, that life could not be better than it once was, albeit different."

"I'm scared," I whispered. "I don't want to screw up anymore. I can't handle any more pain."

"Let me ask you something—can you make peace with whatever pain is currently holding you back?"

I hesitated. "I don't know."

"Do you want to?"

"Y-yes, I think so."

"That desire is all you need. If you take steps toward it, even if it feels like you're walking into an abyss, even if you are unsure of the outcome, moving forward will serve you more than remaining stuck. Take my death as proof. Fight for life, even if you do not understand it. Fight for it because you've been blessed with the ability to." He smiled. "I am finally at peace with leaving this world knowing that my existence has helped bring you on this journey."

"Is this it, then? Is this goodbye?"

"As you said, I existed to you before through stories. I will continue to in some other capacity after I am gone. The lines between reality and imagination, the past and the future, life and death—they are not as stark as you may think." A small fly landed on his hand and crawled to his fingertips. "It may seem terrifying when the structures that seemingly hold this world together come undone, like a finished painting that separates into its composing colors. But it just proves that you are holding a very tiny brush over this limitless canvas. Choose wisely how you use it."

The Singer—my Ajoba—raised his head toward the sky. A heavy wind began to accrue, whipping the grass in the meadow until each blade flew up and softened into tiny droplets of green paint. The daisies, the sky, and the rest of the environment followed suit, morphing into shapeless strands that, when collected together, formed a giant tornado of colors that spun and churned around us. Before long, my Ajoba's body gently dissolved into the mesmerizing whirlwind, as he permanently detached the part of himself that clung to this world and transcended into the vast, unfathomable abstract.

Stuck in the eye of the storm, where I could still feel the ground beneath me, I closed my eyes and clutched my knees to keep from flying away too. I needed to find Vaishu Mavshi before Suhail Mama got to her. It was the only way I could forgive myself. I was too close to give up.

When I opened my eyes, I was back in the meadow. The world was calm. My Ajoba had vanished, but in his place was a small dirt trail leading out of the grass. I couldn't go back to the cottage and risk Marissa kicking me out. So, I stood up and started down the path, trusting that I was headed in the right direction, even if I didn't know where I would end up. I was keen to escape the forest of isolation holding me hostage, just like my Ajoba had after being held captive for so long.

CHAPTER 33

A FALLEN MATRIARCH

I COULD SMELL the salty air before I saw the ocean. The path led me beyond the flowery meadow to a cliffside—a hard, rocky formation with a steep drop to crashing waves below. Milky-white froth billowed up from below, staining my jeans with tiny drops of water. I stopped for a moment to gaze out, reminding myself of how trivial my trepidation was in comparison to the scope of the world.

The path curved away from the cliffside. At the very end of the trail was a small building enclosed by a metal fence. As I neared, I realized that I'd arrived at an elementary school. Colorful murals depicting kids playing basketball and hopscotch were painted on the walls. Little handprints were imbedded on seashell-themed tiles around the front entrance. Children's screams came from the other side of the building, and I followed the boisterous noise to the back playground.

It was the end of the school day—or since it was the middle of summer, the end of some sort of camp or summer school. Most kids were packing their bags to leave, while others were still playing with their friends. They were scattered across the monkey bars, slides, and four-square boxes, engaging in perpetual, feral movement. Their faces were lit up with energetic smiles.

Vaishu Mavshi emerged from behind one slide and helped a child off of it. She was wearing a white linen shirt and denim jeans. She had wrinkles across her forehead and neck, as well as streaks of gray hair near her temples, but the exuberance in her expression made them almost unnoticeable. Her movement was easy and relaxed. She appeared younger, as if she'd shed the burdens and afflictions that had been aging her. She bent down to the child—a small, plump girl with pigtails—and whispered something in her ear. The girl grabbed Vaishu Mavshi's arm and pulled her into a tight hug. Vaishu Mavshi's smile grew bigger, and she let out a sprightly laugh.

When Harsh Kaka had detailed Vaishu Mavshi's disappearance, I'd assumed she would be cooped up in a decrepit place, not taking proper care of her health or appearance. If she had been distraught enough to leave him, I would never have expected her to be in any sort of fit condition. But the Vaishu Mavshi that I saw on that playground was the exact opposite of what I'd envisioned. She seemed happier than I ever remembered her being in my childhood. From afar, one wouldn't have been able to guess the tragedies she'd had to endure. I felt a sudden urge to turn around and walk away. Maybe leaving the Town had been the right decision for her. Who was I to disturb her new life? If she'd found peace, then why should I be the one to take it away?

Before I could retreat, a middle-aged blonde woman in a wool cardigan appeared before me and blocked my view of Vaishu Mavshi. "Excuse me, sir, are you here to pick up a child?"

"What? Oh, um, no," I replied, trying to sidestep her.

She quickly blocked my path again. "Are you with the afterschool programs?"

"No, I'm … uh, I'm just looking."

She crossed her arms and scowled at me suspiciously. "Excuse me?"

"No, no, I didn't mean it like that. I'm not looking at the children. I mean, I guess I am, but that's not why I'm here."

"I'm letting you know that I have security on speed dial." She reached into her pocket and removed a cellphone. "Unless you want further trouble, I suggest you leave immediately."

"Wait, there's no need for that." I took a step toward her and tried to swat the phone down.

She jumped back in fright. "Don't come any closer to me!"

A few children paused their antics and curiously watched the escalating situation. Vaishu Mavshi turned toward us. The woman before me was prattling on about how she wasn't getting paid enough for this, but I tuned her out. The second I caught Vaishu Mavshi's widened eyes, everything else happening around me became irrelevant. Her lips parted in confusion.

"I came to speak to her," I said, pointing at Vaishu Mavshi.

The blonde woman's eyes followed my finger, but Vaishu Mavshi lowered her face and turned away from us. She took the little girl she'd been playing with and led her toward the building.

"Doesn't seem like she knows you," said the blonde woman.

In a desperate attempt to prevent Vaishu Mavshi from leaving, I yelled at the top of my lungs, "Mahi is dead!"

Vaishu Mavshi stopped. Her head tilted slightly in my direction. Then, she let go of the little girl's hand and hurried into the building. My heart plummeted, and I stood in shock. My worst fear had come true. She did not want to speak to me. She did not even want to look at me.

"That's it," said the lady in front of me. "I'm calling security."

"Wait, wait. I'm leaving," I replied.

I backed away from the playground. The teacher slowly lowered her phone, peering at me with narrowed eyes until I was no longer in sight. I walked toward the front of the school.

An abundance of minivans weaved through the parking lot, picking up students near the entrance. I checked to see how long it would take me to get back to Vaishu Mavshi's house, but my data was especially slow.

A large part of me was disappointed and ready to walk away, but I'd come too far to back down. Vaishu Mavshi had seen me now. She knew that I was alive and looking for her. If she still rebuffed me after I attempted to speak to her, then I would respect her decision. But I could not expect forgiveness from her as easily as it had come with Harsh Kaka.

With my renewed resolve, I strode inside the building, scanning the nameplates of teachers outside each classroom. Vaishu Mavshi had been an obstetrics nurse in the Town, so it was of no surprise when I found her name by the nurse's office. The door had a small center window covered by translucent shades. I knocked and heard a shuffle of footsteps inside. The blinds parted slightly, revealing a fraction of Vaishu Mavshi's face. Once she realized who was knocking, she dropped the blinds and let them cover her again. Her shadow was still visible, so I knew she hadn't moved away from the door.

"How did you find me?" she whispered.

"Kiara Mami helped us find your cottage," I said. "After that, I kind of stumbled onto this school."

She was silent.

"May I come in?" I asked.

"I can't …"

"I'm sorry I yelled the news about my mom. That's not how I wanted to share it. Please let me see you."

Vaishu Mavshi let out a shaky breath. "It's not that I don't want to talk to you, Akash. I do. I want to see your face. But I'm scared if I do … I will fall apart again. I almost did when Suhail told me about Mahi's death. I can't have that happen again."

"He told you already?"

"He called me last night."

Kiara Mami's efforts had been in vain. Suhail Mama had already gotten to Vaishu Mavshi.

"Did he ask you about the house?" I asked.

"Yes."

"Please tell me you're not signing it over."

"He's right. It carries too much history."

"What about Harsh Kaka? He's been keeping it for you."

"I told Suhail not to do anything until he's found another place. Harsh can keep all the money from the sale. I don't want it."

"You know he doesn't care about the money. He just wants you home."

Vaishu Mavshi did not reply immediately. After a moment, she said, "For years, I held myself responsible for the well-being of the household. I took care of everyone, not because it was required of me, but because I wanted to. Looking after the family was the center of who I was. But that house … it's just a reminder of my failure."

"You didn't fail. Things happened that were out of your control."

"I should have known. I should have seen the cracks that were forming in our family and prevented them."

I raised my hand to the window and hovered it over her shadow. "Vaishu Mavshi, I'll say one more thing, and if you still don't want to see me after that, I'll leave. I know how hard it is to face the ones you love when you're in pain. It took me a lot longer to come back here than it should have. I thought for the longest time that it was better for all of us if we were apart. That way, I didn't have to look at you and be reminded of how I could have prevented Sagar's death, or how we left you and Harsh Kaka when you needed us the most. But this separation was crueler than I expected. I watched it eat my mother up. It almost took me as well. I came back because I believe there is still hope for this family, whatever broken pieces of it are left. I don't think we can forgive ourselves unless we do it together."

I waited for a response, but none came. I continued, "Still, I want you to be happy. If you think being away from the Town is best for you, then so be it. If you tell me to leave, I will never come looking for you again."

I held my breath tightly in my chest. The AC whirred over the tense silence.

Vaishu Mavshi finally whispered, "Please go."

I dropped my hand and bowed my head. "Okay."

Her shadow vanished. I left the school and found the path that took me toward the cliffside. For the first half of the walk, I was tormented by a sense of disappointment and defeat. Her decision stung me. I was heartbroken that she could not even face me, and probably never would again. Even more than my own rejection, I was consumed with thoughts of Vaishu Mavshi's future. As put together as she'd appeared, her grief had been audible during our conversation. She would continue her life with the sorrow festering within her. I wished that instead of promising to leave, I'd continued to persuade her.

When I reached the ocean and stared out at the sweeping sheet of blue once again, I bundled up my distress and released it in a long, steady exhale. I thought back to the beginning of my journey. Before reaching the school, I had been filled with uncertainty in myself and my ability to face Vaishu Mavshi. But I had done it, and I'd meant every word I'd said. My family and my life in the Town were an essential part of my childhood, and thus, an essential part of me. I could not live without acknowledging that, and I didn't want to anymore. Being back in the Town, reconnecting with the people who had been so formative in my early life, was helping me recognize myself after I'd lost all understanding of who I was. Undergoing this quest to bring my family back together brought me hope after a period when I didn't believe hope was possible anymore. By attempting to repair the relationships that had seemed too daunting to ever touch again, I was fighting for a future where the prospect of happiness, peace, and forgiveness was possible once again. I wasn't going to let Vaishu Mavshi's decision dismantle this. She'd made her choice, but I'd also made my own. I wouldn't spiral again. I would figure out another way to move forward with those who were willing to accept me back into their lives.

When I reached the meadow, my phone began to buzz. I pulled it out of my pocket and saw that I had service again. There were five missed calls from Mayuran and another one incoming.

"Hello?" I answered.

"Finally, you picked up!" cried an agitated Mayuran. Piercing screams were coming from behind him.

"What's going on? What's that noise behind you?"

"It's a fucking shitshow over here. After you left, your aunt started having contractions. She said to ignore it because apparently false ones happen a lot. Something called Brexon. No, Braxon? Fuck, what was it—"

"Mayuran, it doesn't matter. What's happening now?"

"Her water broke."

"Oh, shit! Take her to the hospital!"

"I was going to, but something's off. Her contractions are really intense. She can't even get up. I've never seen someone go into labor, but this doesn't feel normal. She literally thinks—"

Kiara Mami yelled out, "I swear to God I'm going to give birth in this damn house!"

"Well, yeah, what she just said."

I panicked. "Call an ambulance!"

"I did, but this house is so far from everything that it's going to take them some time to get here. They're giving instructions to Marissa over the phone in case it progresses." Another scream rang out behind him. "Fuck, I feel like I'm gonna yack."

"Stay calm. Don't stress her out."

"Come back quickly, man. I need your help."

"I'll be there as soon as I can."

I hung up and took off toward the cottage, almost laughing at how the madness of life progressed without interruption. Instead of letting the chaos deter me, I now ran directly toward it.

CHAPTER 34

LIFE AND DEATH

UPON ARRIVING AT the cottage, I followed Kiara Mami's high-pitched shrieks to the bedroom. Mayuran was bent over against the wall, clutching his thighs. Kiara Mami was lying on the floor atop a heap of spread-out towels. Her upper half was propped up by pillows taken off the bed. She'd assumed a birthing position, with her knees pointed up. She was breathing in short, punctuated bursts and brushing sweat-drenched curls away from her rosy face. Marissa was kneeling before Kiara Mami, balancing the landline phone in between her own shoulder and ear.

"How's it going in here?" I asked.

"Oh, Akash, thank God!" Kiara Mami cried out, stretching her arm toward me. I sat beside her and received a tight, pain-inducing grip on my hand.

"Emergency medical services are on their way," said Marissa. Despite her calm voice, the worried creases in her forehead revealed that she was equally overwhelmed by the experience. "Based on her contractions, I think the baby is going to start crowning soon."

"Don't *saaaaay* that!" Kiara Mami wailed. "Why does this happen to me? Why couldn't I just have a normal birth like everyone else on this planet?"

"How did this happen?" I asked.

Marissa handed me a towel to wipe the sweat off Kiara Mami's face. "They said she's going through rapid labor. It happens rarely, but it's not unheard of."

"What can I do to help?"

"I'm not even sure what I'm supposed to do. I take care of senior citizens, not pregnant women."

"Can I bring some more towels? Or water?"

"Yes, yes, that would be good. Your friend knows where both are."

"Don't leave," bawled Kiara Mami.

"I'll be back in a moment," I assured her, using gentle force to release my hand from hers. Mayuran accompanied me out to the hallway.

"You good?" I asked him.

He shuddered. "Man, that was some scary shit. She was talking to me about baby names, and then all of a sudden, she started screaming in pain. It happened so fast."

"I'm really glad you were with her," I said, placing a hand on Mayuran's shoulder. "Where are the towels?"

Mayuran pointed to a cabinet by the kitchen. I removed fresh towels from it and searched for a water bottle. Once I found one large enough, I filled it up and rushed back to Kiara Mami's side, situating myself in the same position I'd been in before. For a few minutes, the room was relatively calm. Kiara Mami's breathing slowed, and she eased into her pillows. I patted her forehead with a hand towel, absorbing any droplets of sweat before they fell on the rest of her face.

Suddenly, Kiara Mami shot forward and howled as another contraction began. Mayuran, who was hovering by the entrance, ran out of the room, clutching his stomach. Marissa massaged her temples with concern.

Kiara Mami tugged my collar so that my face was an inch

away from hers. Her pink eyes implored me for help. "I can't do this, Akash," she whispered. "It hurts too much. This is not the way it was supposed to happen."

I rubbed her hand. "The paramedics will come soon, Mami. We have them on the phone in case anything happens. It'll all be okay."

"You don't know that. What if I don't get through this? What if the baby doesn't make it?"

"Don't think like that. You and the baby are going to be fine. We're all here to help you."

"He's right," a voice said from behind me.

I spun around and saw Vaishu Mavshi standing at the doorway, holding her nursing tote bag in one hand and car keys in the other. Her eyes were scanning the room, taking in the scene before her.

"Vaishu Tai, you're here!" shrieked Kiara Mami.

"I rushed over the second I saw that Marissa paged me."

"I'm so sorry," I said. "We didn't get a chance to leave."

"There's no time for that now." Vaishu Mavshi dropped her bag and approached us. She took over Marissa's spot and knelt between Kiara Mami's legs. "How are you feeling, Kiara?"

"Like I'm about to die. I can't move."

"Looks to me like precipitous labor. Help is on the way?"

"They're on the phone now," said Marissa. "They got lost on their way here, so I'm guiding them through the shortcut."

"Good. Lucky for you, Kiara, I have years of experience working in obstetrics."

"I love you," cried Kiara Mami. "You know that, right?"

"It's very important that you stay calm. We want to prevent any tearing from happening."

"Tearing! Oh God!" Kiara Mami's eyes rolled back as she convulsed into rapid exhales. She shot back up. "Oh crap! Suhail! I completely forgot. He needs to know."

"I'll call him right away, Mami," I said. "Where is your phone?"

Kiara Mami pointed to her purse on top of the bed. I searched through it until I found a diamond-studded cellphone. "I'll be right outside. Is there anything else you need?"

"Open the front door and wait for the paramedics," replied Vaishu Mavshi. She grabbed Kiara Mami's hand. "We've got this."

Kiara Mami nervously laughed, tears pouring out of her eyes. I gently shut the door behind me and searched for Suhail Mama's contact. He picked up after the second ring. "What's up, Kiara?"

"This is Akash."

"Wha—um, okay? Why do you have Kiara's phone?"

"It's a long story, but you have to come immediately to Vaishu Mavshi's place. Kiara Mami is in labor."

"What!" he sputtered. "How- I—"

"Just come as soon as you can."

"Is she okay?"

"She will be. Vaishu Mavshi is taking care of her."

"I'm leaving right now. Hey, Akash?"

"Yeah?"

"Thanks for calling."

"Of course, Suhail Mama."

He cut the call. I unlocked the front door and left it open as instructed. I began to walk back toward a stricken Mayuran, but my attention was diverted once I saw my Aaji. She was still sleeping, unaware and unbothered by the havoc that was happening around her. I edged into her room and went to her bedside. There was a chair right beside her, likely where Marissa usually sat. I fell into it, weary from the events of the day.

My Aaji's eyes fluttered open. Her face scrunched up as she adjusted to the light and absorbed her surroundings. She unsuccessfully tried to hoist herself up.

"Wait, Aaji," I said, adjusting her pillow. "Let me help you."

She frowned at me in confusion. "Where is Natasha?"

"Who?"

"Natasha. Natasha," she said insistently.

"You mean Marissa?"

"Hm?" Her voice was distant, as if she could not recognize the mistake she had made.

"She's in the other room. She'll be here soon."

My Aaji's dementia had progressed significantly since my childhood. It was unclear whether she even comprehended who I was. I was trying not to let the lack of recognition affect me, but it was painful to look in her vacant eyes and not see overflowing love like there used to be.

My Aaji's head slowly swiveled toward the multicolored flowers blooming outside of her window. "*Kithī sundar dista aaheth.*" How beautiful they are looking.

I leaned back in my chair. Even though Kiara Mami's occasional howls punctured the silence, the room was still. Late-afternoon light fluttered in, creating dancing shadows of petals in front of my feet. There was no television in the room, which struck me as odd, given that my Aaji used to be glued to the screen in our old house. Her days had been occupied with stories, either from shows or of her own composition. However, without the reliability of her memory, she had no other option now but to be an observer of the present moment. There was something so pensive about her choosing to stare at the flowers instead of the vast assortment of photos in her room. Even without the same cognizance a healthy memory would have provided her, she still desired and cherished beauty. Her connection to it, to the depreciated here and now, was arguably stronger than a person who is constantly bogged down with regrets of the past and expectations for the future.

In one of the most climactic moments of my life (which I can now proclaim writing this chronicle years after the fact), I mirrored my Aaji and became an observer. Time slowed down tremendously when I removed myself from the storm. I had seen innumerable flowers before in my life, but none looked as stunning, as fragile, as serene and mysterious as those trembling outside her window did. The paramedics rushed in at some point, and Mayuran led them to Kiara Mami's room. I did not get up. And then, again, when Suhail Mama frantically stumbled in front of my Aaji's doorway, I nodded to my left without so much as shifting my posture. I am not sure how long my Aaji and I sat in silence, but life continued to turn, push, and figure itself out as it always did. The only difference was that I could situate both my body and mind in that chair, watch the events unfurl in front of me, and soak in every second of it without losing myself in the confusion. I was able to grasp at the present moment alongside my Aaji and, in consequence, recognize how magnificent it was to exist—and to persist.

When the sun had lowered and fireflies began to flicker in a disorganized cluster above the flowers, Mayuran came to the doorway, his hair matted, a grin on his lips. He didn't need to say anything. His expression told me that my time on the periphery had come to an end. I followed him down the hallway to the other bedroom, counting myself lucky that, unlike my Aaji, I still had the ability to look back on this momentous day whenever I wished. Because of this blessing, I knew that the beauty I was presently witnessing would abide for as long as I was able to recall it.

The air inside was stuffy and humid. The medical team was quietly packing up their equipment around Kiara Mami, who was still lying on the floor. Marissa was sitting on the bed, and Mayuran went to join her. Vaishu Mavshi was separated from everyone else, hidden in a dim corner of the room. I approached Kiara Mami. She held a small bundle wrapped in blankets. Suhail Mama was crouching down beside her, cradling her head with his arm. Their crimson cheeks glistened with tears.

"Would you like to hold her?" asked Kiara Mami.

I nodded.

She passed her daughter over to me. I received the bundle gingerly, afraid of inflicting harm. The newborn's circular eyes curiously examined me. Rolls of drooping fat made it difficult to distinguish her face from her neck. She had a few tufts of hair sprouting off her scalp, but she was bald for the most part. Her skin was radiant, completely unmarred.

"I was so worried, honey. Thank God you're okay," Suhail Mama whispered, nuzzling Kiara Mami's hair. The business tycoon had withered, and in his place stood the affectionate uncle I'd known and loved. Kiara Mami leaned against him, shutting her eyes and receiving his warmth. The room was saturated with intimacy, sprung from the joint effort of birthing this child.

"We should head to the hospital soon," said one of the medics.

I handed the newborn back to Kiara Mami. Vaishu Mavshi had quietly disappeared from her corner without anyone noticing. I slipped out of the room to look for her. The front door was wide open. Vaishu Mavshi was leaning against the hood of Mayuran's truck, gazing up at the sky. I joined her.

"What are you thinking about?" I asked.

"The first time I saw Sagar … Did you know that he didn't cry when he was born? Instead, he had a very mischievous smirk on his face. I should have known then how much trouble he was going to cause me," she said, chuckling. After a moment, her smile wavered. "I was angry the last time I spoke to him. I wish to God that I hadn't been. Rather than scolding him, I should have told him how much I love him."

"He knew, Mavshi. You were an incredible mom."

"I thought moving away would help numb the pain. For a while, I convinced myself that it did. I missed the laughter and screams—the whining too—and needed those sounds to replace the sickening silence. I would go to work, play with the kids, and fall in love with each of them. But then, they would leave me at the end of the school day and return to their real parents. No matter how much I wished they would, no other child could fill the void Sagar left behind."

She lowered her head, arching further into a stoop.

"My heart …" she continued, her voice cracking. "My heart was so heavy. I couldn't bear the weight of it. I thought it would be better to feel nothing than to feel too much. But seeing that child … seeing how much love she is surrounded by … and realizing how much I wish to give to her." She paused. "I want to feel again. But I'm afraid I won't be able to handle it. I've always been one to use my head first. In matters of the heart, I never know the correct way forward."

I reached over to her bony hand; intertwined my fingers with her slender ones; pressed my thumb deep into her rough, calloused skin. I clutched the same hand that had raised me, fed me, nurtured me, disciplined me, and loved me, hoping the memory of my touch would convince her of her strength as well as the support that was waiting for her should she choose to accept it. She stiffened at first but did not draw back. Eventually, her hand relaxed in mine.

The temperature was cooling down, but I could still feel the sticky, sweaty summer heat plastered all over my body. As the sun continued to set, rose and lavender light billowed out across the giant dome above us. Faint stars twinkled in the distance. The vibrant sky looked as if it had been plucked out of the Imagined. If it hadn't been for Vaishu Mavshi's hand assuring me how concrete and tangible that moment was, I could have easily believed that the dreamlike colors were fabricated. Like my Ajoba had said, everything I considered separate was more connected than I could ever possibly understand. I'd accepted by then that the mind and the world were too expansive, too bewildering, to fully uncover in the short period I was allowed consciousness. But if it was true that lines could be blurred and crossed, and disparate facets of the world could converge, then I earnestly believed that my mother, my Ajoba, and Sagar, in whatever form they were in, were watching this pivotal reunion and beaming at the birth of a new era for this family. I felt, standing under that marvelous sky, as though I were caught in the midst of a beautiful intersection between life and death.

CHAPTER 35

THE PAST, THE PRESENT, AND THE UNKNOWN

"DOES IT LOOK even?" I asked, applying the last piece of tape.

Mayuran leaned away from the base of the ladder, causing it to wobble.

I clutched on to the roof's rain gutter and retorted, "Let me fall to my death, why don't you."

"Sorry, sorry." He recorrected his stance and gripped the side rails. "Looks good to me."

I cautiously climbed down the steps. Mayuran and I stood back to observe our work. For sentimental reasons, Kiara Mami had ordered a banner from the same place she'd bought one for her wedding stage. "It's a Girl!" was printed in swooping letters against a nauseating hot-pink background. The sign was unattractive enough that the asymmetrical strips of blue masking tape holding it up were relatively unnoticeable.

"I think we did a pretty good job," said Mayuran, turning around and surveying the rest of the tables we'd set up in the backyard earlier that morning. Harsh Kaka was circling one of the center tables and placing party favors on each chair. Kiara Mami's father, Manav Ajoba, lounged near him and was mid-rant about how taxes and welfare were ruining this country.

Kalpana Aaji paraded out of the house. Suhail Mama was trailing behind her, struggling to keep up. He balanced multiple trays of appetizers on each arm, winded from the amount he was carrying.

"Put them right over there. Now be careful, Suhail. No, no, not like that," chided Kalpana Aaji. She motioned for him to straighten the trays out on the table so that they were parallel to each other. Suhail Mama misunderstood and lifted one of the trays up. Kalpana Aaji huffed in frustration. "Just give it to me. I have to do everything, it seems."

Harsh Kaka walked over and patted a bemused Suhail Mama on the back, a brief display of their ongoing reconciliation. After Kiara Mami's unprecedented birth, most of us in the cottage had rushed to the nearest hospital. Vaishu Mavshi and Marissa stayed behind to be with my Aaji. I called Harsh Kaka in the car and told him the news. I didn't expect that he would come, given his feud with Suhail Mama, but he immediately asked what the address of the hospital was and said that he would figure out a way there, despite not having a car. True to his word, he arrived a couple hours later and bestowed a warm kiss on top of the infant's head.

"She's beautiful, Suhail," he said. "Congratulations on a wonderful addition to the family."

Suhail Mama nodded appreciatively in response. His eyes hadn't left his daughter's face since we'd arrived at the hospital. They sparkled with a devoted fondness that only comes from paternal love. He would often place his ear on her chest, confirming to himself that her breathing was normal. The tender side that he'd almost shed was steadily reemerging with newfound fatherhood.

To keep with Maharashtrian tradition, Kiara Mami insisted on throwing a naming ceremony for her daughter. Harsh Kaka suggested hosting it at our house in the Town, declaring that it was the most fitting location to welcome a new family member. Suhail Mama's pride caused him to waver, but after seeing Kiara Mami's enthusiasm over the idea, he quietly conceded. Over the following week and a half, we all pitched in to help organize the event.

Kiara Mami emerged from the house with her daughter. She made sloppy kissing noises and cooed to the swaddled infant, "You're *soooo* cute, you know that? How can you be this cute? Can you wave to your big brothers for me?"

Mayuran covered his eyes and cried out, "Peek-a-boo!" The baby gazed at him with startled fascination.

It made me happy to see Mayuran in a cheerful mood. After his ugly confrontation with Ratnam, he'd temporarily shifted into the house with me and Harsh Kaka. He would check in on his father once a day and come back from these short visits weary and depressed. Despite having made it clear from the beginning that he needed space, he still had to rebuff Ratnam's constant pleas for him to return home. Luckily, Mayuran had options on where he could stay in the meantime. Kiara Mami had taken a strong liking to him after their time together in the cottage. She'd offered her and Suhail Mama's house as an alternate shelter, remarking that having someone to chat with while at home with the baby would prevent her from losing her mind.

As for my next steps, I'd decided after much discussion with Harsh Kaka that the best path forward would be to return to Fremont, retake the classes I had flunked out of, and get all my belongings in order. After that, I could decide whether I wanted to reapply to the arts college in Florida, explore other universities, return to the Town, or choose a completely different path. With the money my father had given me, I had enough to support myself while I finished high school. The second summer school term was about to begin, and though I'd made sure to stay back for the setup of the naming ceremony, my flight to SFO was booked for later that evening. I was delaying my goodbyes, unable to handle separating again so quickly after reuniting.

During the week and a half between the birth and the naming ceremony, I'd made calls to those in the Bay that I'd needed to apologize to. My first ones were to Ravi and Eva. I thanked them for being such wonderful friends and disclosed the truth about Sagar's death and the ensuing aftermath. In typical Ravi fashion, he replied with nothing more than a resounding "Damn." Eva stumbled through a tearful, incoherent speech where she praised my courage and honesty. Although I understood only a fraction of what she said, I appreciated the sentiment.

Luke was by far the toughest call I had to make. Given how abruptly I'd cut him off, I was afraid that he would not receive my apology well. I avoided it for a few days but finally forced myself to dial. He picked up immediately.

"Akash?"

His voice threw me off. Everything I'd rehearsed was wiped from memory. "Luke, I- hello- I mean, I wanted to say ... whew."

He chuckled. "Slow down, sir. I can't understand anything you're saying."

I took a deep breath. "I want to apologize for how everything went down between us. I, um, I know I didn't handle things very well. My mother passed away earlier this year, and I went through an incredibly rough time after. Still, it's no excuse for how I treated you. I am so, so sorry."

He was silent.

"Luke?"

"I'm here. I'm just ... processing."

"This is a lot to dump on you."

"I wish I knew."

"I should have told you."

"No, no, I'm not blaming you. I'm just sorry that I couldn't help in any way."

"Ghosting you was the worst thing I could have done. I know my actions might not be the most telling, but I really care about you."

After another long pause, he replied, "I care about you too."

"When do you leave for college?"

"In a little over a month."

"Can I see you before you head off?"

"Yeah, I'd like that. Got a few new pics of Yusuf Uncle I have to show you."

"You're never going to leave that man alone, huh?"

"Never."

Packing for the Bay Area had been much easier after the phone calls were completed. I was sure in my decision, and there was nothing more I had to fear by going back.

While Mayuran and Kiara Mami entertained the newborn, I checked the time. "Guests are going to start arriving soon."

"Did Vaishu Tai ever confirm if she was coming?" asked Kiara Mami.

In a traditional Maharashtrian naming ceremony, the father's older sister usually hears the baby's chosen name first. The parents whisper it in her ear, and she then repeats it in the baby's ear before announcing it to the rest of the guests. Suhail Mama had asked Vaishu Mavshi if she would do the honor, but she'd expressed wariness over attending an event with other people from the Town, saying that she wasn't sure if she was prepared to face them just yet. I'd offered to fill in for the role of the paternal aunt in the event that she did not show up.

"She said she would think about it," I replied. "I haven't heard anything since then."

"Do you still want to go ahead with the plan?"

"I think so. I'll go upstairs and get it."

I wanted to release my mother's ashes before the naming ceremony began. Given the family's recent reconciliation and my imminent departure, I felt strongly that this was the right time to let go. I'd invited Vaishu Mavshi to join, and though I knew it would feel incomplete without her, I was prepared to move forward either way.

I went to my mother's old room and obtained the urn. I was standing at the top of the staircase, ready to head back down, when a familiar voice stopped me.

"Marissa, can you take her outside? I'll be there in just a moment."

My heart soared at the sound of Vaishu Mavshi's voice. I crept down a few steps until I caught sight of her, Marissa, and my Aaji. Marissa pushed my Aaji's wheelchair toward the kitchen, leaving Vaishu Mavshi alone in the living room. Vaishu Mavshi sat on the couch and gazed at the room. She ran her hands over a pillow and then along the coffee table. Her expression was pained as she soaked in the memories that were embedded in the furniture, just like I had when I first returned to the house.

"You came," I said, descending the remaining stairs.

She nodded, still looking around at the room.

"How are you feeling?"

"Words can't describe," she whispered.

"I understand."

She noticed the urn. "Is that …?"

"Everyone is waiting in the back. Are you ready to join them?"

She nodded again and followed me out. Kiara Mami's squeals of joy warmly welcomed us. Suhail Mama embraced Vaishu Mavshi and thanked her for coming. Harsh Kaka hung back at a far-off table and stole shy glances at her. After the initial greetings, Kiara Mami began to lead Mayuran, Marissa, and her parents back into the house. I insisted on her staying, but she said that this moment should just be for immediate family. The rest of us in the backyard stood in a horizontal line. Vaishu Mavshi positioned my Aaji's wheelchair on my left side. Harsh Kaka and Suhail Mama situated themselves on my right. They all watched me expectantly, their hands folded. I stepped forward and removed the top off the urn.

"I hope she finds peace."

I pointed the urn toward the ground, but a gust of wind redirected the tumbling ashes and changed their course toward the sky. Each particle flickered in the sunlight, sparkling like little diamonds against the bright blue.

———

Soon after, the backyard was replete with guests. We gathered everyone around the baby's crib to begin the ceremony. Once the priest completed his chants, Kiara Mami whispered the baby's name in Vaishu Mavshi's ear. Vaishu Mavshi leaned down to the newborn and repeated the name in her ear before declaring it to everyone.

"Aaruni!"

The name snaked through the mouths of each guest, as they massaged the three syllables, felt out the weight of the word, and associated it with the tiny girl sleeping in the crib. Applause broke out, inadvertently waking little Aaruni. Kiara Mami picked up the wailing infant and aggressively rocked her. As Aaruni's cries became more agitated, Vaishu Mavshi leaned over and planted a light kiss on her forehead. The crying immediately ceased, prompting another round of applause from the crowd. Vaishu Mavshi blushed, and Kiara Mami hugged her with relief.

Once the guests dispersed, I made my rounds through the various tables, pleasantly surprised by the number of familiar faces that were scattered through the backyard. Many of those who still lived in the Town were present. Simran Aunty and her posse of salon workers formed an exclusive group to gossip about those at the event. Bhaskar Uncle situated himself at a corner table and was bombarded by old friends who wished to greet him. Mayuran was his dutiful aide and fetched him refreshments throughout the afternoon. A few who were no longer in the Town also unexpectedly showed up. Aneesa Aunty, who had moved with her husband to Long Island, gave me a big hug and informed me that she was still teaching elementary school, though she stated that no other class would compare to the ones she'd instructed in the Town. Mariam and Musa Mahmood found silent company with the other elders. Adi Deo, the cardiologist that my Aaji used to harass for free medical advice, appeared with his son, Kunal, and bragged extensively about the latter's admittance to Harvard.

The bountiful, overlapping conversations spanning a myriad of languages reminded me of the way the Town used to be. Seeing the people of my past come back together, even if just for an afternoon, made me realize that this community would still exist as long as human connection continued. I thought about my conversations with Priya in early middle school where I'd found myself at a loss to describe what bound the Town together. Each family hailed from distinct parts of South Asia, had their own set of customs, and carried unique religious and cultural labels. The Town was a constructed entity, an imagined space, originally composed of immigrants who'd needed companionship in an unfamiliar country. Although my Ajoba founded the Town so its inhabitants could be reminded of the places they'd left behind, an entirely new beast was created, one where certain traditions were preserved while others were altered or forgotten, and Desi cultures seeped into one another to the point where they became somewhat indistinguishable. The move had prompted people who would not have met or associated with each other had they remained in their homelands to exchange and learn from one another. The identity of the Town could never be summed up in a simple answer because it had been invisibly evolving since its creation. This conflated community had charted its own path in a land that regarded it as homogeneous, without any models that it could look to for guidance.

Even though the Town was constructed, the friendships that were formed, the experiences that were exchanged, and the new ways of life that were navigated together, were all undeniably real. The naming ceremony proved to me that the Town, which I now considered a collection of people rather than a geographic area, would reconfigure itself once again to exist within the forthcoming years, even if proximity weakened. Future generations would replace the old, traditions would continue to be modified and taught as best they could be, and culture would be reshaped over and over again, as this group of immigrants evolved further away from their places of origin. The Town was undergoing a similar transformation to that of a child progressing to adulthood. I'd only been able to figure out what I considered important from my childhood once my memory was altered, manipulated, and mutated in the Imagined, and I'd been left with scattered fragments to sort through. Likewise, once collective memory of the homelands had started to decline, the Town had been compelled to come undone. Our community could only determine what would become of us next amid this unraveling. The exposed cracks, fissures, and imaginary lines were showing us that culture and community could not remain stagnant, in the same way that memory couldn't either. Just like my Ajoba had taken fragments of his life in Bombay and used them to construct the Town, I, and the other Townsfolk, would take fragments of the Town wherever we went next. This vital, albeit scattered, passing down of cultural values, stories, and traditions would weave generations together and ensure that memory of the mother countries would never be erased.

At some point in the afternoon, Suhail Mama pulled me aside and apologized for using the news about my mother's death to try to buy the house. He said that he was horrified by his actions and that he'd already apologized to Harsh Kaka. Returning to the house as a father helped him realize how important family had been in his upbringing. He said that he would drop his efforts to buy out the cul-de-sac but warned me that other hungry buyers would replace him. Reconstructing old properties in valuable locations was a sought-out endeavor for developers, and the house would not be impenetrable forever. I thanked him and said it was better knowing that at least my uncle wasn't the one attempting to tear it down anymore.

While strolling through the party, I noticed a captive audience of children surrounding Harsh Kaka. I walked close enough to make out that he was sharing the story of how my Ajoba founded the Town. He was telling it exactly how my Aaji used to at Town events. Most of the children had not heard it before, which was evident by their audible reactions and engaged expressions. I grinned, happy that my Ajoba's legacy was still being passed down. Vaishu Mavshi was sitting at a nearby table, positioned away from Harsh Kaka's line of sight. She wistfully watched him and the children.

After another hour of celebration, it was time for me to start toward the airport. I said my goodbyes to the Townsfolk as well as to my extended family. Kiara Mami pinched my cheeks and insisted I call her the second I landed. I kissed my Aaji's hand, to which she responded with a slight smile, one that possibly hinted at recognition. Mayuran, on the other hand, awkwardly shook my hand without making eye contact and said that he was glad we'd reconnected. His farewell was underwhelming, but I was caught up in such a flurry of good-byes that I couldn't dwell on it for long. At the last minute, one final issue presented itself. Harsh Kaka and Vaishu Mavshi's whereabouts were unknown. They were not in the backyard, and no one had seen them leave. As the boarding time for my train rapidly approached, I decided that I would collect my luggage and then try searching for them again.

I went inside the house to the upper floor, gathered my suitcase, and looked around my mother's bedroom one final time. My throat clenched as I thought of how much she would have enjoyed an event like this. I left the room and shut the door gently on my way out.

As I walked down the hallway, I heard noises coming from the room I used to share with Sagar. The door was cracked open. Vaishu Mavshi and Harsh Kaka were inside, huddled together on the edge of Sagar's bed. Harsh Kaka had his arm around Vaishu Mavshi as she wept uncontrollably into his shoulder. She did not try to hide her face like she used to when I was little. She allowed the raw, exposed, guttural sobs to escape without suppression. Harsh Kaka stroked her hair and kissed her forehead. Although I did not wish to disturb this intimate moment for them, I knew I had to say goodbye before I left.

I knocked on the door. Harsh Kaka waved me in, and Vaishu Mavshi wiped away her tears.

"Is it already time for you to leave?" she asked.

"Sadly, yes," I replied.

"You'll be back soon, right?"

I nodded. "I want to thank you both for helping raise me. I ... I always considered you to be my second set of parents."

Harsh Kaka beckoned me to join. I walked over and embraced them.

"We are so proud of you," said Harsh Kaka.

"Thank you for bringing us back together," whispered Vaishu Mavshi.

I bent over and touched the ground before their feet. They each placed a hand on my head and gave me their blessings. With my last goodbyes said, I left the house and started down the cul-de-sac.

"Wait!" a voice called.

I turned. Mayuran was running toward me.

"Hey, what's u—"

He grabbed my face and kissed me. Suddenly, I was eleven years old again, discovering his chapped lips and the faint cigarette smoke on his breath. I locked my arms around his neck and kissed him back.

He broke away. "I wish you weren't leaving."

"Mayuran ..."

"It's all good. I'll be here, waiting for you. Don't forget about me until then, okay?"

"I couldn't even if I wanted to."

He backpedaled to the house, watching me all the while with a foolish grin. As I turned onto Main Street, a dizzying warmth spread through my chest, a potent feeling, akin to that of a child discovering their very first crush.

———

Suhail Mama had offered to drop me off at the airport, but I'd refused, saying that I didn't want to pull him away from the party. Although I'd considered taking the long public transit route that began with the City bus, I no longer felt it necessary to avoid the train station. I calmly bought a ticket, climbed up the stairs, and walked onto the platform. It was nearly empty, a complete contrast from the last time I had been on it. The mechanical whirring of the tracks and the bored yawning of the other waiting passengers yielded a monotonous, dreary atmosphere. I decided to treat my environment with as much indifference as everyone else on the platform seemed to.

The announcer's voice burst through the loudspeaker and notified us that the train would be arriving shortly. When it pulled in, I carried my luggage inside and chose a seat by the window. I sat down and looked out at the platform. It was mostly cleared out, except for one remaining person. He stood a few feet away from my compartment. His bowl-shaped haircut glistened under the glow of the translucent roof, and his long eyelashes were visible even from afar. He was staring directly at me in his pure, unaltered form. I clutched my seat in confusion. Was I back in the Imagined? I thought that I'd recovered from the terrifying experience in San Francisco when the Imagined and physical world merged. I was sure that I'd regained control of my reality.

Although I was expecting the station to separate into paint at any second, nothing unusual happened. I frantically looked around to confirm that I was still on the train. My hand was clutching the seat so tightly that a sharp pain began to develop in my wrist. I was incredibly aware of where I was, so, how was I seeing him? How was he before me?

I tried to stand up, but the train jolted forward and caused me to fall back in my seat. The doors closed, preventing me from stepping back on the platform to confirm if he was real. I hesitantly pivoted back toward the window. He was still there. Sagar, the fixed one, the unchangeable one. The one who never wanted to grow up, and the one who never had the chance to. I understood at that moment why it had been so difficult to leave him and the forest behind and why he was the only person who existed within my Imagined. Sagar, and the juvenile part of myself reflected in him, had always been the root of my search, even when my visits weren't driven by an evident desire to find him. Until I reconciled with my independence, until I determined how to persevere in spite of life's vicissitudes, I would always want to regress to a state of naivety and impressionability. But looking out at the platform, I knew I was finally equipped to evolve beyond my apprehension of the unknown.

At long last, I peered into his brown eyes and saw my guilt, my fallen innocence, my completed childhood, and the loss of bygone days. I saw what the world had blessed me with and also cruelly snatched away. I saw the things that subsisted and the things I could never get back. And I saw Sagar for who he had been, and not the figment I held on to.

I was certain that this would be the last time I'd see him, that as soon as the train pulled away, I would be relinquishing him and the Imagined for good. The train started to advance slowly, and I kept my eyes on him for as long as I could, straining my neck, until he and the station were no larger than specks in the distance. Then, when I was ready, I turned around and faced forward.

ACKNOWLEDGMENTS

WRITING THIS NOVEL was a long and challenging process, causing me many moments of self-doubt during an already turbulent period of my life. I am unbelievably grateful to those who have assisted me, personally or professionally, over these past four-and-a-half years. I was motivated to see this lengthy project through solely because of your guidance and support.

My most important acknowledgment is reserved for my parents, Ashwini Kantak and Mukund Srinivasan. Thank you for your unwavering confidence in my artistic abilities, especially at times when I was unable to find it on my own. I don't know what I did in my previous life to have such dedicated, encouraging, humble, and selfless parents. No words will ever be able to capture the immeasurable amount of gratitude I have for you both. I am wholly the person I am today because of you. Thank you for loving me.

I would like to express my appreciation to all of the professionals and collaborators who worked on this project. Thank you to my developmental editor, Sohini Ghose, for helping tune up my chapters with well-thought-out comments; to my beta readers—Anisha Anisetti, Samantha Lee, Sayali Ranadive, and Varun Menon—for taking the time out of your busy lives to provide me invaluable critiques; to my copy editor, Joe Pierson, for your attention to my grammatical errors; and to my proofreader, Michael Sandlin, for reading with a sharp eye. Thank you also to Nicole Fegan for doing a final, final close read before publication.

Some other professionals I would like to thank: Xavier Comas, for creating the most beautifully fitting cover art I could have hoped for this project; Euan Monaghan, for your exquisite typesetting and interior design; and Sharika Thiranagama and Kirisayini (Kesie) Uthayavannan, for your insights regarding Sri Lankan Tamil names.

My sincerest thanks to my university friends: Shanzeh Faheem, Diya Correa, Shwetha Ganesh, Kasvi Malhotra, Samantha Lee, and Anisha Anisetti. You have seen me from the first draft to the last and wholeheartedly supported me every step of the way. Thank you for lifting me up in my lowest moments and believing in me even when the project end was still far off in the future. A few other close friends I would like to thank include Aarthi Mahesh, Drishti Vidyarthi, Adya Mohanty, Alyzeh Hussain, Misha Hassan, Aparajita Pathak, and Neha Annamalai. I feel very fortunate to have you all in my life.

Family is the heart of this novel, and I would be remiss not to acknowledge the impact my extended family has had on me and this project. Thank you to the Ranadive Six, and your beautiful collection of children and grandchildren, for teaching me the importance of kin and culture. I especially want to thank Deepak Ranadive, Radha Ranadive, and Asha Vaidya, in addition to my grandparents—Aaji, Ajoba, Thatha, and Paati—for your warmth, affection, and righteousness. I hope one day I can pass forward these qualities to my children with as much grace as you have to me.

There are a few special locations that I believe deserve a mention. Sadly for my bank account, I am quite the coffee shop writer. My deepest thanks to Kaldi Coffee & Tea and Suju's Coffee & Tea for being my creative sanctuaries. The Town was inspired by multiple South Asian hubs across America. Thank you to the diasporic stores, restaurants, and events in Fremont, Artesia, and Edison for keeping me connected to a subcontinent that's thousands of miles away.

I would like to conclude by mentioning the unparalleled influence Indian classical music has had on this novel. Thank you to my old teacher, Suparna Dangi, for introducing me to this art form. Though I was never meant to be a professional singer, Hindustani music has played a huge part in my life, motivating me to start this novel and find the patience to see it through.

In this respect, I credit the late Smt. Kishori Amonkar for indirectly teaching me the discipline, rigor, emotional depth, and mindfulness needed to pursue a creative path. For the first three years of writing this book, I was unable to begin my session unless I was simultaneously listening to Kishori Tai's music. I played the same ragas over and over again, and still, I would always find in her voice the meditativeness needed to untether myself from my environment, concentrate on the page, and lose myself in Akash's story. My relationship with art, and what I hope to achieve with my writing, is largely influenced by Kishori Tai's commitment to her craft. Because of her, I believe the journey of any artist has to begin with a search for the self, with trying to understand one's position in this unstable world. Writing this novel was my way of embarking on an emotional quest for understanding, and I've evolved immensely through the process. Thank you, Kishori Tai, wherever in heaven you are, for proving to me the necessity of art, of emotion-based art, in an era that prioritizes commercialization above all else. I am forever indebted to you and the invaluable body of work that you've left behind.

Made in the USA
Las Vegas, NV
15 December 2024

14248240R00316